Bow's Boy

a novel

RICHARD BABCOCK

SCRIBNER
NEW YORK LONDON
TORONTO SYDNEY
SINGAPORE

SCRIBNER

1230 Avenue of the Americas
New York, NY 10020

For information about special discounts for bulk purchases,
please contact Simon & Schuster Special Sales:
1-800-456-6798 or business@simonandschuster.com

Text set in Bembo

Manufactured in the United States of America

1   3   5   7   9   10   8   6   4   2

Library of Congress Cataloging-in-Publication Data

Babcock, Richard.
Bow's boy: a novel/Richard Babcock.
p. cm.
I Title.

PS3552.A174 B69 2002
813'.54—dc21

2002073342

ISBN-10: 0-7432-278-X
ISBN-13: 978-0-7432-278-5

"Bye Bye Blackbird"
(Lyric by Mort Dixon, music by Ray Henderson) copyright © 1926

For my mother, Elizabeth B. Babcock,
and in memory of my father, Richard F. Babcock

CHAPTER 1

G. Bowman Epps and Ginger Piper died the same day, the same morning—maybe, I sometimes imagine, at the same instant. Neither could have known the fate of the other: They were nine thousand miles apart and hadn't spoken in months. In a purely physical sense, their deaths were unrelated. Still, the same day. My father used to place great significance on coincidences like that. The anomalies of life entertained and finally terrorized him. Not that you could pin him down to any specific meaning of events like these. He simply believed the past—and, worse, the future— were talking to him personally. He had what you might call a hot view of life, and probably because of that, I've tried to cultivate a cold one. The simultaneous deaths of Bow and Ginger were chance, no more—though I'll go to my grave believing their last thoughts were of each other.

They were stars, of sorts, of our small town, Laroque, Wisconsin— thrown together in a way that was probably inevitable, despite their differences. Bow was a rich, scarred, overweight, middle-aged lawyer; Ginger was thirty years younger, a splendid high school athlete, a talented, charming, rather mysterious boy from a bitter family. Overall, I think, each saw in the other a grace, a sort of beckoning of possibilities, that raised them and ultimately pulled them apart.

My name's Charlie Stuart. I'd known Bow—or, at least, known of him—for as long as I could remember. To every child in Laroque, he was an unspoken moral lesson: Money can't inoculate you against misfortune. Bow was the son of a banker, the richest man in town. But an early bout of polio had left Bow with a bum right leg and a laborious limp. As if that wasn't enough, when he was four, the family cook knocked a pot off the stove, splashing boiling oil onto the side of his head. Doctors saved the eye, but the scar was permanent—folds of flesh that seemed to be melting from Bow's right hairline to his jaw. He was a dozen years ahead of me, and as a child I remember watching him around town, a fat, lonely, bookish boy dragging his foot along the sidewalk, his scar lighting up bright red from exertion. Eventually, he went east to college, then came back to earn a law degree in Madison. When he returned to Laroque as a young lawyer, he had a wife, a plain, slender woman with pale skin and dark hair. She stayed perhaps five years, by the end barely venturing out of their house. There was a miscarriage, and shortly after she left.

By then, Bow was wedded to his law practice. He handled criminal appeals, almost nothing else. Some wretched fellow would get convicted of robbing a liquor store, and Bow would take the man's case up through the courts, arguing any procedural error that might overturn the verdict. He was good at what he did; over the years, he made a lot of the criminal case law in Wisconsin. Of course, there wasn't any money in it—most of his clients were indigents, assigned to Bow by the state, which paid a small fee for the work. But he was an only child and his parents had left him a small fortune. His life lay in the thick transcripts of court proceedings that piled up around his office above his family's bank. He'd disappear for days, poking through a trial record. I think the neatness of the process satisfied him—disorder reduced to, say, nine hundred pages of type. And from a desk that looked out over the Agnes River and the grubby street of bars and bait shops that lined its bank, he could pick over and second-guess every tactic, every ruling, every moment that counted.

I hooked up with Bow several years after his wife left. He found me one day at the county courthouse, where I used to sit through trials, enjoying the cheap drama. I even sat through a few of my own—nothing serious, public inebriation, that sort of thing. Bow had seen me around town, and he remembered my father. For years, Bow had battled with his own father, an imperious man as cold as his treasured sheets of financials, and in Bow's mind he and I belonged to a select fraternity of tortured sons. He offered me a job and I became his assistant—his secretary, investigator, chauffeur, companion. He didn't mind if I vanished for a few days every now and then on a bender, and he wasn't above offering me an occasional drink if he thought it would brighten my spirits. My beloved Lucy, who knew me through this time, thinks Bow stole years of my life, but though I respect Lucy's judgment on virtually everything else, she never really understood how it was between Bow and me.

I first met Ginger Piper while I was working for Bow. At the time, in addition to his law practice, Bow ran a small collection business—not that he needed the income, but he bought the paper cheap from the bank, and I think he enjoyed the anthropology of it, dipping into the life of the town. He gave it up after a year or so, but at one point a man named Errol Piper turned up as one of the deadbeats. Piper had taken a loan to buy a used truck from Harry Bigler Motors and then stopped paying. Often enough, a letter with Bow's name on it was sufficient to bring in the money, but in this case, two or three letters had been ignored. One of the tricks with deadbeats is to catch them in front of their families—sometimes the shame works outright, and other times, the wife, the kids, the grandparents start asking later whether that embarrassing bill has been paid. So one evening about dinnertime, I drove out for a visit.

Errol Piper's home sat one road off the highway in a scraggly forest of pines. He'd probably built the place himself—it appeared to be one of those lifelong projects, an expandable shack with tarpaper siding and small, dark windows. This was late spring, the weather had started to soften, yet bales of straw still circled the base of the house, holding in a bit of heat. I parked on the pine-needle lawn and knocked on the door. A woman opened it cautiously, and before she could object, I pushed inside. In the dim light, she made a hollow, shadowy figure with her arms folded protectively across her chest. I asked for her husband, and in a moment Errol Piper stepped out of a room in back. He stood a slender six feet tall or so, and with a face so cool and withholding he seemed almost ascetic.

"That truck don't run right," he said when I explained why I was there.

"Why didn't you take it back?" I asked.

"Wouldn't of done any good. Bigler knew it was bad when he sold it to me."

"Well, you've had it for a year now. You've got to pay up."

"Hasn't been a year," he said, as if that settled the matter.

"Look, where is the truck?" I said. "Show me what's wrong with it and maybe we can make an arrangement."

Errol Piper looked at his wife. "I don't have the patience for this," he announced, then turned and walked away.

I followed him into the kitchen, a low-ceilinged space cluttered with a mix of appliances and furniture—an old sink-and-stove combination, a ragged sofa, a plywood wardrobe painted pale green and bursting with clothes. Piper was sitting at a round table with two children.

"You better find some patience," I said noisily, "because Mr. Epps is going to haul you into court." Of course, I knew Bow would never bother to do that.

Piper didn't look up from spooning a milky soup into his mouth. The room was oppressive. The soup had a dense, fishy smell, and the light fixture on the ceiling bathed everything in yellow. I stood there awkwardly, not knowing what to do. Then I happened to glance at the smaller child, a boy I'd noticed so far only as a burry black haircut. He was staring at me intently. His face had a kind of glow, as bright as a new dime, so full of interest and candor that I had to fight an urge to explain to him why I had barged into his family's house during dinner. Instead, I fled, past the ghostly mother and into the night.

That was Ginger Piper. He would have been eight or so then, and it was another eight or nine years before he and Bow struck up together, in the spring of 1966. That seems so long ago, the memories are sepia toned. The three decades between then and now feel like a great divide. Some people say this country changed course when John

Kennedy was shot, others say it happened with Vietnam. A case can be made for either, but for a little place like Laroque, the change didn't come so much from an event as from a feeling, a slow-turning, unarticulated revision of attitude. At some point—1967, 1968—as we watched our televisions or read the Milwaukee *Journal* or talked over drinks at the Wanigan, it occurred to just about everyone in town that we were all alike. Young or old, rich or poor, man or woman—the differences, the separations that seemed a natural part of life, no longer counted for much. Distances were breached. The wait was over. Something happened to someone in New York in the morning, it was on television in Laroque that night—it had happened to us. Someone got something in Los Angeles—we wanted it, too. The same promises, the same rules (or lack of rules), applied to everyone.

As Bow would have put it, we were all equal, and equally reduced. He was a Menckenite (after one of his heroes)—a simultaneous advocate of civil liberties and privilege. But I'm not talking in a political sense here. (After all, I come from a family of virulent Democrats. My father's letters to Senator McCarthy were ferocious enough to draw visits from the FBI.) I'm talking about a mood, a shared assumption, and I'm only trying to make the point that when Bow and Ginger struck up, Laroque was a place vastly different from the one it became just a few years after.

Of course, by appearances, Laroque hasn't changed much—it's still the shell of the boomtown it had been just over a century ago when the lumber business was humming in northern Wisconsin. French trappers founded the town on a rocky bluff overlooking the Agnes River. By legend, the bluff was favored as a campsite because breezes up there kept the mosquitoes down. Though the first white homesteaders built up high, development settled along the river, particularly as lumbering flourished. At one time, three great mills snarled away along Laroque's stretch of the Agnes, as huge patches of white pine forest were cut clean. Today, the open-again, shut-again Hanson Door Company is all that survives.

Even so, the legacy of the town's heyday echoes in countless ways, some real, some rankly commercial. Above all, the past is there in the glorious gingerbread Opera House that sits in the center of town.

Bow's grandfather helped build the place. He came out from the East as a young man and founded the Laroque State Bank. The business thrived with the town, and soon he and Laroque's other fathers decided they needed a symbol, a kind of monument to their success. With an opera house, they had some antique civic notion about bringing culture to the muscled, sweaty immigrants who cut the trees and sawed them into planks. More to the point, the town's leading men wanted a place to show off the splendid baubles they'd bought their wives. In any case, an architect was imported from Philadelphia, and in 1890 or so, Laroque acquired its only true landmark. Even today, with the building shuttered and peeling, I'll occasionally see a cluster of visiting fishermen marveling over the elegant Victorian structure. They stare at the cracked and rotting tilework that borders the roof. They consider the tall, silent bell tower, now held vertical by a spider's web of chains and wires. Sometimes, they climb the steps and pound on the thick, wood doors, though who knows why they think they'd be admitted. They seem to imagine that this proud building is a kind of ghost castle put there for their amusement, like the Pitch-'n'-Putt outside of town, or the Pioneer Log Cabin Village, built in 1972.

The lumber business started to move west even before the building went up, but the Opera House carried on for decades. In the twenties, my father brought his muse and his demons out from New York, to manage the place and put on shows. He was a great talker and finagler, and the performances he directed were historic, in their way. People from Milwaukee and Minneapolis and as far away as Chicago used to come by train; on summer weekends, even during the Depression, McGill's Hotel was packed. From my boyhood, I remember those nights in bursts of intense light—the milling, whispering crowd on Main Street; the reek of exotic perfume; the sparkle of jewels and of bright, freshly polished black shoes; above all, the Opera House, glowing like a Chinese lantern, drawing life from the forest blackness.

A few years ago, when the town was hoping to get the Opera House going again, someone put up some money to restore the great canvas curtain that draped its stage. Over the years, the front of the curtain had been painted and repainted dozens of times with advertisements for Laroque's stores and businesses. By tradition, though, the back had been signed by the cast of each show. When the restorer finally got down to business, the crackling canvas was found to carry names like Katharine Cornell, Lenore Ulric, Walter Hampden, Orson Welles, Herbert Nelson, and countless others, famous then but now long forgotten.

I hadn't forgotten. The stars would eat at our house, gossip about Broadway, make remarks about the locals—not knowing, or not caring, that my mother was a local girl—and then move on, often as not taking my father with them. He'd come back a week or so later, just in time to save his job and mount another show. But he eventually wore down all of us, the town and his family. It was Bow's father, the chairman of the Opera House committee, who finally fired him. The shows had petered out by then. This was 1942, when I was twelve— what my father's personal wars hadn't finished off, the wider war had. He disappeared overnight. Mr. Epps came to the house to explain what had happened, and this time Dad was gone for years.

The Opera House never recovered. After the war, they used it for town meetings or the occasional school play, but it sat empty for months at a time. Then, in the fifties, during the baby boom, when classroom space was tight, they braced the stage, opened up the sides, and turned the place into the high school basketball court. The theater posters in the lobby came down, replaced by pictures of the team's best players. A big, black electric scoreboard was hung at the back of the stage. On Friday nights during the season, everyone came out— this was before they built the regional school south of town—and the Opera House again became the center of life, an ornate pile of mortar and brick, still stretching, reaching into the sky, heedlessly pulling us along.

Chapter 2

I keep hearing about this boy," Bow said.

"This boy?"

"The basketball player."

"Oh, him. He's good."

"Is he a shooter?"

"He's more like a smart player," I said.

"Oh, Christ." Bow shifted heavily in the passenger seat and stared out the window of the car. It had been snowing on and off all day, thick, soggy, late-winter flakes that burdened the trees and clogged the roads. Bow's wide, boaty Bonneville held the highway well, but I had to concentrate hard on the driving.

"He's got a decent shot," I said.

"If he's not a shooter, he's not worth much," Bow groused.

"Just wait," I offered, uselessly, since Bow had obviously analyzed the matter to his satisfaction.

I steered wide around a snowplow scraping along on the edge of the pavement, and the Bonneville fishtailed slightly before sliding back into our lane.

"Slippery?" asked Bow. He was forty-seven years old, but he had never learned to drive. He liked to say he was too stupid to learn, but what he meant was he couldn't be bothered by it.

"Wet."

"Listen," he said. "What do they call him again?"

"Ginger Piper."

"Ginger?"

"Yes."

He rolled his eyes for my benefit, indicating, but not outright saying, "These people and their names."

We were on our way back to town to see the Laroque High School Lumberjacks play the Kawnipi Blue Jays for the county title. That day, I'd driven Bow over to the state prison in Lovington, where he'd met with several prisoners and collected Jack Barragan, whose conviction for holding up a Skelly station in Beauville had just been overturned. The prison staffers didn't dislike Bow, but they tended to resent his victories, and they were slow about getting Barragan's paperwork together. By the time we'd dropped him off at his mother's house in Wausau and made our way through the snow back to Laroque, it was after eight.

As we turned onto the Turner Bridge, the car's headlights swept over the Agnes, dense with thick, dirty-white islands of drifting ice. Ahead, two figures, smudges in the snow, were making their way on foot. I slowed going around them and recognized Archie Nye, a local thug who liked to call himself a half-breed. He was wearing a flimsy black jacket with the zipper pulled to his chin and the collar turned up. I didn't recognize his pal. Both were hunched over against the snow and the wind, alone in the dismal landscape. Across the bridge, beyond a dark line of buildings, the spotlighted bell tower of the Opera House shone through the thick air.

"The game's probably started already," Bow said.

I dropped him off in front and parked down the street. We bought tickets in the curlicued box office at the entrance on the first floor. The lobby and the basketball court were actually one story up, and we had to climb the lovely, curving staircase. By the top, Bow was wheezing and needed a quick breather. The thick double doors to the auditorium were closed, but we could hear the patterned roar of the crowd, rising and falling with the action of the game. When Bow got his wind again, we entered and stood at the back. The balcony, once my favorite place in all the Opera House, hung over us heavily like a wasp's nest under the eaves. The air had the dense, sweet odor of the inside of an old fur glove. Down in front, the basketball made thundering drumbeats on the stage. Every seat was filled.

After a minute or so, the vice principal of the high school, Alvin George, noticed Bow, and he sent a student out to get two folding chairs. During a time-out, Mr. George led us down an aisle and set the chairs up on the side in front next to the stage. Just above us, the Kawnipi cheerleaders were kicking their way through a routine. The girl on the end noticed Bow. The exertion of the stairs had turned his scar bright crimson; beneath his thinning strands of pale brown hair, his round face was jaggedly two-toned, giving it an almost Cubist aspect. The cheerleader stared and fell out of step, bumping into the next girl.

Several people called out greetings from the seats behind us. Bow waved without looking back and sat down with relief. I helped him shed his overcoat, and we stuffed it under his chair.

A buzzer sounded, ending the time-out. The ten boys who'd been playing drifted onto the court. They were already dripping sweat. Kawnipi had a star, a skinny boy with enough of a reputation that he went simply by his surname, Slagle. He had a loose, jangly way of moving and a sleepy expression on his narrow face. Slagle was one of those natural players you used to see every now and then in small towns—a simple kid who didn't look like much until he had a basketball in his hands, and then he had a skill that seemed beyond training, beyond confidence, something God-given.

Slagle's team had the ball, and he trotted up the court toward us, guarded by a Laroque player named Billy Johnson, a Chippewa boy. After several passes, the ball ended up in Slagle's hands about ten feet from the basket. He did a dance step, faking right, spinning left, losing Billy Johnson, then, in the same sequence, jumping to shoot, his long, bony arms snapping like pennants in the wind. The ball swished through the net. The auditorium erupted. Half the people were from Kawnipi.

"There's a shooter," said Bow.

Ginger Piper played guard for Laroque. He was wiry and small, and, when he played, concentration wrung the softness from his boy-ish features. Unlike Slagle, he had to work to get it right, and his job was to lead the team, guiding the ball around the court, translating the ancient, static, and nounless plays of creaking old Coach Gour-don ("Pass, see? Then run here. Cut, cut. Pass. See? There. Pass. Cut. Down. Pass. Cut. Shoot!") into something resembling the modern game.

Ginger dribbled the ball quickly into Kawnipi territory and then played catch with Billy Johnson for several seconds. When the boy guarding Ginger stepped too close, Ginger darted around him, drib-bling into the thicket of players under the basket. The Kawnipi team converged around him, and Ginger plopped the ball to tall, plodding Karl Nygaard, who easily laid it in.

"Hey, not bad," said Bow. He recognized Karl. The boy had painted Bow's house the summer before.

The ball came back upcourt toward us, and Slagle scored with a long, effortless shot. Kawnipi was already ahead by six points. Bow fidgeted. The folding chair looked ominously delicate beneath him.

"You comfortable?" I asked.

He grunted.

"If it gets bad, let me know, and I'll see what I can find," I told him.

Slagle dominated the game. He made four more shots without a miss. Finally, someone tossed him the ball on the edge of the court, just above us. He faked and made a move, but as he pivoted, his gaze swept low across the auditorium and tripped over Bow. The ball bonked off Slagle's foot and bounced out of bounds. Slagle took a few steps back downcourt, then peeked once over his shoulder, con-firming the odd blot in the tapestry of faces.

"I'm the best defense we've got," said Bow glumly.

By half-time, Kawnipi was ahead by nine points. Bow wanted to take a few puffs on a cigar, so we made our way along the side aisle toward the lobby. The press of people pushed me against the wall, damp from the heavy air. Since they'd started using the place for bas-ketball, the original fleur-de-lis wallpaper had begun to brown and curl at the seams. The stately brass sconces were corroded and dull.

In the lobby, Bow made his way to an open window and blew waves of cigar smoke into the night air. The snow had stopped. Down below, people spilled noisily onto the Opera House steps. A few smokers in boots had wandered across the plaza on Main Street to the little triangular park with the war monument, where their orange-red cigarette tips bobbed and jerked in the dark.

Across the room, someone waved and called out. Boyce Rensinger, who owned the drugstore, pushed his way through the tangled crowd, trailing a sour, stocky man I didn't know. "Looks bad, don't it," Rensinger said to Bow, after giving me a frosty nod.

"Nine points." Bow shrugged as if it were nothing.

"Slagle's too much for the Indian."

"You're probably right," Bow said wearily.

Rensinger shifted his weight from one foot to another. The stocky man with him was trying not to stare at Bow's face.

"This here's Bill McCloud from over in Knife Lake," said Rensinger, sounding apologetic. "He wanted to meet you, Bow."

Bow stuck out his hand and, after a moment's hesitation, McCloud reached out and shook it. Rensinger waited for the hands to drop apart, then he said, "Bill here has a nephew who was working at that Skelly station the night Jack Barragan held it up. He wanted to talk to you about the case."

Bow let a stream of cigar smoke float up out of the good side of his mouth. He knew what was coming.

McCloud squeezed closer. "The son-of-a-bitch held a shotgun to that boy's head," McCloud said. His voice sounded hoarse, scratched by the words. "That was my sister's kid. He could have been shot. He pissed in his pants, and that son-of-a-bitch Barragan just stood there and laughed."

"I'm sorry," said Bow.

McCloud edged closer, gaining confidence. "Not so sorry you didn't defend the son-of-a-bitch," he rasped. "Not so sorry you didn't get him out of jail."

"See here," said Bow. "Your gripe is with the police. Your nephew's identification was worthless after the cops had paraded Jack in front of him with handcuffs on. There was the problem."

McCloud curled his shoulders and set himself. He wanted emotion and now Bow was sliding away with logic. "Don't give me that crap. You know Barragan did it. You know he did. The son-of-a-bitch oughtta be shot."

"Well, before we shoot him," Bow said mildly, "we ought to give him a fair trial."

"Yeah, well . . ." McCloud's speech got choked off in his throat. His tongue snaked out of the corner of his mouth. Rensinger sensed the next move and stepped in.

"See, Bow," he said flabbily, "all Bill here is really getting at is how guys like Barragan keep getting off on technicalities. It's not you he's mad about, it's these goddamned technicalities."

Bow smiled weakly. He waited for effect. When he spoke, he'd dropped his voice to a low roll. "There are no technicalities," he pronounced, jabbing gently with his cigar. "There is only the law."

How many times had I heard him say that? He was every bored actor who'd ever stepped on a provincial stage, hamming his way through a script he disdained, milking a line for an audience he despised. Still, Bow's delivery was impeccable. McCloud's mouth softened, his lips moved as if to tremble. This was a fight he couldn't win. He stepped back.

"I still don't understand why a rich guy like you is defending scum like that," he said, trying to cover his retreat.

"Okay, okay," said Rensinger, taking his friend by the arm. "You've had your say. Now, let's get back and win this game." He looked miserably at Bow. "Sorry to bother you, Counselor. Talk to you later."

McCloud gave up on Bow and glared at me, then let himself be led off into the crowd.

"Nice work," I told Bow when Rensinger and his pal were out of hearing. "For a minute there, I thought he was going to pop you."

Bow rolled his eyes. "Mencken put it best: 'Injustice is relatively easy to bear; what stings is justice.' " He was used to getting abused for his work and his politics, despite being a dedicated Republican and even ginning up a show of enthusiasm in 1964 for Barry Goldwater, with whom Bow shared deep misgivings about government.

But other Republicans distrusted Bow. They couldn't reconcile his criminal defense practice with his otherwise conservative views. Bow occasionally tried to explain that a true conservative held to principles, such as the right to a fair trial, no matter who asserted them. But serious Republicans seemed to think Bow was putting something over on them. And maybe they were right, in a way. Bow was a lawyer, not a politician.

He turned and leaned out the lobby window again, slowly blowing cigar smoke, a kind of neutral blessing, over the people on the steps below. After a minute or so, he said, "What would your father think, Charlie? These crowds, this commotion—wasting his beautiful building on a basketball game."

"He liked audiences. They made him feel at home. I don't think he much cared what the occasion was."

"He'd feel the difference," said Bow, putting out his cigar, carefully crushing the fire against the windowsill outside. "No matter what else you say about him, Malcolm Stuart was a cultured man."

Once, in the late thirties, just as the whole world was starting to go to hell, Broderick Crawford brought his acclaimed Broadway portrayal of poor, slow Lenny in *Of Mice and Men* up for a show in the middle of the week. Broderick Crawford is remembered today, if at all, as the gravelly voiced star of the fifties TV program *Highway Patrol,* but his Lenny was momentous, and my father talked him into gifting Laroque with the show. At the end of the play, after Lenny had cried he could "see it"—see that imagined, sweet, green patch of land across the river—and his buddy, George, in an act of mercy, had shot him in the back of the head, and the heavy canvas curtain had clunked down, scattering a fine snow of tiny paint chips on the stage, the Opera House audience, these big, fleshy working people, these dour white blonds in their black suits and black hats and their plain Montgomery Ward dresses, had sat silently in their seats for at least a minute, trying to fill up again with the energy to go on. Backstage, I found my father alone in his office. His eyes were on fire and he couldn't speak. He hugged me to his chest, so I could smell his smoky breath and feel the nervous twitter of his heart. "Now, *that's* acting," he managed to whisper.

Bow inspected his cold cigar, then stuffed it into his top jacket pocket, the charred end sticking up like a boutonniere. "Malcolm Stuart was no philistine," Bow continued, "and that's more than you could say for my old man."

Back in the auditorium, three trumpets, two trombones, and a drum pumped out the U.W. fight song. The teams were warming up, heaving rainbows of balls at the two baskets. Boyce Rensinger came up, drops of sweat zigzagging down his forehead. "I'm sorry, Bow," he shouted over the band. "I had no idea."

"Don't worry about it." Bow waved him off.

"He's the brother of a vendor, a guy who sells me lotions and things. He gives me great deals." Rensinger continued shouting though the band had stopped. "You know how these things work."

Bow nodded. His pale eyes drifted off to the corner near us. Archie Nye and his pal, the two men we'd seen crossing the bridge earlier, had made it to the game. They were whispering intensely to each other. "How's your son?" Bow asked Rensinger.

"Great, great." Rensinger lowered his voice, grateful for the change of subject. "He loves it. He's shipping out next week."

"It's heating up again over there."

Archie Nye's hand fluttered and dropped something into his friend's palm, and the two of them hurried out, unlit cigarettes dangling from their mouths.

"You know how kids are," said Rensinger. "They want to be where the action is. This Peace Offensive worried him. He was afraid Johnson was going to call the whole war off before he could take a shot."

"I don't think that's too likely," said Bow.

"No, there's too much at stake."

The buzzer sounded for the start of the second half, and Rensinger hurried off to his seat. Coach Gourdon had made a change at halftime: Now Ginger Piper was guarding Slagle, even though Ginger gave away three or four inches. A Kawnipi guard with an anachronistic brown crew cut dribbled the ball downcourt—away from us this time, since the teams had switched ends. He found Slagle with a pass in the corner. For a moment, Slagle's long arms held the ball tauntingly above his head. Ginger took a ritual swat, and with that, cashing in on the smaller boy's wasted effort, Slagle was off. He dribbled once, then whirled, jumped, and shot. His pointy elbows and knees vanished into the fluid ease of his motion, his angular body turning into something smooth and animal, Pinocchio brought to life. The ball clanged off the old metal backboard and dropped through the net.

"They can't stop him!" screamed a man just behind us. "He's unconscious!" Bow slapped the air around his ear, as if chasing a mosquito.

Ginger brought the ball upcourt, his face skewed in irritation. The change of assignments at half-time meant that Slagle was now guarding him. Once Ginger crossed the centerline, he passed the ball to Billy Johnson, who threw it to one of the forwards, who tossed it, perhaps a bit too hard, to Karl Nygaard, whose big, flat, paddle hands couldn't hold on. The ball bounced through wickets of legs and arms before Billy Johnson grabbed it, his eyes bugging, hardly believing his good luck, and quickly laid it in.

Going back downcourt, Ginger stayed tight at Slagle's shoulder, never letting him get more than a few inches away. Under the basket, Slagle wove around his teammates, trying to break free, but Ginger kept up, trailing so closely that after a while he seemed almost an appendage to the taller boy, a physical burden, Slagle's hump. The other Kawnipi players passed the ball among themselves, but they'd spent a season in service. Now, with their star unreachable, they got frustrated and careless. The crew-cut guard threw the ball away.

"That's the secret, don't let Slagle touch it," Bow said to no one in particular. Above us, Karl Nygaard spindled himself up to tap in a rebound. Bow slapped me on the knee. "Now we've got a game," he said.

By the end of the third quarter, Laroque had cut the Kawnipi lead to two points, and Slagle had scored only once more. The fluid had drained out of his movements, and his face had turned pinched and pouty around the lips; he looked like a fish, a smallmouth bass. Ginger, meanwhile, was gushing sweat, leaving great puddles wherever he paused and trailing a team of small boys wielding soggy white towels to mop up.

"He's gonna wash away," said Bow.

The teams traded baskets. Slagle bumped Ginger off on a pick and got away long enough to pull in a pass and take an awkward shot that hammered around the rim and fell in. Back at our end, Slagle the fish puffed after Ginger, who angled under the basket, cutting around his teammates, and slipped free for a layup.

The auditorium had turned into its own, closed ecosystem, overheated and short of air. A hazy fog, the gray on the edge of the horizon on hot summer days, seemed to separate us from the churning rows of students in the balcony. Bow kept his suit jacket on, but he loosened his collar and mopped his forehead with his handkerchief. The side of his face pulsed red.

With less than a minute to go and Laroque ahead by a point, the Kawnipi coach called a time-out. The auditorium exploded in noise. Everyone stood. The squads of cheerleaders tumbled onto center stage and tried hopelessly to organize the chaos. Mr. George, the vice principal, strode out with a megaphone and warned students in the balcony not to stomp their feet, the vibrations could damage the supports. The band rose and attacked "On, Wisconsin" again, the trombonists swinging their instruments like swords. The Kawnipi coach drew something on a small blackboard and screamed at his players. Coach Gourdon bleated out a few, sparse commands. Above our heads, the great ball of a chandelier, hanging over what had once been the orchestra pit, swayed gently, the tinkling of its glass jewels lost in the white noise below. Bow was right: The screams, the sweat, the inflated emotions—basketball games were an affront to the memory of this place. A temple of order and insight had been turned into a supermarket of shared glory. Even the players, their faces pale and sullen, their eyes avoiding their teammates', seemed to recognize that their performances had been swiped.

But Bow was in thrall. "Keep the ball away from Slagle," he recited with a lilting singsong. "Keep the ball away from Slagle." Without looking, he swung his arm to grab me. "Where are you, Charlie?" he called, pulling me beside him.

Kawnipi had the ball. A stocky, frightened sophomore threw it to the crew-cut guard, who stood dribbling out near the midcourt line while the rest of the players scrambled underneath the basket. The ball drummed on the hollow stage. Slagle kept squeezing past picks, but Ginger pushed through after him. Both boys looked exhausted, gray ghosts sliding around their teammates. Ginger's arms flailed the air, and Slagle batted back at them, trying to clear his view.

With a few seconds left, Slagle finally ran to midcourt, circled the crew-cut guard, and snatched the ball before Ginger could get a hand in. Now Slagle had a half-step advantage. He dribbled four times toward the basket before Karl Nygaard ranged up, his big, clumsy arms waving like loose antennas. Slagle's left foot pounded the floor and he sprung up, floating, suspended, a bird drifting on an updraft in the dense Opera House air, ten thousand hours of shooting the ball at a tinny rim hammered on the side of his family's barn coming down to one automatic uncoiling of those snaky arms. The ball popped through the basket, and by the time Slagle's feet were on the floor again, the fish had disappeared; his face had that old, skinny Slagle nonchalance. No sweat: He was unconscious. Ginger crumpled to his knees and slammed the stage with his palms.

"Well, shit," said Bow.

Coach Gourdon scuttled down the sideline to signal for a last time-out. There were two seconds left.

In the commotion, Bow stretched, arching his back and spreading his arms. "I need room," he said, and I slid away.

The auditorium settled quickly. The Kawnipi fans were celebrating, but there seemed fewer of them suddenly, and their screams had the freedom to carry and echo. The clammy air, with its close, human fragrance, was almost an embarrassment. People started packing to go, picking up empty popcorn cartons and paper cups. Bow took his calendar out of his inside jacket pocket and pretended to consider his schedule.

Onstage, Ginger was the last player to come back to the huddle. Coach Gourdon gave him a reassuring slap on the rump with his arthritic old arm, and Ginger took his place in the circle of his teammates. After a few seconds, he glanced up at the electric clock, the little white bulbs curling into that desolate "2." The color was returning to his face and his eyes were clear. He looked at the floor, then glanced up at the clock again. Was it my imagination, or was there a kind of glow about him, an aura in the gloom? Qualities of light are acute to eyes tortured by alcohol.

"Watch this," I said to Bow.

"Huh?" He fumbled and put away his calendar.

The buzzer sounded and the teams came back on the stage. The auditorium was almost quiet. Under the far basket, the referee handed the ball to Karl Nygaard, who wrapped his big hands around it, then waved his arms stupidly above his head. Ginger, who'd been standing close by, suddenly broke away, dashing down the sideline with Slagle right behind. Nygaard finally cocked one arm and heaved a football pass upcourt. The ball sailed past Slagle's ear and Ginger caught it over his head just in front of the midcourt line. He dribbled once, then dropped his right shoulder and shot-putted the ball, getting his legs, his back, and his whole arm into the effort. The ball arced high over the court, heading for the basket just in front of us. At first, the ball seemed to hover, floating like a moon, a light, graceful thing, gentle and familiar. But as it peaked and began to descend, it picked up speed, growing fat and heavy, becoming a huge, deadly rock, a meteor. It was coming straight at Bow. The buzzer sounded a frantic, nasal warning. I grabbed Bow's arm, but I couldn't move him, and still the ball held its murderous course, faster, heavier, meaner, until it dived exactly through the net with the sweet swishing sound of a fireworks rocket, and I felt for a moment something approaching the awe and longing of that night when I was a child and Broderick Crawford had struck my father dumb.

"Jesus!" gasped Bow.

In the tumult, we worked our way out along the side aisle. People were moving in all directions, gaily bumping and pushing one another. Bow put his unlit cigar in his mouth as a kind of prow and tried to tack his way through the crowd. We were halfway down the curling stairway to the ground floor when above us, in the lobby, someone shouted. There was quiet and then a chorus of screams, and the crowd, packed and tangled like a huge, many-jointed insect, began to surge forward. A panic was on. Everyone pushed, trying to rush down the stairs and outside to safety. I got lifted off my feet and crushed against two men in front of me. Bow grabbed the railing to keep from falling. People shouted, warning others to hold up, but still the crowd above pressed forward, fighting to escape. I didn't know what was happening, but, like everyone else, I'd read about the terrible hotel fire in Iowa a week or so before, and I sniffed the air for traces of deadly smoke. Clinging to each other, Bow and I maneuvered down several steps, feeling our way with our feet. Gradually, the crush started to relent. The crowd held itself and eased down the stairway, a pulsing, two-hundred-footed creature taking tiny, awkward children's steps. Finally, it burst through the front door and scattered on snowy Main Street.

Someone said that Archie Nye and his friend had argued in the lobby. A man insisted that Archie had pulled a knife. No, he was corrected, the buddy had pulled the knife. "This is worse than Vietnam," said a woman with a high, laughing voice.

Back in Bow's Bonneville, we joined a line of traffic puttering down Main Street, working its way through the mob of pedestrians. Bow had been subdued since the game ended, and now, vacantly watching the people flock through the street, he said softly, "I'm pooped, Charlie."

"You almost got crushed in a stampede."

His head rocked gently, and for a moment I imagined he was again following the splendid arc of the basketball. The outcome of the game seemed to have depressed him, as if there were only so much heroism to go around, and now more of it had been spent.

His heavy, awkward body was bundled in a thick black overcoat. His bum leg poked out stiffly under the dashboard. In the passenger-side window, I could glimpse the blurred reflection of his scar. Despite his money, everything ordinary about his life seemed to entail grueling effort, and he only got by, as far as I could tell, by being the hardest man, in will and character, that I have ever known.

He sighed as I turned up Summer Street toward his home. "Maybe we should have a drink," he said.

CHAPTER 3

The morning after the basketball game, everyone down at the Wanigan, the local diner, was talking about Ginger Piper and his shot. Most people didn't know much about the boy, only what they'd observed on the basketball court and what they'd heard: He was one of the top students in his class. Growing up outside town, he'd gone to a one-room, rural elementary school, one of the few still scattered around the county, so he hadn't spent much time in Laroque until high school. A couple of the fellows at the Wanigan knew that Ginger's mother had died several years before. Now he lived alone with his father, whose demeanor apparently hadn't brightened much in the years since I'd met him trying to collect a debt. "I don't think the old man even goes to the games," said Clyde Dawson, whose daughter was a cheerleader. "Can you imagine? Having a son like that and not paying attention."

"Yeah, his dad's a real prick," agreed Rita, the diner's longtime waitress, who was weaving among the tables, filling coffee mugs. "He comes in every now and then. Never smiles."

"Maybe that's why the boy's so cool," suggested Boyce Rensinger. "I don't think he ever doubted he'd sink it. And afterwards, he was the calmest guy out there." Boyce snorted. "Hell, I think I was more excited than he was."

The Wanigan—named for the mess hall in a logging camp—usually did a lively business on Saturdays, but this morning the place was packed. The half dozen tables scattered in front were jammed by witnesses to the Great Shot. Another line of testifiers was propped against the trophy wall, where Eli Warzonek's forty-nine-pound muskie, a Laroque treasure caught in the Agnes in 1942, hung mounted on a polished slab of oak. I'd stopped in to get some sweet rolls to take back to Bow's office, but my buddy Ox Mueller was sitting at the counter, lurking on the edge of the conversation, and he called me over. "You there last night?" he whispered. "Unbelievable, right?" Ox's big, puffy face glistened with excitement.

"I'll tell you what that shot means," pronounced Tom Mitford, who owned a haberdashery. "It's money in the bank, that's what it is. The Packers win on Sunday, my sales go up on Monday. Never fails."

"That's right," Rita the waitress agreed. "I see the same thing here. We ought to pay that boy a commission."

"Remember when Eisenhower came through in the fifty-two campaign?" Mitford continued. "Laroque got mentioned in every newspaper in the country. I sold more suits that fall than I ever did, before or after."

"That's politics," someone pointed out. "This is sports."

"I'm talking about the psychological impact."

Ox agreed, nodding thoughtfully. He was a huge man, and years ago he'd had a career as a semipro boxer. Thick, slow, immovable, he was known as a guy who could take a punch. Now the talk of glory had stirred something in him. He gazed up toward the trophy wall. With the layers of drifting cigarette smoke, Eli Warzonek's great muskie seemed to be swimming through the air. "Jeez, would you look at that monster," Ox marveled softly. "You bring in a fish like that and you're set for life. I mean, mentally speaking. You've made it."

Outside, yesterday's weather had left a couple of soggy inches of snow on the ground. I was headed down Main Street with my bag of sweet rolls when an old dark blue pickup rolled past and parked in the A&P lot. Ginger Piper sat for a moment behind the wheel, as if collecting himself, then climbed out and slammed shut the truck's door. It had barely been twelve hours since the stage of the Opera

House had erupted around him, but now, bundled in a maroon winter coat and clomping along in a pair of rubber-bottomed boots, he looked reduced, more childlike than in his Lumberjacks uniform, as if the props of his life, the layers of clothing and the rusting pickup, conspired to hold him earth-bound. He waved to the boy shoveling snow in the A&P's parking lot and tromped into the store. Out of curiosity, I followed.

Ginger yanked a shopping cart from its nesting row and started down the dairy aisle. He was obviously making the weekly family shopping run: a half gallon of milk, a dozen eggs, four sticks of butter. He went to the items immediately, familiar with the routine. The store was busy, the narrow aisles clotted by carts, and Ginger was quickly accosted—a Little League coach, a high school teacher, a couple of fellow students, a dozen or so people in all. They stopped to congratulate Ginger, many of them introducing themselves and offering their observations about the game. Mitford was right: There was a connection between sports and politics, and Ginger could easily have been a candidate out massaging the voters. He responded politely to everyone, shaking hands, nodding and laughing. But all the while he kept moving along the aisles, still shopping, casually plucking an item off a shelf and dropping it into his cart.

He was a handsome kid, with fine, coal-black hair combed neatly back and small, even features. He still had the startlingly bright, open face that I remembered from a decade before, but watching him now, I sensed that the boyishness was transitory, as if his face was on the verge of change, and that if you saw him in five years, all traces of the boy would be gone. Already, when his expression occasionally turned serious, he had a starkly new look.

The cramped A&P conveniently organized itself with four aisles, so you could start on the east wall and shop your way methodically west, up and down the rows, concluding with a final swing past the meat department on the opposite wall and landing at the two checkout counters in front. As Ginger moved past the glass trough of frozen meats, he tossed a few packages of pork and chicken into his cart and then picked up a steak. Just at that moment, the A&P's young assistant manager came up, and he and Ginger began to chat.

They clearly knew each other. Meanwhile, Ginger absently slipped the steak under his arm and pushed the cart to the checkout counter. The conversation continued through the checkout line, and soon chunky, motherly Mrs. Fremont, the cashier, joined in. Still talking, Ginger emptied his cart onto Mrs. Fremont's conveyor belt, but he kept the steak under his arm. He wasn't hiding it—the package was plainly visible, tucked up in his armpit, as he used both hands to transact his purchases, digging a wallet out of his back pocket and counting out the bills. I kept waiting for one of the three of them— Ginger, the assistant manager, or Mrs. Fremont—to realize what had been overlooked, but they all chattered away, completely focused on their conversation and oblivious to the pricey package of meat. Finally, Ginger scooped up his two brown paper bags of groceries— the steak still under his arm—bid good-bye, and shouldered out the revolving door. If one of the store employees had suddenly awakened, of course, nothing would have come of it: They would have laughed at their absentmindedness, and Ginger would have paid for the steak. Watching the incident unfold, I had no idea whether he'd simply forgotten the package or swiped it by design. I went to the A&P's front glass window as Ginger trudged through the parking lot, hugging his bundles. When he set the bags in the back of his truck, I half expected him to realize what had happened and come running back to the store. But, no, he simply tossed the steak into one of the grocery bags with the same nonchalance he'd used in carrying it. Then he climbed in the truck and drove off.

Whether he knew it or not, he'd just committed the perfect crime.

CHAPTER 4

B ow worked out of a space on the second floor of the Bank
Building, looking out over the bars of River Road and the
churning Agnes just beyond. The room had been his father's
secondary office, a private redoubt where he entertained his secretary and mistress, Miss Sinclair. Mr. Epps had installed an imposing
oak desk and a long, undulating sofa that took up one whole wall,
and he'd put in an adjoining bathroom, complete with a huge
clawed tub. Once when Bow was young, he'd come looking for his
father and surprised him there, soaking in the tub, while Miss Sinclair perched stiffly on the edge of the toilet seat, taking dictation.
Now the office was lined with law books. Bow still used the oak
desk, and I sometimes spent the night on the sofa. A bust of Oliver
Wendell Holmes Jr., the great, aphoristic lawyer, anchored a bank of
file cabinets on one side. Holmes was one of Bow's heroes, along
with Mencken, and Winston Churchill, and, of course, that god,
Vince Lombardi, the coach of the Packers. Above Holmes, an oil
painting of Bow's father hung from the wall. The painting had been
downstairs for decades, but when the bank redecorated with some
bright fifties optimism a few years before, someone had decided that
bald, dour old man Epps was bad for business, and Bow had inher-
ited him.

As Bow's assistant, I sat under that portrait at Miss Sinclair's old desk, a squat hunk of wood topped by a typewriter. One of my principal chores was to answer letters from inmates. Bow's reputation had blossomed inside the state's prisons, and he got a steady flow of requests for help getting out, a dozen or so a week. Though we always responded, most of the letters were easily dismissible—pleas from men who had missed the deadline for filing or had already exhausted their appeals and, now, with the advice of their cellmates, had concocted elaborate theories of the injustices they'd suffered. One day that spring, though, the mailman dropped off a letter that piqued Bow's interest. It arrived in a long manila envelope—page after page of yellow legal paper, each sheet covered, front and back, with precise, tiny handwriting, two lines filling each allotted line on the paper. The writing was almost impossible to read, but the effect was of something lacy and decorative.

Bow spread the sheets before him and sent me out to the dime store to buy a magnifying glass. Poring over the pages, he ascertained that the letter came from a man doing time at Lovington for burglary. "His name's Gary Fontenot," said Bow, rather pleased with his deciphering. "See, here's his signature." At the bottom right of the last page, Bow pointed out two thin, wavery dashes, bacilli squirming across the paper. The first was preceded by a miniature *G*, the second by a tilted *F*. The graceful, hopeless precision of the writing must have echoed something that Bow felt about his own work. "It's remarkable, isn't it?" he said, admiring the yellow sheets splashed across his desk. "So perfect. Not a word crossed out. Think of the effort."

"But impossible to read," I pointed out.

"It's as if the actual argument only exists in his mind," Bow said wonderingly.

The week after Ginger sank his shot, Bow and I drove to Lovington to meet Gary Fontenot, the first time we'd been back to the prison since springing Jack Barragan. The old facility sat on a small, treeless hill, a barren empire surrounded by high, barbed-wire fences. The original building stood neatly square, but additions over the years had oozed out in all directions, creating a squat, formless blot of architecture. A brick smokestack, long ago painted white, towered over the campus, visible for miles around.

Bow and I checked in at the perimeter gate and again at the guard station at the entrance to the main building. We emptied our pockets and put all the contents in small metal boxes. An old guard named Clarence, who'd been admitting Bow for years, searched his briefcase and then patted down the two of us. Clarence asked whom Bow was visiting, but the guard didn't know Gary Fontenot. "They come and go, then come again," Clarence cawed, shaking his head.

"You must be about ready to retire," Bow suggested.

"If I retired, I'd just sit around," Clarence explained. "I do that here, and they pay me for it."

"Good point," Bow conceded, rolling his eyes for my benefit.

Gary Fontenot turned out to be a sinewy little tough guy with a thatch of blond hair bobbing over his forehead and an elaborate tattoo of an eagle on the inside of his right forearm. We met him in one of the prison's small, airless interview rooms. He was sitting at a scarred wood table, and he didn't bother to stand or even to offer his hand. Like most of the inmates we met over the years, he didn't show any reaction to Bow's elaborate scar. Bow insisted that was because the convict population was more accepting of freaks; I always suspected that criminals simply didn't care enough about other people to register a response.

"How are you getting along?" asked Bow, trying to get acquainted. He and I had settled into metal chairs on the other side of the table.

Fontenot shrugged. "Same."

"How many times have you been inside?"

"Once before here. Once down at Oswego." He didn't look directly at Bow when he talked, instead aiming his conversation somewhere over Bow's left shoulder.

"Food as good as ever?" Bow asked, smiling.

Fontenot tilted back in his chair, looking faintly amused. He gave the impression he'd be happy to sit there all day, talking about nothing.

"How old are you?" Bow continued.

"Thirty-four."

"You got any family?"

"A sister. She's downstate somewhere. I haven't talked to her for a while."

"Never been married?"

"Nooooo." He shook his head. The idea was preposterous.

Bow reached down and unsnapped his briefcase, taking out Fontenot's letter. "Well, I've looked this over as best I could, but I'm not sure what to make of it."

"Oh, don't bother with that," said Fontenot, waving his hand dismissively. "That's just a lot of bullshit."

"What do you mean?"

"It's bullshit."

Bow studied him for a few seconds. Fontenot rocked up and back on the rear two legs of his chair. "Didn't you write this?" Bow asked.

Fontenot nodded.

"You obviously put a lot of time in on it."

"I thought about it later. It's worthless. I ripped up my copy."

"You made a copy of this?" Bow asked.

"By hand."

Bow studied him again, then folded the letter and put it carefully back in his briefcase.

"I don't know nothing about the law," Fontenot offered.

"I wouldn't expect you to."

"A guy here was telling me stuff, giving me cases to mention." The letter was peppered with citations from law books, each neatly underlined. "But he didn't know nothing either."

"Did you pay him something?"

Fontenot considered for a moment, then nodded.

"Do you still want to appeal your case?" Bow asked. "We'd have to file a notice soon."

The wood table was narrow, and it occurred to me that Fontenot kept tipping back in his chair because the seating arrangement pushed us a few inches too close for his comfort. "Sure," he said after a few seconds.

"I've glanced at the transcript," said Bow, "and it looks like you got a pretty fair trial. Judge Borofsky is a pretty good judge for this state."

Fontenot looked directly at Bow. "See, it didn't work out like I wanted," he said.

"Obviously not."

"There was a big mistake."

"You know about the attorney-client privilege, don't you?" Bow said. "Everything you tell me is confidential. It can never come out in court."

Fontenot thought for a moment. "See, I didn't do what they said." He seemed to be fighting a smile. "I mean, I've done other things, but not this."

Two cops had pulled over Fontenot at three one morning because a brake light was out on his car. The cops asked him to step out, and, searching the glove compartment, they found a box of jewelry that had been stolen several days before from a house in Northrop. They opened the trunk and found a carton of burglary tools. At the trial, Fontenot claimed he didn't know anything about the jewels or the tools—he'd loaned the car recently to a man he'd met in a bar. Afterward, he couldn't find the man or remember his name. The jury was out forty minutes before convicting Fontenot on all counts.

"Well, guilt or innocence is only one of the issues I consider on appeal," Bow said, "and it's usually not on the top of the list."

Fontenot rocked vigorously. Squeezing the table for support, he flexed the muscles in his forearms; the tattooed eagle was flying. "How long will it take?" he asked.

"Depends. There may be no grounds, in which case I'll let you know. How much time are you doing?"

"Five to seven."

"We'll have an answer before it's up."

Behind us, in the corridor outside, a guard shuffled past, tapping his nightstick on the wall, unnecessarily announcing his presence. Aside from a peephole in the door, the only window in the room was a small square of unbreakable glass set in concrete and fronted by bars. The pathetic little patch of gray sky only worked to churn my claustrophobia.

Bow asked Fontenot, "You got something to do if we can get you out of here?"

"Have some fun."

Bow smiled. "Beyond that."

Fontenot shrugged. "I got friends. They'll help out."

"Did you ever learn a trade?" Bow asked.

"I used to be a painter."

"An artist?" Bow was dreaming.

"Houses."

"That's a decent job."

"It was too tempting—standing up there on ladders, looking in people's windows...." Fontenot let the thought trail off and glanced mischievously at Bow.

"I see what you mean," said Bow, nodding gravely. He liked this guy.

When we got up to leave, Fontenot stayed in his chair, but reached out to shake hands. He had a surprisingly soft grip and his fingers felt delicately bony. Bow told him he'd be in touch.

We stayed another hour or so, seeing other prisoners. Afterward, outside, as we walked past a wire fence around the recreation yard, a group of inmates who'd been shooting baskets stopped to stare. Several of them recognized Bow. Someone called out, "Hey! Mr. Appeal!" and Bow waved.

About halfway between Lovington and Laroque, on the edge of a woods outside a little town called Atkins, Bow had discovered a truck stop that made waffles with sour-cream batter. We always dropped in on our way back from the prison. Three rigs were parked in the wet, gravelly lot, their motors running, throwing gray smoke into the chill air. A trail of duckboards meandered through the mud and puddles to the front door of the restaurant. Inside, we sat at a booth and Bow ordered half a dozen waffles.

"I don't like the search in that Fontenot case," he said as he sponged up black-raspberry syrup with an edge of waffle. "What right did the cops have to go rummaging through the glove compartment?"

"What do you think about Fontenot's story about loaning out his car?" I asked.

"An outrageous lie."

On a shelf behind the restaurant counter, a TV playing without sound cut to a report from Vietnam. A reporter in short sleeves talked into the camera while a bedraggled line of GIs filed past in the jungle background. Suddenly, the reporter cringed. He and the soldiers dove to the ground. The picture bobbed and swung dizzyingly as the cameraman apparently scrambled for cover. A shell must have hit nearby, but without sound, the images were simply chaotic, TV run amok. The film concluded with a lingering shot up toward the sky, through the huge leaves of a jungle tree. Bow stared at the screen, a drop of syrup on his chin.

"Still, he couldn't bring himself to be blatant about it," Bow said, getting back to Fontenot's claim of innocence. "He had to hedge it: 'I didn't do this job, though I admit I did others.' There's something in man that hates to lie. It's the lowest sin."

"Some people lie all the time," I pointed out.

"Forget the crazy ones. I'm talking about the normal run of humanity, the good and the bad. Just pay attention. People hate to lie."

Bow signaled for more coffee, and the waitress, a slim, dark-haired woman with a long syrup stain on her apron, brought a pot from behind the counter. "Enjoy your waffles, Mr. Epps?" she asked.

"The best," Bow said. "The best."

"Now, don't you get any more of them prisoners out," she teased. "We was robbed here last week."

"No!" Bow looked alarmed. "Nobody hurt, I hope."

"Nah. They came at night. Broke in through the kitchen door."

"Ah. A burglary."

"They tried the safe but couldn't break it," said the waitress. "So they took two gallon cans of syrup."

"Would've been a shame to leave empty-handed," Bow told her.

The waitress put her head back and laughed. "You always side with the bad guys," she admonished him.

Bow watched her walk behind the counter, his gaze following the pleasant swing of her short skirt. "You know what someone told me the other day?" he said. "I was down at the Wanigan, having a cup of coffee, and they were still complaining about that goddamned Jack Barragan case and this and that. And someone told me my real problem is I don't have a stake in the future. I get all the crooks out because I don't care if the country goes to hell in a handbasket."

"Who told you that?"

"Oh, I don't remember."

"How could you forget something like that?"

"Marcus Laney," Bow admitted.

"Well, shit." Marcus Laney owned the radio station in Laroque and broadcast a late-afternoon show of news and gossip. His conservative views had darkened as his health had started to fail.

"I wonder if he didn't have a point, though, Charlie. I don't have a stake in the future. No family, no kids—I'm really going on momentum."

"Come on, Bow. You know how important your work is. Your legacy is embedded in the law."

"The law changes," he said cheerlessly.

I wasn't used to seeing him moody like this, and I took a moment to study his face, looking for a sign of something physical that might be troubling him. Normally, he was careful about his health. Every two years or so, he would go for a checkup at the Mayo Clinic, in Rochester, Minnesota. I'd drive him there, and he'd stay for a couple of days. Before coming back, we'd stop at a men's store his father had discovered, and Bow would have two new suits made. The suits became his clock to determine if it was time to go to Mayo—he'd make an appointment when the knees and elbows were wearing thin.

Bow was far from a hypochondriac, but it made sense for him to be careful. His father was in his fifties when he dropped dead of a heart attack, walking up Summer Street one day after work. Bow's mother died of ovarian cancer a few years later. Bow would often remark about the sorry health of his family, and he enjoyed posing as a stoic in the face of mortality. Once, when he spotted blood in his urine, he marched right down to the hospital and even strutted for a few days, showing off his courage, waiting for the test results to come in. As it turned out, there was nothing to worry about. "Dodged a bullet!" he exclaimed proudly. Another time, he announced one morning that he'd found a lump in his groin, then worked all day as if nothing were amiss, before checking into the hospital at night. He was back at work the next day, bravely awaiting the doctor's call. Again, negative.

Now, flush with a midafternoon meal, he looked as robust as ever. It had been less than a year since his last Mayo checkup, and I knew he'd resent any suggestion that we move up the schedule.

The waitress came over with the check and stood by as Bow squeezed himself out of his seat. "A few more of those waffles and you'll never get out of the booth," she told him.

Bow paused to catch his breath. "I can think of worse ways to go," he said. He stopped at the cash register to buy a long, thick Dunhill cigar and tossed a dollar bill onto the counter. "It's a dollar fifteen now," corrected the man at the register.

"So, the price has gone up," Bow said, fishing in his pocket for coins. He sounded pleasant, but I could tell he resented it—not the inflation, but the measure of change, of time moving on, erasing accomplishment, devaluing life itself.

Outside, the duckboards clattered underfoot as we walked back to the car. Mud season had begun.

CHAPTER 5

Did you hear? A Laroque boy's been killed in Vietnam." Lucy Braestrup, one of the bank secretaries, stood in the doorway of Bow's office, bringing us the news.

Bow looked up from his desk. "Who?"

"Toby Monck," Lucy said. "He just got out of high school last year."

Bow asked me, "Do I know him?"

"He played on the basketball team. Kind of tall and lanky." Toby Monck had been an awkward forward, always getting tangled up with Karl Nygaard.

"He's Vernon Monck's kid," added Lucy. "You know, he works for the post office."

"How'd you hear?" Bow asked her.

"Everybody's talking about it," she said testily. "The Moncks found out this morning."

Bow sighed wearily, signaling he'd heard enough. Still, Lucy stayed in the doorway. She seemed to want to see how Bow and I reacted.

"What a waste," I said, giving Lucy something to chew on. "He was a nice kid."

"It'll get worse," Bow insisted. "Unless Johnson gets it together, the Viet Cong will just pick 'em off, one by one."

"You'd rather we lose hundreds at a time in a real fight?" I asked.

"Hey, it's a war. Admit it. Get on with it. Joe Alsop was saying the other day that we're paying the price of affluence. We're like what the Romans became—too soft to take care of themselves."

"I can hardly read Alsop anymore," I said. "He reminds me of civics class."

"Jesus, the boy's dead—what are you two arguing about?" hissed Lucy, apparently getting the reaction from us that she'd wanted or, at least, anticipated. She marched off angrily down the hall.

Bow sent me to the library to borrow a high school yearbook with Toby Monck's picture. The boy had a long, elastic face with droopy eyes. "Oh, *him*," said Bow in a burst of recognition. "He doesn't look formed enough to get killed."

In those early days of the war, the dead boy could return to town quietly, without the public agonizing and recriminations that became features of the conflict later. In places like Laroque, a death in service was still considered one of the painful but accepted risks of growing up an American male. Vernon and Elizabeth Monck met their son's body at a military airfield near Milwaukee and rode home with it in the train. A few family friends went to the station for the arrival of the coffin, but most people waited for the service at St. John's Lutheran Church. Reverend Olson, the St. John's pastor, would preside at the event, but Toby's parents wanted one of their son's friends to deliver a eulogy, and they asked Ginger Piper.

The day of the funeral, clouds hung over the town, but a blanket of mild air had settled on the Midwest; in Laroque, all that remained of winter were a few decaying mounds of plowed snow. I brought the Bonneville around to drive Bow to the church, but he shook me off, and we set out on foot.

Most of the town had left for the service. Downstairs, the bank was empty, save for one of the tellers and Joe the guard, in his chair by the door. Outside, a few isolated cars nosed against the curb along Main Street. It was Friday, one of the busiest shopping days; normally, people would be trolling the street for parking spaces. An erratic wind whipped over the river, picking up an occasional sharp edge. With his bum leg, Bow moved so slowly I was afraid we'd be late, but he was determined to hike.

The church lay on the east end of town, about ten blocks away. By the time we passed Veterans' Park, across from the Opera House, Bow had broken into a sweat. We stopped to rest, dropping onto a bench. At the center of the park, a concrete statue of a doughboy gripping his rifle towered over the patchy, moist lawn. The base of the statue was square. One side honored the committee, headed by Bow's father, that had put up the monument in 1921. The opposite side was dedicated to the dead of World War I, and the two other sides held plaques, put up later, for World War II and Korea, respectively. Bow pointed out that they didn't have room now for Vietnam.

Setting out again, he still had the war on his mind. "I really don't get it, Charlie," he said. "Who convinced President Johnson that you can fight a war halfway? We're the most powerful country in the world, and we're getting picked to death."

"Maybe there's not much we can do."

"It's this weird ambivalence that frustrates me. We want to be first in the world, but we want to be nice. A great power, but popular. You can't have it both ways. You can't enforce your will and still expect to be liked. If we were respected, I wouldn't give a damn if we were liked or not."

"I'm not sure that bombing people to enforce your will wins that much respect."

Bow threw up his arms. The strain of the walk had begun to discourage his interest in talking. "What's the use of arguing with you about it?" he said. "Your father was practically a card-carrying member of the party."

"I don't know how I feel about the war," I admitted.

By the time we got to St. John's, the church was crowded and we had to squeeze into the last pew. Mrs. Pangborn, the widow of the man who'd been schools superintendent when Bow and I went through high school, thought she'd captured the seat by the aisle and frowned as she slid over to make room for the two of us.

Down front, beneath the altar, an American flag draped the silvery coffin. The Moncks and their two daughters were sitting in the first pew beside a straight-backed army man in dress blue. A row of pall-bearers, high school boys, including Ginger, all looking extraordinarily scrubbed and pious, stiffly occupied the pew opposite the family.

Hobbled old Reverend Olson, his prized full head of white hair combed into a sleek wave, led the service from a big, cushiony chair beside the pulpit. His arthritis had been acting up, he explained, speaking through a microphone, and standing aggravated the condition; the Moncks had graciously told him to sit. He watched as we rose to sing "What a Friend We Have in Jesus," the music bouncing off the church's bright, unadorned walls, whitewashed every summer by tradition. The Moncks didn't sing, but they stood with that solid, blackened dignity that grieving families seem to draw from each other. The two girls held their heads so close they appeared to be touching.

Reverend Olson led the gathering in a recitation of the Twenty-third Psalm, then gave several readings. (Romans 8:24: "For we are saved by hope: but hope that is seen is not hope: for what a man seeth, why doth he yet hope for? But if we hope for that we see not, then do we with patience wait for it.") When he'd finished, he set his Bible carefully on the floor beside his chair and delivered his sermon. The microphone exaggerated the roughness of his worn, bass voice; if you closed your eyes, the Word of God seemed to be booming directly from the two black speakers hanging on the walls. In twenty minutes or so, Reverend Olson spoke only glancingly of the dead boy—Toby Monck seemed to have made little impression on his pastor. In the last few weeks, however, there'd been several calamities around the Midwest, a bus accident with a dozen or so fatalities, that grisly hotel fire that had helped set off the panic in the Opera House. The news weighed heavily on Reverend Olson and was linked in his mind to the death—by Viet Cong terrorist bomb at Toby's Saigon barracks, as it turned out—of the Monck boy. How can such terrible things happen in God's world? Hard as it may be to accept, the minister explained, untimely death is part of His purpose, too: Without a shadow, there can be no light; without great sorrow, there can be no joy; without doubt, there can be no faith. God is constantly testing us, forcing us to renew our conviction. This young boy's life has not been wasted: Toby Monck's death is a reverse signpost, leading us to Him.

The hard, wood seat made Bow's bad leg stiffen. He squirmed and fussed and at one point leaned over to me. "There are five or six arguments for explaining evil in the world," he whispered, "and this old coot has picked the weakest one." Mrs. Pangborn shushed him, putting a finger to her lips.

The minister finished without a flourish; since he was already seated, there was an awkward stillness while people caught on that the sermon was over. Finally, Ginger Piper realized that his turn had come. He climbed the stairs at the front of the stage and spread several pages of notepaper across the top of the pulpit. He was wearing a black suit, somewhat overlarge and baggy, and his white shirt rode up high around the neck. He gave an impression of great innocence, a schoolboy buried in a man's solemn uniform; I thought of those formal photographs of Civil War soldiers—faded, spotted daguerreotypes, most of them taken, I imagine, before the hopeful boys had ever seen battle.

"I've known Toby Monck since I was in first grade," Ginger started, speaking in a clear, strong alto. "He was always an oaf."

Down front, a nervous, horsey laugh spurted out of one of the pallbearers and carried through the uncertain silence in the church. Ginger paused. He seemed to be steadying himself by holding hard to the pulpit. "The first day of school," he continued, "Toby knocked an inkwell off Mrs. Connor's desk and left a stain on the floor that I think is there still. In fourth grade, or perhaps fifth, doing nothing more than putting his arm in his overcoat, he clobbered Annie Green so hard he gave her a mouse under her eye." Several people in the audience tittered, warming to Ginger's method. "A few years later—many of you will remember this—he sledded down Foster Street into the river and had to be rescued by the fire department. He emerged from that disaster not just an oaf, but—to our little school, anyway—a hero." The quiet laughter in the church expanded, becoming a soft, heaving sigh. Beside me, Bow nodded appreciatively at Mrs. Pangborn.

"Toby grew earlier and taller than the rest of us," Ginger went on, "but he never outgrew his oafishness. Once, at the high school, he tripped on the stairs, fell down half a flight, and took out eleven people. I was there and counted the casualties. Often as not, his shirt was buttoned wrong. He'd scratch his left ear by reaching over his head with his right arm." Ginger demonstrated, and the rolling laughter reached a peak. "He was forever tripping, slipping, dropping things, and bumping into people. And, of course, he was the only Lumberjack player in my memory to score a basket for the opposing team."

Ginger waited expertly as the audience settled. He turned to smile at Reverend Olson, who didn't hear well and appeared somewhat puzzled at the outbreak in his church. "He was an oaf in every sense of the word," Ginger continued finally. "But Toby Monck, my friend, was also loyal, brave, intelligent, and one of the gentlest, sweetest people I've ever known. He didn't join the army to fight a war. He joined—probably without thinking much about it—because that's what most of us do when we get out of high school. He didn't like killing. He didn't even care much for hunting. He worried about himself with a gun in his hand. He knew he was an oaf."

Ginger looked down for a moment and absently straightened the papers in front of him. When he spoke again, his voice had risen by half an octave and gained an edge of urgency. "Now, Toby has been taken away. We hear a lot of talk these days of duty and sacrifice. And, a few minutes ago, Reverend Olson spoke of the role of tragedy in God's plan. I'm afraid those ideas seem terribly distant to me today. I don't know why Toby had to die. He was nineteen and full of life. His country sent him to a faraway place called Vietnam, a land I'd never even heard of until a year or two ago. He was told he was fighting to protect the good people of that country, which, in turn, was part of a larger effort to save us all. Maybe Toby, in his gentle wisdom, understood that. But"—here Ginger turned and nodded to the grieving parents—"I'm sorry, Mr. and Mrs. Monck, I don't."

Another pause. Ginger seemed buried in the immensity of his black suit. The air in the church didn't move. "That discussion, however, is for another time," he continued. "We're gathered here today to recognize that we've lost Toby and to help each other hold on to his memory. For me, there's one recollection—nothing dramatic, just a moment in time—that stands out above all others. It was last year. We'd had a basketball game at Knife Lake, and we were coming back in a school bus. We'd lost. It was late. Most of the team was moping or sleeping. I was sitting next to Toby, near the back. The night was clear and a full moon was out, and when we'd pass a lake, there'd be a shimmery, silver reflection in the water. Toby had been quiet for a long time, just looking out the window, but suddenly he turned to me and said, 'I can't imagine living anywhere but Wisconsin.' " Ginger caught his breath and let his eyes sweep over the audience. "That was my friend, the oaf, and that's how I'll always remember him."

Ginger gathered his few pages of notes, signaling Reverend Olson again to take command from his chair. There was a prayer, another hymn, and, finally, we all stood to recite the Lord's Prayer. The organist played "Rock of Ages" as we filed down the center aisle and out into the startlingly mild air. People made a double line down the church steps and along the sidewalk to let the pallbearers through with the coffin. A hearse waited at the curb to take the body to the cemetery, just outside of town.

"An excellent service," said Mrs. Pangborn studiously, as if issuing her judgment on a new vintage. She'd come to the funeral alone and had decided to play out this final act of the event with Bow, positioning herself beside him at the bottom of the steps.

Someone else remarked that the family appeared to be holding up well.

"I understand the youngest girl had to take a pill," offered Ted Morrison, a history teacher at the high school, who was standing close by.

"They're a strong family," said Mrs. Pangborn, shutting down Morrison with a voice recalling that her late husband, the superintendent, had once been Morrison's boss.

The wind came in sharp spring bursts. Mrs. Pangborn's mink collar flapped around her face, as if the little animal were alive and nipping at her cheeks.

"I always think of President Kennedy on days like this," said Mary Harvey, clinging tightly to the arm of her husband.

A woman named Janet Poplar said, "I was worried about Ginger's eulogy. I hope it wasn't too negative for the family."

"Someone should have told that boy to stick to business," said Mike Harvey, speaking loud over a gust of wind. "Vernon Monck is a veteran and proud of it, and he was proud to have his son serve his country."

"Who's he think he is, bringing the war into it?" griped Janet Poplar's husband.

"It was a good eulogy, just not traditional," said Mary Harvey. She added after a moment, "And the Moncks are a very traditional family."

"They seemed to be moved by it," interjected Ted Morrison, who'd been down near the front, with the best view. Mrs. Pangborn or not, he couldn't resist jumping into the discussion.

This time, the grand lady approved. "It was very imaginative, very loving," she pronounced. "An outstanding eulogy, wouldn't you say so, Mr. Epps?"

"Best I ever heard," Bow said, stopping the conversation.

At the door of the church, the pallbearers were moving with their burden onto the landing. Ginger was on the front corner on the left. He grimaced, working to steady the weight. "Oh, those steep steps," murmured Mary Harvey.

The four Moncks followed, with the army representative, his face a plain mask, walking carefully just behind. The procession moved slowly through the silent lines of people. At the end, near the hearse, a little boy recognized the basketball hero. He pointed and squealed, "There's Ginger!" The pallbearers moved along without reacting, loading the coffin into the back of the car, then helping the Moncks into another black funeral car that had quietly slipped up along the curb. For a few moments, people milled, climbing into cars heading slowly east, toward the cemetery. Back the other way down Main Street, toward the Opera House and the park, the roadway looked desolate.

As Bow and I stood on the sidewalk, Reverend Olson came up with the young assistant pastor and offered to give us a ride to the burial in the church car. But Bow said no, he thought he'd paid sufficient respects. He complimented the minister on his sermon, and then the two of us headed back to the office, our eyes tearing sloppily from the wind.

CHAPTER 6

Bow could fall into silences that lasted a few hours or even entire days. He never appeared particularly gloomy at those times. Usually, he was simply lost in thought, constructing a legal argument point by point. Other times, he just seemed to lose the need for conversation—a legacy, I supposed, of a childhood spent without siblings or playmates, alone with his parents in a huge, chilly house. Since I'd grown up with a father who panicked at the least pause in the general hubbub of human intercourse, I appreciated the quiet, once I understood that it didn't mean Bow was unhappy with me. Early on, after a day or so when he'd come and gone in the office with hardly a nodded greeting, I jumped in and asked if I'd done something wrong. Oh, no, he assured me, he just didn't have anything to say.

The afternoon of Toby Monck's funeral, Bow dropped into a silence that lasted until just before he was ready to leave for home. He broke it abruptly with a question: "What do you know about that Piper boy?" He couldn't bring himself yet to say "Ginger." The name was both too silly and too intimate for him.

I told him what I knew: Ginger lived in a ramshackle house a few miles out of town; his father did odd jobs and a bit of farming; his mother had died a few years before.

"Cancer?" Bow asked.

"I suppose so."

"Any siblings?"

"I think he's got an older sister."

Bow fussed with the papers on his desk, pushing them into new piles. Because of the funeral, he was already an hour or so late in leaving. At his home on the Bluff—the same home he'd lived in most of his life—his housekeeper, Mrs. Gehrke, would be waiting with dinner, some steaming, potato-rich concoction that she'd spent much of the afternoon preparing. "He's a remarkable story, isn't he?" Bow went on. "Growing up in a hardscrabble family like that and yet having such gifts. That eulogy was very sophisticated."

"But you're a hawk on the war."

"Oh, he's all wrong about Vietnam. That's not the point. The point is that it was well said and very gutsy, challenging convention—challenging all of us." Bow cocked his head. Sometimes, when the light and shadows caught his scar just right, he seemed to be winking at me.

"I think he won some kind of a school oratorical contest last fall," I said.

"Really? I've been thinking," Bow continued carefully. "Maybe we should hire him to help out this summer."

"Help out?"

"You know, do a little research, give you a hand with the paper-work."

In the summer, when the courts slow down, there frequently wasn't enough for me alone to do, and I didn't relish the thought of sharing what was there. "How's he going to help with research?" I asked.

"Anyone can learn to use a law library."

"A high school student?"

"I could have taught you, Charlie, if you'd wanted to learn." When pushed, Bow never hesitated to turn ad hominem.

"Well, why don't you ask him?" I said sullenly. "He could probably use the money."

"Here's the thing." Bow avoided looking at me. "I'd like you to ask for me."

"Why me? Why don't you do it yourself?"

Bow fidgeted in his chair. "It might look funny—just stopping him out of the blue," he said.

"I don't know him any better than you do," I protested. "And, besides, he'll know who you are. Everyone in town knows who you are." It occurred to me that Bow was testing me, perhaps even trying to push me away. At the truck stop on the way back from Lovington the other day, he'd fretted about not having a stake in the future. And if he was starting to worry about his legacy, or finding a successor, he'd never make a lawyer out of me. On the other hand, getting me to invite the boy was completely within Bow's character. For all his mettle, when it came to tricky personal matters, he was usually happy to let someone step in for him.

Bow got up from his desk and shuffled to the closet. "Missed Cronkite tonight," he said, putting on his overcoat. "It's getting to be a habit now. Mrs. Gehrke sets up dinner on a tray in front of the TV. Then I get to hear all the bad news. She tells me it's wrong to eat while you're getting riled up, but I wonder if the bile isn't good for digestion."

"You're eating in front of the TV?" For years Bow had put off buying a television, arguing that he was too occupied to fit cowboys and second-rate comedians into his life. When he finally broke down and bought one, he mostly used it to watch sports.

"Kind of a waste of the dining room, isn't it?" Bow said sheepishly.

"I guess if you want to keep up on the news—"

"I must confess," he interrupted, "I've even kept the thing on for a show or two afterwards. Have you seen *Hogan's Heroes*?"

"I've heard about it."

"The head of the German camp—Colonel Klink—they've made him such a moron. . . ." Bow started to laugh, recalling an episode. Quickly, he steadied himself with a sigh. "Oh, well. I guess if the barbarians are taking over the culture, I might as well learn to speak their language."

He gathered up his briefcase. "Staying late tonight?" he asked.

"I thought I'd just finish typing the Spinelli brief."

"When's it due?"

"Next week."

"Let it go, Charlie. Another few days in the pokey isn't going to make any difference to Andy Spinelli. He's probably enjoying the accommodations."

"I'm almost done."

"Suit yourself." Bow offered another tired sigh, absolving himself of any responsibility for spoiling my Friday night. On his way out, he stopped at the door. "About Ginger Piper," he said, looking back toward me, but taking in the whole office as if he were talking to Holmes, his father, the ponderous oak desk, the entire, overfamiliar furnishings of his life. "Invite him up. Let's just talk to him and see what happens."

I told Bow then about seeing Ginger walk out of the A&P without paying for the steak. I explained that I didn't know whether it had been an accident—the moment had passed so seamlessly, it was impossible to tell. Bow listened carefully. "So he forgot to pay? So what?" he said when I'd finished. "He's just a kid. He was probably still reeling from the game. I would have forgotten, too. Invite him up," Bow repeated.

I said I would, if that's what he wanted.

"The boy might make a lawyer," Bow pronounced before heading home to Mrs. Gehrke and her potatoes.

An hour later, Lucy Braestrup, the bank secretary, slipped into the office and flopped down on the sofa. "Were you at the funeral?" she asked. "I didn't see you."

"We got there late. We were in back."

"You and Bow?"

"We walked."

"*He* walked?"

I shrugged. "He wanted the exercise."

Her eyes drifted toward the window behind Bow's desk. With the darkness outside, the pane created a mirror, and I caught her making a quick inspection of her difficult reddish-blond hair, spilling behind her ears.

"You're working late tonight," I said.

"Some contracts had to get out. Everything stopped for the

funeral, then there was a panic." She gave up on her hair and studied me. "What's that you're doing?"

"Just typing a brief."

"Someone innocent?"

"What do you think?"

"Wouldn't it be nice to free someone who really was innocent just once?"

"It probably happens. It's hard to tell."

Lucy scrunched forward on the sofa, the nubby surface hiking her skirt up a few inches. She was twenty-eight and she still had thin, powerful legs. In high school, the coaches had let her train with the boys' cross-country team, though letting her run in an actual meet was out of the question in those days. "What did you think of Ginger Piper's eulogy?" she asked.

"It was strong. He's a smart kid."

"A lot of people were mad. They thought it was inappropriate."

"Did you?"

"I liked it." She hesitated, searching for words. "It was a bit show-offy. It called attention to himself. But the whole event was like that. I mean, I was sitting there, among all these people, and I kept thinking, Why are we here? People die of cancer every day, and we don't stop everything. What's so special about getting killed in the war?"

"Self-sacrifice," I offered halfheartedly. "He gave his life in the service of the country. He died for the rest of us."

"Shit. That boy didn't have any idea what he was doing. Ginger was right about that." She flopped back, sinking into the sofa's ancient, soft cushions. "I'm just sick of Vietnam," she griped. "That's all you ever hear about. You can't turn on the radio, the TV, without getting another report. We're winning, we're losing, so many died last week. Isn't anything else going on in the world?"

"Why don't you take a side?" I suggested. "Protest. Write some letters. Do something about it."

"People get so heated up. I wish you could just . . . ignore it." She gave herself a moment to cool down. "Do you think I'm awful?" she asked.

"No."

"Maybe I am." She sighed and stood up. She kicked off her flats and reached under her skirt, unfastening her stockings. Then she rolled each down a leg before dropping back onto the sofa again. "I suppose Bow was all hot and bothered about Ginger's eulogy," she said.

"He liked it. In fact, Bow was so impressed, he wants to hire the kid."

"For what?"

"To work here. You know, a part-time job."

"But what about you?"

I shrugged again. "Bow thinks there's enough work to go around."

Lucy shook her head, and her hair tumbled free from behind her ears. "Charlie, you gotta get out of here," she said. "I mean, look at you. You're thirty-six years old. It's eight o'clock and you're typing his brief. You ought to be writing a book, or running your own business, or *something*, but something more than this."

I didn't respond, staring at the sheet of paper in the typewriter.

"You drink because of Bow," Lucy continued. "I don't know why—the pressure, his great success. Something. But it's Bow. Believe me, Charlie, I've thought about it a lot."

I hated this argument. Lucy and I had been rehearsing it now for a year or so. "That doesn't stand up," I told her. "I drink less now than I did before. Until I started working for Bow, I was drunk all the time."

"You may be more orderly about it now, but it's the same thing. It's just more concentrated. Don't get me wrong. I'm not blaming Bow. He means well. But it's his life you're leading, not your own."

For all the times we had been over this ground, I'd never been able to express to Lucy what a relief that had been—how a life of logic and detail and routine had come as a blessed compass.

"You know what they call you?" Lucy said, speaking carefully now. "The men in town? 'Bow's Boy.' I've heard them say that."

This was something new, an insult she hadn't fired before, and she watched with some apprehension to see how I'd react. In fact, it was easy to stay calm. I'd heard Boyce Rensinger himself call me that when he didn't know I was standing behind him.

"Bow's been very good to me," I said softly.

"Yeah, the two of you can sit around up here and complain about your fathers together." Now she was cross, irritated that she hadn't got a rouse out of me. "The Bad Fathers Club. Ha, ha, ha. What fun." She was still holding her rolled-up stockings, and for a second I thought she was going to throw them at me.

I got up from the typing desk and walked over to the sofa. "Why do you care?" I asked, standing in front of her.

"I don't," she said sharply. "It's just frustrating watching you."

I knelt before her and buried my head between her legs.

"Charlie!" she screamed. Then she laughed. "Charlie, that's so inappropriate."

I lifted my head for a second. "Why inappropriate?"

She closed her eyes dreamily. "I guess that's not the word I mean." She started massaging the back of my neck with a wad of stocking. After a few minutes, she lifted me, putting her hands under my arms. "I want you inside me," she said.

The sofa was a big, sagging hunk of wood and cushion, wide and low slung, like an old blue rowboat. It was plenty comfortable for two, but so soft that maintaining effective leverage was tricky. Lucy and I rolled onto the floor to finish things off.

An Oriental rug covered the hardwood, but it was cold down there. Afterward, Lucy pulled me back onto the sofa, and we lay half naked, pretzeled together. She said, "I wonder if Bow ever notices the spots we leave on this thing?"

"I doubt it," I told her.

Outside, under the window, a couple of drunks were passing between bars on River Road, arguing noisily. I thought I recognized the voice of Ox Mueller. "Women don't care about that!" barked the other voice at one point. They were having a philosophic discussion of the sexes. It had to be Ox.

Lucy and I clung to each other, breathing softly while the voices of Ox and his buddy faded down the street. It seemed that if we moved an inch, the deepening chill of the room would touch us.

After a while, Lucy said, "You know, none of the Moncks cried today. Even the two girls. Isn't that strange?"

"Maybe. It's hard to tell how people will react."

"I thought it was strange." Lucy considered a moment, then corrected herself. "I thought it was sad. It made me really sad."

I worried she was going to cry, so I stretched to nuzzle her, but she turned away, and instead I buried myself in her rich, unruly hair.

CHAPTER 7

L aroque sprawls for more than a mile along both sides of the Agnes, straddling the river from the Gooseneck Rapids on the east end, past a curving stretch of water below the Bluff, to the ruins of the old Monson Mill in the west. For all that distance, there's a single bridge—the Turner Bridge—crossing the water.

As it happened that spring, a state engineer making a routine check found a crack in one of the stone pilings, and the span was immediately closed for repairs. Several large oil drums, painted orange and weighted with concrete, blocked both ends of the bridge, and traffic was diverted to the newer, steel-girder structure—the Tinkertoy Bridge, as the kids descriptively named it—that the state had put up a quarter mile west of town. The Turner remained open to pedestrians, though, and since there was something novel in being able to wander all over the roadway, particularly as the Agnes churned and spat below with the spring melt, the closed bridge became a favorite hangout.

I found Ginger Piper there late one afternoon, a few days after Bow had given me my assignment. Ginger was surrounded by a crowd of students—boys and girls, most of them wearing Laroque letterman jackets, light blue with white sleeves, and all of them laughing and talking loud and hopping around, looking, with their coloring and their edginess, like a flock of excited tropical birds. I didn't want to wade into the group, so I leaned against the bridge railing and tried to catch Ginger's attention. He was standing beside a pretty, slender girl with large, dark eyes and dark hair to her shoulders. With the noise of the river and the kids all talking at once, it was impossible to hear what was being said, but it struck me that Ginger and the girl were a kind of royalty in the group, the centerpiece of the commotion. At one point, the girl reached over and placed her hand lightly on Ginger's forearm, while still smiling out at the friends around her. The gesture could have been borrowed from an English court scene.

After a minute or so, Ginger saw me wave. He didn't seem particularly surprised, but as he left the group, he leaned over to say something to the girl. For a moment, the talking around them stopped.

"I know you," he said pleasantly after I'd introduced myself. "You work for G. Bowman Epps, Esquire." He'd seen Bow's name on the sign on the Bank Building, and he was having fun with it. "What's the G stand for?" he asked.

"George."

"Ahhh." He smiled and nodded.

"Bow was very impressed with your eulogy the other day," I told him.

"I'm flattered," Ginger said. "I guess."

"He'd like to meet you. He's looking for someone to help around the office, and he thought you might be good for the job."

Ginger studied me for a moment. He had extraordinarily light brown eyes, the color of walnuts, and I realized that it was at least in part the lightness of his eyes, against his olive skin and dark hair, that gave his gaze its transfixing power—the luminescence that I'd noticed the first time I'd encountered him in his family's home.

"I play baseball," Ginger said evenly. "Practice starts tomorrow."

"Something could probably be worked out."

"What sort of help does he need?"

"Paperwork, research. He can explain it all to you."

"I'm not sure I have the time."

His resistance confused me. I'd been working for Bow so long the advantages seemed obvious. "Why not come up and talk to him?" I suggested.

Ginger paused. "It seems funny," he said softly.

I thought I caught something in his voice. "It's nothing like that," I said.

"No?"

"Macy."

Ginger fought to hold back a smile. Macy Cunningham was an elegant Chippewa woman who ran a small brothel at her farmhouse. I drove Bow up there most Wednesday nights. "That's not what I meant," said Ginger. "I meant funny that he sent you to ask for him."

"What's funny about that?" It griped me that this kid, this teenager, with his poise and his reserve, had a way of putting me on the defensive.

"Why didn't he ask himself?"

"He can be formal like that. Come up to the office and see for yourself."

"Will you be there?" Ginger asked.

"Yes."

He glanced back at his friends. The prancing and chatter now centered on the girl alone, but she kept looking our way. "Sure," said Ginger. "I'll try to get out of practice early."

"Good." We considered each other. "Who's the girl?" I asked.

Ginger broke into a smile. "Macy's grandniece."

It was hard to dislike him, cocky or not. "See you soon," I said.

When I was ten yards down the bridge, Ginger called after me, "I remember when you came out to our house." But I pretended I couldn't hear him over the sound of the river.

He didn't show up at the office the next day or the day after that, and Bow started to get edgy. "Do you think he's coming?" he asked. "Are you sure he understood?"

I assured Bow that the offer was too good to pass up, but as the afternoons slipped by without a visit, I think Bow started to wonder if I'd defied him and not conveyed the invitation in the first place. "You know, Charlie," he told me, "even if I hire the boy, it won't make any less work for you."

I tried to act as if the thought had never occurred to me.

Bow spread his arms, indicating the unordered bookshelves of collected cases, the piles of transcripts stacked on every horizontal space. "There's plenty here to go around."

He spent most of the time writing and rewriting a rebuttal brief, keeping me busy at the big Selectric typewriter. Lacking any economic imperatives in his work and, for the most part, any serious deadlines, Bow had let his perfectionism expand over the years to a level that was almost eccentric—the slightest logical bump in his argument, the most insignificant clumsy language, would be the occasion to tear the brief up and start again. But those few days waiting for Ginger were excessive even by Bow's standards. At first, as he handed me the pages to retype, he carefully explained how he was refining his argument. But after several run-throughs, he gave up the pretense. He simply dropped the neatly typed brief—now marred by his scribbled improvements in blue ink—onto the top of the typewriter. "Sorry," he said over and over again.

Finally, late Monday afternoon, five days after I'd talked to Ginger on the bridge, Lucy poked her head around the office door and announced that Bow had a visitor. "He came in through the bank," she grumped. Ginger appeared behind her, dressed crisply in his letterman jacket and a brown crew-neck sweater. "Go on," Lucy told him. Ginger hustled into the office with a hitch in his stride, a teasing skip. It took me a moment to realize that it was directed at Lucy, not Bow. "You boys have fun, now," she said as she disappeared.

Bow stood and beckoned Ginger onto the sofa, the only free space to sit. "Since all my clients are locked up, I've been able to save on furniture," he explained.

Ginger looked uncomfortable. He perched on the front edge of the cushion, his knees together, while Bow talked about his work. He explained about appeals—how he'd scour the transcript of a trial, sometimes thousands of pages long, looking for mistakes that could have influenced the outcome. Then he'd try to persuade an appeals court that the conviction should be tossed out.

"But what if the man is guilty?" Ginger asked.

"He still deserves a fair trial, doesn't he?"

"But doesn't that bother you—helping someone get off who deserves to be punished?"

Bow laughed. " 'Deserves to be punished'! You sound like you believe in some higher justice. If you listened to old Reverend Olson, you'd think that we all deserved to be punished."

"Maybe," conceded Ginger with a smile. He was starting to enjoy this give-and-take.

"Listen," Bow said. "I believe in the process—making our justice system, as imperfect as it is, as perfect as we can make it. The best way to do that is to take appeals very, very seriously."

"So you don't handle trials?" Ginger asked.

"I've never been in a trial courtroom. I wouldn't know where to begin."

"But isn't that where all the fun is?"

"Depends on what you think is fun," Bow said. "Besides, I don't have it here for that kind of work." He jabbed a thumb into his stomach.

"I see." Ginger's eyes skipped around the office walls and settled on the portrait. "Your father?" he asked Bow.

"That's right."

"He used to own the bank, didn't he?"

"He was president."

"Ohhh."

"Do you recognize that guy?" Bow asked, pointing to the bust of Holmes.

Quickly—too quickly, it seemed to me—Ginger rattled off a quote: " 'The life of the law has not been logic: it has been experience.' "

Bow looked at me, then back at the boy. "How'd you know that?" he demanded.

Ginger shrugged. "It's famous. Oliver Wendell Holmes is a famous man."

Bow turned to me again, bouncing his jowls, mugging his astonishment. "Did you hear that, Charlie?"

I nodded, and I kept my suspicions to myself: The boy had done some research in preparation for his visit.

"Did they teach you that at Laroque High?" Bow asked Ginger.

He shrugged again. "I don't know where I learned it," he said.

"Do you know anything about Holmes?" Bow asked.

"Just that he was a great judge."

"His father was a madman."

"What?" said Ginger.

"He was a blowhard of incredible proportions."

"I didn't know that."

"Oliver Wendell Holmes, Senior, was a writer and a doctor, quite famous in his time, but principally a blowhard." Bow glanced at me. "Isn't that right, Charlie?"

I nodded dully. Sometimes Bow and I were like an old married couple who know each other's stories by heart.

"The old man was impossible," Bow went on. "A nonstop talker, a compulsive babbler of puns and doggerel. He'd get so worked up spouting his word games that he'd practically be drooling. And he was constantly writing poems about his son. Wendy. That's what the old man called him. Wendy, short for Wendell. Can you imagine? Every time Wendy burped there'd be a new poem."

"How did Wendy like that?" Ginger asked.

"He hated it," said Bow, leaning over his desk, his voice dripping agony. This was the part he relished. "It took him years to forgive his father. Maybe never. The greatest jurist in American history, constantly harboring the most intense personal resentment you could imagine."

"Jeez." Ginger slid back on the sofa, easing away. He stared at poor Wendy's head, a lifetime of humiliation suddenly apparent in the sculptor's touch. "Why do you keep the thing around?" he asked reasonably.

Bow sat back, lightening up. "Someone gave it to me—the state bar association, in appreciation for my work. No one knows the real story of Holmes. Anyway, I kind of like it after all these years. And he was a great judge. . . ." He let the thought trail off.

A grainy late-afternoon light had settled into the office, a suggestion of spring's occasional harshness. Ginger's fresh presence suddenly seemed out of place amid the mess of transcripts, the apple-sized dust balls under the sofa, the air stained with stale cigar smoke.

Bow must have sensed the same thing. "Is it getting dark in here?" he asked me. "Why don't you turn on the overhead light."

I hopped up and flicked the switch, and the room turned garishly yellow. "Better," said Bow.

For the next few minutes, Bow explained to Ginger the job he had in mind—retrieving documents, looking things up, copying papers—the same sorts of things I did for him.

"I'm flattered," said Ginger after listening to Bow's pitch, "but I don't see how I'd have the time. I've got baseball this spring, and I'm supposed to work on a road crew for the county highway department this summer."

"Squeeze me in when you can," said Bow. "I'll give you five dollars an hour."

Ginger nodded solemnly. The road crew probably paid half that. "I don't know the first thing about legal research," he said.

"It's all library work. Once you know the system, you can find anything. And it's simple. I can teach you in a day."

Ginger crossed his arms and avoided looking at Bow. He gave the impression of someone who wanted to resist, but sensed that more excuses would be insurmountable bad form. "Well, sure," he said at last.

"Fine," said Bow heartily. "Come back any time, and we'll get you started." He stood. The interview was over. Ginger bounced up to shake Bow's hand, then retreated toward the door.

"What you said at the funeral the other day—it was very moving," Bow told him.

Ginger paused beneath the stony gaze of Bow's father. "Thank you," he said. "I meant it."

"You know, you're all wrong about the war. The solution's not to pull out, but to go in hard."

"You think so?"

"I trust history."

"I'm not surprised." Ginger gave his voice a slight singsong, eliminating edges, avoiding—for now, anyway—the risk of an argument.

"Charlie here will show you out the back way," Bow said, sitting down again.

Ginger followed me down the concrete stairwell, avoiding the bank on the first floor. Outside, in the dusk on River Road, the bars with their neon signs had a gay, holiday look. Ginger said, "Five dollars an hour. Not bad."

"How did you know that Holmes quote?" I asked.

Ginger buried his fists in his pants pockets. "It's famous."

"Somebody tipped you off."

Ginger twisted, fidgeting. "I don't think I'm smart enough to do this work," he said.

"Listen," I said. "Whatever you do, don't embarrass Bow."

"Would you?" the boy shot back.

"Of course not."

"Then I won't either."

Across the street in one of the bars, someone suddenly jacked up the volume on a jukebox. "The Ballad of the Green Berets" wailed out an open door.

"I gotta go," said Ginger, and he whirled and hurried off.

CHAPTER 8

Every father has a song, and my father's song was the old Broadway tune "Bye Bye Blackbird." He'd sing it all the time—or, actually, what he'd sing was the chorus, which was either the only part he knew or all he cared about:

> Pack up all my care and woe, here I go, singing low
> Bye Bye Blackbird
> Where somebody waits for me, sugar's sweet, so is she
> Bye Bye Blackbird.
> No one here can love and understand me
> Oh, what hard-luck stories they all hand me.
> Make my bed and light the light,
> I'll arrive late tonight,
> Blackbird Bye Bye.

I'd walk past the bathroom and the melody would waft out, hummed through a beard of shaving cream. In the car, the song was like a stone in the hubcap, repeating methodically with the turning wheels. My mother had a way of tuning the thing out, but when we'd come over a hill and face a long, straight stretch, I'd see the distance not in spatial measures, but in repetitions of the song—about one and a half to the mile, if the traffic was light. In my memory, the song floats over my father like an aura, as intimate as the stinking French cologne he used to splash on every night before a show or the brown, ribbed-cotton bathrobe he lived in for years after he came back home.

Once, hoping for some insight, I did a little research and found that the song was written for one of the minstrel reviews popular in the twenties. "Blackbird" was a slang expression for a Negro singer, but the rest of the words were just romantic nonsense, at least as far as I could discover. After my father died, though, I found myself singing his song in odd moments, and I began to appreciate that it had been a kind of mantra for him, the mortar filling the space between his thoughts. There was sentiment, defiance, hope in that song, and I came to understand how important it had been to him.

That spring, when Ginger started working for Bow, I was living in three places. My principal home was a studio apartment in the old Greenwater Hotel in Indian Town, the low, mosquito-plagued neighborhood across the river. I'd been staying there for five or so years, since my mother died and I'd sold the house. I also spent a number of nights on the sofa in Bow's office. He didn't care—in fact, I think the hidden, banker's side of his nature appreciated the idea that the space was in use twenty-four hours a day. Or maybe he just liked having someone up there at night to look after his beloved transcripts. In any case, he cleaned out a file drawer for my clothes and personal items, and I'd sleep over a couple of nights a week— usually after I'd been out drinking on River Road and the walk back over the Turner Bridge seemed too much to handle.

When the weather turned warm, I also spent time at a place called the Spirit Light Lodge, thirty or so miles northeast of Laroque on Crow Lake. It was a fishing camp, and I picked up spare cash working as a guide. I'd organize my outings around Bow's schedule, but he didn't mind if I was away for a few days, especially during the summer, when the judges went on vacation and the appeals business slackened. Besides, I think Bow recognized that the work was good for me. The Spirit Light's owner, Bob Morgan, was a devout Baptist. He didn't ban drinking at his camp, but, with his style, he tended to attract a quiet clientele, not the usual sporting crowd. If my party was just going out for a day trip, I'd bunk in the dormitory cabin with the other guides and the rest of the hired hands. But sometimes the party would want to camp out for a few days, and then we'd pack gear and stay on Crow or on one of the other lakes in the area. I enjoyed those camping trips. There's nothing ambiguous about being a guide—certitude is the very nature of the job. I'd be the first out of the tent in the morning, starting the fire and making breakfast, and the last in bed at night, after the dishes had been washed in the lake and the embers doused. I knew the weed beds where the heavy-jawed muskies preyed and the rocky shores favored by smallmouth bass. I could take a party anywhere it wanted to go. If the fish didn't bite, that was understandable; I never met an honest fisherman who blamed the guide.

Business was good at the Spirit Light that spring of 1966, and I stayed there more than usual. It wasn't so much that I resented being at the office when Ginger was around, but the formula had changed; I wasn't as important. I suppose I hoped Bow might notice my hint of a boycott, though he never let on that he did.

Once school let out and the baseball season ended, Ginger came to Bow's office most evenings after work. By the middle of June, he'd quit his summer job with the county and was working for Bow full-time.

"He's better than a law clerk," Bow said one day early on. "Works harder and costs less. I'm actually going to start taking a heavier load because of him."

"That ought to please the District Attorneys' Association," I said.

"He's got a natural legal mind," Bow went on, ignoring my joke. "With six months of tutoring, I could get him past the bar exam."

Ginger started out doing simple clerical chores—filing papers, corresponding with inmates, proofreading briefs. Some of it was work that I would otherwise have done, some of it had simply gone undone in the past. Within a week or so, Bow took Ginger down to the bar association library on the first floor of the Laroque County Courthouse and taught him how to look up cases and law-review articles. After that, Ginger spent much of his time at the library, copying materials for Bow and even digesting cases—summarizing the essential facts and issues and writing them up in memos. I wondered about the usefulness of those memos. Bow said Ginger's digests were terrific, but Bow was so particular about his work that I couldn't imagine him relying on someone else's research, especially someone untrained in the law. What's more likely is that Bow used Ginger as a kind of advance scout and then went ahead and read the original materials himself; at any rate, the system pleased Bow.

When Ginger was in the office, he'd spend hours reading transcripts. He didn't know enough to spot appealable issues, but if Bow was looking for something specific—the place where a certain fact was established, for example—Ginger could readily find it, saving Bow the trouble of searching through hundreds of pages of testimony. As it turned out, Ginger shared Bow's fascination with those thick, verbatim records, and he'd read transcripts the way some people read detective novels or magazines, sometimes staying late to finish a new one that had just arrived at the office.

Bow found an old desk for Ginger somewhere in the basement of the bank, and workmen lugged it up and shoehorned it into a space along the wall. Soon, Ginger's desk, like Bow's, was piled high with transcripts and with volumes of *Wisconsin Reports,* all the materials sprouting little ripped strips of paper to mark particular passages. The typewriter table, which Ginger and I now shared, had acquired an extra layer of books and papers, in addition to a companion piece— a boxy little bookcase that immediately overflowed with legal materials. On days when all three of us were there, the office felt miserably crowded; every clearing of the throat, every flipped page, came like a whisper in the ear. Bow appeared to be completely at ease, however. He drifted less with Ginger around—there were fewer moments when he'd stand at the window and stare absently over the meager traffic on River Road, fewer half-conscious conversations to punctuate a long stretch of silence, fewer cigars. He'd jolted his routine, and it had given him a fresh burst of energy.

It should have cheered me to see his mood brighten, but I was bothered by the change in him and bothered yet again by my own pettiness. After all the years, I felt I should have moved beyond that kind of resentment. Still, I'd managed to create a careful equilibrium,

balancing my neatly ordered days beside Bow with the entirely separate (and only occasional) nights of drinking. The addition of Ginger to the office upset the homeostasis, tipped me out of my
discipline. The Spirit Light provided restraint, but when I was in
Laroque that summer, I drank more than usual.

Sometimes, I'd go off by myself with a bottle of scotch, sometimes
I'd hook up with Ox Mueller. The bars on River Road were dreary
places full of the same, familiar stories, but they livened up in the
summer, stirred by a constant influx of visiting fishermen. The mix
of locals and outsiders created a natural tension, and there were
always plenty of arguments and even a fight every now and then to
provide diversion. One night that summer when I was in the Loggers' Lounge, Archie Nye pulled a knife out of his boot and sliced
open the stomach of a bushy-haired man from Nashville. Archie
wasn't charged with anything—we'd all seen the argument escalate,
and the Nashville man had menaced Archie first with a broken high-
ball glass—but the sheriff told Archie to clear out of town for a
while, he was bad for business.

The demimonde of the bars operated far below Bow's realm, and
I did my best to keep the two worlds apart. For all Bow's curiosity
about Laroque, I doubt he—or his father or grandfather before
him—had ever set foot in any of the joints on River Road. In those
days, the people who lived on the Bluff never did. And if Bow
noticed that I was spending more nights down there that summer, he
never called me on it, at least not directly.

One morning after I'd put in a few days at the Spirit Light and
then a long night catching up on River Road, Bow found me
stretched out on the office sofa.

"Spend the night?" he asked pleasantly as he opened the window
wide to air the room.

"I didn't quite have the energy to get across the river," I said.

"What do you think of the new, improved sofa? It was looking so
ratty I had Mrs. Foster from the hardware store come up and clean it.
Quite a difference, no?"

I'd been breathing the vapors of Mrs. Foster's cleaning fluid all
night. "I miss some of the old spots," I said.

Bow stood above me. He was freshly shaved, the razor leaving a pattern of tiny nicks and scrapes on the uneven skin of his scar. Years ago, a story had passed among the children in town, untrue but resonant—the boiling oil that had mangled Bow's face hadn't been knocked over accidentally, but flung by Bow's hard father, furious at his clumsy son. Now, as Bow leaned close, I caught a whiff of lemony aftershave. His lengthening hair, blond gone brown now going gray, was combed back in waves above his ears. The collar of his starched white shirt nestled lightly under the folds of his blue pinstriped bespoke suit. I was the itinerant drunk, but I still felt a kind of wonder that he could get himself together, that the simple, domestic details of his life worked. "Let me buy you a good breakfast, Charlie," he offered.

At the Wanigan, four strangers occupied Bow's regular booth in back, so we sat at the counter. "Sorry," said Rita the waitress, explaining the intruders. "They're fishermen from Indianapolis. I wasn't expecting you this early."

"This is fine," Bow assured her.

Rita stared glumly at the fishermen. "They're loud," she said.

"Bring Charlie here some scrambled eggs, and I'll have a cup of coffee," Bow announced.

Rita frowned at him. A bad case of childhood acne had scarred the flesh beneath the corners of her mouth. Over the years, her face had softened, erasing the worst of the ravages, but seeing Bow's scar always stirred her up. "Can't Charlie order his own breakfast?" she groused.

"Scrambled's fine," I said, and Rita walked away.

Bow rotated on the counter stool, trying to get comfortable. "How are things at the Spirit Light?" he asked.

"The same."

"How are the bugs?"

"Down, so far. It's been dry."

"And Bob Morgan hasn't managed to save you yet?"

"He knows I'm a lost cause."

"That's when the Evangelicals get real excited," Bow said.

Rita brought the coffee and eggs. She let the plate clank down noisily in front of me. I ate without talking. Bow looked over a copy of the Milwaukee *Journal* someone had left on the counter. "They've landed a camera on the moon," he said after a while.

"Really?"

After another long silence, he mumbled, talking to himself, "That's right, just bomb the hell out of 'em."

He waited for me to finish the eggs, then he said, "I have to thank you, Charlie, for bringing Ginger into the office. That boy is getting on great."

Bow saw me start at this spot of revisionist history—I'd only invited Ginger up at Bow's direction, after all. Quickly, he pushed on. "I tell you, he'll make a terrific lawyer someday."

"Ginger Piper, Esquire," I mused.

"We'll have to do something about that name," Bow said.

"You know, you two have the same name."

"Huh?"

"George. He's really George. He told me the other day. When he was little, his sister couldn't pronounce it. The name came out 'Ginger,' and it stuck."

"Really," said Bow, sounding bored, burrowing into the paper again. The story irritated him, as if the idea that Ginger had another family—particularly one with enough spirit to adopt an affectionate, childish nickname—spoiled something.

"Actually, something did happen up at the Spirit Light," I said, changing the subject. "A guy caught a twenty-eight-pound muskie."

Bow looked up, faintly interested. He glanced at Eli Warzonek's forty-nine-pound prize on the trophy wall, still the local standard of excellence. "I heard some talk of that the other day," Bow said. "Anybody we know?"

"He was a friend of Bob's. A guy with a church group."

"Your party?"

"No, one of the other guides'. But I was there when they brought the fish in. They strung it up on the dock, and I assumed they were going to take pictures, but, instead, the whole busload of them held hands and started praying, thanking the Lord for giving them this fish."

"That's priceless," said Bow. "It's almost pagan. I wish I had a picture."

"Then they never gave the guide a tip. Bob himself finally slipped him five dollars."

"At least Bob knows who to thank for a big fish."

The bell on the Wanigan's door tinkled, and Tom Mitford, the haberdashery owner, stepped into the restaurant. He quickly surveyed the possibilities and then folded his long body onto a stool beside Bow. "How's things?" Mitford asked.

"Okay," said Bow. "Okay."

Mitford signaled Rita for coffee. "I hear you've got Ginger Piper working for you," he said.

"He's doing great work," said Bow.

"The fellows out at the county were a little upset that he quit his job there."

"Oh, for Christ's sake." Bow looked away.

"It's just that some other kid could have had the job, and now it's too late."

"He's too bright a boy to waste his time cutting weeds on the side of the road."

"Good, hard physical labor never hurt anyone," said Mitford, tripping over his words, probably realizing when the sentence was half out that Bow had never been capable of serious physical labor.

"Come on, Tom," Bow said.

Mitford stirred his coffee. "An agreement's an agreement," he said. "The boy gave his word."

Bow sighed. "Well, I've got to get back to my criminals." He told Rita to put the bill on his tab.

Mitford suddenly worried that he'd chased Bow away. "No offense, Bow," the haberdasher said. "That's just what people were saying."

No offense taken, Bow assured him.

Outside, Main Street stretched emptily toward the Opera House. The shopping wouldn't pick up for another hour or so. Half a block away, Boyce Rensinger was hosing off the canopy of his drugstore.

"Mitford's brother works for the county," I told Bow. "Mitford probably takes it as a personal affront that Ginger gave up the job."

"This town can't stand that he's special," said Bow. "Anything apart from the great heartland heap worries them."

"That's not true. He's a hero."

"Yeah. The boy who sunk the shot. This is different. This isn't a game."

"You talk as if he's the only kid from Laroque who ever amounted to anything."

"Am I the only one who sees it?"

Rensinger spotted Bow and waved, spraying water with the hose. Bow crossed the street to avoid him as we headed back to the office.

I didn't have many occasions to be alone with Ginger, but a few days later, around lunchtime, I ran into him at Veterans' Park. He was sitting on a bench, eating a sandwich and chips, and looking through a copy of *Time* magazine with a story on the cover about the draft, "Vietnam and the Class of '66." He'd been in the law library all morning, and he wanted to know if anything had gone on in the office.

"Same old stuff," I told him. "The mail's late."

"Bow okay? Was he looking for me?"

"He knew you were at the library."

Ginger put the magazine down and pulled the bottom of his tie out of his shirt pocket, where he'd carefully tucked it for lunch. He seemed to enjoy dressing up. He owned two sports jackets—a blue blazer and a gray plaid number—and he wore them on alternate days. Every now and then I'd see him after work on the Turner Bridge, surrounded by a group of grubby friends, his tie loosened and his jacket draped over his shoulder, looking entirely rakish and pleased with himself. "I've been looking up cases for Gary Fontenot," Ginger said. "I think Bow might be able to do something with that car search."

"Bow thinks so, too. He wants to go over to Lovington to see Fontenot again." Over the months, the wiry little inmate had continued to correspond, every letter composed in the same miniature handwriting.

"You know, Charlie, if you're scheduled for a fishing trip, I can drive Bow to Lovington." Ginger fussed with his tie, ironing it with his hand. It occurred to me that the visit by Mrs. Foster and her cleaning fluid might have been his suggestion.

"No," I said. "I'll drive."

"I can do it if you need me."

"I've been driving him for ten years."

Ginger picked up his bag of potato chips. "You want some?" he asked.

I shook my head.

He tossed a few chips in his mouth and crunched them thoughtfully. Nearby, a young mother was picnicking with her two small children in the shadow of the war monument, and a handful of older folks occupied some of the other benches. But the little park was surprisingly quiet for a pleasant June day.

"What do you think about George Hamilton dating Lynda Bird Johnson?" Ginger asked suddenly.

"What the hell brought that up?"

"I saw something in *Time*. I never liked him much anyway, but they seem like a strange couple. A Hollywood actor and the president's daughter. He's so slick and good-looking, and she's no dish, by a long shot. But I guess you do what you have to do to avoid the draft."

"How does dating her keep him out of the army?"

"You think Johnson can't arrange it?" Ginger challenged. *Don't you know anything, you miserable drunk?* He held half a potato chip in the fingers of one hand and defied me to respond. Bow was right, Ginger owned a lawyer's instincts, relishing the argument, pressing his advantage. Talking to him was like navigating a series of small squalls.

"From what I've read, Lyndon and Lady Bird would be just as happy if Hamilton got drafted and never came back," I said.

Ginger smiled and eased up, gobbling more potato chips. Across the plaza, two workmen were hanging from ropes and harnesses on the outside of the Opera House, repairing as best they could the building's graceful filigree. The delicate wood had cracked and chipped in spots—one time the bell tower had been struck by lightning and the entire exterior suffered. A noisy minority on the city council had wanted to save money and just strip the filigree away. After weeks of discussion, the preservationists had won the battle, and now these fellows, brought up from Milwaukee, were trying to restore the art laid down eighty years before by a handful of imported Italian craftsmen.

Ginger noticed me admiring the work and said, "You love that building, don't you?"

"I used to spend a lot of time there," I explained, wondering, How did he know?

"Maybe you're a frustrated actor," Ginger suggested.

"No," I said, suppressing my irritation, "it's just memories."

We watched one of the workmen laboriously lift himself by his ropes and pulleys a few feet higher on the building's wall. "Anna wants to be an actress," Ginger said.

"Anna?"

"You know, Anna Sterritt, my friend."

I recalled the girl who'd been with him on the bridge. "Ah. Well, she's certainly pretty enough to be on stage."

Ginger smiled, thanking me for the compliment. "How are you and Lucy Braestrup getting on?" he asked mischievously.

I kept staring across the plaza, working harder now to swallow my irritation. Whatever Lucy and I had together, we'd tried to keep it to ourselves. I wasn't even sure if Bow knew.

"It's nothing," I told Ginger, and then immediately regretted betraying Lucy just to shut up this wise-ass kid. "About driving Bow," I said officiously.

"Look," Ginger interrupted, "I don't want to mess up the situation you've got with him. You've been working there for years."

"I'm only looking out for Bow's interests," I explained, though that was only half true.

"Of course," Ginger said generously.

Trying to shake the defensiveness I felt, I said, "This has worked out well for you, hasn't it?"

"The job?"

"Yes."

"I'm really loving it."

"And Bow's all right, isn't he?"

Ginger's fine-featured face still had a child's freshness of expression, and it suddenly turned fiercely intense. "He's a great man," Ginger said. "You know what I mean? A *great* man."

I knew exactly what he meant, and, of course, he was right, though it grated in a small way to hear it pronounced so confidently by someone so young. Later, when I told Bow what Ginger had said, Bow was bothered, too, though for a far different reason. There was a famous story: When Holmes told his father that he wanted to be a lawyer, the father, the celebrated poet/doctor, recoiled. "Why, Wendy, why would you want to do that?" Holmes, Sr., demanded. "A lawyer can't be a *great* man." Bow had told Ginger the story, and now Bow wondered if the boy was being ironic, describing him that way. "Wasn't Ginger joking? Wasn't his tongue just a little bit in his cheek?" Bow asked. I assured him that it was not. Bow shook his head. "Why would he say that?" he wondered. "Why would he say that, of all things?"

CHAPTER 9

A s it turned out, all three of us made the visit to Gary
Fontenot at Lovington. I wasn't about to give up my role as
Bow's driver, and Ginger naturally was curious to get a
glimpse inside a prison. The day of the trip fell in the middle of a
June heat wave. I met up with Ginger on Main Street at about eight
that morning, and the boxy electric sign hanging on the corner of
the Bank Building said the temperature had already hit 82 degrees.
There was no wind, and the steady sun gave the river a sweet, slightly
sulfurous smell. The town was preparing for a Lumberjack Day, one
of a handful of street sales organized every summer. Despite the heat
and the early hour, Main Street bustled as merchants set up their
tables and booths on the sidewalks. Ginger and I bought Wanigan
sweet rolls from Rita and took several along to give Bow.

He was waiting in his office. "Miranda, boys!" he cried when he
saw us. "Remember that name: Miranda. And I don't mean Car-
men." He waved his cigar, leaving a trail of smoke. The newspaper littered his desk.

The day before, in what was immediately recognized as a landmark in American law, the U.S. Supreme Court had ruled that police
can't question suspects until they've been warned of their right to
remain silent. From now on, confessions obtained without the warn-

ing wouldn't be admitted in court. For a criminal defense lawyer, this
was a huge gift, a glorious opening for protecting clients. Bow had
been following the case as it moved through the courts, and he had
talked to me about it often, but now he was disappointed that Ginger and I hadn't heard that the ruling had come down.

"We haven't seen the paper yet," I explained.

"God bless Earl Warren," Bow crowed, honoring the chief justice
and author of the decision. "Another great Republican."

Ginger peered through the smoke curling around Bow's head.
"Who's Miranda?" he asked.

"Ernesto Miranda. A rapist from Arizona. His name is on the case,
Miranda v. Arizona. Now he's part of history."

"He'll go free?" asked Ginger.

"Maybe. Who knows? Depends on the other evidence against
him. But the fact is, freedom has won a great victory." Bow looked
from one of us to the other. "This is a day of jubilation."

"Do you still want to drive to Lovington?" Ginger asked. He'd
been looking forward to this trip.

"Yes, yes, yes," said Bow, sounding mildly peeved. What was the
use of assembling a team if you couldn't celebrate together? Ginger
and I were entirely too slow to catch on.

On the way to the car, Bow's enthusiasm bubbled again. He
stopped to chat about the heat with Boyce Rensinger, whose Lumberjack Day table was covered with lotions and soaps, all selling for a
dollar, and then he bought two little airplane bottles of Chivas Regal
from the booth in front of the liquor store. "I'll celebrate yet," Bow
vowed, dropping the bottles into his coat pocket.

Because of the sale, Main Street was closed to cars. I'd parked the
Pontiac a few blocks away, in front of the low-slung brick building
that housed the offices for WLRK, Laroque's radio station. Bow
decided he wanted to stop in and take a look at the stories about
Miranda coming over the wire machine.

No one was patrolling the counter in the station's lobby, so Bow
marched us straight back to the glass closet where an Associated Press
terminal clacked away in intermittent bursts. Bow liked to stay on
top of major breaking news; after the Kennedy assassination, he'd

spent much of the weekend holed up in this cramped, little room. Now he pawed through the yellow paper tumbling out of the machine until he found a story about the case that included long excerpts from the decision. He ripped it off the roll and sat down to read in a metal chair.

Ginger and I browsed through the other stories that had been piling up since the night before. "More Americans were killed in Vietnam last week than South Vietnamese," Ginger said, reading one account. A few minutes later, he handed me a story about a lawyer from Sheboygan, a member of the John Birch Society, who'd given a speech arguing that Senator Joe McCarthy hadn't died naturally—that in fact he may have been murdered by his enemies. "They've finally figured out what your dad was up to," Ginger teased. I'd told him about the visits from the FBI.

After a while, Marcus Laney, the prunish man who owned and ran the station, appeared at the door. "I guess you've been on a roll lately," he said to Bow. "First Dr. Sam Sheppard and now this."

"The Sheppard case is trivial," Bow said.

"He kills his wife and gets away with it. I guess that's trivial in your book."

"He was *accused* of killing his wife. Then the press convicted him, Marcus. We don't know if he did it or not."

"And this Miranda fellow—even though he confessed, I suppose we don't know if he did it, either?"

"You leave a man alone with the police for three or four hours, and they can get him to confess to anything."

"Oh, Christ." Laney scrunched his face. He was about Bow's age, and his spray of boyish freckles had turned blotchy and rough.

"Listen, Marcus," Bow said, reluctantly putting down the AP story. "Imagine that you're some poor, uneducated slob who gets picked up by the cops. The rich guy, who lives in a fancy neighborhood a few blocks away, knows that the Fifth Amendment protects him against self-incrimination and knows he doesn't have to talk when he gets arrested. The mobster, who lives across town, gets picked up by the FBI, which warns its suspects of their rights. So *he* doesn't talk until he's seen his lawyer. But you, because you're poor and dumb and uninformed, you don't know you can keep quiet. So you spill everything. Now, is that fair?"

Laney didn't respond at first or even look at Bow. He watched the wire machine spit out another story. Finally, he said, in his best, deep radio voice, "The trouble with you, Bow, is that you're stuck on details."

Bow was amused. "Well, that's very perceptive of you, Marcus," he said. He beamed at Ginger and me, then back at Laney.

"You miss the big picture," Laney pressed on, resentful that Bow wasn't wounded by the first insult.

"Well—"

"You forget what's really at stake," Laney interrupted, his great, flat voice wavering slightly as he riled himself up. "We're losing sight of the basics, getting carried away by incidental rights and things and ignoring the fundamental rights, like the right to be safe." Laney had a story: His niece, or maybe it was the niece of a friend, had been raped in San Francisco. She could identify the rapist, and the cops picked him up, but for reasons that weren't quite clear in Laney's account, the authorities couldn't make the charges stick. The suspect was released, and, it turned out, he lived in the girl's neighborhood. She'd see her attacker on the street, in the grocery store. It drove her into a bottomless depression, and eventually, she tried to kill herself. She was under care now, but her recovery was uncertain.

Bow listened patiently. He'd heard the story before; it was one of Laney's favorites. Out of politeness, Bow waited several seconds while the clattering AP machine crushed the echo of Laney's last, plangent words. "That's a sad story, Marcus," Bow said finally. "But it's just a story. You and I don't know the specifics of what happened— maybe the girl was hallucinating, maybe she shacked up and later regretted it—we just don't know."

Bow took a breath, preparing himself. Ginger and I shared a glance. We both knew what was coming. "That's the Tyranny of the Anecdotal Argument," Bow crowed. "Logic, linear thinking, plain old common sense—they all get pushed aside in the face of the dramatic story." I'd heard it many times: You can walk a man intellectually from A to B to C, but if he encounters a telling anecdote along the way—usually something involving bathos or pity or imagined pain—chances are he'll spin off in some other direction. Reason is hopeless, impotent when someone has a contradictory story embedded in his head. And so on, and so on. Bow liked to make a spectacle out of his rant, as if it were a kind of party act for the entertainment of the guests. Of course, he was happy to use an anecdotal argument himself if the occasion called for it.

Laney had heard it before, too. "It's not just you, Bow," he interrupted. "I sit here at night reading the crap that comes over that machine. Riots. Demonstrations. Kids blowing things up. And, now, no one likes the cops. They used to be our friends, but not anymore. Now if you're a cop, you're the enemy, and that's all the courts care about."

"Not quite."

"I tell you, Bow, I feel like I'm reading about the end of the world. It's incredible. I mean it. The story of the end of the world, coming right over the wires. Item by item, all the foundations slipping away. Sometimes I think I should go on air and break the news: 'It's Over. Make Your Peace.'"

"Now you're starting to depress me, Marcus."

Laney stopped himself. It was hard to tell how serious he was. My father thought Laney had a natural acting talent and used to cast him in children's roles. One Christmas years ago, his Tiny Tim delighted the whole town. But even as he'd made a success of the radio station, he had grown into a sour adult, twice divorced, recently recovering from cancer surgery. His theatrical instincts had been channeled into his radio program, which allowed him to comment—morbidly, for the most part—on events large and small. Everyone complained, but the whole town tuned in.

Laney turned from Bow and smiled weakly at Ginger. "What's it like having a job with someone who's always rooting for the bad guy?" Laney asked.

"Like doing God's work," Ginger said.

By the time we got to Lovington, the heat was pushing into the upper nineties. Behind the prison walls, the thick air swarmed with pungent odors. The sergeant at the front desk, a heavyset man with a hairy neck, had sweated through his khaki shirt, which now looked almost black. He didn't want to let Ginger in because inmates were limited to two visitors at a time. Bow had to call the warden's office to get an exception.

The guard named Clarence showed up to walk us to the interview room. "Your first time inside?" he asked Ginger.

"Yes."

"I'll give you a treat." Clarence took us on a shortcut through a cell block. Deeper inside the prison, the air got worse. The inmates draped their nearly naked bodies on the bars of their cells, watching sullenly as we passed. For once, no one called out to Bow. Near the end of the block, Clarence swung wide of a cell door. "Stay away from that one," he warned, pointing to a bearish figure covered with a blanket and curled up on a cot. "He throws shit."

The interview room was empty. Because we were late, the guards had taken Fontenot back to his cell. Now, we had to wait.

"Can't you do anything about the air in here?" Bow asked Clarence. "It's like being inside someone's lung."

The guard shrugged. "It's summer."

Fontenot finally appeared, looking impossibly fresh; his light blue prison uniform still had a crease.

"How do you stay so cool?" Bow asked.

"I never sweat much," Fontenot said.

"Well, you're inhuman."

"Who's this?" Fontenot asked, indicating Ginger.

"My new assistant," said Bow.

"What's wrong with this one?" The inmate nodded at me.

"For you, I've got two." Bow mopped his face with his handkerchief. In the heat, he didn't have the patience for Fontenot. "Let's go over a few points on your appeal," Bow said, brandishing his legal pad. "The argument is scheduled in a few weeks."

Fontenot put his hands behind his head and rocked slowly in his chair. "I wanted to tell you to forget about it," he said, glancing for Bow's reaction.

"Forget about it?" Bow asked.

"Yeah."

"You mean, drop the appeal?"

"Yeah."

"Why?"

"I did it. What's the use of playing a stupid game? I just want to serve the time and get it over with."

"What about that guy you loaned your car to, the one you said did it?"

Fontenot winced.

Bow mopped his face again and puffed his cheeks, blowing out air. He waited. Every now and then, a distant shout carried through the building. The dim olive walls of the interview room seemed to be closing in. We weren't in a lung but a jungle, windless and full of rot.

"Has the prosecutor been talking to you?" Bow asked.

"Nah," said Fontenot.

"No deals? A promise of leniency if you ratted out your fence?"

"I wouldn't do that."

"I don't suppose you would." Bow doodled on his legal pad.

Fontenot felt he had to explain himself. "I don't want to waste people's time," he said. "Especially yours. I did it and I got caught. It's simple."

"Not really." Bow kept doodling.

In the corner of my eye, I thought I saw Ginger's head bob. When I looked over, he'd snapped back up to attention.

"It's actually pretty complicated," Bow said. "There are several elements at work here. There's the one that deals with your guilt and innocence and your punishment, and that's the one that affects you directly. But there's also the process, and that concerns everyone, all of us."

Fontenot folded his arms across his chest. Years of petulance had worn away his repertoire of responses to people who were telling him something important.

"We're in a kind of war," Bow went on. "The police and the prosecutors are soldiers for the other side. They're always pushing, pushing, trying to get away with as much as they can. They aren't necessarily bad—that's just the nature of their work. But it's my responsibility, through cases like yours, to push back."

Bow paused. In the heat, his little speech was an exertion. "And it's war, not a game," he continued after a moment, "because all those pushes by the state, inch by inch, case by case, add up. And after a while, you've got a country not at all like the one envisioned by its founders—where the police can beat a confession out of you, or bust into your home at night, or put you away for days without letting you talk to a lawyer."

Fontenot waited to make sure Bow was finished. "Fine," he said. "But that's not my case. I hit this house. I got caught with the stuff. The cops treated me good all the way. I got no complaints."

"But wait." Bow leaned forward. Sweat dribbled down his face. The top of his shirt collar was soaked. "They searched your car. What gave them the right to go pawing through your car?"

"My brake light was busted."

"So? *So?*"

"That's against the law."

"Stopping your car for a broken brake light is one thing," Bow said. "Searching through your glove compartment is another."

Fontenot took a deep breath. My stomach fluttered to see him suck in all that stinking air. "You make things too complicated," he said. "If I'd got away with it, fine. I've done dozens of other jobs and not been caught. I got no regrets. But this time, I got caught, and to me, it's simple, I gotta do the time. Your problem is you think about things too much."

Bow turned to Ginger. "All of a sudden today, everyone's figured me out," Bow said with a laugh.

Ginger perched stiffly forward on his plain wood chair. He didn't appear to be paying attention. Suddenly, he stood up. "I'm sorry," he gasped. The color drained from his face. His voice seemed to be coming from underwater. "The air . . . I've gotta get outta here."

Bow stared.

"He's gonna faint," said Fontenot calmly.

"Jesus," yelped Bow.

Fontenot hopped up and caught Ginger just as his legs wobbled and gave way. Holding him beneath the arms, Fontenot lowered the boy slowly to the concrete floor, then propped him up, so Ginger sat with his legs bent and his head between his knees. "Just breathe deep," the inmate said, kneeling beside him. "The air's better down here."

Ginger pressed his eyes shut, screwing his face into ghostly wrinkles. Fontenot pulled out a clean, white handkerchief and stroked back from Ginger's hairline, running the cloth over the top of the boy's damp head.

I banged on the door for help and soon Clarence came in with a plastic cup of water. Fontenot sniffed it and handed it back. "Not this prison piss," he said. "Get him a Coke." Clarence wheeled dutifully and returned a few minutes later with a cold bottle of Coke. Fontenot helped Ginger take a few tentative sips. Several other guards slipped into the room and huddled around the group of us. They whispered among themselves. "Gary's a good nurse, ain't he?" snickered one. Bow glared at them.

The Coke revived Ginger. He blinked and rubbed his face. The color started to come back. Fontenot helped him to his feet. "God, I'm sorry," Ginger said, looking at Bow.

"Not your fault," Bow said.

Ginger still clung to Fontenot's arm. "I think I'd be better off outside," the boy said.

Bow gathered his jacket and his legal pad. He told Fontenot, "You think about it. I'm not dropping the appeal until I get the word in writing from you."

Fontenot sat back down in his chair and looked out over his half smile.

"I think I can win this case," Bow told him.

Clarence hustled us out and locked the door, leaving Fontenot alone in the middle of the room. The quickest way out took us back through the cell block. This time, the shit-heaving inmate stood at the bars. He was a boy, not much older than Ginger, with a huge, round face. He watched us hurry past, his hands safely in front of him.

Outside, the day seemed improbably bright and scrubbed. Ginger sat on the curb at the parking lot. He put his head in his hands and sucked in big gulps of air. I realized I'd been renewed myself.

That's one of life's gifts, I suppose—how someone else's misery can distract.

After a while, we walked over to the Pontiac, then had to stand on the baking pavement, flapping the car doors, waiting for the interior to cool. Ginger kept trying to apologize.

"I've never fainted," said Bow, trying to divert him. "What's it like?"

"It felt like everything had run out of my head, like my head was empty. My body weighed a ton."

"That's me all the time," said Bow.

Ginger still looked bruised; his lips had a purplish hue. "I hope I'm not claustrophobic."

"You'd know," Bow told him.

Behind the fence in the recreation yard, a handful of inmates threw up lazy shots at a basket. The ball clanged against the metal backboard. Through the shimmery, overheated air, the gray prison, patterned with tiny, barred windows, looked abandoned—the husk of an empty hornet's nest, a dead animal you'd find on the road.

Back in the car, Ginger asked, "What's gonna happen to Fontenot?"

"I think he'll come around," said Bow. "I think he understood what I was talking about."

"I wouldn't count on it," I interjected. Even after he'd stepped in to help Ginger, Fontenot's cocky disregard for Bow rubbed me the wrong way.

"Meaning what?" said Bow, irritated.

"Meaning nothing. It's just a fact: Fontenot doesn't have the foggiest notion of your sense of justice."

"There are no neutral facts, Charlie. Facts are just pieces of arguments."

I shrugged. "I'm not arguing. I'm just saying that guys like Fontenot are basically out for themselves. He probably wants to drop the appeal because he's decided he's better off in prison."

"Well, I think I can make use of his case." Bow turned to Ginger, who was stretched out on the backseat. "You write him and tell him to let us file the appeal. I have a feeling he'll listen to you."

"I bet he will," said Ginger.

"How about it, Charlie?" Bow asked, still seeking my endorsement despite his passing irritation.

"Why not?" I said.

Within a few miles, Ginger was asleep in back. Bow and I shared his little bottles of Chivas Regal, drinking quick toasts to Ernesto Miranda.

CHAPTER 10

Though Bow's father lived his life in a region famed for its hunting and fishing, he never had the least interest in outdoor activities. He was a banker, though, and couldn't pass up a good deal. One year, not long before the stock market crash, he made an unusual, private loan to one of the struggling lumber mills along the Agnes—a transaction secured by a large tract about fifty miles northwest of Laroque. The mill limped into the Depression, then collapsed, and Mr. Epps collected one of the biggest private parcels of uncultivated land in Wisconsin, thousands of acres of woods and lakes. Over the years, the property got sold off and whittled down, but the sizable chunk that remained eventually passed to Bow. He wasn't any more interested in hunting and fishing than his father had been, but he appreciated the outdoors for its beauty and solitude. Once a year, usually in September, after the frost had killed off most of the mosquitoes, he and I would take a four-day canoe trip around the landholding, camping on the lakes and catching walleyes for dinner.

The summer that Ginger worked for him, Bow decided to push up the itinerary—he'd take his trip in July, and this time the three of us would go. At first, Ginger hesitated, though he didn't have a good excuse. "Why wouldn't he want to come along?" Bow asked me. "I'd think he'd jump at the chance."

"Maybe he's got a better way to spend a summer weekend than paddling around a wilderness with two middle-aged guys," I suggested. But I sensed that Ginger wanted to avoid the forced intimacy of a camping trip—the days spent together, the evenings around a fire. There'd be no escape. He knew that Bow was growing increasingly invested in him, and I think Ginger realized that a camping trip, with its shared adventures and challenges, would tie them together irrevocably. With a little prodding from Bow, Ginger eventually did agree to go, but he had probably been right to hesitate, because after that trip, there was no escape for either of them from the other.

The evening before we were to leave, Ox Mueller and I prowled the bars on River Road, but I bailed out early and headed to Bow's office, where I planned to spend the night. Back at the Bank Building, I noticed a light coming from deep within the offices on the first floor. By entering through the alley, then going up to the second floor and down the back staircase, I could get to the bank without tripping the main alarm. As I suspected, Lucy was at her desk, curled over a stack of papers. For several seconds, I stood in the shadows and watched. She looked utterly self-contained in her labor. Surrounded by darkness, wearing a lacy blouse frilled up around her neck, a single funnel of light from a desk lamp illuminating the concentrated effort in her face, she could have been a study for an Old Master painting illustrating faith. Just as I decided to slip away, leaving her to her work, she sensed my presence and glanced up.

"Charlie!" she called out, barely startled. "I didn't think you were around."

"Why are *you* around?"

She dropped her pencil onto the desk. "Because *someone* has to look over these loan applications. They're amazing. The references don't check out, the addresses are all wrong, whole sections are blank. But does the bank give a shit? No, it just hands out the money. Sign on the dotted line. You should tell your friend Bow—one of these days he's gonna wake up and find the vault in his bank is empty."

"I don't think he'd care much."

She leveled me with a glare. "Don't kid yourself."

I pulled up a chair in front of her desk. "It's eight-thirty," I said. "How much longer are you going to work?"

"I suppose I could call it a day." She sighed and started stacking the papers on her desk. "Why are you here?" she asked. "On a nice, rainy Thursday night like this, I would think you'd be out running around."

I told her that we'd be leaving at dawn for the camping trip.

"It's a little early in the season, isn't it? You usually go in the fall."

"Bow wanted to go. I think he wanted to get it in before Ginger was back in school."

"Ginger Piper's going, too?" She sounded genuinely surprised.

"Yeah."

"Bow's really got the hots for that kid, doesn't he?" She saw that she'd offended me and quickly added, "I mean, he's really intrigued by him."

Beyond Lucy, a tidy row of chunky desks disappeared into the darkness, a line of tanks guarding cold secrets. "Listen," I said. "It's still early. Why don't you come upstairs with me. I'll be gone for the next four days anyway."

Lucy dropped her chin into her hand, looking weary. "I don't know. I should probably get back to my mom. I didn't tell her I'd be out late." Lucy still lived with her mother, a frail woman I'd met only a handful of times. "Besides," she added, plucking at the billowy collar of her blouse, "I feel so grubby. I've been in these clothes for over twelve hours."

Inspiration suddenly struck. "We can take a bath in Bow's bathtub," I proposed. "It's huge, like a swimming pool!"

"Charlie!" She was in high school again, tempted but mortally shy.

I stood and walked behind her, bending to kiss the top of her head. "Come on," I said. "It's a beautiful bathtub with clawed feet. It deserves to be used." She leaned back against me, relenting. We stayed that way for a few seconds, propped against each other. My gaze floated over the first loan application in her neat pile, a handwritten entreaty filled out in blocky black letters by Errol Piper, Ginger's father.

Filling the tub generated great clouds of steam. Lucy and I stripped in Bow's office, then stood around inside the bathroom, waiting for the tub's water level to rise, hardly able to see each other through the warm, soupy air. The tiled walls and floor dripped with moisture, and we were soaked in sweat and condensation. With her features washed out by the steam, Lucy had a kind of unitary completeness, a looming presence, and I was vividly aware that she was easily as tall as I, five-ten or so. Finally, when the time came, she took my hand and we helped each other step gingerly into the tub. She laid her head at the broad curved end, and I tucked mine beside the gold-plated spigot.

We lounged there, waggling toes in each other's face. The tub felt extravagant. Built specially for Bow's father, it was half again the size of a normal bathtub and sat up like a throne on its clawed feet. Lucy wondered out loud if Mr. Epps had dawdled in it with Miss Sinclair years ago; then, remembering the portrait of the somber, fleshy old man, she vowed to put the thought out of her mind. After half an hour or so, I maneuvered around to her end and spooned her. We tested three or four positions, rolling around the tub and splashing water onto the floor. But with the slippery surfaces and our wet bodies, balance was tricky and the action difficult to sustain. Finishing was impossible, more awkward even than on Bow's spongy sofa. So we finally climbed out and made a satisfying bed of towels on the damp tile floor.

Afterward, Lucy asked, "Do you think this is how life on land developed? Some lady amoeba wants to get off, so she drags her man onto hard ground?"

I told her it sounded possible.

"What time do you suppose it is?"

I felt perfectly warm and comfortable, lying on the wet towels, Lucy stretched on top of me with the top of her head just beneath my chin. "Around nine-thirty," I said, underestimating, hoping to hold her a bit longer.

She shot up. "My God, I gotta go. My mother will be frantic."

After the steamy bathroom, Bow's office felt cold. Lucy hurried to get dressed. I poured myself a nightcap from Bow's office bottle of

Chivas Regal. "Will you be camping the same place as always?" Lucy asked.

"Yeah. Bow's property. We'll move around a bit, depending on the bugs and the fish."

She paused in buttoning her blouse and looked at me. "Does it bother you to bring along Ginger? This was always your trip with Bow."

"Not really. Bow and I have lots of time together. And besides, I like the kid. I can see why Bow admires him." I decided, as I spoke, that I was telling her the truth.

"I see Ginger around every now and then," Lucy said. "He has such . . . vitality."

While she primped in the reflection in the window, I said, "I noticed that Ginger's father is asking for a loan."

She swung around abruptly. "Did you see the application on my desk? Those are confidential documents."

"I wasn't snooping, I couldn't help it. It was just a glance."

She returned to the window. "I can't imagine how he'll get it," she said. "He doesn't have a regular job, he's hardly got any income. And he wants the loan to start a Christmas tree business. Do you think Wisconsin needs another Christmas tree vendor?"

"Maybe Bow will help," I said.

"Bow never pays attention to what goes on in the bank—except to deposit his dividend checks." Lucy sighed. "But what do I know?" She grabbed her handbag. "Do I look okay?" she asked. "Will my mother guess?"

Steam escaping from the bathroom had wilted the starch in her blouse and turned her skirt into a clingy swatch of cloth. Her makeup had washed away, and her hair had exploded into a corona of red-blond curls. Anyone past puberty could guess what she'd been up to. "You look perfect," I told her. "She'll never know."

"'Bye, Charlie," she said, hurrying out. "Have fun with the boys." She blew me a kiss across the office, and then she was gone.

Ginger was sitting on the steps of Bow's house just after sunrise the next morning when I walked up Summer Street from the office. His father had dropped him off half an hour earlier, Ginger explained, but he hadn't rung the bell—he didn't want to wake Bow. "He's up," I told him, and laid on the button. Bow appeared in his usual camping garb—once-a-year blue jeans and a khaki English fishing shirt covered with pockets. I tied Bow's red canvas Old Town canoe onto the top of the Pontiac and loaded the other equipment and provisions—most of it stuffed in backpacks—into the trunk. The morning was muggy. Hot, patchy sunlight occasionally broke through the clouds, but it looked as if we'd be rained on before the day was out.

The trip to the property took ninety minutes. The highway streaked through open, gently rolling fields, languorously inhabited by small herds of Holsteins, blotches of black and white. Nobody in the car said much. Ginger slouched in the backseat. His dim and puffy eyes suggested he hadn't got much sleep the night before. Bow fought the lazy tedium by turning on the radio. The news was all Vietnam: A Marine raid in the Central Highlands had surprised a Viet Cong unit, killing a dozen. Peking was protesting that an American bombing raid had strayed into Chinese territory. Richard Nixon was stumping for Republican candidates in Ohio, arguing that Republicans could end the war. A band of demonstrators in Manhattan had broken into a recruiter's office and dumped red paint on the files.

The report of the demonstration set Bow harrumphing about faddish, selfish college students. The chaos of protest annoyed him. He'd heard a report: A sociologist had tested some students at an antiwar rally and ninety percent couldn't locate Vietnam on a map. "Ninety percent!" Bow cried. "They hadn't even done their homework."

The remark settled in the car like a dare. After a few seconds, Ginger piped up, "Why do you need to find Vietnam on a map to oppose the war?"

"So you can argue intelligently. So you can defend your position. So you can show you're not just along for the ride. That was Coach Lombardi's point, and it applies to all aspects of life: Everything starts with discipline. You've got to have discipline to enjoy freedom."

Bow's blast pressed Ginger into a corner of the backseat. So far, he had avoided talking about the war around Bow. At first I thought Ginger was simply being polite, staying away from a subject that he knew divided him from his patron. But later I suspected that Ginger's reticence was designed for his own protection. He felt so passionately about the war that he couldn't bear the thought of losing an argument over it, and he knew he wasn't equipped yet to take on Bow. Ginger's approach—emotional, intuitive—was exactly opposite Bow's fierce application of logic and history. But beyond that, I think Ginger understood earlier than the rest of us that, here at home, the argument over the war was something more—it was becoming an argument over your fundamental beliefs, even over how you lived your life. And he wasn't yet ready to put all that at risk.

Now, in the car, he simply stared out the window, letting the pregnant silence slowly deflate. We made the rest of the trip without talking.

After about an hour of driving, the farms gave way to pine woods. The highway swept past the forest wall, broken here and there by an isolated house or a patch of commerce, a log-cabin bar or a gas station/bait shop combination. A few miles outside a town called Ridgefield, I turned down a rutted gravel road that led to a lake called Bent Pine. There was no easy access to Bow's land. You could hike in over an old logging trail that circled the lake, but the most direct route was to paddle across Bent Pine, then portage the canoe and camping equipment to the sprawling chain of lakes that belonged to Bow.

The Pontiac bounced down the road for a half mile or so, the canoe thudding heavily on the roof, until the trail paused at a tired boat landing. On the right, an old, round-topped silver trailer lay in the shadows of the trees. A shingled wood shack had been appended to the trailer's side—though perhaps the shack had been there first; it was impossible to tell. Beyond the shack, and scattered back as far as the eye could see, stretched a teeming collection of junk—wood vegetable boxes piled shoulder high; two whole rusted sinks sitting one on top of the other; a rotting wood armoire filled with shoes and jars and old magazines; bundled newspapers; old lamps; a naked bedspring leaning on its side. On and on the stuff continued, spreading among the pines as if it were some kind of natural undergrowth.

A gray-haired lady in a yellow housecoat watched us from an old kitchen chair in front of the trailer.

"Let's go pay our respects to Mrs. Hennepin," said Bow.

I parked the car off the road. Fallen pine needles covered the ground and choked off vegetation. Mrs. Hennepin's front yard was a cushiony blanket of brown.

"How are you, dear lady?" asked Bow expansively.

"Good," she said, pleased to see him. She could have been any-where from sixty to ninety, but it was hard to imagine that her round, weathered face had ever looked young. She was shucking peas, catching them in a blue glass bowl between her knees and throwing the husks in a pile at her feet. The small mountain of bright green husks sparkled against the dead pine needles.

"And how's the fishing been?" asked Bow.

"Worms," she said. "If you're after walleyes, they're eating big worms that move a lot. Lures won't do."

"Well, I better take a container of those worms, then," Bow told her.

Mrs. Hennepin put down her peas and walked over to a battered white refrigerator plugged in with an extension cord that ran through an open window of the trailer. She took out a cardboard coffee cup, pulled off its plastic cap, and used her finger to stir the moist, dark earth inside. "Plenty of big ones in there," she said, hand-ing the container to Bow. He quickly passed it to me.

"We're going out for a few days, and we'd like to park the car here," Bow said. "Do you mind keeping an eye on it?" He'd folded a ten-dollar bill neatly and now he slipped it into her pea-stained fingers.

She smiled and nodded without looking at the money. "You're early this year," she said.

Bow shrugged. "The call of the wild."

"You're going to get eaten by mosquitoes," she warned.

He waved her off. "I don't taste so good."

Ginger had wandered over to admire the labyrinth of junk behind the trailer. Several paths led off and disappeared among the assorted heaps and piles. "You sure have a lot of stuff," he said when he returned.

Mrs. Hennepin put her hands on her hips as if noticing the mess for the first time. "My husband wouldn't throw anything away," she explained. "He believed you never could tell when something would come in handy. So, I just got in the habit of saving. It's crazy, isn't it?" She smiled sheepishly.

"Not at all. Makes sense," said Ginger.

"He was good with his hands and he could make things," she went on. "Pieces of that Hudson there went into our next three cars." Far in back, the stripped hulk of a sedan had rusted the color of the pine needles. "With me, though, it's just a habit. I haven't thrown anything away since he died."

"How long ago was that?" Ginger asked politely.

"Twelve years May."

"Whoa. That's a lot of garbage."

She held up a green finger to correct him. "Not garbage. Trash. There's a difference. The garbage goes, the trash stays."

"Right," said Ginger.

We took the canoe off the car and slid it into the lake, then loaded it with gear. In the past, I'd paddled stern and Bow had taken the front, but this time, because we were three, Bow had announced he was riding in the middle, pasha style. Ginger and I built a soft throne for him out of the packs, and he climbed shakily on board. Ginger sat in the bow and I pushed us off.

After half an hour, we pulled up on the other side. The portage to Bow's property was about a mile, a tough hike along an animal trail that had been borrowed occasionally over the centuries by humans. I took the clothes pack and shouldered the canoe, while Ginger made a sandwich of himself with the food pack on his back and the tent pack in front. Bow followed up with the tackle box and the long aluminum case for the fishing rods. We kept to Bow's pace, so the going was slow. In the dampness of the woods, the mosquitoes swarmed, and we covered ourselves with repellent.

The logging company that once owned the land had numbered its lakes instead of bothering to name them. The system may have been practical once, but as lakes had been sold off, the logic disappeared. Bow owned Lakes Eleven, Fourteen, Seventeen, Eighteen, Twenty-two, and a weedy little puddle called Perch Lake that sometimes dried up in the summer. Lake Seventeen was the closest, and we reached it in under an hour. I set the canoe down on the edge of a thick tongue of gray granite thrusting into the water, and we loaded up and set off again. The sun had given up, and the clouds hung heavily. Along the shore, the treetops held a few ghostly traces of the morning fog. The air over the lake was so cool and moist that it seemed almost edible, an icy soufflé with a clean, faintly vegetable taste. It felt good to pull hard on the paddle, and for a long time, nobody talked. Once, Bow signaled us to stop. Rolling out of the trees, a boom, too sharp for thunder, echoed briefly around the lake. A gunshot, perhaps, or a distant jet muffled by the clouds. The sound faded and we went on.

At around noon, we stopped for sandwiches on a tiny rock island, then we paddled for another hour or so and made a short portage in to Lake Eighteen. The sky was getting heavier, and the long, narrow body of water twisted away in front of us, a slice of silver diving into the foggy distance. About a third of the way up the lake, we stopped for the night at a spot where the rocky shore climbed quickly to a small plateau. Bow and I had been camping there for years, and I'd built a functional little fireplace out of stones. In the past, however, we'd always come after the fall frost had wilted most of the foliage from the underbrush. Now, Ginger and I had to use a camp saw and a hatchet to clear a place for the ancient green canvas tent.

As drizzle began to fall, we each set to our individual tasks. Ginger assembled the fishing rods. I went down to the edge of the lake to build a live box, a corral of stones in the water where we could keep walleyes we'd caught until we were ready to eat. Bow gathered firewood. The rain picked up, drumming a steady background to our chores. Moving around camp in hooded, olive-colored rain parkas, working quickly and hardly talking, we looked like brothers in an ancient religious order, tending our timeless business.

After a while, Bow came down to the shore. I'd taken off my boots and was wading around in the water, scooping up handfuls of gravel to fill in the outer wall of the live box. "Cold?" he asked.

"Not like September." The lake water actually felt almost soupy against the rain-cooled air.

"If it rains tomorrow, I think we might lay over here for a day,"

Bow said. "We can paddle down to the end of the lake and try to hook a muskie."

"Sure."

Bow watched a loon swoop down on the water, flopping and tumbling when it hit the surface. After a while, he asked, "You enjoying yourself, Charlie?"

"Yeah."

"I forgot to pack the scotch."

I stood up. My back had stiffened from bending over and lifting stones. "So?"

"I'm sorry, I just forgot."

As someone who never passed a waking moment without knowing the nearest source of liquor, who never made a move without calculating its relation to the possibility of alcohol, I found it unthinkable that anyone could forget a bottle of scotch. Maybe Bow really had forgotten, or maybe he was making a point. In any case, I'd noticed the bottle was missing when we packed, and I hadn't said anything.

"I just goddamned forgot," Bow repeated.

"I'll manage," I told him.

For an hour or so before dinner, Ginger and I stood on a high rock a few yards down shore from the campsite and cast into the deep water. Mrs. Hennepin was right: We didn't have any luck with a variety of lures, but once we switched to her worms, we caught the interest of a school of young walleyes. By six, the rain had stopped and the live box was churning with fish.

Bow enjoyed cooking over a campfire. He got the fire going and boiled water for potatoes, while I filleted the walleyes, using a paddle as a cutting board. Bow breaded them and fried them in butter, and we ate around the fire. "He's dull as hell to catch, but there's no fish that tastes better than a walleye," Bow said.

Ginger and I grunted our agreement.

"Tomorrow, we go after muskellunge," Bow told Ginger. "If anyone can find you a muskie, Charlie can."

We washed the dishes in the lake and strung the food pack from a tree branch to discourage raccoons. Then Bow boiled more water for coffee, and we sat around the fire. The clouds were coming in dark and low again, and the forest around us was already black. Bow lit a cigar. "Well, boys, not bad," he said.

The mosquitoes were bothering Ginger, so I threw some fresh pine on the fire to generate smoke. Still, the insects circled, searching, waiting, a kind of droning fog. Ginger pulled the hood of his poncho over his head, and every few seconds, he beat the air in front of his face. "Why don't they bother *you*?" he finally asked Bow in exasperation.

"Maybe the cigar helps," Bow suggested, though the cigar had nothing to do with it—Bow just didn't pay mosquitoes much attention.

"I've never seen them this bad," said Ginger.

"This is nothing," said Bow. "Charlie, tell him about Ernest Aavang."

Ginger hunched himself farther into his hood. In the shadowy light, his eyes seemed to be peeking out of a cave.

I explained that Ernest Aavang was an old guy who lived alone in a shack by the Agnes. The place didn't have screens, and one night about twenty years ago, the mosquitoes got so bad Aavang took off all his clothes and ran outside screaming and jumped in the river.

"Did he drown?" Ginger asked.

"They pulled him out," Bow said, finishing the story, "but that was the last we saw of him."

"There's an Aavang at the high school," said Ginger. "Jane Aavang." Bow looked at me. "Well, Charlie?"

"I think that's Ernest's granddaughter."

"Charlie knows everything about Laroque," said Bow.

"Not really," I protested.

"He's an archivist." Bow had been calling me an archivist ever since he learned I'd spent my two years in the army filing papers in the records division of the Defense Department. The idea seemed to comfort him, and perhaps it gave some justification to our relationship. Since I wasn't a lawyer or an intellectual, he enjoyed assigning me some other status.

"Do you remember my mother?" Ginger asked me.

"Sure. Not well, but I remember her."

"When did she die?" asked Bow.

"December 14, 1957," said Ginger. "I was eight."

"That's tough."

"She had a stroke. She died instantly."

"She was young for a stroke," Bow said.

We stared at the fire, glowing orange. The grinding chorus of mosquitoes filled the silence.

"I found her," Ginger continued. "She was lying on the floor in the kitchen. She'd been holding an egg, and it had splattered beside her. First thing, I cleaned up the egg. I don't know why. I knew she was dead."

"There's a presence of mind you have at that age that you lose later on," said Bow.

"How well do you remember her?" I asked.

"She could be sitting right here," said Ginger. "Sometimes I can feel her holding my hand."

I tried to turn over my memory of the thin, timid woman I'd met at Ginger's house that night. "You have a sister, too, don't you?" I asked.

Ginger nodded. "Six years older than me. She finished high school and moved to Texas, where my mother had some relatives. We hardly ever hear from her."

"What about your father?" Bow asked. "He's still around, and he must be proud as hell of you."

"I suppose he is," Ginger said.

"And after you made that shot. He must have been thrilled."

"He wasn't at the game. I had to tell him the next morning."

"And?"

"He said it was about time something went right for our family. It was about time for our luck to change."

Bow thought about that for a moment. Finally, he tossed the dregs of his coffee onto the fire. The steam and ashes spun up into the night sky. "Parents are gods," he said. "Good or bad."

Across the lake, a loon gave out a long, hooting call, the wilderness signal of more rain.

"Sing your father's song, Charlie," Bow demanded. "It wouldn't be a night in the woods without your father's song."

I have a strong voice, something I picked up from my mother, who, early on, performed musical numbers in my father's shows. Three times I ran through the song, the third time joined by Bow and Ginger. We shouted the melancholy words into the darkness, across the lake. When we'd said our last good-bye to the blackbird, a distant wail floated back. An echo? A trespasser? The loon again, answering our call? Man or beast, we didn't know.

CHAPTER 11

The muskellunge hunts the shallow water, hiding in the cattails and cabbage weeds, making quick work of the innocent perch, walleye, and sucker that happen by. There is no more ferocious freshwater predator. An adult muskie, twenty or thirty years old, can reach forty or fifty pounds (typically, the females exceed the males, a nice touch). The record catch is just under seventy pounds—the size of a ten-year-old boy. Compared with a lovely blue-green trout, say, or even a plump walleye, the muskie is an ugly fish, with leaden coloring, a narrow body that carries its weight back in an awkward potbelly, and that shockingly huge jaw, nature's mockery of any notion of proportion or restraint. Muskies are vicious, hard to find, tireless fighters when hooked, and smart, probably the smartest fish in the water. For nights on end, I've heard men prattle on about strategies to catch this elusive creature—how you should reel in the line with a rhythmic jig; swing the lure in a figure eight as it draws close to the boat; smear a strip of uncooked bacon across the hooks. I've listened to the hours of arguments over the merits of assorted lures—bucktails, jerkbaits, crankbaits, spoons, poppers. It's all hopeless. By my lights, the muskie strike is best treated as an act of God— a test, a trial, perhaps an opportunity, but nothing you can control or even anticipate. It will come to you.

In the morning on the lake, the fog was back, so thick you could barely see a pine ten yards away. I got up first and started the fire. Bow crawled out of the tent a few minutes later and cooked up some bacon and eggs. By the time Ginger joined us, emerging from the mists like the ghost in *Hamlet,* Bow and I were already loading the fishing gear into the canoe. We paddled hard through the fog down the lake to an area where the shore flattened and the cattails jutted out of the water like a field of young corn. Once there, Bow and Ginger did the fishing, casting over and over into the weeds, while I kept the canoe moving slowly along the shore. They were both using light spinning rods, a sporting style of equipment. If either of them hooked a muskie, landing it would be tricky.

We passed maybe an hour with no action. In the muffled stillness, their lures plopped deliciously onto the glassy surface. A light breeze moved the fog around. Every now and then, you could see the dark smudge of a rocky point farther down the lake where the shoreline rose. As the morning lengthened and the fog slowly lifted, I kept the canoe aimed at that rocky point as a marker for orientation. When we got closer, I began to notice the horizontal forms on shore that usually indicate a campsite.

In the bow, Ginger saw the same thing. He leaned forward, straining to see. "Someone's there," he said.

We all stared through the shifting fog.

"They shouldn't be," said Bow.

For several minutes, I stroked hard, then let the canoe glide toward shore. In the dense air, the silence had a kind of weight.

"I see a tent," said Ginger.

Other blurred shapes began to harden. There was a rock fireplace, a rough log table, an aluminum canoe turned on its side.

"Pull in your line," said Bow softly.

Bow and Ginger set their rods in the bottom of the canoe. I nosed us forward until the bow scraped against the rock shore, the first hard sound we'd heard in several hours. With the noise, I expected the tent flap to fly open, but nothing in the camp moved. For a few seconds, we sat in the canoe and stared. To the side, on the low rocks, a long, straw-colored gill net had been spread out to dry. "Poachers," I said.

Bow moved to get up. "Let's look around."

"I'm not sure that's so smart," I said.

"Why not?" Bow was talking loud, hoping to roust whoever was here. He was looking for a confrontation, but he was wary of surprising someone. "They're trespassers. I want to run them off."

"That boom we heard yesterday—they might be using dynamite."

"So?"

Draped in fog, the camp looked funereal. Near the fireplace, someone had cut down several saplings, leaving the tops of the thin stumps raw and white.

"Let's look around," Bow repeated.

Ginger hopped out and gently pulled the front of the canoe up on shore. He offered his hand, and Bow hauled himself up, stepping awkwardly onto the rocks. He did a little jig, getting the circulation going in his legs. "Come on, Charlie," he said. "I bet it's just kids."

If Bow and I had been alone, we probably would have stayed away, maybe mentioning the poachers to the sheriff when we got back. The presence of Ginger changed the dynamic. I sensed that Bow was being a little showy, a bit more aggressive, because of the boy. I sat for a moment in the back of the canoe, registering a small protest. Finally, I climbed out. Ginger and I carried the canoe a few yards up from the water. It thumped against the rock when we set it down, but the heavy air smothered the sound. Mosquitoes swarmed around our heads. Ginger pulled up the hood of his poncho. "Damn mosquitoes probably drove whoever it was away," he said.

I was the experienced woodsman, so it was up to me. I shuffled through the camp, making as much noise as possible. The tent was pitched just off the rock outcrop, on the edge of the woods. It was new—a sleek, green, expensive piece of light nylon. The flaps were closed but not tied. I reached down and pulled one back, then quickly stood aside. Nothing. I knelt and peered in through the mosquito netting. Two sleeping bags were lying side by side, unfurled and mussed.

"Well?" called Bow.

I stood up. "Nobody. Two bags."

Bow and Ginger wandered around the camp. I walked back to the

fireplace. It was simpler than ours, just six rocks in a semicircle. With
a stick, I stirred the damp ashes and uncovered the long skeleton of a
fish. Bow came up and looked over my shoulder. "They caught a
muskie," I said. The fish's huge head looked up at us vacantly with its
flat, toothy smile.

"Who eats muskie?" said Bow. With all its bones, the fish is almost
inedible.

Nearby, someone had left a pile of trash—charred bean cans, an
egg carton, orange rinds, several dozen empty bottles of Old Style,
some of them shattered. "This pisses me off," said Bow.

Ginger called out from the woods. Behind a line of thick bushes,
he'd found a battered red pickup truck. An old logging road led off
through the trees, and the truck's tires had left a clear trail in the soft
earth.

The bed of the truck had been fitted with a covered plywood
box, crudely hammered together. I unlatched the plywood door in
back. Inside, a great black-and-gold mound of walleyes rested on
blocks of ice. "My fish," said Bow.

Ginger reached in and hooked one of the walleyes through the
gill with his finger, holding the fish up. "Three pounds," he said
before tossing it back on the pile.

"There's a hundred dollars of fish in there," I said.

Bow told me to look in the cab. The floor was muddied and littered with old papers and empty cans. I rummaged through the tools
and maps in the glove compartment and found an invoice for lumber from Stone's Hardware made out to Archie Nye. I hadn't seen
Archie since the night he cut open the man from Nashville in the
Loggers' Lounge. Bow studied the paper. He recognized Archie's
name—everyone in the county knew that name. "Fuck the Fourth
Amendment," Bow said, stuffing the document in his shirt pocket.
"I'm taking it. Now, let's get out of here."

When we came out of the woods and down the slope toward the
water, Archie was sitting on the bow of Bow's canoe. Beside him,
cradling a shotgun, stood the slender, dark man who'd been with
Archie at the basketball game. We stopped, but Archie stood and
motioned us to come down.

He was a tall, slickly handsome man with a mouthful of horsey teeth. He and I had known each other from the bars for years; we'd even guided together a few times at the Spirit Light until Bob the owner had fired him. Now, a panicky thought jolted me: Had I told Archie about Bow's property? I couldn't imagine being that indiscreet, but the fishing here was good, and who knew what I said when I was drunk?

"Was that you singing last night, Charlie?" Archie asked, when we got close. Watching his lips pull back to expose those teeth was to suffer a kind of assault. "Awful." He shook his head. "Awful, awful, awful."

"You shouldn't be here," I told him.

Archie kept smiling. He nodded toward his companion. "This here is Bill LaSoeur. He's not like me. He's a real Indian, full-blooded."

LaSoeur stood at an angle to us, his legs apart and his body corkscrewed under his poncho. His face was narrow, and his hair was light for an Indian's. I didn't like what I saw in his eyes, dark almond slits that looked almost glassy, reflecting back the scene around him.

"This is Bowman Epps," I said. "He owns this property."

"Sure, sure," Archie said. "How are you, sir?"

Bow crossed his arms across his chest. "Now, see here," he said. "This is private property. These are my lakes and my fish."

Archie let his teeth disappear slowly behind his lips. The process was astounding in its way—all that ivory and bone, packed, hidden; I kept waiting for his mouth to burst open again, like an overstuffed suitcase. After letting us study him for a few seconds, Archie said, almost spitting, "No, *you* see here, Mr. Epps. You messed my camp, and nobody has a right to do that." He took several deliberate steps forward, and LaSoeur fell in on his rear flank. Archie was wearing a red lumberjack's shirt and blue jeans tucked into rubber boots that came almost to his knees. He was known for carrying a knife, and he saw me searching his body fruitlessly for the telltale bulge; for a moment his eyes flashed, registering a private victory.

Bow uncrossed his arms but didn't say anything. Even as a boy, he'd probably never been in a physical confrontation.

"Let's get out of here," I said.

Archie held his hand up and moved closer to Bow, an arm's reach away. "You messed my camp," he repeated. "The question is what I'm gonna do about it."

"That's not the issue," Bow said softly. "The issue is you trespassed and stole my fish. Let's get that straight."

"Come on, Bow," I said. I tugged on his sleeve.

"How can you own fish?" asked Archie, spreading his arms wide, opening his palms to the sky. "I don't get that. A fish is one of God's creatures, not man's. Right, Billy?" Archie didn't take his eyes off Bow. LaSoeur grunted, his fingers playing on his shotgun.

"Now, I do know about messing a man's camp," Archie went on, his voice deep and lugubrious. "That's real serious, Mr. Epps. Charlie here can tell you that." Archie let his hands float down the sides of his shirt and brought them together in front, with his thumbs hooked over his belt.

The redness was pulsing on Bow's face. "All right," he said. "Let's go." He took a step to the side, but Archie slid over, blocking him.

"Where do you propose to go?" Archie asked. Behind him, LaSoeur edged back and stood in front of Bow's canoe, the shotgun pointing ambiguously over our heads. LaSoeur's fingers kept writhing like worms over the stock and trigger mechanism of the gun. It was only midmorning, but I wondered if he was drunk or stoned.

Bow stared at me. He took a deep breath and waited. But I had no solution. Worse, the pain of seeing Bow like that, agonized and out of control, gripped my throat.

So far, Archie had ignored Ginger, but suddenly the boy piped up. "Don't you know who this man is?" he asked. Ginger edged a bit to Archie's side, creating a small diversion.

Archie glanced over.

"You know him, don't you?" Ginger persisted.

"I seen him around," Archie said.

"He's the famous lawyer."

"Uh-huh." Archie pivoted and stepped quickly past me to plant himself exactly in front of Ginger. It was the old bar fighter's game, standing too close, making the other man back away.

Ginger didn't move, though he leaned back, looking up at Archie, who was almost a head taller. "He's the kind of friend you ought to cultivate," Ginger said.

"I don't really like lawyers." Archie's lips crept apart, forcing those teeth on Ginger.

I kept glancing between Archie and LaSoeur, watching their hands. I didn't think Archie would kill us over fish, but LaSoeur looked hopped up enough to do something crazy. And as my mind played out the compromises and half steps, I couldn't see the way out. They'd know how to hide our bodies so we wouldn't be found for days, maybe ever. By then, they'd be long gone. "Let it go, Archie," I said softly. "We're getting out of here."

He waved a finger, smelling of fish gut, in front of my nose. "Don't move."

"You never can tell when you'll need a lawyer," Ginger continued brightly. Archie stared at him. "Someday you might want to draw up a will," Ginger added.

"A will?"

"Sure." Ginger cocked his head. "To leave your heirs the money you're gonna make from stealing Mr. Epps's fish."

Archie's eyes wandered around Ginger's face. After a few seconds, he reached behind Ginger's neck, gripping him gently, the way you might touch a child. Slowly, he pulled back the hood of Ginger's poncho. Ginger's head looked tiny in Archie's mitteny hand. "You're the boy who made the shot, aren't you?" said Archie.

Ginger nodded slowly. With his eyes he quickly searched for Archie's other hand. He'd heard about Archie's knife, too.

"I lost a lot of money on that shot," Archie said.

"Sorry."

"I bet you didn't know that, or you wouldn't have made it, right?"

"That's hard to say." Ginger tried to shrug, but he couldn't—Archie was squeezing the back of his neck.

I thought of all the times I'd seen Archie drunk and sloppy in the bars around Laroque, of the times I'd got drunk with him myself, and I wished I'd smashed a bottle into the side of his head.

Suddenly, Archie's hand dropped down to Ginger's shoulder. "I'm not stealin' those fish, hotshot. I'm gonna buy 'em." He let go of Ginger and reached into his back pocket for his wallet. "What do you think those fish are worth, Mr. Epps?"

Bow glanced at me. "I don't care about the money," he said quietly.

Archie held out his wallet, thumbing through a packet of bills. "No, no, no. I'm not gonna steal your fish. Tell me what they're worth."

Bow started to protest again.

"Give him twenty-five dollars," I said.

Archie thought for a moment. "Sure, that's fair," he said, peeling out a twenty and a five. Bow stuffed the bills into the shirt pocket over his heart.

"Hey, Billy," Archie called over his shoulder. "This here's the boy who made that goddamned shot."

LaSoeur swung his head in an arc. His eyes seemed to be rolling around inside.

"That shot was *painful!*" said Archie, flashing his full smile.

"It was luck," said Ginger.

"Fucking shot." Archie looked around, at Bow, then me, then back to Ginger. "What are you doing with these two?" he asked.

"I work for Mr. Epps."

"You do?" Archie turned to Bow. "Does he do good work?"

"The best," said Bow solemnly. "The best."

"Listen," Archie told Ginger, mustering all the earnestness he could squeeze into his face, "here's the most important thing about a job—get there on time. You remember that. Be there early and you'll do great."

"Right," said Ginger.

"Isn't that right, Mr. Epps?" Archie looked hopefully at Bow.

"That's right," said Bow.

Archie tucked his wallet back into his pocket. "Well, we were just leaving," he said. He called to LaSoeur to pack up the tent. LaSoeur dropped his shotgun onto his shoulder and marched sullenly up the bank.

Archie followed us to Bow's canoe and offered to shove us off. We put the canoe in the water, and I climbed out to the stern. Archie steadied the front while Bow made his way to his seat, crouching and working to keep his weight even. "Easy, easy," Archie coached. When Ginger was settled in the front, Archie gave the canoe a push, and it scooted off backward.

We sat for a moment without paddling. Up the bank, the fog closed in on LaSoeur as he folded the tent. Archie stood at the edge of the water, watching us drift away.

"Where'd you hide it?" Ginger called.

Archie laughed and shook his head. We were fifteen feet away now, still drifting, leaving a gentle wake in the black water. With a sweep of his arm, Archie reached behind his back at belt level and then quickly swung his hand forward. "Here you go, hotshot," he called. As Archie faded into the fog, a Polaroid in reverse, he leered at us from behind a wide blade, dull gray beside his teeth.

CHAPTER 12

With a half hour of paddling, we came to the end of the lake, to a pebbly inlet fed by a creek. This was territory favored by the smallmouth bass—a lively but more predictable fish. Ginger got out of the canoe with his rod and stood on a flat rock, casting into the shallows. Bow and I drifted and fished from the canoe. The fast, chilly creek stirred the milder water of the inlet, setting off currents on the surface that spun the boat in a gentle pirouette.

Bow sat hunched over in front, staring at the angle his fishing line made with the lake surface. I was afraid he was brooding, and I couldn't help feeling that the confrontation that morning had been my fault, as if Archie and his pal were something I'd thoughtlessly inflicted—a virus I'd carried, some mud I'd tracked in.

Once the canoe had drifted out of hearing of the shore, however, Bow suddenly spoke up. "Ginger really deflated things back there, didn't he?"

"I think Archie was looking for a way out," I said.

"Still, you and I couldn't push the right buttons, Charlie." Bow shook his head slowly, radiating admiration. "There's a knack there for reading people and situations. It's almost as if he knows how things are going to turn out and plays it accordingly."

The canoe spun slowly on the water. Sometimes it seemed as if Ginger's successes around Bow were built on my own shortcomings.

"Did you notice what Ginger said last night about his father's reaction to the shot?" Bow asked. "The old man said it was about time something good happened to the family. Can you imagine? Having a son like that and still feeling you were getting a raw deal in life?"

"His wife died. He doesn't have any money. I can see why he'd be discouraged."

"But to have a boy like that! I'm not a parent, but it seems to me you have a duty to help him live up to his potential, an obligation." Bow twisted in his seat to face the stern, defying me to argue. Fortunately, the awkward position defused his energy and he soon turned back to his fishing line.

"Do you want to tell the sheriff about Archie?" I asked after a few minutes.

"Why bother?" said Bow curtly. He would have preferred to talk about Ginger's heroism.

"Archie might come back."

Bow shrugged. "It's over."

The smallmouth were biting, and among the three of us, we caught and released about half a dozen that morning. Around midday, the weather started to change. The cloud cover disappeared and the sun burned off the fog. In the rising heat, the fish stopped feeding. We lunched on sandwiches, then paddled back at a leisurely pace. Against the pine horizon, the sky was a rich, summery blue. Bow dozed off, his hands folded over his stomach. When we passed the rock promontory, Archie's campsite had vanished; even the lazy fireplace had been scattered to nothing.

We stayed another night on Lake Eighteen and in the morning packed up and portaged over to Eleven, following another old logging trail that wound over a craggy hill. The clear weather held, and after setting up camp, Ginger and I took a swim, lounging on the sun-warmed surface of the lake.

Late that afternoon, with the sun low in the sky and six nice walleyes churning up our live box, we made a final pass at finding a muskie. I paddled Ginger and Bow across the lake to a low, weedy bay. Five years before, Bow had hooked a young muskie along this shore. Now Bow and Ginger sat in the canoe and cast along the edge of the weed bed. Bow was using a Rapala, a graceful wood lure designed to resemble a minnow. Ginger had fixed his line with an old, red Daredevil, a spoon-shaped hunk of metal that flashed through the water and wasn't so much intended to fool a predator fish as to taunt it. For over an hour, I steadied the canoe while they pitched the lures into the water. We hardly spoke. Behind the trees, the sun sprayed orange across the western sky. The lake turned flat as glass, the surface broken only by floundering insects or an occasional fish gulping a meal. In a day, we'd be back in town, and I'd be within easy reach of a bottle of scotch, but at a graceful moment like this, it was simple to calm my anticipation. It occurred to me that maybe I should just move into the woods—get a cabin out here and make a life of it. There'd been stories lately in the paper and in *Time* about groups of kids rejecting the comforts of civilization, getting closer to nature, going back to the land, as they put it. Maybe that was my answer. I wondered if I could talk Lucy into coming along.

Ginger tossed his Daredevil twenty yards in front of the canoe, the same general area he'd dropped it fifty or a hundred times before. The lure hit flat on the lake and skidded, and suddenly the surface exploded in a chute of water and the silvery-green side of a fish.

"You got one," I said.

"Jesus Christ, it's huge," muttered Bow.

Striking the lure, the fish had jumped. Now, back in the water, it charged off furiously, pulling out Ginger's line and dragging the boat. Bow reeled in frantically to avoid getting tangled, and I aimed the canoe in the direction of the fish's course, trying to take some pressure off Ginger's line. The boy lifted his rod, urging the fish away from the weeds, and the thin stalk of fiberglass bent almost double. Still, the fish didn't slow or change direction. "What test line are you using?" Bow asked.

"Ten pound, I think," said Ginger.

Bow let out a low whistle.

"He can bring it in on that," I said. "We may have to beach the canoe to land it, though." Out on the lake, we'd never get a fish that size into the boat. I'd already started searching for a flat spot of shoreline where we could easily pull up.

"It's gotta be a muskie, right?" said Bow. Except for the flash of scales during the strike, we hadn't got a look at the fish.

"Could be a big northern," I said. The northern pike is a muskie relative, a common fish held in low regard.

"Come on, Charlie," Bow growled.

The fish had been skirting the bed of weeds, but now it paused and shook its head, trying to spit out the lure. The tip of Ginger's rod darted side to side. He turned several cranks on his reel, retrieving a few feet of line. Then the fish took off again, angling right, swimming out to deeper water. The canoe slipped forward. "Ride 'em, cowboy!" Bow cried, scaring up a pair of ducks that had been cowering near the shore.

The fish made a big semicircle, heading toward the middle of the lake, then swinging back, realizing its best chance of escape was in the weeds and fallen logs along the shore. For twenty minutes, we followed behind. Ginger's line dived into the water and disappeared ten yards from the canoe. Every now and then, he'd feel an easing of pressure and reel in a couple of feet.

South of the weed bed, the shore was clogged with thick, low bushes, broken for one small stretch by a rocky beach. If I could ease us to the beach, we could park the canoe, and Ginger, working from shore, could coax the fish into the shallows and pull it onto land. The fish was clearly tiring. Ginger was reeling in, one slow crank at a time.

"I just want to see the son-of-a-bitch," said Bow.

I ruddered the canoe toward the beach. We were maybe forty feet from shore. With the sun sinking, the lake was black, except on the far side, near our campsite, where the water gorgeously reflected back the orange sky. As far as the eye could see, we were the only disturbance on the surface.

Ginger's fish knew it was losing the fight. I marveled for a moment at the kid's luck, if that's what it was. He sinks the winning shot, lands a job with the richest man in town, defuses a violent confrontation, hooks a monster fish. It was as if not just Bow, but God, had decided he was special.

Ginger's line entered the water close to the canoe now, and at any moment, I expected to see a huge, gleaming flank slide past the boat, our first view of the beast since the strike. "Keep a taut line," Bow warned.

The fish had one run left. It dove sharply under the canoe, catching Ginger by surprise. His rod bent almost double again. The line screeched out with a frantic, awful noise. Suddenly the noise stopped. Everything was still. Ginger reeled in quickly and his line popped out of the water, snapped just above the lure. The colorless filament floated above the surface of the lake, drifting and twisting on the imperceptible air currents, looking impossibly thin and delicate, a sexual pun.

"Goddamnit," moaned Ginger.

Bow hissed, "Shhhhhit!"

The three of us sat in the canoe, staring at the dangling line, half expecting the fish to appear again. The stillness was unsettling.

"You know," said Ginger after a while, "I almost feel relieved it got away."

That night, we dined on the walleyes we'd caught earlier in the afternoon, then sat around the fire. In the morning we'd portage back to the car. Bow was feeling expansive over the success of the trip. "Good fishing, good weather," he said. "Even a little danger. Every outing needs that. If Archie hadn't come along, we'd have had to invent him."

Across the lake, the moon was a huge circle of light, just above the treeline. The water and all the woods around it were lit in shades of silver and gray.

"I have an idea," Bow said.

Ginger looked at him from deep inside the hood of his poncho.

"Have you thought about what you're going to do for college?" Bow asked the boy.

"Not really."

"You've got to plan these things."

"I used to figure I'd go into the army for a couple of years, get the GI Bill. But Vietnam's changed that."

"Take the deferment," Bow told him. "Don't be a fool."

"I'm surprised to hear that from you," said Ginger carefully.

"I may be a hawk, but I'm not an idiot," Bow said. "The way they're fighting this war—you could get killed."

"Or kill someone else."

"Well . . ." The point, off the line of the argument, temporarily threw Bow.

"I may apply for conscientious objector status," Ginger said.

"Forget it. You don't have a case. You've got to be a pacifist, with a religious background."

"I probably am a pacifist about Vietnam."

"Doesn't count. You've got to oppose all wars, all violence. You can't pick and choose. The draft board would throw you out in a second."

"Would you have fought the Nazis?" I asked Ginger.

"The world is different today," he said.

"Don't count on it," said Bow.

Ginger poked the fire with a stick, and a funnel of sparks soared up into the darkness.

"What was your idea?" I asked Bow.

"I think Ginger should go to Columbia, my old school."

"Whoa!" said Ginger.

Bow shifted his weight, trying to get more comfortable. I'd hauled up a log for him to sit on, but it couldn't have been pleasant. Still, he seemed invigorated by the trip. He looked more agile than I'd seen him in years. "You'd be a fool to miss the chance," Bow continued, somewhat defensively. "You'd be right there in New York. All the excitement of a big city."

"No, no, I appreciate the thought," Ginger said, backtracking. "But, for Chrissake, my grades aren't even that good."

"What are they, *A*'s and *B*'s?"

"Around there."

"They'd kill to get you," Bow said solemnly. "Believe me, they'd kill. And it's not just Columbia. Yale, Harvard—they'd all want you. I only mention Columbia because I could probably make things a bit easier for you there. But I know the way those schools work. They get a million applications from the usual places, and they're dying to find the kid with promise from some obscure spot on the map."

"It's a long ways away," Ginger said.

"An overnight train trip."

"And expensive."

"You'd get a full ride. Besides . . ."—Bow let his voice drop and slide a bit; here was the real point of the conversation—"I'd be willing to pick up whatever was left over."

"I couldn't do that," said Ginger.

"Call it a loan."

"I couldn't."

Bow snorted, dismissing the objection. "Charlie," he said after a moment, "how long do you suppose it's been since a boy from Laroque went to one of the Ivy League schools?"

"You were probably the last, Bow."

"I don't know," said Ginger. "I'm not sure I'm really the type."

"What type?"

"You know . . . rich."

"That's a lot of crap," said Bow. "Maybe it was true once, back when F. Scott Fitzgerald was tearing around, but those days are long gone. Now they want variety."

Ginger absently swatted at mosquitoes. "I don't know," he repeated. "Up until a year or so ago, it never even occurred to me to go to college. Now you're talking about Harvard and Yale."

"They're just schools."

"But they're really for the elite," Ginger said.

"You *are* the elite," cried Bow.

The two of them fell silent. Bow's smugness on this whole subject rankled me enough that I foolishly piped up. "The boy's just saying that some things seem a lot easier from your perspective than from his."

Bow scowled at me. In the flickering light, the scarred side of his face was all ridges and shadows, a moonscape that slid into darkness. He was genuinely angry, and I realized then how alone he felt in his admiration for Ginger. The camping trip had cemented it. He'd found someone who suggested his own solitary greatness—or perhaps it was only the idea of greatness Bow set for himself. Whatever, he thought Ginger possessed it, and now Bow held the lonely job of nursing it forward against life's banalities. All of Laroque appreciated the boy and acknowledged his talents, but Bow felt isolated and embattled in the depth of his esteem.

Late that night, I woke up in the tent. A mosquito was buzzing around inside, and I waited patiently until its delicate silhouette became visible against the wall, then I crushed it with my hand. After a while, I crawled forward and pressed my face against the netting in the tent door. The outside air felt fresh and cool. I could hear the occasional sound of the lake—a fish or a family of ducks, perhaps, splashing the surface. Somewhere out there, Ginger's muskie was hunting, the captured Daredevil hanging from its mouth. I stayed against the netting for several minutes before lying down again. On one side, Bow was on his back, snoring heavily. In his sleeping bag, he seemed enormous, a huge, unwieldy mound of flesh. On the other side, Ginger was a wisp, hardly more than a riffle in the downy cocoon. For a long time, I couldn't fall back asleep. The heat of their bodies, their breath against the flimsy walls of the tent, the close fragility of it all—I lay anxiously on my side, waiting for the first light of morning.

CHAPTER 13

Ginger wrote twice to Gary Fontenot at Lovington, and about a week after he sent off the second letter, Fontenot responded with a note, addressed to Ginger, care of Bow. If anything, Fontenot's miniature script was getting smaller; we all examined the envelope and marveled that an untold number of postal workers had made the effort to stare down the fine, serrated markings and translate them into a workable address. Someone, probably a clerk in Laroque, had finally scrawled "BOW EPPS" in heavy letters on the front. Inside, Fontenot's message consisted of one short sentence: "Go ahead appeal the goddamn thing."

Bow sent Ginger down to the law library to find every reported case in the country involving a search after a traffic stop. The next afternoon, Ginger flew into the office, waving his yellow legal pad. "There's a great case right here in Wisconsin," he crowed. "*State v. Hodges.* All the evidence got thrown out. The conviction was overturned."

Bow considered the boy fondly. "My old friend *Hodges,*" Bow said.

Ginger looked stricken. "You know it?"

"Bow knows every case," I said.

"I even know the lawyer who handled it," Bow explained. "He's from Milwaukee. A pretty astute fellow."

"Don't you think it's on target?" Ginger was fighting hard against his disappointment.

"If it was so great, why do you think the trial judge ignored it and admitted the evidence against Fontenot?"

"The judge was wrong," answered Ginger.

"We've got to do better than that."

Ginger took a deep breath. The legal pad in his hand was covered with scribbled notations of cases.

"Sit down," said Bow. "Let me give you a little lesson."

Ginger's eyes skipped around the office as he appeared to contemplate escape, then he dropped lumpily onto the sofa. A stack of transcripts that had just been delivered slid onto the floor. Bow waited while Ginger stacked them again.

"Obviously, the key issue for us is the search of the car," Bow began. "If we're going to get Fontenot's conviction overturned, it will be because of the search."

"Right," said Ginger, a bit too quickly.

"The cops said they stopped Fontenot because his brake light was busted. Then they searched the glove compartment and found the jewels, which led them to open the trunk, where they found the burglary tools. If the search of the glove compartment is illegal, then the fruits of that search—the jewels and the tools—can't be admitted as evidence, and the state can't make a case." Bow waved his arm in a vague salute. "There you have our Fourth Amendment at work: 'The right of the people to be secure in their persons, houses, papers, and effects, against unreasonable searches and seizures, shall not be violated.' The courts have decided that the only way to enforce that right is to exclude any evidence that was seized as a consequence of an improper search. That's what's known as the exclusionary rule, and it's probably the biggest so-called technicality of all."

Ginger nodded. He'd picked up these fundamentals from reading the cases.

"So our goal is to show that the cops acted improperly in pawing through the contents of Fontenot's glove compartment," Bow continued. "Was that search 'unreasonable' in the Fourth Amendment's terms? You've already seen that there are dozens of cases around the country that have asked that question under circumstances a lot like ours. Never exactly the same, but close. The first thing you have to remember is that traffic cases are special. Judges don't like cars. They move around, they disappear. They're not like houses. A house isn't going anywhere, so a judge can insist that the cops come to court and ask for a warrant before they search the place. That way the judge himself can decide whether the search is reasonable. But with a car, it's gone before an officer can get to court and get a warrant, right?"

"Right."

"So the judges tend to side with the cops in car cases. There's where we start. With the odds stacked against us. Now, as for Fontenot's lawyer—who actually did a pretty good job, I think—he cited the *Hodges* case, but the trial judge decided it wasn't controlling. Why? Let's look at the facts. The *Hodges* search took place in the middle of the night in Milwaukee. Two cops pulled over a car for speeding. So far, it's basically like our case. The driver was this fellow named Hodges. Right away, he hopped out of his car and came back to meet the cops. They all stood around in the street. The cops had never seen Hodges before. He was a Negro, but for all they knew, he could be the governor of Ohio. Still, one cop spun him around, leaned him up against the patrol car, and frisked him. Nothing. Meanwhile, the other cop went over to Hodges's car. Now, remember, there was nothing at all suspicious about the car. It had been going too fast, that's all. Everybody speeds once in a while. But the cop started rummaging around and reached under the seat, out of sight, and pulled out a bag of marijuana. Bingo. Hodges was nabbed for possession.

"Without the marijuana, of course, there'd be no case," Bow went on, "so, on appeal, Hodges's lawyer tried to get the stuff thrown out as the fruit of an illegal search: What right did the cops have to go rooting through Hodges's car?" Bow paused. "Are you with me so far?" he asked.

"I think so," said Ginger.

"Charlie?"

I nodded.

"Good. Well, there's a long line of precedents holding that there are three justifications for the warrantless search of a car." Bow counted them off on his fingers. "One, to prevent a wanted criminal from escaping. Two, to prevent the destruction of evidence. Three, to protect the arresting officers from injury. Clearly, one didn't hold here—Hodges wasn't a wanted criminal, at least as far as these cops knew. Similarly, two didn't work—until the search, the cops had no idea there was any evidence around to be destroyed, and you can't do a search on unsubstantiated hunches. But three! said the DA. The search was justified to protect the officers.

" 'Forget it,' said the appeals court. The officers weren't in any danger. They'd already frisked him. What was Hodges going to do? Go back to his car after he'd been released and *then* pull out a gun and start shooting? No way. Get reasonable. Good-bye, marijuana. Conviction overturned."

Ginger stared at Bow with that flat, vacant look people sometimes get watching television.

"Am I going too fast?" asked Bow.

"I think I've got it."

"Okay. Now, let's look at Fontenot's case. Again, the cops justified the search by saying they needed to protect themselves, just like with Hodges. As I said before, the two cases start out the same: It was the middle of the night. Two cops spot Fontenot with a traffic violation and pull him over. Now, notice how the differences start. In our case, both cops testified that they knew Fontenot. They knew he'd done time, and one of the cops had even arrested him once for a burglary in a case that got dropped. See, that's a potential problem: Fontenot was a well-known criminal. The cops had a right to be nervous."

Ginger nodded solemnly.

"Now, things get worse. In *Hodges,* they were all *outside* the car when the search was made. In our case, Fontenot stayed in the driver's seat. One cop came to Fontenot's window and checked his license. The other, being cautious, went around to the passenger side of the car. They had him surrounded, true, but think of it: With one quick motion, he could reach under the seat or flick open the glove compartment, and in an instant he'd have a gun in his hand. Can you blame the cops for being nervous? Of course they'd search the car! It's only reasonable, right?"

"They could've asked him to step out," said Ginger.

"What?"

"Step outside the car. Then they could frisk him if necessary and be done with it."

"Come on," said Bow, feigning irritation. "You can't demand, in retrospect, that a cop behave perfectly. They're out there on the front lines, making split-second decisions. You can't come around later and claim that they should have done it just a little better."

Ginger pressed himself deeper into the sofa.

Bow quickly lightened up. "But that's a good point," he said. "Let's keep that in mind. Maybe we can use it."

Ginger's jaw slowly began to churn. He was chewing a wad of gum, though he'd hidden it in his cheek during the height of Bow's performance. "You sound like you should take the prosecution's side," Ginger said.

"That's the way you've got to approach these cases," Bow explained. "You've got to tear apart each little point and look at it from every angle. It's a discipline of mind. You'll get it."

The two of them stared at each other. Since the canoe trip, Ginger had been more at ease around Bow, less the eager acolyte. He'd even spent more time hanging out in the office. Still, he hadn't seen this side of Bow, the lawyer/teacher/actor, in full command of his material, and Ginger seemed to be reading it as a slight rebuke. "Okay," Bow continued quickly. "What we want to do is retell this story in a way that takes the burden off Fontenot, that makes him seem more sympathetic. We need to give the court an excuse to throw the evidence out. See, the search in this case probably *was* unreasonable under the Fourth Amendment, but the trouble is that Fontenot is guilty as shit. We know that and the judges know it. Even if we make a compelling argument on the law, they aren't about to let him go unless they think some serious injustice has taken place."

"You mean, you can't win even if you're right?" said Ginger.

Bow sighed. "The court figures, Fuck him, he did it, so what if his trial was a little tainted—unless there's a good legal point to be made."

"Is there?"

"Perhaps. It's in the facts."

"The point?"

"It's always in the facts."

Ginger looked at me and shook his head.

"The cops knew Fontenot. They knew all about him, about all his arrests and convictions. They knew he was a habitual burglar. But they also knew something else." Bow threw up his arms. "He's a pussycat! In fifteen years and twenty arrests, he's never had a single violent incident. Look at the record. Never even been found with a weapon. He breaks into people's houses when they aren't there. He's harmless. The cops knew that. They knew that a hundred times better than they knew a thing about Hodges, for example. For all they knew, Hodges could have wired his car with an atomic bomb to blow up all of Milwaukee. But Fontenot? Fontenot's a naughty boy, but he's absolutely harmless. Am I right?"

"Right," said Ginger, grinning in admiration.

"Charlie?"

"Right, Bow," I said.

"There's a simple reason why those cops searched Fontenot's car: They were harassing him."

"Because he's an ex-con," said Ginger, jumping ahead.

"The cops probably spotted him driving by and figured they'd pull him over to see what they could find," Bow continued. "I wouldn't be surprised if one of the cops himself knocked out the brake light after they stopped him. They were out to harass him, and that's exactly what the Fourth Amendment is supposed to prevent."

Ginger hopped up from the couch. I'd never seen him so animated. "No wonder Gary always returns to a life of crime—the cops won't give him a chance to be a free and honest man," he blurted.

"Well, maybe, maybe," said Bow, nodding and laughing at Ginger's excitement.

"Really!" Ginger insisted, a little too ardently, I thought. He'd listened patiently to Bow's step-by-step analysis of the appeal, but his enthusiasm only fired at the argument that Fontenot had been treated unfairly. The details didn't interest Ginger as much as the larger (less strictly legal) point. The boy's reaction was probably understandable for a teenager untrained in the law. But his eagerness bumped in a slight way against Bow's approach. Bow liked Fontenot, too, but not with any real caring—Bow just wanted to use him to tinker with the justice system.

Now Ginger stood in the middle of the office, his lithe body tensed as he waited for Bow to agree with him that, burglar or not, Gary Fontenot had been given a raw deal. Bow hesitated—he'd spotted something in the boy's reaction, too—but he simply steered the argument back to more quantifiable facts. "How many people do you think get stopped for traffic violations every year in Wisconsin—two hundred thousand?" Bow asked. "Three hundred thousand? Do you think the cops search every one of them? If they tried, drivers would be so pissed, we'd have a revolution on our hands."

Ginger nodded and sat down. This was Bow's terrain. Ginger knew enough to let Bow lead the discussion.

"And here's where we can use your point. Even if the cops had some misguided concern about whether Fontenot was armed, they had an easy solution: Ask him to get out. Frisk him. Both things are overdoing it, but they might be considered reasonable, under the circumstances. Certainly, though, it doesn't make sense to go rummaging through a man's car when you have a simple, less violative, less obnoxious way to check him out." Bow leaned back, beaming and spreading his arms, being perfectly reasonable. "That's just not the American way."

Ginger waited to see if there was more. Finally, he said, "Where do we go from here?"

"Bring me more cases," said Bow. "Not just car searches, but searches where there's discrimination, where the cops are only going after Negroes, for example. I think there's a line of cases in New York. And see what you can find about the harassment of ex-cons."

Ginger headed for the door. It was after four and the law library would close in under an hour. Abruptly, he stopped. "Why do you need me?" he asked. "You could sit down right now and write this off the top of your head."

"It's all preparation," Bow said. "That's where I try to find an advantage. The state's got more people, smarter people, working on these cases. Plus, the law is usually on their side. All I can do is out-prepare them. That's my only hope."

As Ginger turned again to go, he caught my eye, then tried to hide the smile teasing his face. I had to hand it to the kid—he appreciated great art. Bow had put on a gorgeous performance, and he'd played his modesty beautifully—it made you wonder whether he believed it himself.

CHAPTER 14

Well, Bow, it's been a while," said Macy Cunningham, talking through the screen door to her kitchen. "I was beginning to wonder where you were."

"Here and there," said Bow. "I've been busy."

"It's a mistake to be *too* busy, Bow." Macy was studying us under the strong outside light above the door. Her fine, dark features were only faintly visible through the screen.

"And I'm getting old, don't forget that," Bow said. He pawed at the doormat with his foot. "Can we come in?"

Macy tilted her head slightly, as if considering. With Macy, there was always a shadowy moment before anything significant was said or done. A menagerie of night bugs darted and buzzed around the light. "Well, of course," she said finally, pushing open the door. "And you, too, Charlie. You know you're both welcome."

The large, well-kept kitchen was dimly lit by a bowl-shaped overhead fixture. Beneath it, Macy's friend Bill Addy was sitting at a red Formica table, drinking coffee. Some high-pitched chattering drifted down through the floorboards from one of the rooms above our heads.

"You don't mind sitting a minute or two?" said Macy, pulling two chairs over from the wall. "Can I get you some coffee?"

Bow and I sat down beside Addy. "We're in no rush," said Bow. "Sit down yourself. Don't worry about the coffee."

Macy swiped with a sponge at the counter beside the sink. She was wearing a red silk dress with puffy sleeves and a graceful, low neckline. Her white-gray hair was swept back from her face.

"I heard you went camping," said Macy, putting the sponge down and sliding into her chair. Her dress made a slippery sound, something strange and tantalizing.

"Just for a weekend," said Bow. "Who told you that?"

"Someone," said Macy, frowning, trying to remember. "Wasn't it someone?" she said to Addy.

Addy nodded solemnly. He was drinking coffee out of a teacup made of thin porcelain and decorated with pale pink roses.

"Weren't the mosquitoes bad?" asked Macy.

"I'm told so, but I hardly notice anymore."

Macy smiled. The wrinkles on her face made dark brown lines, so vivid and fresh it seemed you could wipe them away with a damp cloth. "And how is business?" she asked.

"There'll always be crime," said Bow. "I'm in demand."

Addy cleared his throat. The sound seemed to be coming from somewhere deep in his chest. "This Richard Speck," he said. "The guy in Chicago who killed all those nurses. I bet he's impotent." Addy looked around the table and his eyes sparkled.

Above us, someone was walking on the wood floor.

"How's *your* business?" asked Bow.

"The farm doesn't do so well these days," Macy said. "It takes more work than I have energy for."

"It's a good thing you've diversified."

Macy turned her head away—punishing Bow, in an affectionate way, for the remark. "Things are slow all over," she said.

When we'd come in, a car and a pickup had been parked in the driveway. Twenty years ago, there would have been half a dozen men or more waiting around downstairs at Macy's on a Wednesday night.

Addy said, "Speck had nine girls to choose from and couldn't make it with any of them, so he killed them all."

"Oh, hush about that awful man," said Macy.

"This area's never been any good for farming anyway," said Bow. "Once they took out the white pine, there was nothing left, just hunting and fishing."

"We have to develop the tourist industry," said Macy.

"That's already old. People can fly to Las Vegas or Canada as easily as they can get here."

We listened to the sound of footsteps coming down the stairs, and in a moment two men wearing pastel polo shirts walked into the kitchen.

"I hope you gentlemen enjoyed yourselves," said Macy.

They nodded and mumbled and hurried out.

"See, tourists," said Macy when they were out of earshot.

"From Illinois," said Addy.

"That's not far enough," said Bow. "To make it work, they've got to come from all over the country."

"Maybe it will happen," said Macy, without sounding as if she expected it.

We chatted for a few more minutes, and then Macy said to Bow, "I think there's someone who'd like to see you in Room Three." Bow nodded and stood up. To me, Macy said, "Why don't you try Five."

"See you in a bit," said Addy.

The stairway wound from the parlor outside the kitchen to the second-floor hallway. Bow used the wood banister to help haul himself up. At the top, he stopped and pulled from his inside pocket a thin silver flask, a German antique his father had picked up on a trip to Europe. Bow took a swig of scotch, then handed the flask to me. The metal felt warm and slightly moist from riding near Bow's chest. I put my head back and took a long drink, closing my eyes, letting the scotch slide down the back of my tongue. For a moment, my head swam with the taste and the scent of the liquor.

Bow ironed his slightly unruly hair with his hand and straightened his tie. "Am I presentable?" he asked. The side of his face was flushed from the stairway and the scotch, and the barely contained globe of his stomach strained against the one controlling button of his suit coat. I couldn't imagine a girl who wouldn't be startled and perhaps appalled to see him in the doorway.

"You look great," I told him.

He clapped me on the back. "Well," he said, "once more unto the breach, dear friend." I watched him knock, then slip around the door into Room Three.

Room Five was at the end of the hall. I knocked once, then went inside. A young woman with curly brown hair was sitting with her legs crossed at a small desk, studying her face in a vanity mirror. She was wearing a pair of lacy shorty pajamas.

"Hello," she said, talking to my reflection in the mirror. "Have I met you before?" She had a cheerful, schoolgirl's voice.

"I don't think so." I sat down behind her on the carefully made bed. "I haven't been around in a few weeks."

"This is only my third time here," she said. Several jars of cream were open on the desk before her. She was reapplying her eyeliner. "We drove up yesterday, and we'll go back tomorrow morning, in time for the weekend."

"Do you like it here?" I asked.

"Macy's nice. And at home, I'd just be sitting around. Things don't really get going until Friday night."

"Home?"

"Milwaukee."

"How's this compare?"

Her eyes got huge in the mirror. "It's so *rural*."

I came up behind her, cupping her breasts with my hands and resting my head on her shoulder, nuzzling her neck below her ear. She was wearing a strong, sweet perfume, and again my head swam.

"Not too close," she said to the mirror. "I've got a cold."

When I went back downstairs, Macy and Addy were working a crossword puzzle together. Addy had the habit of licking the tip of the pencil before writing anything down, and his lips were marbled with graphite.

Bow appeared in a few minutes, still looking slightly flushed. Macy stood up. "Can you stay for a second?" she asked. "There's something I'd like to discuss."

She led us off through the parlor to the darkened living room. We stood in the doorway while she walked around turning on lights.

The room was spacious but the shades were drawn, and Macy's collection of heavy, oak furniture suggested a funeral home or a faded London men's club. In busier times, this is where Macy and her guests would gather and wait.

Bow and I sat on an undulating maroon sofa, and Addy dropped into an easy chair. Macy disappeared for a moment and returned with a tray holding glasses and a decanter of scotch. After she'd poured us each a shot, she sat down opposite Bow and me on a matching sofa.

"I want to draw up a will, Bow," she said. "I have a nephew in Minnesota with a wife and a baby. He's in the army and he's about to go to Vietnam."

"It sounds like he's the one who needs the will," said Bow.

Macy gave him a polite, joyless smile. "If anything happens to me, I want to make sure his family is cared for."

"That can be arranged."

"There are others. . . . It's very personal."

"No problem."

"I don't want to have to worry about it ever again."

"I'll find a good lawyer for you. Everything will be taken care of."

"I want you to do it," said Macy.

Bow shook his head gently. "I've never drawn up a will in my life, Macy. I'll find someone good."

"You," she said. "I've thought about this a lot—a lot."

"It's all she's talked about for the last two weeks," Addy volunteered.

"Hush," said Macy softly.

"You don't understand," Bow explained. "Just because I'm a lawyer doesn't mean I can do everything a lawyer can do. It takes practice and familiarity with the law. I haven't studied trusts and estates since I took the bar exam."

Macy was perched forward on the sofa, with her hands in her lap and her shoulders back. She held herself absolutely still. "I've known lots of lawyers," Macy said to Bow, "but this is personal, and if you'd do it, I wouldn't worry." She talked as if being saved from worry was to be returned to life. I wondered what sort of secrets Macy had guarded over the years that she'd only entrust the details to her old friend Bow.

Bow contemplated the last drops of scotch in his glass. "Well, hell," he said finally. He avoided looking at me. I'd been listening to him turn down work for ten years, and now he was embarrassed to admit he was embarking on something new.

Macy's smile seemed to flow through her body, softening all the angles.

Addy hopped up and poured refills for Bow and me. He'd been a cop somewhere once, but for as long as I could remember, he'd been coming around to help out Macy on nights when her place was open.

Bow put his head back and tossed down the second shot, then he shook himself, reacting to the blast of alcohol. "I guess it's mostly a matter of filling out forms," he said, wiping his mouth with the back of his hand. "I'll get my new assistant to dig them out. You'll have to promise not to sue for malpractice if I make a mistake."

"She won't be around to know," said Addy with a hacking laugh.

Macy signaled with her glass, and Addy hopped up again to pour scotch for Bow and me.

"I do appreciate this, Bow," said Macy.

A silence weighed down around us. Bow reached over to a side table and picked up a framed photograph that he'd been admiring— an old sepia print of a young woman with strong Indian features and wearing a dark, high-necked dress. "Something new?" he asked.

"I rediscovered it in the attic," said Macy. "That's my grandmother when she was a girl. She spoke three languages, French, English, and Chippewa. French because she was taught by French nuns. She used to pray in French, go shopping in English, and talk Chippewa at home."

"She's lovely."

"I've been making an inventory of all my things," said Macy. "I want to make sure they're properly distributed."

"That'll be helpful."

"You should do the same thing."

"I suppose," said Bow. "I'm the last of the line, like a whooping crane. The Last of the Eppses."

Macy flinched politely. "Don't you worry about your things?" she asked.

"Charlie here can pick through the stuff. I'm more worried about keeping my work going, but now maybe Ginger will want to do that." Bow looked at me. It was the first time he'd out-and-out suggested that Ginger might actually carry on behind him.

"Ginger?" said Macy.

"My assistant."

"I thought Charlie was your assistant."

"He is," said Bow. "Ginger's helping out this summer."

"He's the boy who made the shot," said Addy helpfully.

Macy looked baffled.

"A basketball star," Addy explained.

"I don't follow basketball," Macy said.

"He's a friend of your grandniece," I offered, recalling the pretty, dark-haired girl who'd been with Ginger on the Turner Bridge that afternoon.

Macy's expression softened into a smile. She turned to Bow. "You should look up your family," she said. "I feel much better now that I did."

"The Last of the Eppses," Bow repeated with a flourish, still identifying with the whooping cranes.

Macy frowned at him.

Outside, a car pulled into the driveway, crunching gravel. The headlights hit the drawn shades, disrupting the moody shadows of the room. Bow and I got up to leave. "Call me and make an appointment," he told Macy. "Bring in the inventory of what you own. Financial stuff, too."

She ushered us out through the kitchen. On the flagstone path across the lawn, we passed Macy's new customer, a short man in a coat and tie. He noticed Bow's limp and stood aside. We nodded at each other in the darkness.

In the car, Bow and I handed the flask back and forth until we'd emptied it. The road was a series of flat, straight lines that made right-angle turns around fields. There was only a quarter moon, but the sky was clear.

"How was your girl?" Bow asked after a while.

"Nice. Very young."

"Mine, too." In the distance, a boxy farmhouse spilled a small circle of light on the even ground. "I'll tell you something strange, Charlie. Lately, when I'm doing it, I think about my wife."

"Is that so strange?"

"I haven't seen her in fifteen years."

"So?"

"And we were never that great together."

"You were young."

The Pontiac was a pleasure to drive on nights like this, holding down the deserted road with its weight and its easy horsepower. I locked the left wheels on the broken white ribbon in the center of the pavement and kept my eyes straight ahead.

"What do you think it means?" Bow asked, watching my reaction.

Betsy Epps had a pale, delicate face and thin black hair. Bow met her while he was at Columbia. He wasn't her first choice, but after her other boyfriend broke off their engagement, she'd accepted Bow's offer. He had finished law school by then, and he brought her back to Laroque, moving into the big house on the Bluff, which had been empty since Bow's mother died. Betsy worked part-time at the library. I used to see her flitting around town, always alone, always carrying several books or magazines under her arm. I didn't work for Bow at the time, but from what I gathered, she'd been so unhappy that it was a relief when she moved back East.

"I wished we'd had a baby," Bow said abruptly. The visit to Macy combined with the booze had unplugged a whole reservoir of sentiment and memories, and Bow was reeling back and forth over his life, mixing hope and regret. I was sorry I'd brought him out to Macy's that night. Having sex provided a close enough encounter with mortality without adding talk of wills and legacies. "What do you suppose it means?" Bow asked again.

I told him I couldn't figure it out.

We watched a car come up and flash by. After it had disappeared, Bow asked me to pull over so he could take a leak. I parked on the soft shoulder beside a cornfield and turned off the engine. Standing by the road, we pissed into a gully that ran between us and the corn. The moonlight gilded the tops of the plants, creating a silvery lake that stretched off as far as we could see.

Bow tucked himself in, then stood looking out over the field. He swayed slightly, feeling the effects of the scotch. He'd drunk more than he was used to. "Look at that corn," he said, sweeping his hand across the horizon. "Hundreds of thousands of plants, all from the same seeds, the same soil, the same weather, none deviating more than—what?—five percent from the others. That's nature, Charlie. That's life."

"That's corn."

"And what would you say if one year there was a single plant that sprouted fifty percent, a hundred percent higher than the others? Just out of nowhere. A miracle seed. Wouldn't that get you just a little excited?"

"You're asking a lot of the kid."

"How do you explain?" he insisted.

I shook my head, a needless gesture, since Bow was absorbed in the corn. "Explain! Explain!" he shouted, imitating Lear, his voice sailing out over the shimmery field.

After we'd climbed heavily back into the car, Bow blustered, "Damnit, Charlie, I work all my life doing what I think—what I know—is right, facing nothing but scorn from the people around me. And then someone comes along who gets it, who really gets it. I'm excited. Can't you understand that?"

"Great. I'm pleased for you. But why are you getting upset with me?"

"Because I know you, and I know you're sitting over there brooding like a Puritan elder, and, goddamnit, I want a reaction!"

"I've got none, Bow. I mean, I like Ginger, and I think he's a remarkable kid, and I'm happy you're excited. Everyone should be excited sometime."

"But not you."

"I have my moments."

I could feel Bow relaxing, the great bulk he carried, his burden, easing and sinking into the Pontiac's plush vinyl seat. "You know who you remind me of?" he said a little farther down the road. "Not all the time, but sometimes? You remind me of my father."

"Please," I begged.

"Hah!" He slapped me on the knee. "My father," he repeated, satisfied, and he turned to look out the window. The black wall of a pine forest was closing in on us. I didn't tell him what I'd been thinking, what had emerged like a remembered dream from my blowsy sense of the evening—that at moments like this, Bow was *my* father, returned.

CHAPTER 15

As that summer unfolded, with the Lovin' Spoonful proclaiming "Hot town, summer in the city" on every airwave, with *Gemini 9* cruising overhead and the first miniskirts distracting mankind back on earth, the war stayed far away from Laroque, for the most part—a worrisome though mostly abstract concern; a civic issue, a debate question. Toby Monck's death never became a warning or a symbol of some larger conflict. After high school got out in late spring, a dozen or so young men signed up for the armed services, just as their brothers and fathers had done before them, and at least an equal number of boys waited apathetically to be tapped by the draft. Laroque was more backwater than much of the country, of course, but I suspect the same attitude prevailed almost everywhere outside Washington and perhaps New York. Vietnam hadn't yet become the pervasive agony that it would be in just a year or so, and it certainly wasn't yet a shibboleth—"You for or against the war?"— for the kind of person you were.

Looking back more than three decades later, Vietnam seems like a hurricane of events, clearing everything in its path. But I sometimes now have occasion to wander through old copies of the newspapers and magazines of the midsixties, and I'm always startled and saddened at the coverage the conflict received—not the lack of it, but its haphazardness. The papers ran stories virtually every day, but the editors often buried them inside—articles about battles in unpronounceable provinces or accounts of the jockeying among the circle of men around President Johnson. The myopia is humbling, but, of course, the country had countless other preoccupations. A headline referring to war could as easily have sat above a story on Johnson's War on Poverty. The explosion in Watts the summer before had pushed the "Negro problem," with its undercurrent of threatened violence, onto the national agenda. At the Wanigan, people were far more likely to grumble about, say, the tortured pace of repairs on the Turner Bridge than to reflect on the baffling reports coming back from an obscure country. That would change soon enough, but as yet we didn't even know the glossary—pacification, defoliation, napalm, body count, kill ratio, and so on, words that would eventually become like weapons themselves—to make the arguments immediate and personal.

Though it was often on their minds, at first Bow and Ginger spoke only occasionally of the war. Unless he was bored, Bow didn't seem eager to provoke Ginger, and, as I've said, I suspect that Ginger was cautious about testing his beliefs. But after the canoe trip, and as they grew more comfortable with each other, they began to probe and tease, knowing they disagreed. Even then, Ginger remained tentative, often taking the tack of trying out various lines of argument. Every now and then he'd lob a fresh point at Bow, and the two of them would tussle as they tried to work the idea into their already settled positions. I used to wonder about Ginger's sources of information, since the Milwaukee *Journal,* our main link with the outside world, offered spotty reporting at best. One day at the Wanigan, Marcus Laney, his voice heavy with concern, confided to Bow that he'd spotted Ginger in the library reading a copy of *The New Republic.* "What in God's name is wrong with that?" Bow demanded. Laney just shrugged, as if the answer were apparent and Bow was being his usual contrarian self in denying the obvious.

Today, the arguments between Bow and Ginger sound nostalgic, almost comforting, like lines from dimly remembered songs. But at the time, they were fresh and raw and almost endlessly compelling, given our pained inability to understand what was really going on.

Bow's defense of the American position typically centered on two fundamental but related arguments. First, he rattled off a series of agreements Washington had made with the government of South Vietnam promising to defend the country in the event of outside aggression. ("The sanctity of the contract!" Bow would crow. "A cornerstone of capitalism and democracy!") Bow was old enough to recall vividly the shameful images of Neville Chamberlain backing away from defense pacts to appease the Nazis. The lesson was clear: Sooner or later you have to stand up to a bully, and the sooner you do it, the easier it will be. By this line of reasoning, North Vietnam was essentially a surrogate for Communist China (as experienced hands like Joseph Alsop repeatedly assured us). Bow didn't particularly hold to the domino theory, the notion that if South Vietnam went Communist, all of Southeast Asia would topple (the idea was too fatalistic for him). For Bow, it was sufficient that South Vietnam itself was at risk after Washington had agreed to defend her.

Here, Ginger would interrupt: But those agreements were signed with a corrupt and undemocratic government in Saigon. Why do we owe it any support?

Bow: Because that's the government the world community recognizes. Global order would collapse, the world would fall into chaos, if Washington stood by promises only to regimes it deemed honorable (assuming it could find any at all).

This line of argument usually segued into Bow's more heartfelt point, that the United States had to stand fast in Vietnam to maintain its special role as a world leader—and, indeed, to defend and encourage freedom everywhere. The country had emerged from World War II as the bulwark of democracy. Nations looked to America as both symbol and protector; more important, so did the oppressed, the wretched peasant who dreamed of one day breaking the shackles of totalitarianism, whether in Asia, Eastern Europe, or South America. Holding this position of global responsibility, America could not falter in its resolve. It had to show it would stand up for freedom and democracy, not shrink from the cost. Again, the lessons of history were paramount: The country's failure to step up to a global role after World War I led directly to the catastrophe of Nazi aggression, halted only by England's (and Churchill's) steadfastness in the darkest hours of world conflict.

If Bow's main points were relatively straightforward and grounded in history, Ginger's arguments tended to circle and tilt toward the emotional. He didn't assert that the United States had stepped into what was essentially a Vietnamese civil war—an analysis that wasn't yet current enough to reach a high school senior in a small Wisconsin town. Rather, he talked about the mounting loss of life, given the questionable importance of Vietnam in the global scheme of things. He pointed out the corruption and cruelty of the South Vietnamese government. And he brought up the continuing reports that the war wasn't being won, that even American firepower couldn't subdue a guerrilla movement. He came close to what would turn out to be (in my mind, anyway) the strongest argument by the doves: that the war was simply unwinnable, and therefore wrong to pursue. For someone like Bow, with his keen sense of the past, it was unthinkable that the United States could be thwarted by a tiny, backward country; Ginger found that result absolutely possible.

"Even Richard Nixon was saying the other day that we could end up losing more men in Vietnam than in Korea," Ginger pointed out once, after the former vice president had passed through Wisconsin drumming up support for a future race.

"But he wasn't saying we should turn and run," Bow responded. "He meant let's toughen up and get this thing over with. Say what you will about Tricky Dick, but he knows foreign policy."

"It may not be that easy, though—just a matter of more bombs and soldiers," Ginger pressed. "And, meanwhile, the killing goes on."

"You talk as if the fact that someone gets killed should end the argument," Bow said. "War is an extension of foreign policy—politics by another means, as Clausewitz put it."

"Well, if Clausewitz said it, then it's true." Ginger rolled his eyes. Bow's learned sources annoyed him.

"Unfortunately, people get killed in war," Bow continued. "You remind me of the boys at Oxford in the thirties. One time, they took a vote and declared they'd never fight to defend their country, since war was stupid. It was a lovely sentiment—and entirely understandable, given that so many of their older brothers had been slaughtered in the First World War. But it was incredibly naive. And, of course, they fought gallantly against the Nazis when the time came."

"Well, I don't know that much about history," said Ginger, regrouping. "But in World War Two, the question of good versus evil seemed a lot clearer than it is in Vietnam."

"It seems clearer now, from a distance. Believe me, the issues were grayer at the time."

"Come on, Bow. The Nazis were thugs, that was obvious. They were beating people up back in the beer halls of Bavaria." Ginger had been reading his Shirer; Bow was impressed, but he stifled a smile and went on the offensive.

"You think Ho Chi Minh is a kindly old grandfather? A proto-democrat waiting to free his people? Believe me, there'll be a blood-bath in the South if he takes over. And then you can kiss good-bye any semblance of freedom." To his credit, Bow was always less anti-Communist than antidespot.

"Colonel Ky isn't exactly Thomas Jefferson," Ginger said weakly.

"At least there's some suggestion of an open society in South Vietnam. Look at these protests by the Buddhists. You think Ho would allow that? He'd crush them in a moment. I grant you Ky is no sweetheart, but at least he knows the rules and we can keep some pressure on him. In the South, people can speak out and move around. In the North, you're a worm, you don't have anything. Where would you rather live?"

"You're fine in the South as long as you've got money or connec-tions. If not, you're a worm there, too—maybe worse, since you have to watch the elites getting all the breaks."

"You extinguish freedom, and it's hard to get the embers going again." Bow glanced at me; he'd surprised himself with his burst of lyricism.

"So we'll kill them all until they're free," Ginger shot back.

Bow started to respond, then thought better of it. A prickly silence dropped between them. But within seconds, the tension popped. They could play this as sport, after all. They ended up laugh-ing, admiring each other across the office or the booth table at the

Wanigan or the seat of the Pontiac—I can't recall anymore where the argument took place. In fact, virtually the same argument probably erupted in half a dozen places that summer, when the war was still far removed. What strikes me now, these many years later, is that Ginger, more than Bow, sensed the undercurrent—felt that there was something personal at stake, something that suggested an essential difference between Bow and him. I doubt the boy could have articulated how or why, though his early reticence and reluctance to commit to Bow suggests to me that he worried about it. Maybe he even realized that it could lead to trouble. He didn't yet have Bow's talent for making arguments abstractions, apart from himself.

But that analysis of the situation comes in hindsight. At the time, I only remarked on how much Bow and Ginger each belonged to his own side—how their choices about the war seemed utterly wrapped in their personalities and couldn't possibly come out any other way.

CHAPTER 16

The district appeals court sat in a town called Waterville, about a two-hour drive northeast of Laroque. In the early sixties, the state had tried to give an economic lift to the area by rebuilding the Waterville courthouse. While the old facility had been an amiable Gothic redbrick structure filled with cavernous court-rooms, its sprawling replacement featured big aqua tiles outside and the low-slung, utilitarian shape of an elementary school. Inside, there were more courtrooms than before and they were smaller, but the acoustics were so misconceived that microphones had to be installed for the judges, lawyers, and witnesses. Bow had come to dread his appearances there.

On a muggy day in August, he, Ginger, and I climbed into the Pontiac and headed for Waterville so Bow could argue Gary Fontenot's appeal. We made the trip without talking. Bow sat beside me in front, reviewing the brief he'd submitted to the court a few weeks before. Ginger rode in back, studying copies of some of the decisions that Bow was going to cite. Since we kept the Pontiac's windows open to hold off the heat, legal papers flapped and flew around the car the whole way there.

In Waterville, we parked in the dull shade of an oak that had survived the laying of the vast new parking lot and trooped through the sultry air into the courthouse. The guard in front seemed pleased to see us: With the docket thinned for the end of summer, the place had turned gloomy and quiet.

Bow's punctuality had brought us there early, so we waited in the Counsels' Lounge, another innovation of the new building. We'd been alone for five minutes or so when a young blond woman edged open the door and looked around. She burst in when she saw Bow.

"Oh, Mr. Epps, what a pleasure to meet you," she cried, grabbing his hand before he could get up from the table. "You're such an inspiration. I can't believe I've got to argue against you." She was tall and large-boned, and she moved with broad, awkward gestures. Bow looked overwhelmed. "I'm Sally Morrison, the assistant state's attorney," she went on. "You talked to my class in law school. We studied all your cases. You're a genius."

Bow carefully retrieved his hand. "Hardly," he said, smiling. "But thanks for the flattery. What law school was that? I move around."

"Madison. I just graduated last year. This is only my third case." She pumped her arms, which seemed to have the effect of raising her voice. "And I'm up against *you*."

"If you're such an admirer, why are you working for the state?" Bow asked.

She grimaced. "They gave me a job."

Bow shook his head at me. "See how the odds are stacked against us?"

"Are these your partners?" she asked, looking from me to Ginger and failing to perceive Ginger's age.

"Assistants," Bow said.

"Gee. I'm here alone."

"You'll do fine."

"I'm pretty nervous," she said with a giggle.

"Just remember, you know more about the case than the judges do."

"Really?"

"They don't bother to read the briefs."

"They don't?" She looked stunned.

"Not before oral argument."

"Wow."

"Anyway," Bow said, "this appeals panel is a nice old crew. And they'll like you. Two of them used to be prosecutors."

"I'm still nervous." She tried not to stare at Bow's scar. "Can I ask you one more question?"

"Of course."

"What did you think of my brief?"

"Excellent," said Bow. "Very professional."

"Really?" She struggled to control her smile.

"Of course."

"Gee, thanks, Mr. Epps." In her excitement, she leaned over and gave him a quick peck on his good cheek.

By the time we migrated down a long hallway to the courtroom, Gary Fontenot was already sitting in front, unfolded in a chair beside two sheriff's deputies. Inmates weren't usually brought over to hear their appeals argued, but Fontenot had a good record in prison, and Bow's request had been granted. "For Christ's sake, sit up straight," Bow told him. "I brought you here so the judges can see that you're a fine, young citizen."

Fontenot exchanged smirks with the deputies and then pushed his narrow butt back in the seat, stiffening his spine. He'd put together what passed for a serious outfit—a dark suit jacket, clean gray work pants, white shirt, and a thick, black tie that crept out from under the shirt's yellowy collar.

"How's life in Lovington?" Bow asked as he unpacked his papers on the small defense table.

"Okay," said Fontenot diffidently. The two deputies laughed.

"How's your mom?" asked Ginger.

Bow looked up from his papers. Ginger and Fontenot had been exchanging letters, but this was the first Bow or I had heard of Fontenot's mother.

"Real weak." Fontenot dropped the wise-guy pose with Ginger. I realized that he never pulled it with the boy. "They're gonna put her back in the hospital."

"Let us know if there's anything we can do," said Ginger.

"We're just waiting for the end now," Fontenot said.

Bow wasn't at his best that day. I wondered later if Ginger's presence had distracted him. After all, this was Bow's arena, his basketball court, and he may have been overeager to demonstrate his own brand of heroism. It's equally possible that he was simply uninspired by the issues in the case or just weary from the sticky weather. At any rate, he was a beat slower responding to questions from the judges, and some of his answers lacked the usual clarity. The difference was hardly apparent, and he still dominated the courtroom, but after years of listening to him argue, I could sense that he was off. Once, after a rapid exchange with the judges, he paused and turned toward the back, where Ginger and I were sitting on one of the new, padded benches. The exertion of the argument had raised the color on Bow's scar but also dampened and puffed out his entire face, eliminating years of wrinkles and other erosions of age. The transformation was startling—he'd been tortured back to childhood.

Part of Bow's problem was that the appeals panel had actually come prepared for once. Two of the three judges—the two former prosecutors—had read the briefs carefully. They knew something about car searches, and, after years of listening to Bow lecture them on the rights of defendants, they seemed eager to draw the line.

"Come on, Mr. Epps," interrupted one of the judges, Desmond Lawrence, during Bow's presentation. "I don't think you're being intellectually honest with us. One whole line of cases you cite is from house searches. But we're talking about a car here. Surely, there's a difference."

"There is, Your Honor. . . ." Bow had anticipated this objection, but he couldn't head off the judge.

"You don't need a license to live in a house, right?" Lawrence pressed, his voice metallic and piercing through the microphone.

Bow nodded slowly, resigned to the inevitable speech.

"And no one ever got run over by a man driving a house. You can go home and drink yourself blind, but you can't do that and drive a car. A car is a dangerous machine that the state regulates carefully. Why shouldn't we treat the search of it differently from the search of a house?" Lawrence had played football for Wisconsin, and he had the loud, trampling style of a coach.

"You're right about regulation," Bow said briskly. "I cited the house cases to make the point that our search-and-seizure rules are based partly on the *expectation* of privacy. When you're sitting at home, minding your own business, you expect to be safe from having the police burst in and tear the place apart. The same when you're walking down the street to the grocery store. The men who wrote the Fourth Amendment had probably never dreamed of a car, but they did understand the fundamental importance of that sense of security."

"I don't know," Lawrence interrupted again. "Thomas Jefferson probably dreamed of cars. He thought of just about everything else. Haw, haw, haw." The judge's blustery laugh ricocheted around the courtroom. He beamed at his colleagues, pleased to show off his wit.

Bow smiled indulgently, but I knew he was furious at himself for giving this bozo a wedge to break in.

The other former prosecutor, frail, excitable Eugene Ratz, cleared his throat, and the dismaying noise rattled through the sound system. "But the police didn't stop your man maliciously or even randomly, Mr. Epps," Judge Ratz said. "He was driving a heap, and the cops stopped him for cause. He had the stuff he stole right there in the glove compartment. Why should he be able to hide behind the Constitution? He brought this on himself."

Bow nodded agreeably. "It might be different if the goods had been in plain view, if they'd been sitting out on the backseat, for example," he said. "But they were out of sight. The officer had nothing to go on but his suspicions."

"Well, bravo," bellowed Lawrence. "There's one smart cop. He should get a raise, right? We honor our doctors who can sniff out a disease, right? The great diagnosticians. Why impede a gifted cop who's just doing his job?"

This was too much, even for Ratz. "He's got to have more to go on than suspicion," the judge gently reminded his colleague. Then, to Bow: "But I still wonder about the safety issue. After all, it was late at night, and these officers recognized the defendant. They knew they were dealing with a past felon. Couldn't you argue that they had good reason to frisk him and search his car, just to protect themselves?"

"But they knew Mr. Fontenot was nonviolent," Bow said, gesturing toward his client. Fontenot looked intensely uncomfortable under the sudden scrutiny, and the two deputies grinned as if they were sharing a dirty joke. "They knew they had nothing to fear from him," Bow went on. "There'd be more risk with an utter stranger."

Judge Ratz extended a bony hand from the sleeve of his black robe and pulled the microphone close to his lips. "What are you trying to do, Mr. Epps? Set up a rule that if the officers know the driver, they can never search his car?"

"No," Bow insisted. "The rule is they *can't* search." He paused. From the bench, the three judges draped in black looked down on him like vultures waiting for a lost calf to expire. "This just eliminates their supposed exception in this case."

Sally Morrison turned out to be quite good on her feet. Her presentation was smooth and strong—the microphone was superfluous—and she maneuvered through her arguments with easy confidence. The judges were pleased, grinning loopily and offering encouraging comments. As she turned to gesture, making a point, the front of her black silk blouse pulled apart, unveiling a lovely white sliver of lacy bra. The criminal justice system was a tight fraternity of aging men, and she was an exotic counterpoint, a bright revelation. Watching her perform, I felt exhausted for Bow.

Afterward, she scurried across the parking lot to catch up to us. "Mr. Epps, it's been such a pleasure being in court with you," she panted. In one hand she had a big leather briefcase, and an accordion folder was crushed under the other arm. A small band of perspiration glistened on her forehead.

Bow was taken aback. For a moment I thought he didn't recognize her. The moist, heavy air was almost disorienting after the chill of the air-conditioned courthouse. "Why, Miss Morrison, the pleasure was mine," he said, recovering. "You were a wonder in there."

"I was *so* nervous."

"You were a wonder," he repeated.

She put her briefcase down on the pavement and hugged the accordion file with both arms. "Can I tell you something?" she asked.

"Of course."

"I really prefer the defense side. I'm a Democrat, you know."

"Bow's a Republican," Ginger told her.

She cocked her head. "You're kidding," she said. Bow and Ginger and I were already dripping sweat, but her little band of perspiration never moved.

"The Constitution doesn't care about politics," Bow told her.

"But I'm surprised." She blinked wildly, flirting.

The four of us stood in the circling heat and watched as a side door on the courthouse opened and Gary Fontenot was led out in handcuffs. One of the deputies had brought a state car up close to the building and Fontenot climbed in back, followed by the other deputy. Ginger waved as the car pulled away.

"Maybe sometime we can work together," said Sally Morrison.

"Any time," said Bow, turning quickly and heading for the Pontiac. "Any time."

The car was an oven. Bow swatted at the air with some legal papers, trying to concoct a bit of a breeze. "We should have left the windows open," he said. "Nobody around here has enough ambition to steal a car."

Under way at last, we fell into a dull silence again until we were past Waterville's necklace of gas stations, tire stores, and welding shops and back on the winding road to Laroque. Finally, Ginger asked how Bow thought it had gone. Bow grunted and mumbled something cheerless.

The boy leaned over the back of the front seat, looking hurt. "You seemed convincing to me," he offered.

"Unfortunately, you don't count," Bow said. "For the defendant to win a case like this, you can't just be convincing, you've got to be overwhelming—you've got to *embarrass* those old fools into going your way. Otherwise, they won't bother."

"Well, what happens now?" asked Ginger.

"Nothing, for a couple of weeks. They've got to write the decision. We'll see how it reads. I'll decide then whether there's any hope of taking it up to the supremes. This one may just be a loser." Bow looked at me. "If it hadn't been for that weird letter, I don't know that I would have taken it on in the first place."

Ginger sat back. After a moment, he asked, "What will happen to Gary?"

Bow was overheated and frustrated, and he didn't think before he responded. "If he gets out or not, it won't make any difference. Guys like him don't have much of a life span. They all seem to die young. Right, Charlie?"

"Right."

In the rearview mirror, I saw Ginger brace, as if to say something, then stop himself. Some of the papers he'd brought along flapped in the wind.

A few days later, when I was walking with Ginger to the Wanigan to pick up some lunch, I took the occasion to ask him why he felt so drawn to Fontenot. After all, Ginger had been helping out on other cases over the summer, though none had moved along as quickly as Fontenot's. I thought the boy might deny that he had any particular interest in the burglar or brush me off, but instead he was eager to talk—he'd obviously been thinking about it himself. "This may sound strange," Ginger told me, "but I think he's basically a good guy."

"Just bad breaks?"

Ginger shot me a sidelong glance, deciding whether to be annoyed. "I'm not that naive," he said softly, choosing patience. "But I think Bow's right—Gary never really had a chance to go straight. And aside from the burglaries—a pretty big exception, I'll admit— but aside from them, he's all right, he means well." The boy thought for a moment. Up and down the street, as if answering an alarm, the Wanigan regulars were leaving their stores, heading for the diner. "Besides," Ginger added after we'd taken a few more steps, "I guess I'm just kind of amused by him, by the way he thinks."

The boy turned and slowed to watch my reaction, hinting, I thought, that only a superior sensibility would recognize Fontenot's special qualities. It occurred to me that Ginger and Fontenot were physically similar—bodies slight and coiled, without a wasted molecule. And they had a similar kind of presence, always giving the impression that they were holding something back, forcing you to commit—though, of course, Ginger was much more subtle about it.

When I didn't say anything, Ginger continued, "We've been writing back and forth, you know."

"All those tiny squiggles—your eyes must be killing you."

"Oh, that stopped long ago. Now his writing's big as ever. I'll show you when we get back to the office." The boy bubbled with pride. "It's absolutely normal."

"Well, I wouldn't get your hopes up too high for him," I warned. "Bow was pretty discouraged by the way the oral argument went."

"I bet he'll win," said Ginger flatly. "At the appeals hearing, I was watching the judges when Bow talked, and when he made his key points they all nodded. They didn't do that with the girl."

"They nodded?" I didn't try to hide the skepticism in my voice.

We'd come to the door of the Wanigan. A lunch crowd was milling at the register.

"You could barely see it, but they did," the boy insisted, his patience giving way. "I've got more confidence in Bow than you do, Charlie," he blurted angrily, swinging open the diner's door, leaving me standing outside.

CHAPTER 17

Charlie, wake up." Someone was shouting at me from inside a metal drum.

"Charlie, it's me. Wake up." Now I felt a claw digging at my shoulder. "Charlie! I've got some coffee for you."

My eyelids scraped open. I was lying on my back, on something firm but spongy. A swarming pattern of fuzzy red lights, perhaps a UFO, circled far above.

"Here." Each word—another explosion from the drum.

I turned my head slightly and felt a rush of vertigo, then I blacked out.

When I woke up again, Lucy Braestrup hovered inches above me, so close I could smell the Pepsodent on her breath. "Thank God you're all right," she said, sitting back.

I stared at her. The blackout had been mildly recuperative. " 'All right' is a relative term," I told her scratchily.

"I thought you were dead." She sounded matter-of-fact about it. "Here, drink some coffee."

It took an effort to sit up enough to pour a shot of the scalding, tasteless liquid down my throat. I could feel it ravaging various internal organs until it settled in a bubbling pool in a corner of my stomach.

Lucy examined me. "Why don't you lie down again," she said.

By now, I recognized my surroundings: the tarted-up lounge of Jack Amani's Rainbow Supper Club, a few miles outside Laroque. Ox Mueller had driven me there. The last I remembered, Ox and I had been drinking shots of tequila and arguing with some other patrons about Vietnam, but that had turned into a discussion of the guy in the Texas tower who'd shot all those people, and the talk had finally evolved into a debate over whether the current Packers were better than the old Colts. Every argument in a Wisconsin bar seemed to reach the Packers eventually.

"Do you see any sign of Ox?" I asked Lucy. She'd pulled up one of the chairs from the dining room and was now sitting quite primly beside me.

"He's over there." She nodded in the direction beyond my feet.

"Is he alive?"

"He's been snorting."

"Snoring?"

"Snorting," she corrected, and then demonstrated.

"How did you get here?" I asked.

"Jack Amani called me," she said.

"Does *he* know about us?"

Lucy smiled wanly.

"Thank God he didn't call Bow," I said. I sensed the unkindness as soon as I uttered the remark, but it was too late.

Lucy flinched almost imperceptibly. Her eyes gave her away. "Bow doesn't drive," she pointed out. "And Ox's wife couldn't help because he had the car." Lucy paused to take a sip from the coffee cup, making a face as she swallowed. "Jack called me when he was closing up."

"What time was that?"

"A little after two. He woke me up." I shut my eyes, unable to look at her. She continued, "He left the key under the mat out front and some coffee on the stove ready to be reheated."

"What time is it now?" I asked.

"About seven-thirty."

"You've got to get to work."

"I've got a few minutes."

I took a deep breath and opened my eyes again. "I'm so embarrassed," I told her.

She smiled at me but waited, letting me dangle for a few seconds. Finally, she said, "I've seen you like this before. And, anyway, I wanted to see you. There's something I want to tell you."

I didn't like the sound of that. "What?" I asked.

"Oh, it can wait a bit while you pull yourself together," she said mysteriously. She kneeled down and helped me lift my head for another swig of coffee. Her hand felt warm and soft on my neck. Incredibly, the coffee had turned from scalding to ice cold in just a handful of seconds.

"Let's just talk," she said, sitting up in her chair again and balancing the coffee cup and saucer on her knee. "The effort will help you recover."

"Talk about what?"

"Oh, I don't know." She rolled her eyes. "Why don't you tell me something about your mother."

"Why?"

"Because you're always talking about your father, never your mother."

"What can I say? She was sweet, loving, generous. A wonderful person."

"Then why do you only talk about your dad?"

"Because he was the one who tormented me."

Lucy's light blue eyes, almost turquoise, darkened at this observation. "That's awful," she said. "The one who's good gets overshadowed by the bad one."

"That sounds like one of Bow's favorite sayings—'The barbarians always win in the end.' "

"I don't believe that," said Lucy petulantly. "The barbarians are all gone, along with the Visigoths and the Huns and all those other ancient creeps. Civilization is moving forward." She didn't sound entirely convinced. "I saw your pal Ginger with his girlfriend the other day, down on the Turner Bridge," she said, quickly changing direction.

"He's not exactly my pal. But I've seen the girl. She's pretty."

"She's beautiful, really lovely. And he's beautiful, too. They were holding hands and talking, looking right at each other. They looked like two angels. I couldn't take my eyes off them. And I felt something, Charlie—I couldn't tell if I was thrilled or really, really miserable."

Ox stirred just then, erupting in a series of ferocious snorts, as if a huge, oily motorboat were starting up on the edge of Jack Amani's dining room.

When he quieted, I asked Lucy, "Was that what you were going to tell me?"

"Oh, no, no, no," she cried, her mood brightening.

"Well?"

She put the coffee on the floor and folded her hands in her lap. She was wearing a short black skirt, rather daring for the bank, and I enjoyed the neat lines of her thin, tanned knees.

"I've got a boyfriend," she said.

Lying on my back on Jack Amani's heavy-duty, faintly smoky smelling carpet, staring up toward Lucy and beyond, to the UFO, which turned out to be a string of red Christmas lights, inexplicably still entwined—and lit!—around a wiry chandelier, I was able to repress any visible reaction. Which is how I wanted it to be, since I had no claim on Lucy, and, in fact, I'd never once thought of her in any kind of a permanent way. Still, she'd now done something to my stomach, which was roiling silently.

"Anybody I know?" I asked.

"His name's Ed Gable, and he lives over in Gadsden. He's buying a little cabin upstream on the Agnes. In fact, I met him at the bank when he came in to get a mortgage."

"That's nice." I waited. "What's he do?"

"He's a policeman."

"A cop!" I spat it out.

"I knew you'd say that." She turned away angrily.

"But why a cop?"

"Why not?" she hissed, turning back. "I suppose you'd rather I went out with some rapist or murderer, one of those monsters you and Bow love to set free."

The commotion roused Ox, and he unloosed a steady outpouring of liquidy grunts and moans.

"No," I told her. "It's just . . ." But, of course, I had no defense. "A habit from my work," I said, wilting. "You know—the cops are the bad guys. A stupid reaction."

"There are decent cops, too."

"Of course."

"Ed is one."

"I'm sure."

"I wanted you to know because this means, well, no more . . ."

"I know. You don't have to say it."

"Thank you." She stood up. She'd accomplished what she'd intended. "Do you want a ride back to town?" she asked. "I need to get to work."

"Sure." I climbed shakily to my feet. Now my head was pounding *and* my stomach was a mess. "Think we can give Ox a ride, too?" I asked. "Maybe he better come back for the car." Underfoot, the carpet felt amazingly springy. There were probably worse places to sleep.

Lucy and I stood over Ox. He was an enormous man, a bunker of flesh. Stretched out on the floor, his body twitched in a sort of rhythmic pattern from head to toe. "How do you pick *him* to go drinking with?" Lucy asked.

"He just seems to be there."

I bent down and started shaking Ox's shoulder. Pretty soon Lucy and I had him on his feet, though his eyes were half closed and he wasn't talking yet.

"He's huge," groaned Lucy, teetering under one log-sized arm. "The Packers could use him."

We managed to cram him into the back of Lucy's little blue Corvair. She drove us to town, and I hauled out Ox on River Road, in front of Duffy's. I took him around back, out of sight, and propped him up against a wall until I could bring him some coffee and food. By the time I walked back to the front again, Lucy and her Corvair had scooted away. So I set out on foot for the Wanigan. I was feeling more lucid now, and I considered what Lucy had told me. How long had we been seeing each other? Two, three years, but never formally, no dates or anything, just stolen moments here and there. Still, three years. I thought about my reaction, or nonreaction, to what she'd told me. It had to do with Bow, I decided. He'd seen a light in me, and I'd responded. Now I concentrated so much on him that it probably almost eliminated the chance to think about anyone else—as if in owning my head, Bow occupied my heart as well.

CHAPTER 18

In early September that year, just after school started, a young man named Andy Stanziale became the second Laroque boy to die in Vietnam. Andy was two years out of high school and within a week of returning to the States when a single, isolated mortar round landed at his feet at a base camp near Kontum in the Central Highlands. The army couldn't explain why the Viet Cong would fire one shot at a well-fortified camp that otherwise had never been attacked. But there you had it: Andy was killed instantly.

The death raised several delicate issues in Laroque. The Stanziales were outspoken anticlerics and refused to have anything to do with a church. As the story went, Andy's grandfather had been a tailor in Italy who made vestments for the Vatican and came to believe that the priests were cheating him. He fled to this country, renouncing organized religion, and the antagonism held through the next generation of the family. Andy's father was a quiet milkman, but he happily paused in his rounds to rail against Roman Catholicism and other supposed inhibitors of American freedom. The election of John F. Kennedy almost panicked him. Given those views, holding his son's funeral in a church was out of the question.

At the same time, though, in just the few months since Toby Monck was killed, the Vietnam death ritual had grown more elaborate. The state VFW had formed a special funeral unit that it wanted to send along. And Laroque's congressman, a first-termer, who'd been an early, strong supporter of the war, hoped to give a speech. Neither of these outsiders expected to proceed without the imprimatur of a religious authority of some sort. And, in fact, a number of people in Laroque—who were otherwise understanding of the Stanziales' idiosyncrasies—felt they couldn't adequately express their grief without the invocation of God.

The mayor and some of the town's other leading citizens helped the Stanziales sort through the possibilities, and in the end it was decided to hold the service in the Opera House. Reverend Olson would open the proceedings, then leave the stage to sit in the audience. The congressman, a lawyer named Michael Wilcox, could make his speech. Andy Stanziale's younger sister, Rose, a gifted violinist, would supply the music. And, once again, the grieving family asked Ginger, who'd played baseball and basketball with Andy, to speak in his memory.

I don't know whether anyone hesitated because of Ginger's opposition to the war or his skeptical remarks at Toby Monck's funeral. Chances are, by then, Ginger's antiwar comments had either been dismissed or accepted—what stood out was his generous recollection of his friend. Or perhaps the Stanziales themselves had turned against the war. In any case, I'm sure they felt that a eulogy from Ginger—this glowing young star of the town, with his remarkable speaking gifts—would serve to honor their Andy.

The day of the funeral was bright and warm for September, a tantalizing reminder of the season slipping away. The fire siren sounded at quarter to eleven that morning, calling people to the service; many of the stores downtown closed.

On Main Street, Bow and I fell in with the crowd, which was shuffling toward the Opera House at about Bow's normal pace, slowed by the numbers of people and the melancholy of the occasion. Up ahead, the VFW had strung Veterans' Park with flag banners and placed wreaths around the base of the war monument. A color guard stood on the top steps of the Opera House. After a few blocks, Morris Pogue, Laroque's gray, owly optometrist, came up. "It never gets easier," Pogue said.

"Hello, Morris," cried Bow, who'd obviously been thinking about something else. "What doesn't get easier?"

Pogue's dark, round eyes seemed to shrink, retreating from the horror. Suddenly Bow understood. "Oh, never, never, never," he said, recovering. "It's heartbreaking." He took Pogue gently by the elbow and guided him up the Opera House steps, past the soldiers standing stiffly at the entrance and beneath the huge American flag hanging from the same fat, ancient nails that used to hang hand-painted pennants celebrating my father's productions.

Inside, Pogue diverted greetings with his air of fierce purpose, and we made our way upstairs. The auditorium was about three quarters full, a generous turnout for a funeral, but deflating for anyone raised in the theater. I glanced around for Lucy, but didn't see any sign of her.

Bow found three seats for us on the aisle, ten or so rows back. Onstage, in front of the curtain, several folding chairs and a lectern stood in grim isolation. Half a dozen flags drooped from poles. With the religious trappings eliminated, the arrangement seemed merely civic, suggesting a candidates' debate or a school assembly. Pogue, a widower without children who had found solace in the Methodist Church, was put off. He examined the space darkly. "There's no coffin," he said.

"I think they had a cremation," Bow told him. "This is just a service."

"You'd never know someone was dead," Pogue rasped.

Soon the color guard trooped down the aisle, boots thumping against the worn carpet, and stopped at attention in front of the stage. The Stanziale family filed in through a side door and sat in two rows of seats reserved by a red velvet ribbon. They were a dozen or so people over several generations, all covered in black. Huddled together in their seats, murmuring among themselves, they made a striking, inky swatch in the mottled fabric of the audience. "Italians know how to *dress* for funerals," Bow whispered to me, out of Pogue's hearing.

Onstage, Reverend Olson's pale face peeked out through the crack in the curtain. After a moment, he stepped forward to the lectern, more sprightly than he'd been at Toby Monck's funeral, his arthritis soothed by three months of summer's heat. Behind him,

Congressman Wilcox, Rose Stanziale, and Ginger solemnly took their places on the gray metal folding chairs. The Opera House fell into a musty stillness, the silence broken only by the creaking and wheezing of the old spring seats.

The service moved along quickly, starting with comments by Reverend Olson. Whereas at Toby Monck's funeral the minister had found purpose in the boy's death, this time he found honor. Andy Stanziale had loved his country and understood the obligations of citizenship. He died fulfilling his duty, an example to all young men in these troubled times. In any great culture, it falls to the strong to sacrifice, to offer the last full measure of devotion. In that way, the weak are drawn to the community ideal.

The minister's argument was graciously secular, with references to Lincoln instead of the Bible. His becalmed arthritis allowed him to stand for the duration, and he played his resounding bass voice—always his greatest asset as a preacher—with a rejuvenated skill. When I was a boy, my nonbelieving father would occasionally dress me up and take me to a crowded service at St. John's just to hear Reverend Olson perform. Time and illness had worn down his gift, but now it was as if the Stanziales' atheism had freed the minister from the tired strictures of his calling, and he was liberated to exercise his great instrument to its creative limits. At the end, after a thundering call to learn from the sacrifice of Andy Stanziale, when Reverend Olson finally hobbled off the stage to a seat down front, the Opera House audience wanted to explode in applause. I don't think anyone paid a whit of attention to what he actually said.

With smart timing, Michael Wilcox waited until the minister was safely off the stage and beyond concern before hopping up to the lectern. Wilcox was a small, nimble Democrat who'd coasted to Washington on the Johnson landslide of 1964. Though Wilcox wore tweeds and horn-rimmed glasses, affecting the slightly academic air of the crowd around President Kennedy, Johnson was said to be fond of the young congressman. In turn, Wilcox was unendingly appreciative of the man who'd made his election possible. There'd been talk that the president himself might make a campaign stop for Wilcox later that fall.

As it happened, Wilcox had served in the Pacific in World War II with one of Andy Stanziale's uncles. Though the congressman had never met Andy, he began by ascribing the same soldierly instincts of the uncle to the nephew. Wilcox had an immature, slightly buzzing voice, and he droned on for a time about the Stanziale character. It was generic material; soon he was accompanied by an orchestra of creaking seats. But when he moved to a discussion of Vietnam, his intensity picked up; the audience returned. He'd made this speech before, and he was rather good at it, though his defense of the war was probably more vigorous than needed, given the audience. Wilcox believed firmly in the imperialist intentions of Mao's China and in the domino theory. But his heart seemed to be in the same place as Bow's—holding to the more abstract argument that America's greatness would dissipate if Washington backed out on a commitment to an ally. Loyalty, constancy, courage, self-sacrifice: These were the qualities of a strong and lasting country.

"President Johnson understands the terrible sacrifices being asked of great people like the Stanziale family and of towns like Laroque," Wilcox pronounced, hugging the lectern. "No doubt, there will be more sacrifices ahead, though I hope none so painful for this brave little town. But if we don't draw the line here, then where? If we don't stand up for what we believe in now, then when?"

The audience, though attentive, seemed to grow sullen under the outpouring of polemics. Why this campaign speech at a funeral? Pogue's narrow, white hands churned in his lap. A few rows over, Mrs. Pangborn, who'd sat with Bow and me at Toby Monck's funeral, ratcheted up her chin a few millimeters, leaving no doubt that her approval was far from won. On the other hand, Bow was pleased; the congressman made his case well, and, anyway, Bow had never liked the oafish Republican incumbent whom Wilcox had beaten.

"We've made a promise not just to the free government of South Vietnam, not just to our other allies around the globe, but also to boys like Andy Stanziale," Wilcox pressed on, his voice revving. "Do we now tell Andy's parents that we've changed our minds? That this was all a mistake? That protecting democracy in a small country many miles away isn't worth the trouble after all? Of course not. Our support of the president means Andy did not die in vain. This fine young man, this true American hero, made his commitment, ladies and gentlemen. Now it's up to us to make ours."

Bow leaned close to my ear, carrying the smell of his morning cigar. "Not bad for a Democrat," he whispered.

From far in the back, someone broke into a spasm of coughing, splintering the silence and demonstrating the splendid acoustics of the auditorium. People in front turned and gawked, trying to catch a glimpse. For a few seconds, there was a scuffling of feet, and then the great wood doors neatly sliced off the sound.

Wilcox, still at the lectern, seemed momentarily pleased behind his horn-rims—his prose had ignited this fit? "Now," he said, as the audience settled its attention on the front again, "I'd like to bring on another fine young son of Laroque." Ginger was on the edge of his chair, a few folded pages of yellow legal paper in his hand. "Even out in Washington last spring, I heard the news of the shot, but this morning is the first opportunity I've had to meet the Laroque Lumberjack who made it." Wilcox turned and in a fatherly way waved Ginger to step up. "Ginger Piper was a teammate of Andy's, and the Stanziale family has asked him to say a few words in memory of his friend."

Since school had started, Bow and I had seen less of Ginger; he still came around several days a week, but usually it was just to drop off some research or pick up a check from Bow. He rarely stayed and often as not seemed to be in a bit of a rush. We hadn't talked to him at all since hearing the news of Andy Stanziale's death.

Now, in his black, baggy suit, Ginger looked almost stocky next to the little congressman. The two of them danced an awkward minuet of shaking hands and moving past each other on the stage. Ginger laid down his papers and gripped the edges of the lectern. "I'm honored to speak on behalf of Andy," he began quickly, sounding a bit ill at ease. "As Congressman Wilcox said, Andy was a true American hero." Ginger paused and looked out over the audience. "But to me, he was a hero because he was friendly, cheerful, funny, and gentle. As a soldier in Vietnam, however, I worry that Andy was less a hero than a victim."

Bow glanced at me, smiling and shaking his head. Onstage, Wilcox was slow to catch the drift; he still wore his campaign grin. "This is the second time in six months that I've been asked to speak on behalf of a teammate who was killed in this war," Ginger went on. "That basketball team only had twelve players on it. Today, two of them are dead. Statisticians would tell us that that's a terrible coincidence, but how much more coincidence do we have to suffer before we ask ourselves if this war is worth it?"

Now Wilcox understood. He looked as if he'd bitten into something sour. Ginger took out a handkerchief and mopped his forehead. In front of him, the Stanziales were frozen, gravestones draped in black. The auditorium felt airless.

Ginger launched into his criticism of the war, familiar to me now from his arguments with Bow. The speech went on for several minutes. While the boy's eulogy for Toby Monck had been woven with references to the dead teammate, Ginger's comments this time drifted away from Andy Stanziale and stayed polemical, doubting official government accounts of the war and questioning President Johnson's optimism.

Congressman Wilcox took the references to his patron hard, fidgeting in his chair, crossing and uncrossing his legs, glaring at Ginger and then letting his head swivel solemnly so the audience could read the fury on his face.

By now, the hundreds of friends and neighbors of the Stanziales who'd come out to the Opera House were losing their patience. They wanted soothing lamentations, not argument, not more of the drumming debate that was becoming inescapable outside the Opera House walls. In front of us, heads bobbed together, people talked. Mrs. Stanziale broke down, slumping forward, her shoulders rolling in swells with her sobs. "Enough, already," Bow whispered to me, referring to Ginger.

Finally, the boy came around to his finish. "Something like this, the death of my friend Andy Stanziale, makes me feel powerless," Ginger said, his voice, always thin, starting to crack. "I don't think Andy should have died. I don't think any more Americans should die for Vietnam. I wish there was something I could do—we all could do—to stop this war. My one hope is that Andy's death could be a message to officials like Congressman Wilcox to take back to Washington and to the president, a message that says enough people have died. If that could happen, then Andy Stanziale would be a true American hero."

Ginger had rallied for the rhetorical finale. His voice had strengthened and deepened, and the words sailed defiantly over the low-grade rumble of conversation starting to fill the auditorium. Everyone had an opinion. As Ginger gathered his notes and slipped back to his chair, Pogue leaned over, his sad, worn face an overripe grapefruit bobbing at Bow's chest. "Where did he get the ... idea," Pogue stuttered, struggling to put words behind the anger and suspicion. Bow ignored him.

"He's always opposed the war," I told Pogue.

Mrs. Stanziale continued to sob. A tangle of black-draped arms reached out to comfort her. Her despair was a trigger, and the noise in the auditorium rose, feeding on itself in a kind of rebellious disrespect for silence.

Meanwhile, Andy's sister Rose approached the lectern. At fifteen, she was a small, wispy girl with the straight lines and uncertain features of a child. Her dark hair was pulled into a tight ponytail and her black, ankle-length dress looked several sizes too big. She stood awkwardly at the front of the stage, holding a golden-brown violin that seemed huge in her hands, impossibly beyond her strength to control. After a moment, she flung her head back, whipping her ponytail out of the way, and tucked the instrument neatly under her chin. She began to play the Adagio from Bach's First Sonata for Solo Violin, the opening, beautifully hesitant notes searching through the vaulted space above our heads. Soon the notes were rushing out, filling the auditorium, luring us up out of the worn, creaky Opera House seats and out of the tired, old building itself into the free, clear skies above. As a crescendo rose, her thin child's arm pumped furiously at her instrument, blurring the line between grief and creation. The gorgeous music was inhuman in a way, a rebuke to words and logic from a tiny angel. And when she had finished, bowing, still fresh and composed, the Opera House emptied almost silently. People made their way slowly down the winding staircase and through the cramped lobby into the bright September sun and hardly a word was exchanged. Bow and I were well down Main Street, lagging behind the faster-walking crowd, before Bow finally spoke. "He overplayed it," he said crisply. And that was the first time I'd ever heard him criticize Ginger.

Chapter 19

ow, there's someone here to see you," said Ida Klister, the
bank receptionist. She was standing in the office doorway,
looking profoundly put upon.

"It's me, Bow," said Macy Cunningham, peeking over Ida's shoulder. "Remember, you told me to stop up."

"They came in through the front entrance," groused Ida.

Bow stood up behind his desk. He'd been working in silence for
several hours, and he appeared a bit unnerved by the sudden activity.
"You can get here through the alley, then up the stairs," he said
weakly to Macy.

She slipped past Ida, followed by her companion, Bill Addy. Just
behind them, looking uncomfortable at the intrusion, came the
pretty young woman I'd seen with Ginger on the Turner Bridge.
Suddenly, the office was jammed. Bow swatted the air in front of his
face, disturbing the lingering haze of his after-lunch cigar. I scrambled to move papers and books off the sofa.

Ida wasn't finished. "It's awkward having your clients come in
through the front," she told Bow. "I'm not supposed to be away
from my desk." The inflection of her voice and the stapled corners
of her mouth left no doubt that she knew all about Macy Cunningham.

"Thank you so much for your help," said Macy with exaggerated courtesy, driving Ida away.

As the sound of Ida's heels clicked off down the hall, Bill Addy said to Bow, "Don't you own this bank?"

"You can't *own* a bank," Bow told him. "There are too many people involved."

"Heh, heh." Addy's laugh was dry and almost soundless. "Ever since the Waterville Fire Department joined a union," he said, "they practically have to give the firemen a raise each time before they'll put out a fire."

"Well, sit down," said Bow, gesturing toward the sofa.

The three guests silently squeezed onto the soft cushions, Macy and the young woman sitting primly on the ends, Addy sandwiched in between. "You know Bill, of course," said Macy. "And this is my grandniece, Anna Sterritt. I don't believe you've met."

"Grandniece, grandniece," puzzled Bow, sitting down. "How does that work?"

Macy frowned. "What do you mean?"

"You know," said Bow. "What's the relation, the lineage?"

"Oh, here or there," said Macy dismissively. "It's not important."

"Nothin' you could prove," quipped Addy, and this time his laugh hooked a cough deep in his chest. Macy and Anna sat patiently, bouncing gently on the sofa, as he worked to bring his hacking under control.

When it was quiet again, Macy said, looking at me but talking to her companions, "And you both know Charlie, of course."

Anna beamed at me so brightly that I thought for a moment something was going on. She had Macy's high cheekbones, but she was much lighter skinned and her features were softer. The Chippewa connection—whatever it was—was remote.

"I hope we're not interrupting anything," Macy said. "I don't get a chance to come to town much."

"No," said Bow. "Nothing special." He glanced at the transcript open on his desk. "Actually, it's sort of an interesting case," he volunteered. "A woman over in the Meadowland Apartments in Kawnipi says she was raped by someone wearing a ski mask. The cops arrested my client, and he was convicted on her testimony, even though she admits she didn't know him and never saw his face. He was just a handyman who happened to be working around there that day."

"What's his name?"

"Lester Freund."

"Hey, I know him," said Addy brightly. "He's a bad guy, a scary guy."

"Hush," said Macy, not looking at Addy, acting as if she didn't want to acknowledge that he was actually there. I wondered why she kept the old fool around—though it quickly occurred to me that people might wonder the same thing about Bow and me.

Bow frowned, then tore off a strip of yellow legal paper to mark his place and closed the transcript. "How are you doing?" he asked Macy.

"Oh, not well, Bow. The doctor says there's trouble."

"She was in the hospital," said Addy. "Tumors."

"I'm sorry," said Bow. "I didn't know. I don't get out as much anymore. I hope everything's going to be okay."

Macy shrugged. With her vibrant, dark skin and compact figure, she looked the picture of health. "Anyway," she said, skipping forward, "I need that will."

"Oh, Christ." Bow shuffled through the papers on his desk. "Ginger pulled some forms for me."

Macy opened her purse and took out several sheets of onionskin neatly folded into a square. "I've got an inventory of everything I own," she said, unfolding the papers in her lap and ironing them flat with her hand. The sheets were covered with carefully typed lists. "Most of it's stuff that was handed down to me from my family. I didn't provide many new things myself. You make a list like this and you see: Life is mostly just keeping things and passing them on, handing them over to the next round."

"Oh, Macy," said Anna, "you have such beautiful things."

"Sometimes, Bow, I just walk around the house and touch objects," Macy continued. "Especially the wooden things. I just stand there and run my fingers across the top. That Parsons table in the hall, for instance. The wood feels so real to me, like skin."

"Her grandmother gave her that table," said Addy.

Macy's eyes were filling with tears.

"Well, let's see," said Bow. He couldn't locate the will forms. Instead, he picked up a legal pad and prepared to take notes. "Who are your survivors?"

"What do you mean?"

"Who's in your immediate surviving family?"

Macy stiffened. "I've never been married, Bow. You know that."

"Okay," said Bow. "Let's put it this way. Who do you want to leave your things to?"

"Three people," said Macy firmly. "I'll leave the bonds to my nephew in Minnesota."

"He's not really her nephew," said Addy.

"Please, Bill," Macy said, not looking at him.

"Okay," said Bow. "Go on."

"And I want to leave all my furniture and things to Anna. Plus what's in my savings account."

"Okay." Bow jotted notes.

"And the house and property to Bill here."

"That's it?"

"Yes."

"Hmmm." Bow chewed on the end of his pen. "That shouldn't be too tough. How much money is involved?"

Macy took an ancient savings book from her purse and fumbled through the pages. "Right now, $291,463," she said.

"Whoa!" cried Bow, sitting up.

Addy laughed, setting off another hacking fit. Everyone waited for his chest to settle. "And that doesn't include the bonds," he finally wheezed.

"I've always been careful with my money," said Macy defensively.

"Forgive me," Bow said. "It's these times. No one saves that well anymore."

"We all have obligations to the future," said Macy.

"Well, let's see." Bow looked over his notes. "There's going to be a big tax bite. Maybe I should talk to an expert. We might want to put some of this in trust. That might help a bit when the time comes."

"I don't want to do anything sneaky," said Macy.

"That's just taking advantage of what's allowed."

Bow went over a few more points, jumping from one thing to another: The farmhouse was owned outright, the mortgage having been paid off years ago; the important documents were in a safe deposit in a bank in Morris and the key was in the top right-hand drawer of the writing desk in the living room; Macy didn't have any life insurance; her birth certificate had disappeared years ago; she wanted Bill Addy to be the executor.

It was an overcast day, and the low afternoon light sapped the color from the office. With the details of her death being worked out, Macy began to look frail. In her lap, her thin fingers worried themselves into a complicated knot. She'd told Bow she was sixty-six—"As old as the century"—but I wondered if that figure had been chosen for convenience. I'd always assumed she was older than my father, and he'd have been seventy if he were still alive.

During a long silence, the phone rang, and I answered. The clerk from the appeals court was calling as a courtesy. There was a decision in the Gary Fontenot case: The judges had voted 3–0 to reject the appeal. One written opinion and a brief concurrence. The papers would be filed tomorrow. Did Bow have any questions? A trace of smug satisfaction registered in the clerk's voice. Bow towered over these people. I told the clerk to send copies and hung up.

Bow had followed the drift of the phone conversation. "Well, I'm not surprised," he said. "I thought I might pry out one vote, but I'm not really surprised." He'd lost scores of appeals over the years, far more than he'd won. But I could tell he felt set back.

"Can't you just appeal it up higher?" asked Addy helpfully.

"Maybe," Bow said. "But there's a risk there, too. It's one thing to have some bad law coming out of an insignificant little midlevel appeals court. It's another to have it sitting there in a state supreme court decision, for everyone to cite. I think Gary Fontenot is just a loser, and we'll have to leave it at that."

"Ginger will be disappointed," I said.

Bow sighed. "He's gotta learn. You lose more than you win in this business." His tone held a hint of impatience. "But we better call Ginger and tell him. Maybe he wants to tell Fontenot."

"I can tell Ginger," Anna offered suddenly. "I'll be seeing him later on."

"Well, sure," said Bow, studying her as if she'd just walked in the door. "You must know him from school."

She nodded as her eyes darted nervously to me. I wasn't sure whether their romance or whatever was a secret I was supposed to hold.

"How's he get along there?" Bow asked abruptly, his curiosity getting the better of him.

"He's different," she said without hesitation. "He's different from everyone else."

"Meaning what?"

"Oh, he's popular and a sports star and all. But I don't think people realize how different he is."

Bow stared at her stiffly for a few seconds. Anna's cheeks brightened, and she tugged shyly on her short, black skirt. Finally, Bow said, "How?"

Anna stopped fidgeting. "He has no limits."

Bow smiled, pleased to find someone else who understood.

Out of the silence, Addy said, "A lot of people made money on that shot. That was a big payday for Laroque."

"Did you?" I asked.

Addy shook his head violently, offended that I'd misread his character. "I don't gamble. Never did. It's for fools."

Macy was getting restless. She glanced at her watch, a thin band of gold, bright against her skin. "About the will," she said.

Bow pushed himself up out of his chair. He wanted to get back to his transcript. "I think I've got a good start. Send me everybody's name, address, and birthdate. I'll see where we go from here."

Addy and Anna hauled themselves out of the soft cushions of the sofa, but Macy had a hard time getting up. With the effort, a small, violent shiver passed through her failing body. Addy leaned down and gave her his arm, and she rose heavily to her feet. Bow watched intently. For the first time, I think, he realized she was dying, and for a moment his face darkened with the painful knowledge. He recovered quickly, though, and ushered his visitors to the door.

Macy said, "I really appreciate this, Bow. You don't know how it gives me peace of mind."

"It's the least I could do," Bow told her. "You've given so much over the years."

Her eyes narrowed as she tried to decide if this was another of Bow's wisecracks. But he was serious. "We all try to do our best," she said.

The hall outside Bow's office was barren and dusty for lack of traffic. The other offices up there had once been rented to lawyers and accountants, but now all the rooms were empty or used to store bank records. The clouded glass in the doors admitted an eerie gray light that created ghostly shadows. No one could enjoy standing out there for long, and Addy tried to hurry his group up, taking each woman by the elbow. Anna would have none of it and pulled herself free. "It was really great to meet you," she told Bow, shaking his hand.

"My pleasure," he said.

"I'll tell Ginger about the case," she promised. Then she added reassuringly, "He'll be all right."

Bow watched them walk down the corridor, Macy braced awkwardly on Addy's arm. Bow didn't say anything, but I could see his distress. His father had died suddenly walking home from work, and Bow had been in law school when his mother passed away. His life was so insulated that, until now, he'd probably never witnessed close up a body in the end stages of decline. Macy's visible helplessness made his shoulders sag. It sapped his breath, as if approaching death sucked up the surrounding air. Bow limped back to his desk and sought solace in the transcript of Lester Freund's rape trial.

CHAPTER 20

A few days after Macy's visit, I hitched a ride up to the Spirit Light Lodge, figuring to get in a little work outdoors before the cold set in. The camp slowed down in the fall. Bob would get a few fishing parties on the weekends and an occasional group of duck hunters, though he didn't hunt himself and didn't promote the sport. The other workers at the camp were seasonal, so by this time Bob and his wife, Margaret, had the place to themselves. Bob and I spent most of the days battening down the camp for winter—patching up the boats, closing the unheated outbuildings, making minor repairs on the lodge. We hit a nice run of Indian summer, and in the afternoon we'd sometimes finish early and take a canoe out looking for muskie. Bob was an easy, patient fisherman, basically unambitious; dangling a line was good enough for him. He'd sit in the bow, ramrod straight on the hard aluminum seat, wearing the same blue John Deere baseball cap that he'd been living under as long as I knew him. He never talked much, but he enjoyed hearing gossip about local people. Bow interested him, and Bob always had a few questions about Bow's latest cases. I think, in his devout, Baptist way, Bob saw Bow as a kindred spirit, another saver of souls.

Bob also took a special interest in Archie Nye, who'd been

arrested that fall for another bar fight. Archie had worked one summer at the camp, and it pained Bob that the experience hadn't
brought him around to a better life. "I thought Archie was going to
straighten himself out, but he never got the chance," Bob said one
afternoon as we trolled along an inlet on Crow Lake. "He wanted to,
I really think he wanted to, but he could never settle himself down."

I told Bob about our experience a few months before, running
into Archie on Bow's property.

"He does play on the edge, doesn't he," said Bob.

"He's pretty wild."

Bob shifted his cap to wipe the perspiration off his forehead,
exposing a startling crescent of sunless, white skin, luminous against
his ruddy face. "That summer he worked here—I bet you two had
some good times," he said, smiling. Bob had long ago divided the
world into drinkers and nondrinkers, and he assumed everyone in
each camp celebrated together.

"Actually, no. He kept pretty much to himself."

"Well, he sure could find fish," said Bob. "He was a difficult man,
but he could smell the fish."

I'd only planned to spend a couple of days at the Spirit Light but
ended up staying much longer, held by the leisurely pace and the
sweet changing of the seasons. The birches turned while I was there,
golden against the pines for a day or so, until a quick storm spilled
the leaves into fading yellow puddles. The air was filled with noisy
squadrons of geese and ducks, honking their way south, their looping, slithering formations sometimes stretching halfway across the
sky. Late in the afternoon, the sun was hot, but once it slipped below
the treeline, a sharp chill dropped over the water, and Bob and I
would have to paddle hard to beat the darkness. In the evenings,
before dinner, Bob and Margaret would sit in front of the big fireplace in the lodge, reading their Bibles. I'd sit there, too, and for hours
at a time, I never thought about scotch. It even occurred to me one
day that I'd never drink again, that I'd simply run out of the desire.

One afternoon, Bob caught a fifteen-pound northern pike, pulling
him in with a light spinning rod while I maneuvered the canoe
around a weedy inlet. That evening, Margaret baked the fish in tin-

foil, then let it cool, so we could pick out the moist, white chunks of meat with our fingers, avoiding the creature's many bones. Margaret put a bowl of mayonnaise on the table and we dipped the morsels in it before dropping them into our mouths. It was a sloppy, noisy dinner, almost raucous by the standards of the Spirit Light. At one point, I said something that amused Margaret, and when she'd stopped laughing, she said to Bob, speaking of me, "He's like our son."

Bob's thin face clouded, and he asked what she meant.

Margaret was a soft, round woman, not especially pretty, but rather sexy in the confident way she moved around the largely male world of the camp. She and Bob were in their early fifties by this time; I never knew why they hadn't had children. Now she paused and smiled uncomfortably at her husband. "I mean, with the three of us here, Charlie's like our child," she said. "It's fun."

Bob reached over and put his palm on top of her chunky left hand where it was resting on the table. "Don't talk like that," he said softly. "Charlie is a grown man." Then, with his free hand, he reached over and clasped my right hand, squeezing it lightly and bowing his head. We stayed that way perhaps fifteen seconds before Bob let go, and we finished the meal. I excused myself soon afterward and spent a restless night: Was this where I'd ended up after thirty-six years?

I wanted to get back to town, but I'd agreed to guide two Baptist barbers from St. Louis the next day. We stayed on Crow without much luck, and when we came back in, Bob was waiting at the end of the rickety pier. "Bow Epps called," he told me quietly when I stepped out of the boat. "He wants you back in Laroque."

"What's up?" I asked.

We tied the boat to the pier and waited for the barbers to wander off. Bob was vigilant about not interrupting the idyll of a fishing trip with news from the outside. "A fellow Bow had defended escaped from jail and shot one of the sheriff's men," Bob said. "It's pretty bad. The sheriff's man is dead."

"Who was it?"

"Was there a fellow named Fonto?"

"Gary Fontenot?"

"You'd better check with Bow. I wouldn't want to get it wrong."

"Jesus," I said, and Bob nodded solemnly.

With the barbers staying at the lodge, neither Bob nor Margaret could get away to drive me to town, so I hiked out to the main road to hitch a ride. Traffic was sparse, and I didn't get back to Laroque until almost eight. By then, Main Street was empty, the street lamps creating mournful cones of light. Bow wasn't in his office, so I dropped off my gear and walked up Summer Street to the Bluff.

Bow's house was the second in from the corner at the top, a three-story Victorian monster with a brow of filigree and three porches glommed on at different angles. A short lawn in back sloped down to a line of trees. In winter, when the leaves were off, you could stand at the window in Bow's living room and look down on the town proper, ribboned along the river. Inside, the house was ridiculously grand. Bow's grandparents had raised two children there, and Bow was an only child. Yet there were half a dozen bedrooms, a colossal dining room, parlors of various sizes, a study, an upstairs and downstairs library, and two apartments for the long-departed live-in help.

For years, Bow had relied on a daily housekeeper, Mrs. Gehrke, a gray, plump German woman who would come in the early afternoon and stay to make dinner. She met me at the door wearing a red-checked apron. "You want food?" she asked, making an eating motion with her hands. She and her husband, Rolf, had immigrated after the war and she remained insecure about her English.

"What have you got?" I asked.

"Ah, lots of meat, I cook too much." Her hands seemed to describe a cow.

"Okay," I said, and she hurried off to the kitchen.

Bow was in the middle parlor, sitting at the head of a long table, considering a plate of pot roast. A book was propped in front of him on a wire easel. "No television tonight?" I asked.

He brightened when he saw me. "Cronkite's over," he said. "More bad news. And you—how was the fishing?"

"Good. It's been dry. The lakes are down."

"I thought fish bite when it rains."

"Well, it depends."

"You want to know something? Nobody knows. You're a god-damned fishing guide, and you don't know when the fish bite. Nobody knows anything about anything." He cocked his head, waiting for my reaction.

Suddenly, Mrs. Gehrke bustled in carrying a plate mounded with pot roast, boiled potatoes, and overcooked peas that had turned an unpleasant pale green. "Dinner's terrific," Bow told her.

"The butcher—I ask for three pounds, he give me five. He knows I buy for you. He thinks you rich, you always pay." She shrugged.

"Well, we'll manage to eat it," Bow said.

"This is not right. People that take advantage." Mrs. Gehrke crossed her arms across her large, soft bosom and looked as if she were settling in for a serious discussion of the decline of manners.

"Why don't you take some pot roast home to Rolf," Bow suggested. "Charlie and I will clean up the dishes."

That struck her as a good idea. When she was out of the room, Bow said, "She thinks I'd be lost without her."

"Tell me about Fontenot," I said.

Bow pushed back his plate of pot roast, barely half eaten. "It turns out he was a bad guy."

"You sound surprised."

"I guess I am. God knows I've defended killers before, but I met them on my own terms. I knew what I was getting into. Here I thought I was dealing with a harmless crook, a small-timer." Bow took a cigar out of his coat pocket and went through the ritual of preparing it and then lighting up. "The man he killed left four kids," Bow said as the first, heavy puffs of smoke poured out of his mouth.

Gary Fontenot's mother was dying of cancer, so Fontenot had arranged with prison authorities to be taken for a final visit to the hospital where she was staying. It was in Vineland, about a hundred miles northwest of Laroque. The same two deputies who'd brought him to his appeals-court hearing got the assignment to drive him. Fontenot rode alone in the backseat, in regular clothes. The deputies hadn't bothered to handcuff him. On a quiet stretch of road just outside Vineland, Fontenot pulled a knife. He pressed the point into the neck of the driver and ordered him to pull over. Apparently, Fontenot planned to disarm the deputies and escape in the car. He took a gun from the driver, but the second deputy resisted. He and Fontenot struggled for a moment, and Fontenot shot him in the eye. He left the surviving deputy and the dead one on the shoulder of the road and drove off. Later that day, the cops found the car in a thicket of trees on the edge of a field about twenty miles away. Fontenot had disappeared.

I tried to remember the dead man: Both deputies had been big, meaty blonds with the settling bodies of middle age. "The fellow he killed had bought Gary a new shirt to wear for his mother that day," Bow said. "A gift. Gary was wearing it when he shot him in the head."

Bow pushed himself up and wandered listlessly around the table. For years, his father had collected elaborate beer steins, and dozens of them were lined up on shelves around the room. Most were fashioned into men's faces, with corpulent noses and long, curling mustaches. But there was also the headless torso of a naked woman, a horse's ass, a volcanic mountain, many others. Bow hated them. He told me that as a child, he used to dream that the packages his father was always bringing home would contain toys for him. They always held mugs. Now Bow blew smoke on one stein, stirring dust, and straightened several others in their rows.

"The knife is a problem," he said, forming his words carefully. "The cops think someone smuggled it in to Gary. You could hide it in a shoe or maybe put it in a book. The prison had been on lockdown for the last couple of weeks, so they'd searched most of the cells. They don't think he bought it inside, since the weapons inside are mostly homemade, and this was a real knife."

I didn't quite get Bow's drift. "A problem?"

"You and Ginger and I are the only visitors Fontenot's had in the last year."

Mrs. Gehrke stepped in, her head swathed in a purple scarf. "I go now," she said, pointing vaguely in the direction of the driveway. "The kitchen is fine." Her eyes caught the plates of unconsumed pot roast.

"It was a lovely meal," Bow said, rescuing her. "Now you and Rolf go enjoy what's left of the night." With a gallant sweep of his arm, he guided her out of the room, then closed the heavy wood door.

"How much of a problem?" I asked.

"None, really," he said, sitting down again. "They'd like to find someone to blame. The deputies made all the mistakes, of course— they let all the rules slide. But now one's dead, so they'd like to blame an outsider." He paused. "You and I obviously didn't bring a knife to Fontenot."

"And Ginger?"

Bow flicked a crumb of bread off the table. "You don't like him, Charlie," he said.

"No," I answered slowly. "I do like him."

"Ginger was with us twice at the prison. According to records, he went alone four times, the last time about a week ago."

"He went alone?" I was astonished. "Did you know?"

Bow shrugged. "In a way. I knew when he went last time, after the appellate decision came down. He went up to tell Fontenot in person. And he told me then that he'd gone before. He wasn't trying to hide anything."

"Ginger seemed awfully drawn to him," I said. "They did seem to have a kind of bond."

"He liked him," said Bow matter-of-factly. "So did I, or so I thought."

"Does Ginger know the cops suspect him?"

" 'Suspect' is too strong a word," Bow said. "The cops wish they had someone, they wish they had something. They don't even have enough here to build a suspicion. But, yes, I told Ginger, and, natu-rally, he was upset. He's a seventeen-year-old straight arrow, trying to do good, and suddenly he's lining up for a felony-murder rap." Bow sucked joylessly on his cigar. "It's because of me," he continued after a moment. "The cops have nothing to go on, but they'd like to stick it to me, so they make noises about him. They all think if I'd just let Fontenot rot in prison instead of appealing his case, their deputy buddy would be alive today."

Bow and I stared at each other but didn't speak for several sec-onds. We were both thinking about the same thing, but putting the thought into words, raising it to the level of an articulated question, seemed a kind of affront. Finally, I asked, "Is it possible that Ginger smuggled in the knife?"

"No," Bow said quickly. I sensed that his rapid response was less out of conviction than to assure me that he didn't resent the question. More guardedly, he continued, "I suppose it's possible—a young boy who feels passionately about something might not always think through the consequences of his actions. But you know how bitchy they are about searching visitors—you couldn't smuggle in a piece of gum. Besides, he *says* he didn't do it. He was as upset as I was when I told him what had happened. I've never seen him so upset. I thought he was going to cry, and he's not the kind of kid who cries." Bow had grown animated as he rehearsed this defense. Swinging an arm, he'd brushed a chunk of cigar ash onto the worn blue cardigan he'd changed into when he got home. He blew the ash away, but it landed on his pant leg. Finally, he just crushed it, rubbing with his hand until the ash disappeared into the tired fabric. With the distraction of the ash, he hadn't been able to read my reaction. Now he asked, "What do you think, Charlie?"

I answered honestly, "I think Ginger would never do anything to put you in a bad position."

"Yes, I think you're right." He shook his head. "I feel horrible about dragging him into this whole mess."

"How could you know?"

"I suppose I couldn't," Bow said grimly.

After another silence, I said, "Does anybody have any idea where Fontenot is?"

"Probably not far away. They've got bulletins out for him everywhere, and it's all over the news. This all happened a week ago. I waited before calling you. I'm surprised you didn't hear about it up at the camp."

"Bob doesn't take a paper."

"He's not big on current events, huh?"

"He thinks the place should be an escape."

"Maybe they should look for Fontenot up there."

We sat without talking for several minutes. Bow's cigar smoke made a dense, low cloud that gently bloomed and retracted, endlessly transformed by the drafts churning through the house. The old place seemed rock solid, but in fact it was battered and cracked, constantly vulnerable to the weather. Rolf pitched in to do repairs, but the place needed Bow's regular attention, and Bow simply wasn't interested.

After a while, the sound of a siren spiraled out of the silence. Bow and I went to the window, and far below we could see the red, bleating light on a squad car heading north across the river, over the Turner Bridge, open again at last. The town looked innocent from this distance at night, a small casting of twinkling gems, centered on the illuminated tower of the Opera House. Only the black swatch of the Agnes had any gravity.

"This has been a tough week," Bow said, talking to my reflection in the window. "I wish you wouldn't go away for so long." He wasn't angry, but there was disapproval, even blame, in his voice. In his mind, my inconstancy had somehow allowed him to misread Fontenot's character. Bow was nothing if not honest with himself, and yet in a harrowing moment even he sought a scapegoat. Still, I couldn't help thinking he was right: When the office life turned slightly complicated over the summer, I'd fled to the woods. Maybe if I'd been paying closer attention, I could have steered Bow away from Gary Fontenot. I'd never been as charmed by him as Bow and Ginger had; I'd seen his type too many times in prison and in the bars around town. If I'd been more alert, I might have urged Bow to heed Fontenot's own advice to drop the case.

Watching the flashing red light of the squad car disappear in the distance, I gave myself a few moments to collect my thoughts. And then I assured Bow that the season was over at the Spirit Light.

CHAPTER 21

fter I left Bow that night, I walked down Summer Street to town. From the pay phone on the side of Rensinger's Pharmacy, I tried to call Lucy. I'm not sure what I expected; I just felt like talking to her. I let the phone ring ten, twenty times, and no one picked up. Her aged mother was probably asleep, dead to the intrusion. But where was Lucy? Their trim little cottage sat on a treeless street on the east side of town—almost close enough that I could dash down Main Street and answer the damn phone myself.

Finally, I hung up and stood beside the pharmacy, studying the array of greeting cards displayed in the tinted front window. Among the cartoon drawings of birthday balloons and soothing flowers, Rensinger was offering something new, a line of cards featuring pictures of muskies—giant, lead-colored fish, cruising, jumping, lurching for bait, soaring from the flat plainness of the cards with all their astonishing ferocity. The barbarians win in the end, Bow said.

I should have gone home and gone to bed, but I was feeling wide awake and unsettled. It wasn't just Fontenot's treachery; in retrospect, that was hardly surprising. But I knew his crimes would shift the ground for Bow, would lead to changes. The deputy's murder offered for once a real consequence, a grieving family, to substantiate the simmering criticism of Bow's work. Of course, that was unfair—his appeal of the case had nothing to do with Fontenot's burst of violence. But that fact wouldn't reduce the pressure; as Bow liked to point out, logic played an even smaller role outside the justice system than within it.

I tried Lucy again in the empty hope that I'd misdialed the first time. Still no answer. It struck me how often I'd turned to her for comfort. Buried in our occasional sex and bantering arguments was a grounding, at least for me. Now she was gone, and at the Spirit Light, another grounding, they considered me a child. All that on top of Bow blaming me for not warning him away from Fontenot. *No one here can love and understand me,* I warbled to Rensinger's muskies, trying to jar myself with irony out of an onslaught of self-pity. That miserable shot of pathos had been my father's favorite line from the blackbird song. I vowed I wouldn't let it become mine.

At Duffy's, a half dozen or so men were scattered around the tavern.

"Haven't seen you in a while," Duffy said without any enthusiasm. He was standing behind the bar, wiping the counter with a rag.

"I've been laying low," I told him.

"Your boss has got himself in kind of a fix now, hasn't he?" Duffy stopped wiping and watched for my response. His sallow complexion suggested he'd spent too many years indoors under the throbbing lights of neon beer signs.

"Bow will manage," I said. "Listen, I can't stick around, so can you give me something to go?"

"What'll it be?"

"Any kind of scotch."

Duffy surveyed the array of bottles behind the bar and sold me half a fifth of J&B.

"Can I take a glass?" I asked.

He pouted, but handed over a Manhattan glass.

Outside, a low cloud cover kept the temperature up; without a breeze, the night was fairly comfortable for October. At the end of the alley next to Duffy's, a worn path led through the high weeds and grass to the river. I followed it for twenty yards or so and sat down on Jones Rock, a flat outcropping above the water. Around me, pieces of glass and empty cigarette packs glinted in the dim light from River Road. Wisps of fog danced along the Agnes. I poured the glass half full and took a leisurely drink.

It always startled, how good scotch tasted after I'd been away from it for a while. I drank and watched the river. The water moved gently this time of year and gave off the soft gurgles of a baby. After a while, I heard footsteps close behind me, and when I turned, Ox Mueller was standing there, blocking everything in sight. "That you, Charlie?" he asked. "Duffy said I'd probably find you here."

"It's me."

"Can I join you?" He waved a bottle for my benefit, and the liquid sloshed. "I've brought my own."

"Have a seat. But watch out for the glass. The kids have been breaking beer bottles."

Ox landed heavily beside me.

"I was just thinking it's a beautiful night," I told him.

"Hey, you must be reading my mind," Ox said. "I love being outside. When I was a kid, I wished I was an Indian." Ox shook his head. "Isn't that something? I never looked around and saw how bad the Indians had it. I just imagined I'd run around in the woods all day without any clothes on."

Ox refused the scotch I offered and took a swig from his bottle. He was drinking tequila, and by the way he was going on I assumed he'd had a good head start. "In summer, I used to sleep outside," he continued. "Hated my bed. We lived right over there." He made a rough gesture across the river toward the scattered lights of Indian Town. "There." He sighted down the line of his gently swaying arm. "Right there."

"I see."

"We had a little yard out back. I put a pallet down. All summer, Charlie, even when it rained. I'd pull a tarp over myself and just lie there and listen to the rain."

"What about the mosquitoes?"

"They never liked me. Some people, you know, they just have a body odor or something and the mosquitoes don't bother them."

My scotch bottle was emptying quickly, and I did one of those instant calculations of whether I'd need to make another run before the bars closed. It would be close.

"Sounds like you had a pretty good time as a kid," I said. Ox was older than I. He'd been in school with Bow.

"Then you grow up and lose it all," he said. "It goes away."

The fog kept sashaying down the Agnes in patches. In the far distance, I could hear sirens howling back and forth like wolves. The sounds kept drifting in and out, as if someone were tuning a radio. "Must be a pretty big fire someplace," I said.

Ox cupped his ear. "Those are cop cars," he said. Then, as if to explain his knowledge, he added, "I just got out of jail."

"Do you need a place to stay?"

"I figured I might sleep outside tonight, since it's not too cold."

"I'm staying at Bow's office. You can sleep up there if you want."

Ox thought for a moment. "I don't know. I might feel kind of funny, sleeping in a bank."

"The office is upstairs. It's just an office."

"Even still."

"Suit yourself."

Ox stretched out on his side on the rock, bracing his huge bulk against his left elbow. For a long time, we contemplated the night and the river. Every now and then we could hear snatches from Duffy's jukebox. "You didn't ask me why I was in jail," Ox said after a while.

"I figured that was your business."

"You can ask. It don't bother me."

"Well?"

"Drunk driving. I totaled my wife's car."

"That's why you need a place to stay?"

"We hadn't been getting along too good anyway," Ox said. After a pause, he added, "She'll calm down in a little while."

"Was anybody interesting in jail with you?"

"Archie Nye. But they let him out. He made bail."

"I heard he cut up a guy in a fight. The second time this summer."

"He told me the guy's gut was hanging out," Ox said. "And Archie laughed about it. That kind of thing's funny to Archie."

"He's another guy who likes to sleep outside," I said.

"Aw, he's no Indian. That's just something he says to impress people. I knew his mother and father. They were as white as you and me." Ox sounded resentful and took a drink of tequila to console himself. "Say, did Bow ever defend him?" he asked.

"I don't think so."

"'Cause Archie goes on as if him and Bow was best friends."

"You're shitting me."

"I'm not. It's 'Mr. Epps this' and 'Mr. Epps that'—how the two of them are gonna go fishing together, maybe go into business together."

"Bow will get a kick out of that," I said.

"I always thought Archie was full of shit," said Ox.

Upstream a few yards, a loon let loose its strange, gulping cry. Loons are skittish and rarely venture into town; this one must have felt protected by the fog. "Maybe I should head back up for a refill," I told Ox.

"You can have some of mine." His tequila bottle was still half full.

"I better stick to the scotch."

"Well, let's go," he said.

At Duffy's, I stepped inside the doorway. Someone was sitting at the bar and Duffy was alone at the sink washing glasses. I must have looked pretty shaky, because Duffy scowled at me, so I backed out. Down the street, at the Loggers' Lounge, the bartender was a new fellow. I gave him a ten-dollar bill and he carefully poured a generous portion of scotch into my bottle.

"I don't think I'm quite ready to retire for the night," I told Ox. He was happy to have the company, so we walked back down the path to the rock. The deep grass was dewy now. Our pants got damp. Close by the river, you could feel the coolness of the water. I'd misplaced my glass and started swigging from the bottle.

"How come you never got married?" Ox asked me.

"I don't know. Never met anyone, I guess."

"You think it's because you drink?"

It occurred to me to work up some irritation, but Ox didn't mean to offend. "What would drinking have to do with it?"

"As a rule, women don't like men who drink."

"I never heard that rule."

"That's just a figure of speaking," Ox explained. "My father drank and my mother always hated him for it."

"My father never drank much," I offered.

"He was just crazy," Ox said and laughed. He was gulping his tequila now. "I've tried to quit," he said. "Joined AA three separate times. And I loved it. I really did love those people. They cared about me. But I always went back to drinking." He stared out at the night. His pushed-in features gave him an almost childish profile. It was a good face for a boxer, nothing prominent to attract a fist. "How about you?" he asked.

"Huh?"

"Ever join AA?"

"Nah," I lied. Once, years ago, my mother's minister had fished me out of jail and driven me to an AA meeting in Kawnipi. Twenty people were sitting on folding chairs in a church basement painted a dismal blue. It didn't work. AA is for people addicted in part to the fraternity of drinking, and I'd always been just as happy to drink alone. Besides, there'd be no breakthrough for me in standing up and admitting I was an alcoholic—I knew I was one, I agreed with people when they told me so. Only Bow denied it. He used to argue that since I could stay dry for weeks at a time, I wasn't technically addicted—unlike the others, I could choose my moments of submission. But we both knew it was a pinched argument, and after a while even he gave it up.

"Hey, lookit there," said Ox suddenly. He put his bottle down and hauled himself to his feet. Just offshore, an unmanned rowboat drifted downriver, weaving slowly with the current.

"What do you suppose is in it?" Ox asked, getting excited.

"Probably nothing."

"Let's catch it." He jumped off the rock and started pushing his way through the heavy grass and bushes along the bank, following the boat as it moved downstream. Once there'd been paths and roads and even some buildings down here near the water, but now the riverbank was overgrown and mined with collapsing foundations, a barrens more wild than raw nature. Ox made a terrible racket as he went, breaking small branches, crushing the vegetation. He fell heavily and, fifty feet away, I sensed the shudder in the earth. But he just groaned and bounced back up. I followed behind in the path he'd made. The boat still floated along easily, its pirouettes a mockery of Ox's heaving effort.

After fifty yards or so, the Turner Bridge loomed over the river, and Ox stopped in the cleared, gravelly space underneath. He'd gained a few feet on the boat, and he quickly threw off his jacket and kicked off his shoes and socks. "I'm going after it," he called back to me.

"Wait!" I yelled. The currents under the bridge were notoriously treacherous, but Ox ran into the water up to his chest, turning upstream and taking the river face on, the same way he used to dare his opponents in the ring to batter him to their exhaustion. The rowboat came straight for him, and he expected to grab it near the bow. But the boat tricked him, swinging wide and catching a burst of current. Ox lurched, missed, and lost his footing on the slick rocks on the bottom. He went under. Moments later, his head popped up again. When I got to the bridge, he was already twenty yards downriver. He rolled once, and his arm flopped wildly above the surface in a spastic imitation of a swimmer. He was drowning.

The effort to chase him had left me panting and dripping with sweat, and the scotch sloshing in my stomach set off a blast of nausea. Still, I pulled off my boots and jacket and plunged in. The river was strangely warm, and the shock to my system helped clear my head. I felt a small rush of exhilaration as the spiraling current swept me downriver. I'd been a strong swimmer once, but it had been years since I'd been tested. Now I took a few careful strokes, holding my head above the surface. I seemed to skim over the water.

Away from the lights of the bridge, the river fell into blackness. I thought I saw Ox's head and swam toward it. Nothing. A shadow on the surface. I stopped swimming and drifted with the current. I hollered for Ox. Still nothing. I could feel the cold now; it came quickly when I stopped flailing. I thought I heard a shout and started swimming again, but my leaden clothes pulled me down. I hardly seemed to be moving. The water splashing on my face felt jagged, like ice.

Now I had to save myself. Adjusting my course, I put my head down and stroked hard for shore. Poor Ox, I thought. That huge body, sunk like a bag of sand. What would I tell his wife? After a few strokes, my arms went dead. My strength had drained out in seconds, as if something had punctured my gas tank. I tried to float, but I kept sinking. I kicked, but now my legs were dead. It occurred to me: I was going to drown, too. I let my mind curl around the idea for a moment. I was too exhausted for panic. In fact, I wasn't entirely unhappy with the thought, but maybe I didn't quite believe it yet. Yes, I insisted to myself, you're definitely going to drown. This is how it happens. Just relax.

I thought of Ophelia, her body in the water. My father's *Hamlet* was designed around her. Ophelia, all loving and beautiful, played by Becky Parker of Summit Avenue, up by Bow's house. She dressed in white, her hair blond and to her waist. The Opera House was packed. My father told me I should fall in love with her, though she was ten years my senior. I think he was in love with her. Afterward, he told her to go to Hollywood, and she did. What a loss. The whole town was plainer, meaner without her. I saw her once in a movie, a second feature. She was playing a secretary, sitting down, on screen for maybe five seconds. Years later, I ran into her on Main Street, visiting for her mother's funeral. She asked about my father. She was surprised when I said he was dead. She didn't think he would die. Becky was still beautiful, still young. I still loved her. A sweet whisper in my ear: "Charlie." Now she was beside me in bed. "Charlie." We were coming out of sleep. "Charlie." I reached to touch her lovely, soft hair. Cold, sloppy flesh. I opened my eyes. There was Ox, clinging to the boat. "Save me," he said.

I heaved and reached up, but I missed the side of the gunwale, and my hand slapped Ox's face. I slipped under the surface. My head bounced off his knee, and I grabbed him around the ankles. His toenails scratched my neck. I hauled myself up over his soft, giant's body. My face crossed his stomach and it felt like a pillow. Finally, I dragged my arm up and hooked my hand over the top of the boat. "Thanks," Ox said as I hung there breathing heavily.

"I thought you were Becky Parker," I told him. I was coming in and out of my mind.

"Are we gonna drown?" asked Ox. He was surprisingly calm. "I'm cold," he said when I didn't answer.

Behind us, the lights of the Turner Bridge made a glorious arc over the Agnes. The riverbank on this end of town was wild and empty. We were falling off the earth. "Let's kick," I told Ox. I tried to maneuver the boat toward shore. It turned out to be half filled with water, a drift-away, heavy and clumsy. My legs were numb and didn't work right, and Ox couldn't move. My arms ached from holding the boat. "I'm just going to let go," Ox said quietly, and I watched him slide under the surface. I kicked and hit him in the back, and he floated up a few feet away. Water poured from his mouth.

When I let go of the boat, the river pulled me beside him. His massive, dull presence seemed to warm the water a few degrees. I grabbed the back of his shirt collar with my left hand and rolled on my side, lining up beside him. We were spooning. I stroked three times with my free arm, then rested. The top of his head came just under my chin. Three strokes. Rest. He was silent and still. I could have been dragging a mattress. Stroke, stroke, stroke, rest. Over and over. Maybe we'd drowned already, and this was life in hell. Uncomfortable, wearying, but not entirely unbearable. Unending.

I reached to stroke again and my fingers stubbed a rock. I lowered my legs and my knees banged the bottom. In front, I could make out the line of the riverbank, not as black as the water. I crawled forward, my shins scraping bottom. Ox kept pulling me back, the current tugging him downstream. He was waterlogged, a dead weight. Dead weight for a dead man.

Finally, I found a spot where the rocks felt steady, and I stood up, stumbling. The water came to my knees. I heaved once and dragged his body halfway onto the ground, low and weedy here. Then I flopped down myself, snuggling into the mud. Sweat poured off my head, the taste of salt flavoring the mud in my mouth. I passed out.

When I woke up, Ox was snorting. His legs still dangled in the water, so I grabbed him under the armpits and hauled him up a few feet. He opened his eyes and blinked at me. "Jesus, Charlie, I'm cold," he said.

"We gotta get out of here, gotta get dry."

He forced himself to his hands and knees, crouching there like a dog, his head hanging between his shoulders, his hair dripping in strands. He seemed to be thinking about whether he had the strength to get up. Finally, he said, "You saved my life, Charlie."

"Forget it."

"I'll never forget it." He raised his head to look at me. "I'd be dead now."

"What we did was stupid. It's what a couple of old drunks would do. Let's not talk about it."

"Jesus, they might write about you in the *Reader's Digest*."

I grabbed him by the back of the collar again, squeezing tight, pressuring his breathing. "Don't talk about it, you hear?"

He twisted slowly. I felt the immense strength in his shoulders. "Okay, okay."

I put a hand under his arm to help him to his feet. The two of us turned a staggering waltz, then found our balance. Slowly, we plowed through the weeds toward the dirt path above the riverbank, the unfinished extension of River Road. The old Trumble Mill had been down here, one of the last mills to be built on this stretch of the river. One corner of its stone foundation still stood, jutting out of the weeds like the prow of a ship. Someone had laid planks across the top, creating a crude shelter.

"God, I'm sick," said Ox. "I think I still might die."

We were barely making progress, taking tiny, shuffling steps, our backs so stooped our arms seemed to be dragging behind us. Apemen. Maybe we'd never make it back to the road.

Suddenly, a figure rose out of the bushes, arms waving, head shaking, an emissary from the dead come to pull us back under the river. Ox staggered and fell to his knees, pressing his face into my hip.

"They found him!" cried Archie Nye, his eyes glinting wildly, his breath filling the air with the reek of whiskey. "They killed the man who shot the deputy."

CHAPTER 22

The state police caught up with Gary Fontenot on a small farm about fifty miles or so north of Laroque. He had slipped into a barnyard one night, apparently hoping to steal a chicken. But he woke a dog, which woke the farmer, who took a shot at Fontenot from his bedroom window with a .22 rifle. Fontenot retreated to the barn with the farmer and his sons in pursuit. The cops had a hunch they'd found their man and surrounded the place. As they closed in, Fontenot used the last bullet in the gun he'd stolen from the deputy to shoot himself in the head.

For Bow, the news had a particularly troubling aspect: Fontenot had been found about three miles east of Bow's lake property.

The next day, Bow reached Ginger through the principal's office at school, and Ginger came up to the Bank Building that afternoon. He looked spiffy in his school outfit, a blue oxford shirt and khaki pants, but he didn't know quite how to react to the Fontenot news, bouncing from grief to anger to a sort of elation at being so close to the startling sequence of events. At one point, he remarked that all this would never have happened if only the appeals court had decided the case in Fontenot's favor. Bow had heard enough. "There's only one person who brought this on and that's Gary Fontenot," he said sharply. "The appeals court didn't shoot anybody. Gary did that."

Ginger nodded, aghast at rousing Bow's anger.

"The judges decided the case as best they saw fit," Bow went on, lowering the volume. "They did their job, and they did it in a civilized manner, if you will. Gary introduced the barbarity."

Ginger continued to nod, grateful to let it drop. He sat down at his desk, now buried in clutter. The office was like a weed patch—every space not constantly in use was immediately overgrown with transcripts. Absently, he riffled the pages of one, waiting for a moment to escape.

Bow had held off mentioning where Fontenot had been found, and now he watched Ginger closely. "Let me ask you something," he said. "Did you ever tell Gary about my lake property?"

"Where we took the canoe trip?"

"Yes."

Ginger frowned. "I told him about the trip. I went to see him not long after we got back."

"Did you tell him where the property was?" Bow pressed.

"I don't know. Probably, in a general way." Ginger considered some more. "Not specifically, I don't think. Just the general area."

Bow swiveled in his chair to stare out the window behind him. The unseasonably warm weather had produced more fog and a steady drizzle. The world outside was the color of concrete.

"Why do you ask?" Ginger said after a few seconds.

Bow didn't answer; he didn't appear to hear.

Ginger looked at me, his eyes wide with confusion.

"Because they found Fontenot right next door," I told him.

"Was he staying there?"

"We don't know," said Bow, turning back to the conversation. "Maybe the cops can figure it out."

"Maybe it's just a coincidence," said Ginger, grasping.

Bow shrugged and shook his head.

Ginger waited, hoping for some sign of absolution. His crisp school clothes gave him a vaguely collegiate air. I know what a bother those oxford shirts can be, and without a mother, he must have done his own ironing. "I'm sorry," Ginger said finally. "It never occurred to me."

Bow pushed back wearily from his desk. He'd been called about Fontenot around midnight and hadn't slept since. "It's my fault," he said now, his head rolling slightly. "I should have told you that you never share anything personal with a client. They'll use it, or steal it, or make it part of a scam. They're criminals, after all. That's all they know. You've got to keep them out of your life."

Ginger opened his mouth, as if about to plead for Gary Fontenot, and then stopped himself.

"It's my fault," Bow repeated. "But now you know."

"Now I know," Ginger echoed glumly. He stood up; he'd found his moment to escape. As he got to the door, he stopped. "What'll happen to Gary now?" he asked.

Bow and I stared at him. "He's dead," I said.

"I mean, will there be a funeral?"

"Not another eulogy!" cried Bow, exaggerating his horror.

Ginger managed a smile; Bow's semijest was as much absolution as the boy was going to get. "I'll keep my mouth shut," he promised.

Bow waited until Ginger was well down the hall on his way out. "Was I too hard on him?" he asked.

"He was behaving like a seventeen-year-old," I said.

Bow puffed his cheeks with air, then blew it out noisily. We'd all let him down. Fontenot was the worst, of course, but Ginger and I had failed him, too, each in his own way. At that moment, I'm sure Bow was thinking that no one could perform according to his high standards. "I'm glad Gary is dead," he muttered.

A few days later, I ran into Lucy Braestrup outside the Wanigan. "Well, now you've got a mess on your hands," she told me. She sounded almost sympathetic. I wondered if that meant her romance with the cop was souring.

"It's awful," I told her. "Bow's taking it hard."

"What really happened?"

"Who the hell knows? Maybe only Fontenot knows. Or knew." Lucy had wrapped herself in a brown camel's-hair coat, something new, as far as I could recall. The weather had turned nippy, and she'd buttoned the coat up right beneath her chin. "You're looking good," I told her.

"Charlie, I don't look a bit different than I did the last time I saw you." Now she sounded exasperated.

"That's just a figure of speaking, as Ox would say."

"How *is* Ox?"

"I haven't seen much of him lately." I couldn't bear to tell her about our dip in the Agnes. "Listen," I said. "I tried to call you the other night."

"You did?"

The front door to the Wanigan suddenly banged open, and Boyce Rensinger bustled out in the midst of half a dozen other merchants, all bundled in dark, heavy coats, their regular lunch together breaking up. Lucy and I were engulfed.

"Hey, where's Bow been?" Rensinger wanted to know. "Tell him to come around. We've got a lot of questions."

I nodded and smiled.

Rensinger must have had a couple of beers with lunch, because he was full of good cheer. "Tell him he's got nothing to be afraid of. We all know he's in a difficult line of work, ha, ha." The good burghers of Laroque moved on down Main Street in a cluster, dispersing one by one to their stores.

Inside the Wanigan, I could see another wave of regulars about to come out. "Do you want to go somewhere?" I asked Lucy. "Can I buy you lunch?"

She held up a big, white bag. "I better get back. I'm on the sandwich run."

My face must have given something away, because she quickly grabbed my hand and led me over to the wood bench at the Main Street bus stop. The bus had quit running several years before, but the bench, with its graffiti and its ad for Mitford's Bargain Men's Store, was waiting for the weather to finish it off.

Lucy put the bag carefully between us as we sat down.

"Why did you try to call?" she asked.

"No particular reason. I just felt like talking."

She looked at me sideways and laughed. "You felt like *talking*?"

"This Gary Fontenot thing had started to unwind," I told her, as if that could explain it.

"Oh. Well, I haven't been home so much lately," she said matter-of-factly.

Across the street, a handful of teenagers, Ginger's classmates, were lounging on the Opera House steps, smoking cigarettes. With the high school's new open-campus policy, kids seemed to be taking over the town.

I asked her how her romance was going, though by then I could guess the answer.

"Oh, fine." She kept her eyes on the teenagers. "We're going up to Duluth this weekend. Ed has family there."

"Duluth. Now, that's an ugly town. This must be serious."

Lucy turned to me wearily. "I don't know quite how to express this, Charlie, but I'm at that stage of life where I need to nest," she said softly. "I've got a real nesting instinct kicking in."

"And this cop is the best prospect you've got?" I asked.

"Is that how you think of it? As a 'prospect'? Don't you hope there's more to it than that?" Her eyes clouded and she looked as sad as I'd ever seen her. Her disappointments in me were so different from my disappointments in myself.

"Of course," I said. For a moment I considered how far I was willing to go. "I suppose I'm sorry this nesting thing never came up with me," I told her.

"You never paid attention."

"I was too busy drinking."

"That doesn't *begin* to explain it."

I tried again. "But you're talking about getting married. There's a little distance between that and—"

"Just fucking?" I'd never heard her use that word.

"I didn't know what you were thinking," I said weakly.

"Charlie, every woman thinks about that all the time."

"You could have said something."

"I shouldn't have to make an announcement."

"You never even told me you loved me."

"You didn't want me to, Charlie. You didn't give me the chance."

It astonished me how quickly, after all the years of casual sex and glancing conversations, Lucy and I had leaped to matters of the heart. I wondered if it came from the last week's roller coaster of death and near death, or from my realization that I'd lost her.

In any case, I felt winded. We sat watching the teenage tableau across the street. The kids were sprawled like floppy dolls on the steps—languid, posture defying, as if someone had opened the Opera House doors and spilled them out. They were talking loud and lighting cigarettes off of cigarettes. Their heedlessness had a kind of beauty to it. After a while, Lucy asked, changing the subject, "What do you think will happen to Bow?"

"He'll manage. He's smarter than everyone else."

"His problem is that boy, isn't it?" she said. "Bow's obsessed. Do you think it's sexual?"

"No." I shook my head. Bow was right. Nobody in Laroque understood. "Bow likes women, at least to the extent that he bothers anymore."

"Well, he's got to be careful he doesn't get dragged down."

"You're awfully concerned about Bow's well-being all of a sudden," I said.

Lucy stood and picked up her bag of sandwiches. "It's *your* well-being I worry about." She reached down and patted me on the knee. "Take care, Charlie." She strode off behind me to the bank.

For several days, the papers and the TV stations carried panting stories about the death of Gary Fontenot, though, oddly enough, for all the loose talk, none of the accounts mentioned Bow or the connection to his property. Early on, Mary Reimer of the Laroque *Daily Sentinel* called to ask a few general questions, but, as Bow put it, he got rid of her by being as boring as possible. Marcus Laney gassed on about the case on his regular evening radio show, and he pointed out that Bow had tried to win the release of this murderous creep. But Laney's real interest lay in broader comments about the dangers of coddling criminals. He never made much of Bow's connections, and soon enough his attention swung to other areas of moral collapse.

Still, Bow assumed his time would come. He hunkered down in his office, working on briefs. He sent me out for lunch and made me drive him to and from work, avoiding the risk of running into Rensinger or his ilk on the street. Not that Bow was ashamed or felt in any way responsible—he just didn't want to talk until the authorities had ground through their investigation.

The call came early one morning after about a week—Pete Asmus, the Franklin County district attorney, was on the line. I took it in the office. Could Bow come over for a meeting? The deputy's murder and Fontenot's suicide had both taken place in Franklin County; about half of Bow's property lay there. Asmus thought they should talk.

I held my hand over the receiver to relay the message. "What's left to discuss?" Bow told me to ask him.

On the other end of the line, Asmus's voice was layered with irritation. "I've got an officer murdered here, and I want to be able to close out the investigation."

"When does he want us?" Bow asked.

"If not today, tomorrow," Asmus said.

"Tell him we'll be there at ten tomorrow," Bow told me.

The next morning, we couldn't get the Pontiac started; the wires were old and with the dampness in the air, the ignition wouldn't turn over. Johnny Dale finally drove a truck up from Moe's Towing to give us a jump. "Jeez, Bow, that was some monster you were defending," Johnny said as he clamped on the starter cables. "Where do you find guys like that?" Bow was sitting in the front of the car, furious at the delay, and he pretended he didn't hear. "In prison, I guess," said Johnny, answering himself. I gunned the engine, drowning him out.

By the time we got to the DA's office in Waterville—in the same awkward new building that housed the district appeals court—we were half an hour late. Pete Asmus kept us waiting while a succession of aides marched in and out of his office. His secretary, who'd worked in the court system for years and who knew Bow, started fluttering as the minutes passed and still we weren't summoned. "Do you remember Judge Bone?" she asked, trying to entertain Bow. "The skinny one?"

Bow nodded. "He retired years ago, didn't he?"

"Dead," the secretary said. Her curled gray hair was trapped in a fierce permanent that hugged her head like a helmet. "Cancer everywhere. And Judge Shrewsbury, the mean one?"

Bow stared, blinking.

"Dead, too. His liver. He drank a lot." She shook her head, and not a hair moved. "Shrewsbury liked you, Bow. I remember that for sure. All the judges did. They thought you were a bright young man." She lowered her voice confidingly. "Smarter than the prosecutors."

"That didn't last," said Bow.

"And Bob Harrington, the clerk?" the secretary asked.

"Dead?"

"He lives in Florida with his son. I heard he still plays on some baseball team for people over seventy." She beamed. "It's just you and me, Bow. We're all that's left anymore." She was probably twenty years Bow's senior.

At about eleven, Asmus finally emerged from his office. "You're late and I'm late," he said to Bow. "We cancel each other out." He was a trim, athletic man, about Bow's age, but bald, with a thick, broad nose. He was wearing a well-tended gray suit and a blue tie. "Come on in," he said.

When I followed the two of them, Asmus stopped. "Do you want Charlie in on this?" he asked Bow.

"Of course." Bow kept moving.

In the office, the three of us sat in leathery chairs around a circular glass table. Asmus had probably put some of his own money into decorating the place. Over the years, he had moved back and forth between the DA's office and a private practice that grew lucrative, anchored by his role as the leading Republican in the county. He used to float his name as a possible candidate for statewide office, but as he got richer, he got smarter and stayed home.

"Coffee?" he asked. Bow and I shook our heads. Asmus folded his hands before him on the table. He had a deceptively open manner, one source of his great success in front of juries. "I have an enormous amount of respect for you, Bow, and for what you've done for the law of this state." He sounded as if he were following a script. "You and I are often on the opposite sides of things, but our differences are honorable."

"Get on with it, Pete," said Bow.

Asmus didn't flinch. "I wouldn't want to see anything tarnish your reputation or your legacy. That's why I called you here." He waited patiently for a response. Bow tried to outlast him, but finally gave in and said, "Thank you."

Asmus leaned earnestly forward. His big, meaty nose seemed to invite a punch. "You're under siege, Bow. We're pulling together the threads of the Fontenot case, and they lead back to your office."

Bow had assumed it would get to this, though of course he didn't know the specifics. Now he measured his response carefully. "Tell me what you know," he said.

The prosecutor wasn't about to give anything away without some kind of return. "Some of my colleagues think you're part of the problem, Bow, but I've held them back. I said I've known you for twenty years, and it's unthinkable that you'd countenance anything like this."

"Like what?"

"You have a boy working for you, George Piper."

"He's called Ginger, and he helped out in the office over the summer," Bow said.

"How much do you know about him?" Asmus asked.

"He's a local boy. Charlie here has watched him grow up. He's an outstanding student and athlete."

"You don't know him."

Beside me, Bow's bulky body gave off heat. His face was two-tone. "What have you got?" he asked.

"Ginger Piper gave Gary Fontenot the knife he used to escape and then helped Fontenot when he was out."

Bow said nothing. He stared at the DA, as if waiting for more. In the office silence, we could hear voices from the hallways through the shallow walls. The window behind Asmus overlooked the building's grounds in back. Trees had been planted but hadn't begun to mature. The leafless, gray saplings poking out of the brown lawn made the landscape look devastated, Gettysburg after the battle.

"I don't believe it," said Bow finally.

"It's real, Bow," said Asmus.

Bow paused again. "What do you want from me?"

"I want to know you're on our side," Asmus said reasonably. "I want to know you'll cooperate when the time comes."

"Does Ginger know he's a target?" Bow asked.

"I suppose. Like you said, he's a smart kid."

"He didn't say anything to me."

"He wouldn't."

"Have you talked to him?" Bow asked.

"No."

"I've got to tell him," Bow said.

Asmus shook his head. "You can't be his lawyer."

"Why not?"

"You're an appeals lawyer. Besides, there's a conflict."

Bow put his palms flat down on the cool glass top of the table. "Pete, I'm blind here," he said. "Unless you tell me what you know, I can't do you any good."

Asmus took a deep, noisy breath, pretending to consider. "The boy brought Fontenot the knife," he said.

"How do you know?"

"Come on, Bow. Did you or Charlie bring Fontenot a knife?"

"No."

"Ginger was the only one else to visit him. He brought books, things you could conceal a knife in."

"We're always searched."

Asmus shrugged. "It's not that hard to smuggle something in."

"Jesus Christ," cried Bow. "That prison is crawling with weapons. You confiscate them every day."

"We'd been on lockdown," Asmus said calmly. "We'd searched the cells. And this was a real knife, with a leather handle and a four-inch blade."

"Have you got it?"

"No. We're still looking."

"Well—"

"There's more," said Asmus coolly.

"Like what more?"

"You're not gonna like this, Bow."

"What?"

"Ginger set up Fontenot on your place near Bent Pine Lake. Fontenot was using that as his base when they caught him."

Bow thought about that. "How do you know Ginger was involved?" he asked after a while.

Asmus looked carefully at Bow. "I shouldn't be telling you this," he said. "It's not what another prosecutor would do."

Bow waited silently.

"But I know what happened here," Asmus went on after a pause. "And I don't want to play games with you."

"I appreciate that, Pete."

"Do you know Mrs. Hennepin?" the prosecutor asked.

"The bait lady."

"She saw the boy and Fontenot."

Bow nodded. He seemed to be agreeing at last that this was serious. "Is she reliable?" he asked.

Asmus snorted. "Would that lady lie?"

"Did she make a statement?"

"I'll show it to you, Bow, because it's you, and I think you'll know what to do."

Bow nodded. When he looked away for a moment, Asmus glanced at his watch.

"And that's everything you've got?" Bow asked.

The DA's face registered a flash of annoyance. "I know you like the boy," he said, "but you made a mistake with him, Bow. He's trouble and he comes from trouble. His father did time for armed robbery, you know."

Bow looked at me. This was background information I should have produced. "When?"

"Fifteen or so years ago," Asmus said. "Held up a grocery store."

"Come on, Pete," said Bow.

"The boy has a bad streak. He got up at a funeral for a kid killed in Vietnam and harangued the audience about the war."

"I was there," said Bow. "He did it twice."

"Well, then, you ought to know." Asmus stood up and went to his desk. He picked up a sheet of paper, looked it over, and shook his head. Then he brought it back to Bow. "Here's Mrs. Hennepin's statement," he said. "I think you'll see what I mean."

Without reading the document, Bow folded it and stuffed it into his inside jacket pocket. With an effort he stood up, then drifted to the window, leaving Asmus and me at the table. "You like your new building, Pete?" he asked, gazing outside. "The change isn't too jarring?"

"We're getting used to it," the DA said impatiently. He was uncomfortable being in front of his desk while Bow was behind it.

"And you've got the bugs worked out—the air-conditioning, the heating?"

"Yes, yes, yes."

"When do you want to talk to Ginger?" Bow asked abruptly.

"Soon, I don't know." Asmus hesitated. For twenty years, he'd been the only criminal lawyer in northern Wisconsin who was anywhere near Bow's match. "I think it's scheduled."

"Scheduled?" Bow said genially, still lingering at the window. Suddenly, his body stiffened. His shoulders shot back and his spine arched as if he'd been stabbed. I thought immediately: a heart attack. I jumped up just as he spun around. His scar was pulsing and his face was twisted. "You son-of-a-bitch," he barked at Asmus, then slammed the desk chair out of the way and hobbled out of the room. In the reception area, the secretary was filing papers. When she saw Bow coming, bright red and churning his arms for speed, she pressed herself against the file cabinet. "Where's a pay phone?" Bow demanded.

She pointed: down the hall, to the left.

Hurrying his limp, Bow weaved from side to side like a badly ruddered canoe. "They fucked me," he hissed over his shoulder. "They wanted me out of the way. They're probably beating a confession out of Ginger right now. I've got to call the school."

We found a bank of phone booths off a corner of the lobby. Bow squeezed into one and closed the door. Just then several courts let out, spilling lawyers and litigants into the halls. The other phone booths immediately filled up. Suddenly, the corridor rang with voices and cigarette smoke thickened the air.

Bow emerged several minutes later, his face dripping sweat and his shirt soaked. He leaned against a corner of the phone booth and mopped his forehead with a handkerchief. The color had drained from his face with the calming news. Asmus's men had tried for forty minutes to talk to Ginger before finally giving up: The boy had invoked his Miranda rights and refused to say a thing.

CHAPTER 23

E rrol Piper hadn't changed much in the ten years or so since
I'd gone to his house trying to collect a debt. It was hard to
say how old he was. He had a deer's sinewy thinness, and
although he was a few inches taller than Ginger, he stood slightly
stooped, the backs of his shoulders forming a gentle arc. His face was
narrow and longer than Ginger's, and the corners of his mouth
turned down and disappeared into deltas of wrinkles, suggesting a
sort of Calvinist disapproval of everything around him. He moved
stiffly; indeed, there was something almost fragile about him, as if the
percolating anger I'd seen years ago had hardened and turned brittle.
Nothing in his aspect suggested Ginger, and yet as the two of them
stood side by side in the dull lamplight of Bow's office, I sensed
immediately that they were a team, aligned by blood and history
against Bow and me.

Bow had summoned them when we returned from Waterville. By
then, he'd read and studied the statement Mrs. Hennepin had given
the cops. If she was to be believed, Ginger was in the thick of
Fontenot's escape. The old lady said she'd been inside her trailer late
on the afternoon of October 17, the day after the deputy was shot,
when she saw Ginger walking down the road that winds around one
side of Bent Pine. She recognized him immediately as the young

man who'd been with Bow, she told the cops. She thought it odd that he was walking instead of driving. He was carrying a shopping bag and keeping to the far side of the road, glancing regularly at the trailer, as if to make sure no one was watching. She always kept an eye on things going on around the lake, so she slipped out to follow him. He walked half a mile or so along the shore, finally stopping at an old boat landing. There, he put the bag down and sat on the edge of a broken-down pier. For five minutes, nothing happened. Then a man stepped out of the woods. Mrs. Hennepin didn't know him, but later, she recognized him as Gary Fontenot from the pictures in the paper. She told the cops she was standing in a thicket of scrub pines a hundred or so feet away. She watched the two of them talk for a few minutes, then she got worried that Ginger might turn to leave and see her, so she slipped away. Half an hour later, back in her trailer, she saw Ginger go by again, headed for the main road.

"Why would an old lady like that lie?" I'd asked Bow.

"Maybe she's confused," he said. "Maybe she saw something, and the cops persuaded her it was Ginger and Fontenot." Later, he added, "It's just the recollection of one witness. You know how unreliable that can be."

In dozens of appeals over the years, Bow had convincingly disparaged just this kind of evidence. Yet, now, in the middle of an unfolding case of our own, the sloppy and handwritten police notes of Mrs. Hennepin's interview seemed to glow with the truth.

Still, Bow gave no indication that he had lost confidence in Ginger. In the office, he greeted Errol Piper robustly. "You've got a fine son here," Bow told him in a big voice. "We've enjoyed working with him."

"He's a good boy," Piper agreed.

"You should be very proud."

Almost imperceptibly, Piper nodded. He was wearing a maroon wool coat, blackened and frayed at the collar where it rubbed against his neck. Underneath, he had on old, gray work clothes—no youthful blue jeans—though the outfit looked clean and perhaps even starched. In contrast to his father's outfit, Ginger's bright blue puffy down ski parka seemed starkly modern.

I cleared space on the office chairs, and Ginger and his father shed their coats and sat in front of Bow's desk. Bow held out the cigar box, and Piper stared blankly into it, as if trying to figure out what he was supposed to do. Bow calmly took it back and lit a cigar himself, blowing out huge clouds of gray smoke. "Now, tell us exactly what happened with the cops," he said to Ginger.

The boy took a breath. With his father beside him, he seemed younger, the aura he'd acquired—on the basketball court, on the dais, in the backwoods—diminished slightly. But he showed no signs of being intimidated and launched crisply into his account: "At about ten, Mr. Miles, the principal, came and got me out of physics class and took me to a small room near the main office. Two men in suits were waiting there. They said they worked for the Franklin County district attorney. One was named Art and the other Norb—they told me their full names, but I forgot. The one named Norb said he was a lawyer."

Bow interrupted. "Did they show you any identification?"

Ginger shook his head. "I didn't think to ask."

"No matter. Go on."

"They said they wanted to ask some questions about Gary Fontenot. I figured I better talk to you, but they said I couldn't."

"Did they say you were a suspect?"

"No. They just said they wanted to talk. So I told them about the *Miranda* case, and I said I had a right to talk to a lawyer. At first they claimed they'd never heard of it. Then Norb said it only applied in federal courts. Anyway, when we weren't getting anywhere, they finally let me use the phone in Mr. Miles's office, and I tried to call you. But of course you weren't there. So they took me back to the little room and kept badgering me, and I kept insisting I wouldn't talk without my lawyer. They tried a lot of stuff. Norb said that because I was a minor, having the principal there was just as good as having a lawyer, so he brought Mr. Miles into the room. But I knew that was nonsense. And then they began to threaten me—if I didn't cooperate, I'd be charged with complicity in the murder of the deputy and sent away for life. My only hope was to come clean. And so on. Then they said they knew *you* were behind the plot to free Gary and that if I helped them, I'd get off scot-free."

"They came right out with it!" For a moment, it amused Bow to be placed at the center of a criminal conspiracy.

"They were crazy. I was just sitting there in the chair, and they were walking around screaming. Finally, Mr. Miles told them to get out. He'd heard enough."

"Miles did that?" said Bow. "I'm surprised he had the balls."

"You could hear them all over the first floor. People were coming by to see what was going on."

"Noise in the hall," cracked Bow. "Much worse than raping the Constitution." He smirked and nodded at Piper, who stared back as if he didn't have the slightest notion what Bow was talking about.

Ginger edged up in his chair. "What's going to happen?" he asked.

Bow shrugged. "It depends."

"But Gary's dead. What's left?"

"An officer was shot. They want to nail everyone who had anything to do with it. I understand their point of view."

Ginger took this as a rebuff and sat back.

Bow said, "Do you know what they're accusing you of?"

Ginger glanced at his father. I wondered how much the boy had told him. "Helping Gary escape," Ginger said.

"Specifically, bringing him the knife in prison."

"They think *you* did that."

Bow drew slowly on his cigar, then let the smoke drift like an afterthought out of his mouth. "What exactly did they tell you?" he asked.

"They weren't exact. They just said they had reason to believe that you smuggled in the knife, and they wanted me to tell them how."

"They're fishing," said Bow.

"Can they do that?" Ginger asked. He was growing agitated now. He'd probably assumed that once he talked to Bow, everything would be all right. His father, recognizing the urgency in his son's voice, turned deliberately to look at him.

"Prosecutors can do just about anything they want," said Bow. He added after a moment, "We have nothing to be scared of."

"It's so easy to make a mistake."

"Mistakes don't land you in prison." Bow put the cigar down in the big bowl of an ashtray on his desk. I thought I saw a slight tremor in his hand. He quickly withdrew it to his lap. He told Ginger, "They also say you helped Fontenot once he'd escaped."

Ginger's nervous eyes skipped around the room as if trying to spot where this latest accusation came from. "How?" he asked weakly.

"They didn't ask you about that?"

He shook his head.

"They have an old lady who says she saw you taking groceries to Fontenot. The old lady who sells bait near my property."

"She says she saw *me*?" Ginger's voice leaped to the edge of hysteria.

"That's impossible, isn't it." Bow expressed it as a statement of fact, not a question.

Ginger buried his chin in his chest. His face had turned the same waxy gray I remembered from the end of the basketball game eight months before, after he'd chased Slagle around the court for half the contest. "I have to confess something," he said, hurrying so Bow couldn't interrupt. "I went up to your place, your property, without you. Twice, with my father." Ginger nodded slightly in Piper's direction without looking at him. "Once in August and again a few weeks ago. We just camped and fished. We didn't even take a boat. We hiked in. I should have asked you. I was going to. I don't know why I didn't." He gulped air. "I was afraid you wouldn't want my father there. I knew you'd say yes, but I was afraid you ... wouldn't want to."

Bow's years of court arguments had taught him how to assume a deadpan expression in charged moments, and now he worked to absorb this latest bit of news calmly. His nervous hand snaked out of his lap and fussed with the cigar without bringing it to his mouth. Through the smoke-stained air, he said quite evenly, "I wish you'd asked me. I wouldn't have minded."

Ginger shook his head. "I was stupid," he said—though, of course, he'd read the situation correctly. Bow would deny it, but he wouldn't have wanted Errol Piper tramping around his land. Piper came from Ginger's past, from the dark ages before Bow had discovered the boy.

Bow returned to the issue at hand. "The old lady was quite specific," he continued. "She said she saw you the day after Fontenot escaped."

"It was the weekend before."

"She said she saw you carrying a bag of groceries past her shack. She followed you and saw you give it to Fontenot near an old boat landing."

"That was Dad," said Ginger hollowly. "I dropped him off first with the tent and the packs, then parked the truck down the road so no one would know. That was him I gave the groceries to."

Bow regarded Piper, who returned the gaze evenly. "Your father doesn't look like Fontenot," Bow pointed out.

Piper turned to the boy as if expecting an explanation for this piece of the puzzle. The two of them seemed oddly formal with each other, yet respectful, as if they'd come to be acquainted through reputation. "She's an old lady," Ginger said and shrugged.

Bow waited. In the silence, we seemed to have arrived at a dead end so abrupt and final that we'd have to back up and start anew. But then Ginger's face clenched and reddened. He blinked, and suddenly he was awash in tears, losing it with a volcanic intensity, tears spilling down his cheeks and spreading into dark stains on the front of his blue oxford shirt. His shoulders shook with silent sobs. He made no effort to cover himself but just sat there, slumped, his eyes closed, the tears flowing in spasms, misery coming in waves.

Bow stared, horrified. Ginger had always handled himself as an adult—that was part of his attraction for Bow: Here was a boy who bridged the great chasm to childhood. Now, watching him dissolve into raw despair, Bow was completely out of his realm. Piper never moved either, he just sat there studying his son behind that same, permanently pinched mask. Seconds passed. Finally, something gave me a push, an instinct perhaps awakened out there in the churning Agnes with Ox. I got up from the couch and slung my arm across Ginger's back. His head, surprisingly small and light, fell on my hip. In a moment his tears were staining my pants.

Bow said, "Don't worry."

Ginger shook his head, and the tears scattered in a semicircle. "I've let you down," he gasped.

"It's nothing." Bow's voice was heavy and final. He looked empty, the flesh loose on his skeleton. "What's important is you have an explanation for being up on the property. Is there anyone who can corroborate your story?" He hesitated, nodding toward the immutable father. "I mean, besides your dad?"

Ginger took a deep breath, calming himself. I left him and sat down again on the couch.

"Well, work on it awhile," said Bow. He relit his cigar, both hands now shaking as he fought the matches.

From the bottom of the silence in the room, Piper spoke up. "It's not right that my boy gets blamed here," he said. "He's just a boy in these things." His tone seemed to suggest that Bow was at fault.

"I'll watch out for your son," said Bow unsympathetically.

"I don't want him blamed."

"He won't be."

Piper wouldn't let go. "They always try to blame the weak," he went on, "the folks that don't have nothin'. That's how they save themselves, on the backs of the weak."

Bow stared blankly at him, astonished by this burst of polemics.

"Okay, Dad," said Ginger. He wanted to shush his father, but there wasn't a trace of embarrassment or impatience in the boy's voice. I wondered if he actually agreed with Piper's sentiments and was only quieting him because the moment was inappropriate.

"The criminal justice system works on fact, not social theory," Bow lectured, recovering quickly. "Everybody is equal in the eyes of the law. I'll handle the facts here, and we'll be fine."

Piper pushed his chin out a few millimeters, utterly unpersuaded. I could see then, in his reserve and his icy will, the origins of Ginger's rebellious spirit. But Piper dropped the argument, glancing once sideways at his son, then letting his gaze drift down to the top of Bow's desk.

"When does basketball season start?" Bow asked Ginger, trying to lighten the room.

"A couple of weeks. We've started practice."

"Are you guys any good this year?"

"Better than last year, I hope." Ginger forced a thin smile.

"At least last year ended on a high note."

The boy seemed to nibble at the memory of his great shot, and then his face clenched again. "I'm sorry," he burst out. "I've made such a mess."

Bow was probably the least physical person I've ever known, his touching of other people limited, literally, to the unavoidable hand-shake and, of course, the occasional wrestle with one of Macy's whores. But now he stood and walked around his desk. Gently, he put his hand on the top of Ginger's head, stroking softly, as you might a jittery horse. "I don't want you to think about it," he said. "Spend your time thinking about boys' things."

Ginger quietly composed himself. In another minute or so, Bow withdrew behind his desk, and Ginger and his father got up to go. "I'll watch out for your son," Bow told Piper, making a final offering of cordiality. "I'll make sure nothing goes wrong."

Piper hesitated, preparing to say something. His deliberateness gave him a kind of force. "I seen the law do a lot of bad things, and I told Ginger that," he said, hinting that there'd been discussions and even battles at home over whether Ginger should go to work for Bow in the first place. "The law eats up the little guy every time."

"Well . . ." Bow was at a loss.

Ginger looked nervously back and forth between his patron and his father. I couldn't figure out why the boy didn't try to squelch his old man's ungrateful rant, but perhaps I'd forgotten what it is to be a devoted son. Finally, Ginger said, "Come on, Dad," and led Piper down the hall.

Bow sat with his head cocked, following the sound of their foot-steps as if the hollow echoes might tell him something. Finally, he got up from his desk and switched on the overhead light. For a moment, from my vantage, I saw Bow lined up beneath the stern painting of his own father. Though the two of them were built alike, I'd never seen much similarity in their faces. But now, perhaps because I'd been studying the Pipers, I saw the match in Bow's family, particu-larly in the tired flesh around the eyes. The picture had been painted just months before Mr. Epps dropped dead.

Bow said, "You grew up in the theater, Charlie. Was that an act?"

I'd asked myself the same thing, and I'd studied Ginger, looking for a sign—a fluttering of the eyelids, a fidget, a stolen signal between father and son. Nothing. He was seamless. "Beats me," I said.

"If it's an act, it's a good one," Bow pronounced wearily.

Downstairs, the bank had closed. A last flurry of voices drifted up from the alley and from River Road. The day ended so much earlier in those times—by five-thirty Laroque was a ghost town, except for the bars and the Wanigan, and even at the Wanigan, Andy, the cook, wouldn't start a meal after six-thirty. Everyone was at home, behind the porch lights and the pulled shades, where the hours of evening stretched out vacantly.

For an hour, Bow worked quietly at his desk while I finished up some typing and then browsed through the Milwaukee *Journal*. A small article on one of the back pages of the news section related that Martin Luther King, Jr., had again spoken out against the war at a rally in Towson, Maryland. If King was against the war, I suddenly realized, how could I not be? After the endless arguments pro and con, I'd been either too lazy or too stupid to settle on a position. But King stood for goodness unlike anyone else on the public stage. How could I be on any other side?

"You okay?" Bow asked. He'd caught me staring into space, working through the logic of my fresh certainty.

"Just daydreaming." I wasn't prepared yet to test myself.

"You were smiling."

"I was in Florida," I lied.

Bow offered up a perfunctory laugh: Had he figured out what I was thinking?

Suddenly, Ginger appeared in the office doorway, looking anxious and flushed. His legs were bare. He was wearing his down coat over his gym clothes.

"Jesus," said Bow with a start. "We didn't hear you."

Ginger looked startled, too, and almost suspicious, as if he'd expected to find us locked in furious discussion, not just reading and musing like a couple of old guys at the barbershop. He took a step into the room. "Gym shoes," he said, explaining his stealth. "I ran over from basketball practice." He sucked in air. His damp, dark hair hung in strands over his forehead. "There's something else I should tell you."

Bow flinched. He didn't need any more difficult news. "Well?"

"A few times when I visited Gary at Lovington, I sneaked things in to him, cigarettes, stuff like that." The words tumbled out almost on top of each other.

"Stuff like what?" Bow pressed.

"Just cigarettes mostly, and twice Ex-Lax."

"Ex-Lax?"

Ginger shrugged. "He said he was constipated. He always got constipated in prison."

"But couldn't he just get it from the nurse?"

"He said he couldn't. He wanted me to bring some."

"Ex-Lax," Bow repeated wonderingly.

"The prisoners use it to hide or smuggle drugs," I explained. "They put drugs in a balloon or a rubber and swallow it. Then when it's safe they take a huge dose of Ex-Lax to move it through their system. That's why it's contraband. The authorities keep a close eye on the stuff."

Bow winced as he thought through the logistics of the procedure. "How the hell do you know that?" he demanded of me.

"They talk about it down at the county jail."

Ginger insisted Fontenot didn't take drugs. "He was just constipated."

"He could always sell the Ex-Lax," I said. "There's a black market inside."

The boy glared at me.

"Anyway," Bow said. "Cigarettes and Ex-Lax. That's all?"

"Yes." Ginger gratefully turned back to Bow.

"How did you do it? They always search us."

"At first, I put them in my shoes. But the last couple of times, they just said, 'Aww, he's with Bowman Epps,' and waved me through."

"Jesus Christ," cried Bow. "They *always* search me!"

"I got to know the guards a little bit," said Ginger softly. "You know, we'd talk about basketball."

"Waved you through," Bow marveled.

Ginger hugged himself across the chest. "How bad is it?" he asked.

"Lawyers give cigarettes and candy and stuff to their clients all the time," Bow said dismissively. "I've probably done it myself."

"Really?" The brightness returned like an explosion to Ginger's handsome young face. My father would have loved this boy and his artful grasp of one emotion, then another.

Bow hesitated, watching Ginger. Aside from his bright face, the boy looked ludicrous, his skinny legs, splotchy red from the rapid changes in temperature, poking woefully out beneath his blue ski parka. He resembled a child's drawing of a man, all overstuffed upper torso and stick legs, without any waist or hips.

For the second time in a few hours, Bow assured him, "It's nothing."

CHAPTER 24

Macy Cunningham was failing, and Bow threw himself into winding up the work on her will. He'd enlisted the help of a law school classmate in Milwaukee—a trusts-and-estates lawyer—and together they moved around Macy's assets to reduce inheritance taxes. Since Macy was in and out of the hospital, Bill Addy did most of the legwork—tracking down documents, running back and forth with papers to be signed. The prospect of Macy's death had set Addy adrift, and he was in the office almost every day, bubbling with gossip and opinions. Bow couldn't bear him, so the burden of conversation fell to me. I spent most of my time silently counting the ways that Addy was different from me, searching for reassurances that I wasn't talking to a version of myself in a few years.

One day when Bow was at the law library, Addy wandered in and settled on the sofa, glancing through the *Journal*. "I hear Bow and that boy are going to be nailed," he said after growing bored with the paper.

Addy was full of loose talk and speculation. Still, as an ex-cop, he had connections. "Who told you that?" I demanded.

He broke into a coughing fit that held him up. Finally, he reached for the metal wastebasket and spat (a comforting difference: I'd never be that vulgar). "It was just talk," he said, wheezing.

"Where? The Wanigan?" Bow had been avoiding the place, knowing the crowd there would ask a lot of questions.

"I don't remember quite where I heard it," Addy said, turning cagey. "Don't know if it's true, either."

"It's a lot of crap."

"Maybe, maybe not." Addy lit a cigarette (at least I'd laid off that vice). "I didn't tell Macy. Didn't want her to worry about her will."

"Bow didn't have a thing to do with Gary Fontenot's escape."

"That don't necessarily mean anything." Addy took a long drag on his cigarette; the smoke seemed to calm his watery chest. "I seen men nailed when they was innocent as a puppy. There's a lot of people mad about that deputy getting shot, and someone's got to take the blame."

I shook my head and went back to my work, typing a document for Macy. Over the years, I'd learned the language of criminal procedure, but trusts were something else, something clotted and medieval, and I had to proofread my way from word to word.

Silences nagged at Addy (I enjoyed solitude). Sometimes I thought he coughed just to give a room some action. "If they don't get Bow, they'll get the boy," he said.

"For Christ's sake, Ginger didn't have anything to do with it, either."

"I'm not saying he did, and I'm not saying he didn't."

"Well, what the hell are you saying?"

"He's untrustworthy."

"You don't even know him."

"I seen him around. And I seen a lot of boys like him over the years—boys who want to be something they ain't. I don't like 'em as boys and I don't like 'em as men." He stubbed out his cigarette with a flourish.

"Come on, Bill, that's the American way," I teased. "Get ahead, improve yourself. Where's your sense of history?"

Addy wouldn't ease up. "You're supposed to get ahead by hard work, not by latching on to the richest guy in the county."

"I suppose you could say that about me," I told him.

Addy averted his eyes, looking uncomfortable enough that I realized he indeed had said that about me over the years. I added quickly, "That's not what happened with Ginger."

"There's a name for people like him, and it's 'con man,'" Addy said, warming again to his slander. "The girl Anna's the same way— coming around when she sees Macy's dying, sneaking her way into the will."

"I never heard you complain about Anna before."

"I wouldn't around Macy, because Macy's so glad to have her. But I know what she's up to. I seen it a thousand times." Addy shook his head, and that seemed to loosen something in his chest. He started coughing again, bringing up puffs of buried smoke with the phlegm. After waiting patiently for the spasm to subside, he said, "If I was Bow, I'd keep my distance from both of them."

"I'll pass on the message," I told him sullenly.

But when I mentioned the conversation to Bow, he waved it off. "The man's a fool," he said. "Why Macy lets him hang around is beyond me."

"There is talk that they're making a case against Ginger, though," I said. "I've heard it myself."

"Of course there's talk. There's always talk. That's the way prose- cutors work—they poison the air around you, so whether they get you in court or not, they win. Just ignore it."

In fact, I couldn't understand why Bow was being so casual. Sev- eral weeks had passed since the meeting with Asmus, and as far as I could tell, Bow had done nothing with the case, ignoring it, as if he hoped it would simply go away. We knew Asmus's men were out talking to people because word would drift back. Ginger stopped by one day and said the investigators were interviewing his classmates; Bow told him to encourage the kids to talk—we had nothing to hide. Bow didn't even want me to do any investigating on my own. As far as we knew, Mrs. Hennepin was the most dangerous witness, at least for Ginger, but Bow told me to hold off trying to talk to her, saying he thought we should put a little distance between the DA's interview and ours.

As long as the case stayed out of court, Bow seemed to think he could represent Ginger, despite the conflicts; but, worse than that, he hadn't retained a lawyer for himself. When I suggested that getting representation would be the prudent thing to do, he dismissed the idea immediately. "Who am I going to hire?" he demanded. "No one knows this stuff better than I do. If Asmus gets anywhere, I'll find someone. But why drag anyone else into it now?"

Over the years, Bow had grown cocky about being able to maneuver the system, but this seemed something more, something intensely personal, as if he was ashamed of the whole wretched situation and bringing in an outsider would certify that things were out of hand. My prodding only irritated him, and several times when I asked what was happening or made a suggestion, he snapped back, shutting me off. For someone who was proud of his honesty with himself, he seemed to be suffering a remarkable case of denial.

Meanwhile, though, the tension clearly wore on him. One day, I came back to the office and found the lights on and papers scattered over his desk, but no sign of Bow. On a hunch, I wandered down the hall to a warren of old offices and storerooms. Many of them were empty now, abandoned as the bank's record keeping grew more automated and efficient. Bow was standing in a narrow storage room, its walls lined with gray metal shelves overflowing with outdated office supplies—black-bound accounting notebooks, old-fashioned ledger paper, ancient stationery. Bow couldn't really explain what he was doing. He mumbled about looking for something, but he seemed almost disoriented, as if he'd been spinning around and had made himself dizzy. The dusty, windowless room with its throbbing overhead light was oppressive, and I quickly led him away. On the way out, he grabbed a handful of old bank stationery and extravagantly admired the curling, flowery typeface on its heading, an antique style long ago replaced by a cleaner, more modern design. In the office, he put the stationery in a file cabinet and went right back to work. He never mentioned his little excursion again, but every now and then he'd pull out a few of the old sheets for doodling or taking notes.

A day or so after I discovered him in the storage room, I asked when he was planning to visit the Mayo Clinic again. He made a small ritual out of examining his suit, looking for the worn knees and elbows that indicated it was time for his checkup. "Another six months," he said.

"Maybe you should speed things up. You look as if you've lost some weight."

"I do?"

"A bit. Have you weighed yourself?"

"I weigh myself every morning. I haven't noticed anything."

"That's odd. I could swear you're skinnier."

"Maybe the weight's just shifted," Bow suggested.

"Does that really happen?"

"People say so." He thought for a moment. "On the other hand, where would it go?"

"Does your suit still fit?"

He ran his thumb along the waist of his pants. "I guess."

"Well, you don't look good," I said, finally coming out with it. "You've been under a lot of strain. I think you should get a checkup."

"You're right, you're right."

"I mean soon."

"I *will*, Charlie," he said.

I let it drop. It worried me, and my impulse was to nag, but I could hear my mother, toward the end of a difficult marriage, picking uselessly at my father as he sat at the living room desk, raging in his letters at the forces that had conspired against him.

On the Friday after Thanksgiving, Bill Addy called from the hospital. The doctors said Macy might go that day. Could we come over? There'd been a dusting of snow the night before, but the weather had brightened, so Bow and I decided to walk. Main Street was bustling. The vacation from school had brought out shoppers, and cars were backed up and cruising, waiting for parking spots. Across from the Opera House, we paused so Bow could catch his breath. The usual crowd of kids on the Opera House steps stared across the plaza at us, cigarettes dangling. Their fashion tastes favored baggy green army jackets, open in front despite the chill. "No wonder we're losing the war," Bow grumbled.

Laroque Memorial Hospital's three stories of gray stone sat like a huge outcropping on the western edge of town, where Main Street again became Route 21. Like the high school on the eastern edge, the hospital served as a bookend for development in those days; beyond the facility's asphalt parking lot, the river valley stretched out in a narrow checkerboard of woods and fields. Bow and I maneuvered the hospital's heavy revolving door. Inside, a neighbor of Bow's on the Bluff, a small, cheery grandmother named Mrs. Mills, was volunteering at the reception desk. Bow told her we'd come to see Macy. "Why, Mr. Epps, she's in your wing," Mrs. Mills said brightly. The Epps Pavilion honored a hefty donation from Bow's father.

Down a long hall, Bill Addy stood at the nurses' station. "It's all gone to hell," he said. "Macy's daughter is here and she wants to get the money."

Through a door behind Addy, I could see a dark-haired, middle-aged woman sitting by the foot of a bed. Beyond her, Anna Sterritt was standing at the window.

"Who the hell's Macy's daughter?" said Bow, looking at me.

The hospital vigil had forced Addy to cut back on his cigarettes, and his chest gurgled now when he breathed. "Anna's mother," Addy rasped. "Macy gave her up when she was a baby. She never cared about Macy until now, when she learned there was money." Every word was a struggle for him.

"Jesus Christ, Macy could have told me," griped Bow.

"She didn't tell anyone."

"Jesus Christ," Bow said again, his anger turning to wonder.

"It's all gone to hell," Addy repeated. He seemed almost relieved. Life was living down to his expectations.

"Well, a will's a will," Bow said. "She can do what she wants with her money." He asked the young nurse behind the counter if he could go in.

"Let me check," she said, and she padded silently into Macy's room.

Macy's daughter's name was Franny Sterritt. She and her husband both worked for the telephone company. Addy told us that after giving the baby up for adoption, Macy had lost all track of her, but several years ago Anna got curious and found her grandmother. Macy called Anna her grandniece so Anna's mother wouldn't have to be involved.

"Who's Franny's father?" asked Bow.

"Heh, heh, heh." Addy's muffled laugh quickly turned into a coughing fit. Along the hospital corridor, heads popped out to see what was happening. "I guess that could be just about any man in Laroque County," Addy croaked.

The young nurse returned and said Macy's family would be leaving in a few minutes. Bow could go in then.

"How is she?" Bow asked.

"In and out," said the nurse with a practiced look of sympathy. "I don't think it will be long." After a pause, she asked, "Are you a friend, Mr. Epps?"

"He's her lawyer," interjected Addy.

"A friend," said Bow.

"Let me get you something to sit on." The nurse brought out from behind the counter of the nurses' station a small, wire-frame chair. Bow barely managed to squeeze in between its arms.

After five minutes, the family drifted out of the room. Anna hurried up to Bow and introduced her parents. Franny Sterritt was a thickset, plain woman with her hair pulled back in a careless ponytail. Her husband was gray and paunchy. Beside them, Anna looked impossibly mismatched, vivid and shiny like a polished stone.

"I'm sorry to have to meet under these circumstances," said Bow, being carefully polite.

"It reminds you of your own mortality," said Franny. "I hardly knew her, but she was my mother, my own flesh and blood." Franny had a strong, even voice, cleansed of any regional inflections. Early on at the telephone company, she'd been an operator.

"I think she's had a full and happy life," Bow offered.

"She could have written a book," Addy piped up, standing outside the circle of introductions.

Franny ignored him. "I wish I'd got to know her better, but it was hard," she said. "At least Anna got to see her grandmother."

"She had great dignity," said Bow. He paused, giving Franny an opportunity to bring up the will. But Franny just shook Bow's hand again. She excused herself and said she'd be down in the visitors' lounge in case anything happened.

The curtains were drawn in Macy's room and the lamps were off. She lay on her bed in the ghostly half-light, her arms at her sides outside the covers. Her eyes were closed and an oxygen tube ran out of her nose. She was pasty, but her face had puffed up under her medication, eliminating the gauntness brought on by the illness. With her hair down and forming a white corona on the pillow, she looked girlish and aged at the same time, a smooth-skinned ancient prophet. Bow clasped her hand. "Cold," he whispered to me.

But as he squeezed, Macy opened her eyes. Her mouth moved without making a sound.

"Don't try to talk," said Bow. "We're just here to say hello."

Macy's mouth moved again. This time, after a moment, we heard, "My daughter."

"You surprised us," said Bow with a soft laugh. "You're supposed to confide in your lawyer."

Macy's eyes sparked, though she didn't have the strength to smile. "She was a beautiful baby," she whispered.

"Are you happy with our arrangements, your will?" he asked.

Macy closed her eyes and nodded slowly. For a moment, she gathered her strength. "Bow," she said, as she opened her eyes again. She spoke his name easily and seemed to relish it. He leaned close. For a moment I thought he might kiss her. "Bow," she whispered. "It goes so quick."

"I know, Macy, I know." He squeezed her hand.

"I'm floating," she said. Her gaze drifted off and she closed her eyes again. "Floating. Like a feather."

"Just rest," said Bow. He released her hand. "You look beautiful, Macy."

He stood beside the bed. She was breathing silently. The covers heaved slightly over her chest. After five minutes or so, he led me out of the room. "I think she's sleeping again," Bow told the nurse.

"Thank you for coming, Mr. Epps," she said.

Addy caught up with us at the hospital door. "You're leaving?" he asked.

"There's no reason for me to stay," said Bow. "Let me know when it happens."

Addy looked dismayed at the prospect of being abandoned. "But what about her daughter?" he asked.

"What about her? She seemed nice."

"What if she gets Macy to change the will?"

"Macy can't change anything now."

Bow pushed his way through the revolving door. Addy hesitated, then pursued us down the walk. His lips were trembling, his eyes were wild—he already felt the loneliness ahead. "What did Macy *say*?" Addy begged.

Bow stopped. Bundled in his winter coat and braced by the cool air, he looked robust, healthier than I'd seen him in days. "She said she was a feather, floating away," Bow whispered. He lifted his arm and let his hand drift down, slicing gently through the air.

Addy's reddened eyes watched in horror. "Mary, Mother of God," he gasped.

Walking back to the office, Bow seemed more vigorous than before, as if he'd taken to heart Macy's remark about time slipping away. As we got to the Bank Building, he told me, "I think it's time now. Why don't you pay a visit to Mrs. Hennepin."

CHAPTER 25

The snowfall that had dusted Laroque two days before had dropped several inches on Bent Pine. No one since had driven down the gravel road to the lake. Except for a few squirrel tracks, the white floor of the pine woods was clean and unbroken until you got to Mrs. Hennepin's trailer. There, the energetic old lady had trampled the snow all around her home and left trails leading off through her collection of junk.

When I pulled up, she was sitting on a rickety folding chair, bundled against the cold and using a hatchet to break up a wood box, splitting the flat pieces into thin strips of kindling. She paused in her chopping and watched me park the car and walk over. "Nice day," I said. It was cold but clear, and in the fading light the sky was turning a rich blue.

"Isn't it, though." She looked me over carefully. I couldn't tell if she recognized me.

"Is the lake frozen solid yet?" I asked.

"I wouldn't go out there," she said. "I'd give it another week at least. You don't want to fall through."

"No, ma'am."

She gestured toward the water with her hatchet. "A man fell through a few years ago about this time in the season. He got out about a hundred yards and the ice broke. I watched him walking, and then he just dropped. There was nothing anybody could do. They couldn't even get his body out until the lake had froze some more. They had to wait and chip it out of the ice."

"That's rough."

"He might of been trying to kill himself. The police said he was a sad man. And he didn't have any gear or anything like he was going to fish out there. He was just walking." Mrs. Hennepin watched to see how I would handle this story. She appeared to be wearing four or five layers of clothing, including a faded red sweatshirt with a hood that she'd pulled tight around her head. The hem of a blue skirt poked out below the bottom of her coat, and her legs were covered by a pair of brown knit men's pants.

"Well," I said after reflecting for a moment on the dead man, "I guess that's one way to make sure your body's well preserved for the funeral."

She smiled. I'd passed her test.

"It must get lonely here in the winter," I said.

"Oh, the ice fishermen come around on the weekends, and I'm busy. I always got things to do around the trailer." She motioned with her head behind her, where the junk stretched out in mounds and towers under the snow. "Last summer, a man came by and offered me a thousand dollars for everything I had back there. He didn't even want to go through it. He stood here and said he'd bring in a truck and clean it all out. One thousand dollars. He was a scavenger and he knew what he was doing. I said no. I got too many memories back there."

"I don't blame you."

"Everything back there's got a memory attached to it," she continued, sounding like Macy. "What would be left of me if someone took all that away?"

"You're right."

"I don't need the money. I get Social Security and I sell some bait. I don't need much."

"As long as you're comfortable."

"You got to have stuff to remember by, otherwise you're just alone."

I nodded. Suddenly, she reached out and tugged on the sleeve of my coat. "You must be a bit chilled, young man," she said. "You want a little nip to warm up?"

"A nip?"

"I got a bottle of Wild Turkey inside."

"Will you join me?" I asked.

"What time is it?"

I made a small show out of checking my watch. "Four-fifteen."

"No, never before five for me. Five is my time. My husband used to call it oh-be-joyful hour. We'd tick down the minutes." She smiled at the memory. "He was born in London. They have nice expressions over there."

"I think I'll wait, too," I said.

"Suit yourself."

She turned from me and split a few more pieces of kindling. A pine stump, about the size of an overturned washbasin, served as her chopping block. The hatchet was old, and repeated sharpenings had given the blade a fine, wavery sheen. She chopped away with the precision of a metronome, tossing off slices of wood hardly thicker than a straw. When the last board was split, she gathered the pieces into an old wicker basket and, without a word, went into the trailer, which rocked slightly as she moved around inside. I waited out front. The cold was starting to bite.

In about five minutes, she stepped out again. She'd taken off her gloves and was holding something wrapped in a paper napkin. "Do you know what a scone is?" she asked.

"A muffin."

"An English muffin. Try it." As she moved close to hand me the little bundle, her breath hung in the chill air. I picked up a whiff of bourbon.

The napkin covered a triangular piece of dough flecked by raisins. The scone was extraordinarily dense and dry, but I chewed away with as much enthusiasm as I could muster. "Good," I said.

"My husband loved those." She sat down on the metal front step of the trailer. A shaft of sun speared through the trees and made an inviting yellow puddle at her feet.

"Say," I asked, "didn't I read about a shooting around here a few weeks ago?"

"Maybe you did." Her jaw jutted out in a kind of school-yard challenge.

"What was that all about?"

"They shot an escaped prisoner—a few miles from here. He was living right back there, the other side of the lake."

"That's a lot of excitement."

She shrugged. "I'm too old to get excited."

"I don't believe that."

"Eighty-two," she said with a trace of pride.

"That's nothing. You got plenty of time left for excitement."

"Don't need none. I keep busy."

"Did you ever see the guy they shot—the escaped prisoner?" I asked.

"See him?"

"You know, did he come around here?"

She laughed. "I can't talk about that."

I forced myself to laugh, too. "Why not?"

"I'm a witness."

"So?"

She lifted her right arm and flapped it at me. Despite the cold, she hadn't put her gloves back on, and the back of her hand was covered with soft brown freckles. "Listen, young man, my husband was a process server for forty years. He knew all the tricks and a few of his own, and he taught them all to me."

"I guess everybody's a lawyer these days," I said.

"You work for Mr. Epps. I been expecting you." She laughed again. "I been waiting for you for days."

We smiled back and forth. Bundled in her layers of clothing, she looked invitingly warm and round. I knew I wasn't going to get anywhere. "Say hello to Mr. Asmus for me," I told her. She waved from the icy metal step as I drove away.

Back on the main road, I stopped in front of a ragged gray house crowded into a narrow crescent of space cleared from the forest. The surrounding pines seemed to be pushing the house and the tiny front yard precariously against the edge of the highway. The summer before, I'd seen bicycles and toys scattered around. Now I parked and followed a crumbling concrete walk up to the front door. The voices of children rang out from inside. Before I could knock, the door swung open and I was face-to-face with a man about my age. He was wearing blue jeans and a worn green sweatshirt, and he'd missed a few days shaving. An assortment of small children spilled out the door around his knees. "Can I help you?" he asked pleasantly.

"Sorry to intrude, but I was wondering about the lake down there," I said, gesturing behind me. "I like to ice fish, but I wasn't sure about access."

"You mean Bent Pine?"

"Yes."

"Oh, you can go down there whenever you want," the man said. He absently put his hands on the heads of two of his children. "That's public land. Private beyond, but public down there. At least, I think. People from town been fishing there for years."

"Oh, good. I thought maybe the old lady who lives in the trailer down there owned it."

"Mrs. Hennepin? She just sells bait." At the mention of her name, the children stirred.

"Do you know Mrs. Hennepin?" I asked one little boy. He turned away and buried his face in his father's pants.

"I wouldn't go out on the lake yet," the man said. "I'd let it freeze up for another week or so."

"Right. Give it some time. I was asking that old lady about the ice, but I couldn't get a straight answer." I made a motion with my hand as if taking a drink. "You know, she seemed a bit confused."

The man smiled. "You might get a perch or two out of there. Or maybe a little northern. I never had much luck with Bent Pine."

"Do you ice fish?"

"Not so much anymore." He let his eyes drift over his brood of children. "Don't have the time."

"Does that old lady live down there by herself?" I pressed. "It must get pretty lonely for her."

"Every now and then she'll come around with a pie she's baked. She likes the kids."

"She ever baby-sit?"

He shook his head.

"The booze?"

He hesitated, studying my brown Sears hunting jacket and my worn Sears boots; I knew right away that I'd pushed it too far. He stepped back, pulling his kids with him. "Listen, you son-of-a-bitch," he said in a low, controlled voice. "I don't know if you're a lawyer or from an insurance company or what, but that's a sweet old lady down there and you're not using me to cheat her."

"Okay, thanks," I said cheerfully, and I turned away.

"Son-of-a-bitch," he spit after me.

A child asked, "Daddy, why did you swear at that man?"

I drove on into the nearest town, Ridgefield, which amounted to a dozen stores strung out along the highway for fifty yards or so. Angelo's Restaurant was open, so I stopped and nursed a couple of cups of coffee at the counter. For over an hour, I was the only customer. The waitress sat near the door to the kitchen reading a movie magazine. When I got up to pay, I asked her if she knew Mrs. Hennepin, the old lady who lived at Bent Pine. The waitress shook her head. "I don't get around much anymore," she said.

By the time I left, it was pitch black out. The moon hung low and the sky was awash with stars. I drove back toward the lake and pulled off on the side of the highway, just down the road from the turnoff to Bent Pine. Up ahead, the gray house with all the kids was throbbing with light. I sat in the car for five minutes. No vehicles came along and no one from the house seemed to have noticed me. Finally, I took a Polaroid camera out of the glove compartment and started walking down the gravel road toward the lake. Beneath the snow, the frozen ground was rutted and treacherous. In the spring, with the mud, Mrs. Hennepin must have had a terrible time getting her car out. Overhead, the night sky was just a gash through the tops of the pines.

After ten minutes, a pale, uneven glow appeared through the trees, then the tinny sound of voices. In the cold, still air, the metal trailer was like an echo chamber, amplifying the noise inside and spreading it out to the world. The flickering gray light came from a small window on the side. Carefully, I put my face up to the glass. Mrs. Hennepin was asleep in an easy chair in front of a yapping television. She'd taken off her coat, but otherwise she was wearing the layers of clothing she'd had on outside in the afternoon.

I walked around to the end of the trailer and followed a path into the labyrinth of junk. Away from the window light, the snow-covered boxes and sinks and furniture made ghostly forms among the trees. Behind the skeleton of the Hudson sedan, I surprised a small animal, which skittered off through the snow. "Johnny, that's crazy!" buzzed a woman's voice on the TV. The labyrinth hooked around the trailer, and in back another window tossed light onto several metal garbage cans. I lifted the top of one, taking care not to set off a clang. Inside were hundreds of empty tin cans. I checked another: brown paper bags, all neatly folded. A few yards farther into the woods stood a small shack that could have once been an animal shed—a pigsty, perhaps, or a chicken coop. The door had separate top and bottom halves, and the top had fallen off and was leaning against the wall. As I got close, I could smell what I was looking for. I lifted the camera and shot. The flash danced off a thousand facets of glass, a jeweled mountain. Hundreds, perhaps thousands of empty Wild Turkey bottles were piled up to my chest. I waited for the camera to reload, then shot twice more. Each flash sent an explosion of light through the silent woods, but Mrs. Hennepin never stirred.

CHAPTER 26

We were barely into December that year, and official winter hadn't even set in, when the jet stream slipped off-track, pushing a fierce arctic front down out of Canada and across the upper Midwest, creating one of the worst bursts of frigid weather in Wisconsin's history. Records were set for days running. One night, the temperature dropped to 23 degrees below zero, and hit 60 below with the windchill factor. During the day, even in the sun, the thermometer never climbed above -10. The state issued warnings to stay inside. Motorists were told not to drive alone: If a car broke down on an isolated road, you could freeze before help came. For the first time in anyone's memory, the schools were shut because of the cold. The postmaster in Kawnipi set off a commotion by canceling local mail deliveries, giving every editorial writer in the state a chance to invoke the old chestnut, "Neither snow nor rain, nor heat, nor gloom of night stays these couriers from the swift completion of their appointed rounds," which turned out to be nothing official, just the slogan carved across the entrance to the main New York City post office.

For the first day or so, the cold was an adventure. People traded stories about surviving the dash from the parking lot to the warm harbor of the A&P. At the Wanigan, the weather was all anyone talked

about and the mood was almost giddy: We were heroes, bravely standing up against all that nature could throw us. But as the front stalled
and the cold wore on—the deadly isotherms forming a malignant
bulge over Wisconsin day after day on the *Journal's* weather map—you
couldn't help but feel resentful. The cold was an assault, disrupting
plans, forcing changes in lifelong habits, punishing any challenge.
Pipes burst, cars wouldn't start, doors froze shut. To go outside, you
had to bundle yourself clumsily and cover every exposed square inch
of skin. On the street, faces hid behind ski masks or scarves, and ugly
clumps of frozen breath formed on the cloth around the mouth. Even
with the best protection, the cold attacked relentlessly. You'd step outside, and for a moment—in the lee of the building and still carrying
the inside air in your clothes—you'd think it wasn't really so bad. And
then the wind would catch you, ripping through layers of cloth until
you were surrounded by pain and might as well have been standing
naked on a snowy street corner. Inside, with gusts battering the brittle windows, it was impossible not to sense the frailty of the shelter-
ing walls, the precariousness of our manufactured heat against the
unyielding force of the front. "These are the times I believe in God,"
Bow gasped one day as he stepped into the office, radiating the chill
he'd picked up in the thirty-second walk from his car to the Bank
Building.

Macy died in the middle of the cold wave. Bill Addy called one
morning to let us know. With the ground frozen hard as granite, they
couldn't bury her, so Addy and the Sterritts decided to have her cre-
mated. "I couldn't stand to think of her lying there in the morgue
until a thaw," Addy told us. They didn't hold a service, but a few days
later, Addy stopped up on the way home from the funeral parlor
cradling a neat, gray box: her ashes. He seemed more at ease than
he'd been in the last month or so; holding her remains gave him a
kind of grip on her passing. Also, he'd misread Franny Sterritt—she
wasn't after money, she'd just wanted to meet the woman who'd
brought her into the world. Now, Addy told us, when the will
cleared probate and he owned Macy's house, he was going to sell it
and move to Arizona. He wanted a cottage on the edge of the desert
where he could sit outside at night and listen to the coyotes howl in

the distance. "I think Macy will like it there," said Addy, tapping the top of the box with his finger. "There's nothing to keep us here."

With the freeze outside and the criminal investigation looming around us, the days had assumed an unsettled, slightly ominous tenor, and now with Bill Addy bailing out, I couldn't help feeling that we were moving toward some kind of harsh climax, that Bow and I were the last, heedless rebels to stick it out at the Alamo. Even Bow seemed a little wistful that day when Addy got up to leave, still clutching all that was left of Macy.

"Don't worry about the will," Bow assured him. "It'll work out like Macy wanted."

Addy offered some comfort of his own. "They say Asmus is having trouble coming up with much," he pronounced on the way out the door. "That Piper boy is cleverer than they thought."

Bow hadn't heard a word lately from the prosecutor, but several inmates at Lovington had written, warning that investigators were talking to everyone at the prison, tracking down leads on Fontenot's escape. "Watch out, they're trying to pin it on you," wrote an ex–insurance agent named Ole Carlsen who'd shot his partner dead when they fought over dividing the business. Bow had handled the appeal but couldn't get the court to bite on any of the issues. "I of course told them nothing and spoke very highly of your character," Ole confided. Another inmate, a man we didn't know, could hardly wait for the gate to slam shut behind Bow. "Since they say you're coming here, could you look into my case?" he wrote. "A terrible injustice has been done." The fellow went on to describe an appalling incident of mistaken identity; he was almost certainly lying. "I look forward to meeting you and working with you on this very important matter," he concluded.

Bow amused himself by reading the letters aloud to me, but he didn't seem to pay them much attention. Aside from the Polaroids I'd brought back from Bent Pine, nothing about the Fontenot case held his interest. The Polaroids, though, were special. "Very good, Charlie," he mused when I handed them over. He laid the three photos carefully on his desk and studied each with the same dime-store magnifying glass he'd once used to examine Gary Fontenot's tiny handwriting. "This will be very helpful." The crude pictures were almost identical, with a bright star of light in the center where the flash bounced off the glass, and murky, gray forms giving way to darkness around the edges. In the penumbra, the hundreds of empty bottles testified to a powerful drinking habit. Bow put two of the photos in his desk and dropped the third in the side pocket of his suit coat. Every now and then, in the days ahead, I'd see him slip the picture out and examine it quietly, as if it were a prized relic or exotic pornography. Recharged, he'd drop the photo back into his pocket.

By then, Bow's criminal appeals practice had started to dry up. He didn't seek out new assignments, and the judges, perhaps aware of the cloud over his head, stopped sending him cases. For the first time in memory, space opened up on shelves and on other horizontal surfaces in Bow's office as we shipped volumes of transcripts back to the court and no new ones arrived. Bow came in every day as before, and he mopped up on the appeals he'd already accepted. But he spent a lot of time reading the law of trusts and estates and fussing with questions about Macy's will. "I hated this stuff in law school, but I'm starting to get it," he told me one day. "Writing a will is like building a house. *You're* in control—*you* decide how many floors to have, how many rooms, where to put the entrance, and so on. If you mess up, if the roof leaks, it's your own goddamned fault." By contrast, he argued, criminal appeals work was too reactive—he was tired of having his efforts defined by the facts and the rulings embedded in a transcript.

"I thought that's what you liked about it," I said.

"It was simply what I did. I don't think I'd thought about it in twenty years."

"But what about the rights of defendants and cleaning up the justice system?"

"I still believe all that," Bow told me. "What I did was right—it was always right, and I'll always believe that. But now it's someone else's turn."

I let his words echo around the office for a few seconds. Then I said, "Before this whole Fontenot mess, you thought that someone would be Ginger."

"No," he corrected sharply, letting me know that I was close to overstepping. "I never urged the criminal law on Ginger. I never urged anything on him other than to live up to his great potential. That's still all I want." He breathed in sharply through his nose, a strange little reverse snort. "As for me," he said, "I'm enjoying exploring a new area of practice."

I glanced through some of the cases he was studying, disputes about irrevocable trusts passing from one spouse to another, about fractions of property skipping generations to dodge, the dying ancestor hoped, the grasping hand of the inheritance tax. The cases were all beyond me—page after page layered with clauses and dense with phrases of art, endless paragraphs dry and uninviting as an old piece of fruitcake. I missed the human simplicity of the criminal law, which, I pointed out to Bow, comes down to real stories about people and basic ideas about what's fair. By comparison, estate law seemed false and impersonal—though that may have been what suddenly attracted Bow, given the turmoil in his life.

"Nonsense," he said when I gently suggested as much. "This stuff is all about people's lives, real lives. Writing a will is a vote of confidence in the future."

"But listen to this"—and I read a typical passage from a will case so thick with dead language that it bored me even in the middle of our argument.

"So?" he said, giving away nothing. "So?"

"It's impossible to understand."

"No, it isn't. I understood it."

"But you're a lawyer."

"Of course."

"If it's my will, I'd like to know what the hell's in it."

"Fine, Charlie, I'll draw up your will, and I'll make sure you understand every word of it."

"But I don't have anything to leave in a will."

"Sure, you do. Every man should have a will. Bring me an inventory of your assets."

"Do *you* have a will?" I challenged him. "You're the one with assets."

That stopped him for a moment. His gaze softened while he reckoned how far he wanted to go with this. Then he plunged on. "Fine," he announced. "I'll draw one up, too."

Because of the cold, I'd been spending days and nights in the office, venturing out just to chauffeur Bow or to run a quick errand. The evenings were numbingly uneventful. The bars all closed early, lest someone get drunk and wander fatally off into the cold. That left me on my own, and I'd never been comfortable drinking alone in the office—it seemed a kind of desecration after the years of watching Bow work so hard there. For all his tolerance of my habits, I knew he'd feel the same way. But I desperately needed some action, so the day after Bow had suggested that I make a list of assets, I bundled up and walked back over to my apartment in Indian Town, a legal pad tucked under my arm.

An inch or two of light snow had fallen more than a week before, but it had stayed fresh in the cold, so hard and fine that it squeaked with every step. Indeed, the freeze had a kind of sterilizing effect— the entire paralyzed, white landscape looked pure and clean enough to nibble on. "KILLER COLD," the *Journal's* front page had barked that day—eight known dead so far because of the weather, including a teenage couple from Waterville who'd been out driving the back roads for reasons no one could explain, perhaps looking for a place to park and neck. Their car skidded off the road. They tried to walk to help, then gave up and returned to the vehicle. They were found in each other's arms.

The wind had calmed somewhat from the early days of the front, but it still whipped vicious gusts across the span of the Turner Bridge. Below, the Agnes had frozen down to a channel so narrow that a man could jump over it in spots. The slice of open water frothed up luxurious billows of steam against the far colder air. Glancing down, I noticed that someone had left a trail of large footprints across the ice—someone teasing death had walked right to the water's edge. I thought immediately of Ox.

No one was out and about. In Indian Town, I walked down the middle of the street. The cottages and shacks along the way sat lifeless on their cramped plots of frozen lawn, the only sign of habitation an occasional tin chimney stack puffing out gray torrents of wood smoke—undetectable to the nose, since the cold wiped out your sense of smell.

Ahead, my building towered over the block, four stories of pricey, now dirty gray stone, a relic of the moment when the town's prosperity seemed likely to sweep away any faltering neighborhood. A converted hotel, the old place had stood for decades as a fading grande dame, looking down on everything around. In the knife cut of the icy air, her thick walls beckoned, and I picked up my pace. The cold was in me now. My numbed feet stomped along like chunks of concrete. My eyes began to tear, soaking then freezing the scarf around my face; it felt as if I were wearing a frying pan.

Behind me, a lone car, a new dark blue Ford, rolled up the street. The car honked. Something expensive yet cheerless about that model Ford suggested trouble. Another honk, a quick, friendly pop on the horn. I stopped and the car pulled up beside me, driver's window already down. "Charlie? Charlie Stuart?" The man inside looked faintly familiar. "Jesus, I never thought I'd find you out in weather like this." He was thin and ruddy, probably about sixty, his weathered complexion camouflaging what had once been a face full of freckles.

"Yeah?" I said.

"You are Charlie Stuart, aren't you?"

"Yeah."

"My name's Art Genter." He watched me hug myself and bounce from foot to foot. "You want to get in?" he asked, indicating the seat beside him. "I've got the heater up full blast."

Wispy traces of the car's warmth, like tiny eddies in a stream, drifted up through the cold and touched me on my exposed forehead before dissipating immediately. As Art Genter leaned awkwardly across the car seat to unlock the passenger door, his short black jacket pulled up, exposing the holster on his belt. "I've got to get inside," I told him, and I wheeled and scudded up the walk to my building.

Above the entrance, the building's proud name still lived in concrete: Greenwater Hotel. I pulled open the door and found the inside stuffed with dry, hot air; the nervous landlord wasn't taking the chance that one of his tenants—not the most self-reliant group in town—might freeze to death and provoke a nasty lawsuit. Through the glass panel beside the door, I watched Genter steer his car into a no-parking zone along the curb. He pulled a cop's fur-lined winter cap over his ears and followed me inside. "The cold's a bitch," he said, bouncing and slapping himself as we faced each other in the lobby. "Good thing the Pack's playing in Baltimore this week."

I told him he might as well save his breath—I wasn't going to talk to him.

"Hell, I know that," Genter said glumly. "The fuckin' Piper boy won't talk, why the hell does Pete expect you to?"

"He doesn't, does he?"

"That's the thing about Asmus, he never concedes a thing." Genter's tone wavered between ruefulness and admiration. "He's like a fuckin' freight train, he just keeps coming." I assumed this to be a threat, planted to intimidate me, but Genter quickly disarmed it. "He doesn't care about you or Bow. It's just the boy he wants to nail."

Years ago, when a previous team of owners had converted the hotel into apartments, they'd left the built-in oak reception desk in the lobby. Now it was piled with boxes and other junk, but Genter's practiced eye picked it out. "Jesus, would you look at that," he said, walking over and inspecting the massive hunk of wood, taking off his gloves and running his hands affectionately along the dusty grain. "It's just sitting here going to waste." He looked up brightly. "Jesus, would I like to have this in my basement, down by the pool table."

"Maybe you can," I suggested. I mentioned the name of the building's owner.

"And look at this." He scurried over to the old elevator door, hurrying, as if someone might take it before he got there. The door, made of brass molded into twining, leafy vines, formed a gorgeously elaborate gate. The elevator itself required an operator and hadn't run in years. Genter lovingly petted the metal, tracing a vine to the point where it burst into an open flower. Then his eye caught the brass sconce on the wall. "This place is a fuckin' treasure chest!" he exalted.

"It was well built," I conceded. It embarrassed me suddenly that I'd come in and out for ten years without much more than staring at the floor—which, I noticed now, contained lovely and intricate tile patterns.

"And they're just using it as a shithole apartment house," Genter grumped, without thinking. Quickly, he backed up. "I mean, no offense to you."

"No offense taken," I promised. I told him I had some work to do and had to get up to my room.

"Jesus, can I see it?" he asked. "I love this place."

"It's just a shithole, as you put it. There's nothing to see, believe me."

"Aww, come on," he begged. "I'll only take a peek." He pulled off his fur-lined cap. His silky white hair stood up in tufts from the static electricity. I tried to imagine that this eager old coot could be laying a trap.

"All right, follow me," I said.

All the way up the four flights of stairs, Genter gabbed on about his antique-crammed house, the trouble he'd had fitting the ancient pool table into his basement, the trip he and his wife had taken the summer before to inspect Frank Lloyd Wright buildings in the southern half of the state. By the time we got to my room, on the top floor in back, I was puffing while he was still nattering away.

I opened the door and watched him deflate. The original owners had lavished their attentions on the public spaces; the rooms themselves were spare, and I'd hardly contributed much on my own. The place looked almost unlived in, barracks-neat, with a lone copy of the *Journal* yellowing on the night table.

"Furnished, huh?" the cop said.

"Mostly."

He walked over and sat on the bed. Now he was wheezing from the climb. I wanted to apologize for disappointing him.

"Oh, *this* is nice," he said politely, fingering a brass lamp on the night table, a token that a bar group had given to Bow for his good works and that Bow had promptly passed to me. Genter read the inscription and immediately lost interest.

I explained that when my mother had died five or so years before, I'd sold her house to pay off the mortgage and sold or given away the furniture, since I had no place to keep it. I didn't tell him of my subsequent regret at parting with the lovely pine armoire that my mother's family had hauled from the East a century ago and the small writing desk my father had kept in his office at the Opera House. Even their huge oak double bed—gone. In their place, I had a modest savings account, my only insurance.

Genter possessed the kind of spirit that was hard to suppress, even in a grim room at the Greenwater Hotel. "Would you look at that," he said, shoving himself off the bed and awkwardly kneeling beside a bruised steel trunk pushed against the wall under the window. My father had lifted the trunk from a prop room somewhere years ago and used it to collect souvenirs of his career—old playbills, scripts, correspondence, costumes, reviews, books. I'd held on to it under the theory that one distant day it would be amusing to browse through the stuff.

Genter tried to lift the top. Locked, held tight by a thick bolt buried in the side. "Must be pretty important stuff in there," he said. I assured him it wasn't, but for a minute or so, while Genter looked on impatiently, I searched assorted drawers for the key. I couldn't imagine why I'd locked the thing. My mother must have done it, I decided. Maybe she was afraid I'd dump the contents sometime in a drunken snit. I noticed Genter's holster again, and it occurred to me that we could shoot the damn lock off. Then, stirring pennies in a glass ashtray on the dresser, I caught a flash of silver: a small steel key.

The trunk lock clicked over easily and I popped open the lid. Folded neatly on the top lay a stiff, elegant child's suit—a blue jacket and shorts with thick suspenders. "Well, I'll be," marveled Genter. "Little Lord Fauntleroy's clothes."

Actually, it was my costume when I was six and played in *Mint Juleps,* a trifling drawing-room comedy. I'd been little more than a prop, a spot of cuteness on a stage full of adults, but I had a single line, simple though important. I'm in the suite of a southern hotel while my stage parents dress to go out, oblivious to me. As the scene ends, the adults exit suddenly, leaving me alone. A rap on the door. I open it to find a bellboy. "Is this the party that called for the bucket of ice?" the bellboy asks. I pause and glance around the empty room. ("Wait!" my father would scream at me in rehearsals. "Set it up! Wait, wait,

wait!") Finally, after a child's eon, after a hideous, brain-aching silence, I answer innocently: "There's no party here." Curtain. End of scene. ("Again!" my father would cry. "You rushed it! You've got to hold, hold, hold!") And we'd run through it once more. There were at least a dozen major roles in the play, countless scene changes, curtains, and plot points, but I came to believe that all of *Mint Juleps* and its hours of silly banter hung on my one, wee line. *There's no party here.* The words became my mantra, endlessly recited in silence, the last thing in my head before I fell asleep, my first conscious thought on awakening. During the day, I could hardly talk, all other language being crowded out. At night, I dreamed the words. And, of course, the repetition only caused me to speed up when I actually said the line onstage, setting off another tantrum by my father. True actors find comfort in the ritualistic order of a script, but to me it represented a kind of horror chamber, dread leading to failure, and I longed to escape to the safe, real world of randomness and uncertainty.

In the end, I managed, as children usually do. The audience exploded with laughter, the curtain came down, the show went on. But even my father recognized my misery and never cast me again.

Genter lifted out the little jacket, admiring the craftsmanship. I reached over and ran my fingers along the soft felt of the garment. The gold buttons down the front were cool to the touch, as if they'd picked up some of the outside weather. How often had my six-year-old fingers fussed anxiously with those buttons, absently seeking something to do? ("Hands at sides!" my father would scream.) Macy had talked of drawing life from the objects saved from her past, but the trunk and its contents still felt too close, too raw—they hadn't even slipped into the safe zone of nostalgia. Bow liked to call me an archivist, but an archivist enjoys some distance from his records, some question in relation to them, some reverence, even. I was more like a witness, spouting evidence, spilling memories.

I snatched the jacket back from Genter, dropped it in the trunk, and slammed down the lid. The hell with an inventory, I decided. Bow will never make one, either. "Whoa," the cop yelped. "I wasn't going to hurt it."

I told him I had to get back to the office. A spark of suspicion flashed across his watery eyes: Was I hiding telltale evidence in the trunk? But it passed quickly. He offered me a ride.

Outside, the arctic air brought a wave of refreshment after the claustrophobic heat of the rooming house. All along the street in the falling darkness, the silent houses were reviving themselves and glowing with light. The faux-leather front seat of the cop's Ford crackled with cold as we slid in. Guiding the car along the empty street, Genter took a final shot at doing his job. "So, you never saw anything noteworthy between the boy and Fontenot?" he asked.

"Not a thing," I assured him.

"Never heard anything that could be construed as a signal?"

"Never."

He gave up. Turning onto the bridge, the Ford's headlights swept across the frozen tundra of the river and its banks. Laroque felt deserted. I asked Genter if he'd been one of the men who'd tried to interview Ginger. He nodded. "I felt sorry for the kid," he said. "You know, I busted his old man years ago. Writing bad checks. I thought he was retarded at first. Never said a word. Never looked at you. He was the coldest man I ever met."

"Ginger's done amazingly well for himself, considering. Good student. Star athlete—"

Genter interrupted my platitudes. "I was at the game, you know. On the Kawnipi side, though. I used to play forward for Kawnipi myself when I was a kid. I saw him make the shot. And you know what? He didn't get it off in time. The game had ended before the ball left his hands."

"I don't think so. I was there, too."

"I *know.*" The cop drawled the word for emphasis. "I had a perfect view. I tried to talk to the ref about it afterwards, but the place was a madhouse, and he wouldn't listen. Later on, I realized the ref was right. The game was over. People thought the kid had made it. Let it be, you know? Let it fuckin' be."

Genter pulled up in front of the Bank Building. A scrum of bank employees huddled just inside the front door, waiting to make the sprint to their cars. I looked for Lucy, standing taller than the others, but I couldn't find her.

"Well, it was good talking to you," Genter said. He offered me his hand with his glove still on, conventional manners under the cold front. We shook. "Good luck," he offered as I climbed out of the car.

I stopped and leaned back in. "With what?" I asked. "I thought you said Asmus didn't care about Bow and me."

"Pete's a freight train," Genter repeated. Then he reached over and closed the car door in my face.

CHAPTER 27

The cold spell broke after a week or so. The jet stream returned to its normal course, and the temperature pushed up around freezing, which of course now felt balmy. By then, though, the weather had taken a terrible slice out of the Christmas shopping season, and the merchants in Laroque were panicked that they would never recover the lost business. There was talk that a few of the shakier places would close down, leaving debts all over the state. So the town fathers declared a hasty Lumberjack Day, and one gray Saturday, the sidewalks filled with tables piled with everything from gloves to hardware to Christmas tree ornaments.

At around noon, Bow and I stepped out to grab some lunch. Main Street had been closed to traffic, and a sizable crowd milled about downtown, enjoying the burst of freedom provided by the milder weather. A scratchy album of Christmas carols played through loudspeakers strung up on the lampposts. Bow purposefully wove his way straight down in front of the Opera House, where the Wanigan had set up a steam table selling pork pies. Rita the waitress presided over the operation. She had on a pair of heavy boots and a green parka, and she was wearing thick beige leggings under her white skirt. "Haven't seen you in a while," she remarked to Bow when we came up.

"It's been hectic," he admitted.

"Heard your name a lot, though." She cocked her head, raising her dark eyebrows, trying to draw him out.

Bow smiled wanly. He studied her carefully from top to bottom. "I like your leggings," he drawled suggestively.

"Arrrrhhh." She reached out and pinched his good cheek. The skin seemed strangely loose; his entire face slid over his skull. "You're a bad boy," she scolded.

Bow and I took our pork pies on paper plates over to a bench in Veterans' Park. Sitting out on Rita's steam table, the doughy pastry had grown damp and soft; after the first bite, we had to hold the treat with both hands, and even so the gravy inside escaped and dripped over everything. Still, Bow quickly put one away and sent me back to Rita for a second. It was the first good showing of his appetite in weeks.

"Hark! The Herald Angels Sing" warbled through the sound system, and Bow nodded along to the music. Across the street, Boyce Rensinger waved and hustled over. "Big day coming up," he announced. "I'm going to the championship game, if the Pack makes it."

"Lucky stiff," said Bow. "How'd you work that?"

"Drug company. They're flying their best customers out there, putting us up for the weekend."

"Where's the game again?"

"Los Angeles."

"Lucky stiff," Bow repeated, looking past Rensinger to a table where a Girl Scout troop had set up an array of home-baked cookies and pies.

"Now the Pack's just gotta keep winning," said the pharmacist.

"They'll win," Bow assured him.

More people stopped by—the mayor, Marcus Laney, two elderly ladies who'd been friends of Bow's mother. Over the next half hour or so, several dozen acquaintances drifted over to say hello and chat. With his dismay about Fontenot and the onslaught of the cold front, Bow had hardly been out for weeks, and now it had to be heartening for him to see how people brightened in his presence. Everyone had a spot of news—an upcoming trip to Japan, a farmhouse sold and bought, a stock tip that paid off, a nephew back in college. Telling Bow seemed to provide a kind of validation, and of course he was endlessly gracious in enthusing over the latest tidbit, even if he was mortally bored by it. Actually, I should take that back—it was I who grew bored; I never sensed that Bow's interest lagged. Indeed, he seemed to have tireless patience for the effluvium of the town's life.

He probably could have sat there holding audiences for the rest of the afternoon, but eventually Boyce Rensinger came striding back toward us, and this time his round, fleshy face was squeezed red. I had one of those premonitions and knew even before he'd opened his mouth that his news had to do with Ginger. "That brilliant assistant of yours is making a pretty funny scene over on Hutchins Street," Rensinger pronounced. I don't think I'd ever heard his anger tuned to sarcasm before. "He's got a protest going in front of the army recruiter's. He's gonna get himself arrested."

Bow sagged slightly, his shoulders sinking under the weight of his bulky black overcoat. The day had been moving along so pleasantly. Now it took his relaxed mind several seconds to digest this new report of trouble. Finally, he thanked Rensinger and wearily stood up. "Well, Charlie, I suppose we should go investigate," he said without looking at me.

The crowd on Main Street had started to stir. Word of the demonstration had spread, and children ran past us to catch a glimpse. By the time we got to Hutchins, an otherwise forgotten side street, people had gathered in a huge semicircle around the recruiting station, a former shoe repair shop. Bow and I bulled our way through the crowd. On the sidewalk in front, Ginger and two other high school boys were parading up and down, carrying hand-lettered cardboard signs. Ginger's, the biggest and best constructed of the lot, read "Say No to Vietnam." He'd fastened it to a six-foot slat of wood, so it flapped in the breeze well above his head. I didn't recognize the other boys, and their signs—"Get Out Now"; "Stop the War"—looked as if they'd been scribbled out moments before. The lone recruiter, wearing fatigues, watched the show from the doorway of the shop, appearing thoroughly amused. Most of the folks in the street seemed puzzled more than anything, or, at least, they were withholding judgment until something happened. They'd seen it all before on TV—the enraged shouting, the taunts, the rocks hurled through a window. But Ginger and his two young buddies hardly looked like dangerous revolutionaries. They filed up the sidewalk twenty or so feet past the recruiter, then turned abruptly and marched back. Ginger avoided looking at anyone, his dark face remaining blankly intense. None of the three boys said a word. Laroque's first antiwar protest was being carried out to the tinny echoes of "God Rest Ye Merry Gentlemen."

Bow took in the scene for just a moment, just long enough for his face to flush. "It's like squeezing mud," he said almost wonderingly. "You think it's under control and then something oozes out." He made a fist and squeezed, holding it out as if to show murderous felons, ambitious prosecutors, unreliable acolytes slipping through his fingers. Henry Abbott, a bristly young real estate agent, approached, tautly furious, but Bow turned rudely away and put his face near my ear. I could smell the pork pie on his breath. "Bring him up to my office," he rasped before limping away through the crowd.

Henry Abbott was left to vent to me. "Bow got him started on this," he fumed.

"Fuck off," I told him.

I moved along the crowd trying to find an angle of approach. Ginger's choreography had military precision, and even in making a turn his eyes didn't sweep the faces on the street. I spotted Axel Kurtz, the chief of police, standing beside a young officer on the opposite sidewalk, and I edged over beside them. The cops had attracted their own small orbit of buzzing onlookers. "Aren't you going to shut them down?" a man asked. Kurtz ignored the question. The chief was big and dangerously overweight. His black leather police jacket rode high up over the prow of his stomach.

Henry Abbott had followed me, and now he pressed his anger on Kurtz. "Why don't you arrest them?" Abbott demanded.

The chief shrugged. "For what? Walking on the sidewalk?" Kurtz had grown up in a labor family in Milwaukee, and he'd watched his father march countless picket lines.

"Interfering with an army officer," Abbott persisted. "Blocking access."

Kurtz's small, round eyes never drifted from the protest. "Tell you what," he said. "You go on up there and try to enlist, and if they stop you, I'll arrest them."

The young cop with Kurtz let out a breezy laugh.

"Jesus!" Abbott hissed. "What are we paying you for?"

After Abbott had stalked away, Kurtz asked me, "Does Bow know about this?"

"He was here and left."

Kurtz shook his head gloomily. "This boy is looking for trouble," he said.

The younger cop piped up, "Ever since he hit that shot, he's been kind of crazy."

Kurtz said, "He gets all worked up over people dying in Vietnam, and then his own stupid scheming leads to the death of a good man." The chief spoke quietly, as if the truth of the matter were obvious.

There weren't going to be any arrests, any rocks thrown, any screaming students hurling themselves at the cops. Over the next half hour or so, the people in the street tired of watching three boys walking up and down the sidewalk. The crowd drifted away. The recruiter disappeared into the shop. Through the glass front, you could see him sitting at his desk, shuffling papers. The sound system playing the Christmas carols broke down, and for half a minute or so, the lampposts rang with a hideous screech. Then someone shut the music down. I sat on the damp, cold curb while Ginger marched just a few feet behind me, never acknowledging my presence. Finally, the recruiter came out in his overcoat and locked the front door. "See you, kids," he called cheerfully to the protesters and walked off toward Main Street.

One of the boys with Ginger said, "My feet are frozen solid."

The other saw an opening. "My mom's expecting me home," he said.

The two boys stopped, their signs dangling to the ground. The boys were both small, probably a year or two younger than Ginger. The one with cold feet said, "How about it, should we quit?"

Ginger had continued marching, but I sensed it was mostly for my benefit. The handful of people still standing around were chattering with one another, not paying attention to the protest.

I stood up. "Bow wants to see you," I told Ginger as he filed past.

He stopped finally and rested the handle of his sign over his shoulder. He was wearing his standard-issue Sears ski parka, but his navy wool cap looked like something he'd picked up in a surplus store. "I think that's good enough for today," he told his companions.

Cold Feet said, "Do you think we did any good?"

"Nobody enlisted, right?" said Ginger.

Mama's Boy burbled, "There were a shitload of people here, did you see? And Chief Kurtz. I thought he was going to arrest us."

"We didn't do anything illegal," Ginger told him.

I asked Ginger loudly, "Where did you find these tots?"

Under his wool cap, Ginger's face scrunched into an angry fist. "I think that's good enough for today," he repeated to the boys. "Thanks for coming out."

"See you Monday," they called and hurried off together.

When they were out of earshot, Ginger said, "Sometimes you can be a real asshole, you know that, Charlie?"

"Never mind me. You're about to get fired by your lawyer."

"What for? Bow never heard of the First Amendment?"

"Ask him yourself. He wants to see you."

Ginger hesitated but fell in behind me. To avoid the crowds on Main Street, we circled to the Bank Building by way of River Road. Ox happened to be tottering out of Duffy's as we walked past. His huge, veined face lit up when he saw me. "Hey, Charlie, you coming around tonight?" he asked. Ginger slowed reproachfully, waiting for me to respond. No matter how I tried to wall off my other life, it seemed to break out at inopportune moments.

"Not tonight," I told Ox.

Ginger and I took the alley and climbed the back stairway. The bank closed at noon on Saturdays, and now the inside of the building was dark. From the end of the second-floor hallway, the light from Bow's office glowed with a kind of heat. He was waiting at his desk, not pretending to be occupied with anything but this. Ginger walked in behind me, then stood in the middle of the room. He couldn't decide what to do with his bulky protest sign, which seemed to overwhelm and divide the cramped office, so he tipped it upside down and leaned lightly against it, like a workman resting casually on a shovel. "I feel like I've been brought to the principal's office," he said.

Bow's face remained flushed, but he spoke calmly. "Are you completely lacking in judgment?" he asked.

"Did you see the paper yesterday?" Ginger answered quickly. "Johnson's sending twenty thousand more troops."

Bow stared at him silently, an implacable, red-faced Buddha.

"The war is escalating," Ginger continued, "and we're not winning. If we were winning, we'd be pulling men out. But it's just getting bigger. More people are going to get killed, and for what? It's so wrong. And we're helpless to do anything about it." The words spilled out, scattering in defiance of Ginger's normal articulation, fragments of a speech he'd probably been making to himself as he trooped resolutely along the sidewalk in front of the recruiter. "So we've got to send a message to Johnson and the rest of the government. And even if that message starts small, like here, there are protests going on all over the country today, so the world is going to hear what we're saying." With his ski jacket still zipped to his chin, Ginger was getting overheated, his olive skin turning moist under the cuff of his wool cap.

"Right now, I don't give a fuck about the war," Bow said solemnly.

Ginger recoiled but staggered on. "I just can't tuck away my feelings because they're inconvenient," he said. "The war is bigger than me."

Bow asked me, shaking his head, "What movie has he been watching?"

"Really, Bow," Ginger continued, "I really appreciate what you've been doing for me, but I can't just ignore what's going on in the world."

Bow sat with his hands before him on his desk, palms down, as if he had to restrain the ancient chunk of oak from flying up and clawing at the throat of this self-righteous little prick. "Don't you realize how precarious your position is?" Bow asked, his voice just short of a shout. "A stunt like this just provokes Asmus. Twenty people have probably called him about it already. Don't you see that?"

The redness had leached from Bow's scar to the good side of his face, erasing for once the jagged, two-tone effect he carried through life. His lips had turned a deathly purple, and I worried about his heart. "Bow," I crooned softly, meaning to calm him.

"Shut up, Charlie!" he snarled.

Ginger's wiry little body had clenched, and now he looked as if he were clinging to his protest sign just to stay afloat. "But don't you see?" he pleaded. "They're using these false accusations to shut me up."

"So shut up—for a while, at least. At least until this thing cools down," Bow said, quieter now, trying to sound reasonable.

The lowered volume gave Ginger hope. "Why should *I* shut up?" he asked. "They're the ones who are wrong. The war is wrong. Asmus is wrong. Why should *I* give in?"

"Because they've got you by the balls."

"That just makes me want to fight harder."

Bow took a deep breath. He even flirted with a smile. He removed one hand from the homicidal desk and brushed back a few strands of gray-blond hair tickling the top of his ear. He'd avoided the barbershop, too, over the last few weeks, and now he was long overdue for a trim. "Ginger, listen," he said finally. "If you've learned anything from me, it should be this: The job of a lawyer is to win. That's it, nothing more. Win. Win for your client. If you have to make compromises, chip away at your principles, even say things you don't really believe—that's all part of the job. There's no room for absolutes in what I do, and I'm glad, because I don't like absolutes. They're for people who aren't smart enough to see the whole picture."

"Maybe I'm not cut out to be a lawyer," Ginger said.

"I'm just talking about acting in your own best interests here and now," Bow told him. "And in mine, frankly."

Ginger looked down at the floor. Sweat had stained a dark ring around the collar of his ski parka. "You're probably right," he admitted, glancing up at Bow. "I mean, I know you're right. But I get so angry about the war, so frustrated—I can barely describe it. Every day we're in Vietnam, someone else is killed, sometimes dozens of people. Maybe to you it's just an argument, an intellectual thing, but it seems so wrong to me. I hate it."

Bow sat there silently again. I'm sure he was calculating—trying to figure what to pull from the soup of anger and admiration he felt for the kid. After all, Ginger was nothing if not steadfast. He'd first attracted Bow's interest by denouncing the war in another awkward circumstance. Finally, Bow said, "I'll tell you what. I'll help you find another lawyer. This is dumb. I'll get one for myself, too."

Ginger looked stricken. "No, Bow, you've got to handle it."

"You don't understand how dangerous this is. You could go to prison. I could be disbarred."

"You could go to prison, too, Bow," I offered.

"But I'm innocent," cried Ginger.

"So fucking what?" said Bow. "Haven't you learned anything here?" He swept his arm around the office as if the transcripts still littering the room were flesh-and-blood defendants.

"But you don't give up on these guys, and they're *guilty*," Ginger protested.

"Maybe, maybe not," groused Bow. But Ginger had scored a point. I could see Bow notching it up in appreciation. He put his chin in his palm. Sitting there, his face droopy and now drained of color, he looked like one of those Easter Island statues, his whole body consumed in one huge, magnificent, hopelessly ungainly head. "Well, shit," he said after a while.

Ginger flopped down in a chair, propping the sign against the wall. With the confrontation winding down, he finally thought to unzip his parka and pull off his cap.

Bow asked, "When's your next game?"

"Tonight. Kawnipi."

"Maybe we'll go." He hardly sounded enthusiastic. "What do you say, Charlie?"

I shrugged.

"You kids any good this year?" Bow asked.

"No," said Ginger.

"Yeah, I guess I heard that."

They chatted about the team for a few minutes. Coach Gourdon had fainted during a game a few weeks ago. He was back now, the tests had all returned negative, but the frightening incident had thrown another shadow on the team. Ginger thought people weren't coming to the games because they felt anxious watching the old coach scuttle along the sidelines. "Maybe we'll come tonight," Bow repeated.

Ginger took the opening to leave. At the door, he started to thank Bow again, but Bow waved him away, and with that blessing, Ginger was off down the hall so quickly he left behind his sign, still standing against the wall. Bow and I stared at the thing. The tall, neat letters seemed to shout over everything else in the understated room: "Say No to Vietnam."

CHAPTER 28

Bow invited me home for dinner that night, and after one of Mrs. Gehrke's overcooked pot roasts we walked in the sharp evening air down to the Opera House for the basketball game. Because the Lumberjacks were playing Kawnipi, most of the seats were filled, but the place had none of the frantic excitement of the game last March, the match that had climaxed with Ginger's shot. This season, neither team had much to crow about—the Lumberjacks had yet to win a game, and Kawnipi's former star, the great Slagle, was now a reserve on the freshman squad at Madison. Besides, the Packers were too close to the NFL championship for a basketball game to count for much.

Bow and I found seats down front and watched the teams warm up. When the announcer called out Ginger's name during player introductions, a few scattered boos punctured the normal burst of applause. There were more boos as play started, and he missed his first couple of shots. But after five minutes or so, he wove through the Kawnipi defense for a nifty layup, and the crowd yelled and whooped.

Still, the game was dull. Kawnipi moved ahead quickly, and the Lumberjacks' shots kept bouncing off the rim, clanking dismally, creating endless echoes that showcased the glorious acoustics of the building. At half-time, Bow grabbed his coat. "I think I've seen enough," he grumped. "You can stick around if you like."

I decided to go, too. In the lobby of the auditorium, as we were maneuvering through the knots of people, Pete Asmus suddenly stepped in front of Bow. "You're not leaving, are you, Counselor?" he asked, nodding at the overcoat clutched in Bow's arms. Beneath the prosecutor's pumpkin-bald head, shiny in the lights and heat, his smile looked like a gash.

"As a matter of fact, yes." Bow backed up half a step or so, startled at the intrusion. He and Asmus hadn't spoken since Bow had stomped out of Asmus's office. "But I've always got time for you, Pete," Bow said robustly, regaining his composure. "What brings you out to this worthless game?"

"Oh, it's not worthless to me. I find it quite, quite interesting, as a matter of fact."

"Not for the basketball."

"I'm interested in a lot of things." Asmus mugged a cagey smile.

We were being buffeted by the crowd, enough that the jostling would have broken up a casual greeting. But the two of them wanted to talk, and without saying anything, they executed a neat transition, gliding over to the relative calm of a corner near a window.

"What's this I hear about you giving up criminal law?" Asmus asked.

"I'd be a fool to do that," Bow told him. "Crime is a growth business."

The prosecutor complimented him with a short laugh. The cold weather had been hard on Asmus's lips, and they cracked and flaked when he opened his mouth wide. We waited while he soothed them with his tongue. "So it's not true?" Asmus persisted.

"I'm handling Macy Cunningham's probate," Bow confided. "Beyond that . . ." He shrugged.

"You should be on the bench," Asmus pronounced. "That's where you belong."

Bow eyed him closely. Was something being dangled? "You probably have a lot to say about that," Bow said, challenging him.

Now it was the prosecutor's turn to shrug.

Bow said, "What's happened to your investigation of us?"

"It's coming along," Asmus said easily. "These things take time."

"We're getting a little impatient on this end."

"We're just gathering information." Asmus waited. "Your boy Fontenot wasn't too discreet."

"You can't believe what anyone down at Lovington tells you," Bow said.

Asmus's face lit up. "Whoa! I guess you *are* getting out of criminal law."

Bow regretted his remark. "I don't pay much attention to what a defendant says," he explained too earnestly. "I look at how their cases were treated."

Beyond Bow, through the crowd across the lobby, I suddenly caught a flash of familiar blond hair. Lucy pushed through a huddle of teenagers and came into full view. She was wrapped in a snug ski sweater, her long, thin legs in a pair of blue jeans. With her bobbing hair and her taut figure, she gave off a kind of sexual luster, and I got hit with a wave of wonder and regret. My stomach sank.

"Oh, well," Asmus was saying, "we all have our methods."

Lucy hadn't spotted me. She moved carefully through the crowd, as if she were looking for someone. She almost never came to basketball games and used to say that she hated them, that they took her back to high school. I waved. She brightened and waved back and started squeezing her way over.

Bow said to Asmus, "I suppose that was you booing Ginger when they introduced him."

"God, no. I wouldn't want to be accused of polluting the jury pool. Ha, ha, ha." Asmus threw his head back, and the gash of his mouth became a black circle. I'd never seen him so playful. "By the way," he added, once he'd made his point with his laugh, "he sure didn't do himself any favors with that demonstration this afternoon."

"He's just a kid."

"Sometimes," Asmus said.

Bow's right hand slipped into the pocket of his sports jacket. I sensed his fingers fussing along the edges of the Polaroid.

"And how's old Mrs. Hennepin doing?" Bow asked just as Lucy broke through the crowd and stepped beside me.

"Charlie," she said softly. "I thought I might run into you." She reached out and touched the back of my hand. The tips of her fingers felt moist.

Bow and Asmus were too intent on each other to notice her.

"What brings you out tonight?" I asked. Her eyes sparkled and welcomed, and I tried to hold her gaze. But my attention kept being pulled away by the fidgety movements of Bow's hand on the Polaroid.

Asmus was giving a little speech, saying that Mrs. Hennepin was a great old character, that she'd been living out on the edge of Bent Pine for half a century, that she knew more about the history of Franklin County than the folks at the historical society.

Bow listened patiently, then asked, "Does she still stand by her story?"

"I came with a couple of my girlfriends," Lucy told me. "They wanted to do something besides go to a bar."

So, where was her cop? I wondered.

Asmus fired up a shot of indignation at Bow's question. "Hell, yes, she stands by it," he barked. "She has no doubt about what she saw."

I knew I couldn't ask Lucy about the cop, not now; I was so distracted by the test of wits between Bow and Asmus that I could hardly make conversation. She saw me waver. The sparkle in her eyes dimmed. Still, I had to glance back at Bow's nervous hand. "How's work?" I finally blurted stupidly.

"The same," Lucy said coolly.

"I'm just not sure how reliable she is," Bow said with a pregnant drawl.

"Just try her," Asmus taunted.

Lucy looked from Bow to Asmus, studying them as a rebuke to me. Then she took a step back. "'Bye, Charlie," she said.

Bow's hand was cocked.

"No, wait," I said and reached out for her. But my arm flapped in the air. Lucy had disappeared into the crowd.

"Well, you see," Bow was saying, "Charlie here took some pictures." Slowly, he pulled out the Polaroid and handed it to Asmus.

The prosecutor squinted, studying the picture. Then he put on his reading glasses and stared some more. It took him several seconds to digest what he was seeing, but he was good—the playfulness had vanished, but he remained utterly opaque. He could have been examining someone's grocery list. "Doesn't mean a thing to me," he said finally, pushing the picture back at Bow's chest.

Bow wouldn't take it back. "She's a drunk, Pete. I'm surprised she didn't see Fontenot riding a pink elephant that night."

"That's just a cheap trick. You'd be a fool to go after a sweet old lady like that." Asmus kept jabbing the Polaroid into Bow's chest as if he could hurt him with it.

"Keep the picture, Pete. I've got others."

"You've got no center," Asmus told him. "No principles. All you can do is pick, pick, pick. Tear down. I couldn't live like you."

"Keep the picture, Pete."

Asmus finally pulled the Polaroid back. He crushed it in his hand and stuffed it into his pants pocket. "You've got a boy there who's out of control, and you want to fuck this sweet old lady just to save him." His tongue swept his tortured lips. He wanted to go on but thought better of it. Finally, he said, "You've lost me, Bow," and walked away.

Bow watched him burrow into the crowd. "Was that a mistake?" he asked me. "I was taking a risk, showing my hand like that."

"I think you did the right thing." I wanted to try to catch Lucy, but Bow wanted feedback.

"There's a chance I just steeled him," he said. "And what was that about the bench? Was he hinting at a bribe?"

"It sounded like it."

Half-time was ending. We could hear basketballs drumming on the stage as the teams warmed up again. People started filing back into the auditorium. At the door I saw Art Genter, that old Kawnipi forward, jabbering with a team of geezers. "Was that Lucy you were talking to?" Bow asked.

"Yes. I'd like to go catch up with her."

"Go ahead. I'm heading home anyway."

"You sure?" He looked weary again and frail. "Maybe I should get the car," I said.

"No, no, no." Bow waved me off. "Go find her."

I pushed my way into the auditorium. The game hadn't resumed yet, so people were standing in the aisles and milling about. No sign of Lucy. I ran up the stairs to the balcony, where the freshmen and sophomores liked to sit. From the front railing, I could look down over most of the audience. Still no sign of her.

Back in the lobby, I saw Peg Lowden, one of her friends. "She just left," Peg told me, pursing her lips to stamp her disgust. "Abandoned us after we'd planned this night out for a week. She said she couldn't stand to watch more basketball."

I scrambled down the stairway to the ground floor and then pushed through the doors to the outside. Main Street in front of the Opera House was empty. Snowflakes drifted through the cones of light beneath the street lamps. Down the block, where Summer Street climbed up the Bluff, a lone, hunched figure leaned into the hill, dragging a leg, moving so slowly the motion could hardly be called walking.

I sat down on the Opera House steps. The cold concrete came as a welcome punishment. What had Ginger said once? *It's so easy to make a mistake. The moments that matter are so slippery, so uncertain.* I'd spent months, years, weighing an abstraction, trying to decide if I was for or against the war, and then when a real choice came, a choice that counted for me, it passed in seconds. Now Lucy was gone, probably back with her cop.

The snowflakes drifted down lazily, big, round clumps the size of dimes. They'd be gone by tomorrow. The temperature was pushing up. We'd have fog tonight, maybe rain. Then more cold and snow the beginning of the week. More weather. Endless. The frigid concrete felt like a dagger up my ass.

After about ten minutes, Fred Cozad, the old guy who ran the box office, shouldered open the big wood door and tossed a cigarette outside onto the sidewalk. "Charlie?" he said, surprised to see me. "Charlie, you drunk?"

"No, just sitting."

"Well, come on in. The game's getting hot. Bow's boy is leading the Lumberjacks back."

"Bow's boy?"

"You know, Ginger Piper."

"Ahhh." I nodded numbly and followed him inside.

Bow phoned me at the office late the next day. He was at home, watching the Packers game on television. One of Bow's neighbors from his property up north had called with the news: Mrs. Hennepin was dead. An ice fisherman looking to buy bait had found her that morning in her trailer. Her body was frozen solid. She'd died during the arctic front, but they didn't know whether the cold had killed her or she'd just passed away of natural causes. "I'm surprised Pete didn't think about that," Bow mused. "He could have put her up in a motel somewhere. She was awful vulnerable out there."

I asked what this would do to Ginger's defense.

Bow paused. "I guess it's gotta help."

In the background, through the telephone, the TV announcers were screaming. The Pack was on the move. Bow asked what had happened in the basketball game the night before. I told him that the Lumberjacks had actually come back to win the game in overtime.

"No shit," he said. "And Ginger?"

"He scored the Lumberjacks' last eight points."

Through the telephone, the announcers were still shouting. Bow hung up without saying good-bye.

CHAPTER 29

I t didn't take long for Pete Asmus to get back in touch. Late Tuesday afternoon he called Bow's office with an offer: He'd refer the matter to the juvenile authorities. Ginger would have to admit to a crime—probably something to do with the contraband—but Asmus wouldn't push for a stiff sentence; Ginger could probably get away with weekends at the youth facility at Bartlett. And under the rules of the juvenile court, the case would be sealed; if Ginger stayed out of trouble, the whole thing would eventually be expunged from the records.

"He sounded pretty matter-of-fact about it," Bow told me after hanging up the phone. "He wants me to come up on Thursday to sign off on the deal. Christmas Eve. I bet he wants to get this whole thing out of the way over the holidays, when no one is paying attention." Bow was slumped in his chair, his arms dangling at his sides. He'd been expecting this call, but now his relief had taken all the starch out of him. "Anyway, it's the perfect deal for Pete," he continued. "No one can complain that he didn't get a scalp, and yet no one will know what really happened since it's all under seal."

"Do you think Ginger will take it?" I asked.

Bow looked at me as if he hadn't considered any other possibility. "It amounts to nothing," he said. "He'd be crazy if he didn't."

"And what about you?" I asked. "Are you off the hook now?"

"Asmus never had anything on me," Bow said solemnly. "That was just part of his game."

"Some game. He's slandered you all over the state."

"I'm still here, aren't I?"

"Yeah, but the best criminal appeals lawyer in Wisconsin is now doing trusts-and-estates law."

Bow's eyes narrowed, his brow forming a thick, Neanderthal ridge. For all the traumas of the last few months, he couldn't bring himself to admit that he'd let Pete Asmus influence his fate. "That has nothing to do with this," he insisted irritably. "I needed a change. Life goes on." He wiggled his way back up in his chair, reestablishing his lawyerly stiff back. Then he punished me for my affront. "You should think about a change, too, Charlie. No man should do the same thing for ten, twenty years running. Look what happened to our fathers. Sometimes you've just got to change direction."

I told him I couldn't argue with that, but the remark stung. He was right about needing change, but where did that leave me? I'd dedicated ten years to Bow, I'd centered my life on him. I wasn't like Bill Addy, who could tuck a box of ashes under his arm and head into the sunset, relaxed in his sense of completion, his earned right to slide. Nothing for me felt finished, nothing felt settled. Ever since Ginger had appeared on the scene, Bow had been making remarks, hinting that I should move on. But where was I to go?

Later that night, after Bow had headed home, I violated my rule about drinking alone in his office, polishing off half of Bow's new bottle of Chivas Regal, retaliating, brooding.

The next morning, Bow greeted me as if nothing had happened. With the sun glaring off a few inches of new snow, we drove ten or so miles out Route 21, then a short way north on Wendell Road into a scrub-pine forest. I had warned Bow that the Piper house was meager; in fact, the place looked slightly better than I remembered. Since my visit to collect a debt ten years before, Piper had covered the tar-paper walls with wood siding and painted the boards barnyard red, though the color had now started to fade. The siding must have improved the house's insulation, because the foundation was no longer wrapped in bales of straw. At the north end of the house, Piper had added a wood-burning stove with an awkward metal chimney that jutted ten feet or so past the roof peak, high enough to cool falling sparks and diminish the risk of fire. For a moment, Bow and I sat in the car and watched the chimney cough out clouds of heavy gray smoke. "They're burning pine," Bow muttered, grasping for a neutral observation. Even with my warning, he wasn't prepared for the shabbiness of the place.

Ginger had seen us pull up, and he ran out without a coat to greet us. "Something big must be up to get a visit from you two," he said, hugging himself against the cold. "My dad's not here," he added as he led us inside. Despite the sun, the house was shadowed and gloomy. The air held a faint gamy odor. Ginger dropped our coats onto a high-backed chair already draped with garments and took us into the living room. A patchy blue sofa sat in front of the wood-burning stove, and a few plain chairs and a bureau were pressed against the walls, as if pushed there by centrifugal force. A Christmas tree, no taller than Ginger, stood naked in the corner farthest from the stove. Ginger apologized for its appearance. "I was about to hang some ornaments," he explained. "We're late getting started this year."

We'd just sat down when outside a dog erupted in high-pitched yapping. Ginger ran to a small window. "Oh, God, there's Dad," he said. I could hear Piper's angry shouts railing against the racket from the dog. We threw on our coats and followed Ginger back into the cold.

Behind the house, Piper was approaching along a rutted trail that sliced through the pine woods. He had a rope slung over his shoulder, and he was dragging something heavy. An incensed yellow mutt—a runty animal with collie blood—kept nipping at the load. Every few feet, Piper stopped and screamed at the dog, waving his arms furiously. The animal would retreat a few steps but always returned to the pursuit. As they drew closer, I saw that Piper's rope circled the neck of a young deer, recently dead, its slumped body steaming lightly in the cold as if the last traces of life were drifting away. Someone—almost certainly Piper—had crammed snow into the bullet hole behind the shoulder, probably to stanch the bleeding, to avoid leaving a crimson trail.

The dog wouldn't shut up. Ginger hurled a stick, which skidded past its target, kicking up snow. The animal fled into the trees, then stopped abruptly to yap some more from a safe distance.

"Look who's here," said Ginger to his dad, as if Piper had somehow missed Bow and me. Piper didn't pause. His back bent under the load, puffing clouds of frosty breath, he trudged toward a shed behind the house, pulling the deer past our feet. It was an underage buck. Hunting season had ended a month before.

"Where'd you get the deer?" Ginger asked, pressing against his father's silence.

"Found it," Piper said over his shoulder. Dressed in a long brown hunting jacket and with his lean, sinewy body, Piper looked like a deer himself.

We fell in behind him as he hauled his load the last few feet to the front of the shed. Finally, he dropped the rope and straightened up, carefully stretching out his back. "Someone shot it, and it must have wandered away to die," he explained. "I found it back there about a mile."

For all the unlikeliness of the story, Piper wasn't carrying a rifle. If he was the shooter, as I suspected, I couldn't explain why he hadn't brought the rifle back from the woods with him.

The nervy mutt had slinked up to the corner of the house and let loose a fresh barrage of barking. This time Ginger clocked it in the side with a small rock. With a yelp the beast rocketed off through the woods. "The neighbor's pet," Ginger said. "A real pest."

Piper strung up the deer in the shed, looping the rope over a low rafter and tying the end to a metal hook. With its neck stretched out, the animal's soft, moist tongue wedged out of its mouth. The antlers were nubby stumps. The deer couldn't have been more than nine months old. Bow stood close and examined the bullet hole. "One shot," he said. "Didn't take much to bring down this child."

"I thought I heard some shooting out back earlier this morning," Ginger offered. "We get hunters in the woods here all winter."

Piper went about his business, gathering tools—several knives, a small hacksaw, and a shiny hatchet. He would have dressed the deer right then, as we all stood around, but Ginger correctly surmised that Bow needed to discuss something. So Piper reluctantly put down a knife, and we trooped back into the house. Bow and I sank into the sofa. Ginger and his father pulled up chairs. The four of us made a small circle around the woodstove, though Piper's icy reserve sucked all the warmth out of the situation.

Bow got right to the point. The state's best witness had died; Asmus's case was obviously in jeopardy. He could still prosecute, but without a fresh break, it would be harder now. He was offering up the juvenile-court deal as a way to resolve the matter, a compromise of sorts. Bow tried not to oversell the arrangement, but he indicated clearly that he thought it was a good deal. Ginger listened anxiously, slowly edging forward on his chair. Watching his face tighten, his eyes ratchet down in concentration, I knew he wouldn't go for it.

"You mean," he asked when Bow had finished, "I'm going to have to admit I did something?"

"In juvenile matters, there's got to be an underlying crime," Bow explained patiently. "You're acknowledging responsibility. We can draft the arrangement so the acknowledgment is of something minor."

"But I didn't do anything."

"Well, you did. You smuggled contraband—the cigarettes, the Ex-Lax." Bow was working to stay measured.

"But you yourself said that was nothing."

"It's obviously *something*."

Ginger glanced at his father, then at me. "Help me out here, Charlie," he said, so panicked that he imagined I would disagree with Bow.

I shook my head. "I can't."

Bow tried again. "Look," he said. "If you turn this down, Asmus will probably go ahead with the prosecution. He can't just let it go. We could wait until he charges you and see what he's got, but then we'd lose this offer. And I know he's got *something*. He's a good lawyer. There'll be a trial. He'll treat you as an adult. He'll rake you over the coals. You'll lose months. And even if you're acquitted, which is uncertain, there will always be a stigma. A huge, splashy public record will follow you around forever. The beauty of the juvenile court is it will all disappear. Poof!" Bow's thick hands fluttered in the air, and Piper winced, as if he'd been startled by a pheasant taking flight. "By the end of next summer, it will be as if nothing had happened."

"Except that I'll have admitted that something happened that didn't," Ginger stubbornly insisted.

"But no one will know," Bow said.

"Of course they'll know. You can't keep anything secret around here."

It occurred to me that Ginger enjoyed the prospect of a trial, a chance to hold the town's attention and spout his views.

"Can I smoke a cigar?" Bow asked, looking to Piper. Without waiting for an answer, Bow started unwrapping a pricey Dunhill.

Ginger continued, "This will make you look bad, too."

Lighting up, Bow blew huge mouthfuls of cigar smoke around his head. Suddenly, the air belonged to him. "I'm too old to care about that," he told Ginger. "I'm never gonna run for office. I can't bother with what people think. Besides, everybody's got all sorts of crap mixed up in their past. This just qualifies as more of the crap."

Bow's crude logic stirred Piper. "What about the punishment?" he asked.

"What about it?"

"When you're a juvenile they can hold you until you're twenty-one," Piper said. "Ginger's only seventeen. That's four years."

Bow hesitated, slowed for a moment by Piper's fluency with the law. "I tell you, Asmus doesn't care," he said finally. "He just wants to be able to close the case. When we talked, he mentioned weekends next summer at Bartlett, something like that. We can work it out, but whatever it is, it won't be like getting sent away to an adult prison."

"But it's up to the judge, not Asmus," Piper persisted.

"The judge will go along with the prosecutor's recommendation, I assure you."

Piper absorbed this information without registering a reaction, then swiveled to face his son. "Take the deal," he said.

Ginger stared at the floor, rubbing his hands against his blue-jeaned thighs. "No."

The father didn't move, but he seemed to be churning through this defiance. I worried about how he'd respond, but he only repeated, "I think you should take it."

"I can't."

The room lapsed into a kind of stasis, the frustration of the adults equaling the misery of the boy. Nothing moved but the clouds of prickly cigar smoke circling in the drafts just over our heads. It's astounding, really, the level of unseen action ignited by a stove in a cold room. Bow tried one last time. "Look," he said. "This whole thing has been a terrible distraction. What's important is to get it behind you, to get on with your life."

"You mean, you want to get on with *your* life," Ginger interjected.

Bow blinked. The bad side of his face throbbed. In all his years of lawyering and conflict, he'd always had the bolstering advantage of righteousness. No one had ever accused him of selling out.

Ginger kept rubbing his hands on his thighs. He looked as if he were about to fly out of his chair. "I thought you were *defending* me." The word came out as a moan.

"I am, if you'd just think it through," Bow said gently. "I have no hidden agenda here. I'm just trying to give you the best advice I can, based on my experience."

"I know you are," said Ginger, "it's just that I *know* I can beat this thing, I just feel it. And so to give in, to have to go around admitting and apologizing . . . I'm too young for that, do you know what I mean?"

Bow forced the corners of his mouth up, creating an overbroad, clownish smile. "You're too young and I'm too old. How did we end up together?" He looked at me, as if I'd appreciate the paradox.

There was another long silence, broken finally by Piper, his voice mournfully slow. "I think you should listen to your lawyer, son."

"No, no, that's all right," Bow said in a kind of resigned singsong, a voice I'd never heard from him. Somewhere in the aftermath of Ginger's intransigence and the boy's soft insult, Bow had again decided to ignore his own good judgment. "It's Ginger's call. He's the client, ha, ha." The term suddenly struck Bow as funny applied to the jittery teenager sitting on the front edge of his chair. "It's his life," Bow continued, looking at Ginger. "I'll tell Asmus no deal."

The room deflated. Ginger was too startled by Bow's capitulation even to say thanks. Bow pushed himself off the sofa. He wanted to get out of there.

Away from the stove, the air turned chilly. The house leaked heat. Our coats by the door still held the cold. Bow wrapped his scarf around his neck, then paused to consider a family photograph hanging in a wood frame on the wall. The Woolworth in town used to bring a photographer in on Wednesday afternoons, and this was one of those quick color portraits, already faded. Ginger's mother and sister were sitting on a small bench in the makeshift studio, with Ginger standing stiffly beside them.

"That was just before my mother died," Ginger said. "She saw an ad in the paper and took us in. Then we didn't get the photo back until after the funeral."

"A pretty woman," offered Bow from behind his scarf.

Actually, she looked hollowed and worn, as I'd remembered her. Death couldn't have come as a surprise. Perhaps because the mother was so dour, the photographer had missed Ginger's spark. The boy was looking away from the camera, his eyes slightly blurred as if he'd been caught in a blink. But the picture had an odd effect: With the awkward composition drifting off in different directions, your eyes were drawn to Ginger's tiny right hand, which rested supportively on his mother's shoulder.

Bow noticed it, too. "Your hand's so *little*," he enthused, and immediately he was embarrassed.

Now Ginger placed that hand on Bow's sleeve. "You've done so much for me," Ginger said. "How can I ever thank you?"

With his wrap of scarf and his wide black overcoat specially tailored for his girth, Bow looked obscenely fecund, like a tropical fruit that's grown overripe and spoiled. He shook his head. "You can thank me by living up to your potential," he said as he pushed out the door.

The remark was oddly moralistic for Bow, and probably just an unconsidered afterthought, nothing more than the echo of an admonition Bow's father had dropped on him long ago. But as I followed Bow into the cold, Ginger's face had knotted and twisted in pain. I felt an immediate surge of sympathy, a connection—both of us wounded in the last twenty-four hours in encounters with Bow's sharp tongue.

CHAPTER 30

B y the time Bow and I got back to Laroque from Ginger's house, the town was already starting to dress up for the Christmas Revels, the holiday choir festival held every year. Sawhorse barricades closed off Main Street downtown, and in the plaza in front of the Opera House workers and high school kids were building a tower of old, oil-soaked railroad ties for a bonfire. Bow and I sat in a rare Laroque traffic jam before working our way down a side street and finally finding parking several blocks east on River Road. "Your father is still causing trouble," groused Bow as we hiked our way back to the Bank Building.

The Christmas Revels had been my father's idea, and, in fact, it represented one of his great successes. A few years after arriving in Laroque, he hit upon the idea of inviting church choirs in the area to participate in a caroling competition; looking to drum up an audience for his shows, he wrapped the concert around assorted skits and vaudeville routines, all staged on the floodlit steps of the Opera House. Only someone new to Wisconsin and its winters would dare hold a spectacle outdoors at night in December, but my father's ignorance paid off handily. From the first year on, thousands of people turned out, entire families wrapped in blankets and toting folding chairs, filling the plaza and overflowing into Veterans' Park. The bonfire provided modest heat, and street vendors sold cups of glogg, a Scandinavian concoction of hot spiced wine prepared in huge, simmering vats. Over the years, the theatrical elements faded from the show, but the caroling competition was still going strong through the late sixties.

Bow never liked the Revels. His bad leg stiffened with long stretches in the cold, and he was bored by the choir music, which was inescapably amplified throughout downtown Laroque. Indeed, nothing much about Christmas interested him—hardly surprising, given that he had few sentimental memories from childhood and no family with which to celebrate. That afternoon, he dropped into one of his quiet spells, reading at his desk while the sounds of the workmen outside testing the amplification system rattled through the office. Toward the end of the day, Bow perked up enough to make arrangements with me for next morning's trip to Waterville to give the bad news to Pete Asmus. Then he went home, vowing to drown out the carols by turning up the volume on his television.

I bedded down in Bow's office that night—I was supposed to pick him up at seven the next morning—but I lay awake on the sofa listening to the carols rolling through the cool air, the voices blending sweetly in the distance. I was still reeling from Bow's hard remark the day before, and, besides, the music churned memories—the days leading to the Revels once provided rare periods of good cheer in our house. My mother had been a seventeen-year-old blond soprano for the Benfield Methodist Church when she met my father at the first concert, and though, God knows, she later had every reason to regret the encounter, the Revels remained the high point of her year for the rest of her life. Even after she'd dropped out of the choir, worn out by my father's badgering disdain for organized religion, she always attended the concert, standing for the full two or three hours, buttoned into her long winter coat and singing along in a whisper. A few weeks before my father died, and long after he'd been erased from the Revels operation, she took him to the annual spectacle just to remind him what he'd created. He was frail and only fitfully lucid, but she rented a wheelchair and covered him with blankets. I wasn't much help to her in those days, but I sobered up enough to push his wheelchair from our house on Anderson Avenue down Main Street to the Opera House. We planted ourselves on the pavement close to the steps, Mother standing on one side of the wheelchair and me on the other. After an hour or so of the singing, my father started asking in a thin, little-boy voice, "Can we go home now? Can we go home?" "Hush," Mother told him, again and again. "Hush." And we stayed for the entire concert. Afterward, at home, when Mother leaned over to unwrap his blankets, my father creaked forward and with his dry, papery lips startled her with a peck on the cheek.

Now I thrashed and fidgeted on the spongy sofa. Lucy was probably down there, I thought, maybe with her cop, maybe not. She and I had enjoyed the Revels together a few times. She wasn't much of a drinker, but she loved the wine-soaked raisins that sank to the bottom of the cups of glogg. We'd fish around with our fingers to pull them out and then pop them in each other's mouth. Once, we'd got so warmed and sloppy from the raisins that we'd had to abandon the concert early for a fast, rowdy session in Bow's office, pumping away while the rat-ta-tat of "The Little Drummer Boy" tapped against the windowpane. I wondered if Lucy and her cop fed each other that way— the Sacrament of the Raisins, we'd called it. The thought burned, and I thrashed some more. At least they wouldn't be able to dash to a neighboring building to finish it off. Or would they? He was a cop. He probably had keys to just about anywhere.

Falling asleep was hopeless, at least while the singing was going on. Finally, I put on an extra pair of socks as a small measure of protection against the cold and headed down to the street.

From a distance, the bonfire threw an orange glow over downtown, but at the center of the event, the floodlit brightness of the Opera House steps suggested the harsh lighting of a movie scene. One of the bigger choirs, four rows deep and ten or so people wide, had embarked on an ambitious medley of old English carols, most of them completely unfamiliar. I drifted around the edges of the crowd, half hoping to catch a glimpse of Lucy, half dreading what I'd see. Away from the floodlights, faces were hard to read in the throbbing glow of the bonfire. Suddenly, a heavy hand on my shoulder turned me around, and I was staring into a gorge of flesh and ivory, Archie

Nye's smiling mouth. "How you doin', Charlie?" he trilled. He had a glass of glogg in his left hand, and his face had a warm, alcohol blush. "Where's Mr. Epps and the boy?"

"Bow's at home, and I don't know about Ginger."

"I hope they're preparing their de-fense," Archie said. His emphasis on the first syllable seemed designed to give the word a special significance.

"Why's that?" I asked.

"Now, don't play dumb, Charlie. That may work with them rich guys, but you and me are different." Behind his lips, those huge rows of teeth reflected the firelight.

"The whole thing is about wrapped up," I told him. "Bow's got it under control."

"I hope so. He's a good man. I'd hate to see that boy, you know, lead him astray." Archie raised his thick, black eyebrows, hinting he had secrets.

I waited, daring him. He took a swig of glogg, then plunged on. "I knew his father, you know. Errol Piper. I didn't realize until later, after we'd run into you up at the lake. A mean son-of-a-bitch." Archie shook his head gravely. "I didn't like that man."

"The boy's not like that."

"Same blood," said Archie.

We were surrounded by revelers, families, mostly, and Archie was talking loud to be heard over the music. "How's your buddy Bill LaSoeur?" I asked, changing the subject.

Archie's dark eyes widened. "You didn't hear?"

"No."

"Sad story. Sad, sad story." Archie glanced around, suddenly self-conscious about being overheard. Lowering his voice, he said, "A couple of months ago, he was out fishing in the Agnes, and he must have fallen asleep or something, because he drifted right over the Allen Dam and drowned."

"You're kidding." The Allen Dam was a flood-control device—only about five feet high, but the water around it could be treacherous.

"They said he was stone drunk, but I don't believe it; Bill liked to fish too much. It was a week before they found the body. They never did find the rowboat."

I wondered suddenly if that had been LaSoeur's boat that Ox and I had chased in the river.

"It's easy to tell lies about a dead man," said Archie, resenting the defamation of his friend. He threw his head back and poured the last of the glogg down his throat. A handful of bloated raisins dropped into the gorge, and he chewed on them thoughtfully. "Say," he ventured after a few seconds, "I'm looking for a new partner next spring. You and me could do all right together, Charlie."

"Ahh . . ." In an odd way, I was flattered.

"You still work up at the Spirit Light, right?" he asked.

"Occasionally."

"Well, we could do much better on our own. A whole hell of a lot better." He was getting excited.

"I mostly work for Mr. Epps." A slight, shivery spasm, like a small fish, slid from the back of my head to my stomach. Who knew what would happen with Bow and me?

Archie stepped back to look me over. "Yeah, well, we'll see how that turns out," he said, referring to the Fontenot matter.

"I think you better find someone else."

"Think about it," Archie urged cheerfully. He stared at his empty cup. "You want to get some glogg, man?"

I told him I wasn't drinking. He looked at me quizzically. "Right, right," he said slowly. "Well, I'm gonna get a refill." He slapped me on the shoulder. "You take care, now, and think about what I said. We could make some good money."

"Right." I watched him wander off. People stepped aside as he approached.

On the Opera House steps, the big choir had finished and was neatly filing off. Marcus Laney had my father's old job at the microphone, emceeing the event, offering congratulations and patter and introducing the groups. He managed to sound buoyant, raising his lugubrious broadcasting voice half an octave or so. I leaned against the trunk of a maple tree in Veterans' Park, waiting to let Archie get some distance away before moving on myself. In front, the crowd parted slightly, and then Lucy appeared, beaming and striding toward me on her long, athletic legs.

She came up and nuzzled me on the cheek, and I could smell the sweet, cinnamon fragrance of glogg on her breath. "I was waiting for Archie to leave," she told me.

"I was afraid he wasn't going to."

"You two looked pretty intimate," she teased. "I didn't know you and Archie were such good friends."

She was wearing a maroon ski parka, something new, and tight, faded blue jeans. Tufts of her blond hair pushed out beneath a wool navy cap, the same kind of cap Ginger wore. I'd seen pictures of protesters down at Madison in those caps, too. Was it fashion or a uniform? "What in God's name were you talking about?" Lucy pressed.

"He asked me to be his partner."

She stroked my arm. "Now, *that's* a nice offer," she said.

The latest choir—a smaller, less polished group than its predecessor—had returned to the familiar "I Saw Three Ships." As the refrain built up, the crowd quieted. Lucy joined me, leaning against the trunk of the tree. After a minute or so, I put my arm around her shoulder. I wondered if she'd object, but she stayed pressed against my side, looking ahead toward the Opera House. In the floodlights and the smoke from the bonfires, the gorgeous old relic stretched up above the crowd like a cathedral. It surprised me—my pleasure in being with Lucy felt so uncomplicated.

"Does it make you think of your father?" she asked after a few minutes. I knew she was talking about the Revels.

"And my mother," I said.

"That's good."

Lucy eased her head onto my shoulder. A soprano and tenor, remarkably skilled, soloed back and forth through "The Holly and the Ivy."

In the pause between songs, I concentrated on erasing all inflection from my voice and asked, "How are you and your friend the cop getting on these days?"

She lifted her head to look at me. "We aren't seeing each other right now."

"What happened?"

She sank back to my shoulder. "Oh, you know how it is. Some people just aren't a good fit." Her tone of voice suggested she didn't want to talk about it. A few seconds later she said, "I heard you and Bow were going through a bit of a bad patch."

She said it casually, as if one thought naturally followed the other, and I thought then, with a clarity that weakened me for a moment, how utterly misguided I'd been about myself.

"Bow's just changing his practice a little, getting out of criminal law and into trusts and estates, that sort of thing," I said, babbling. The raw bark of the maple pressed into my back. My arm felt dead on her shoulder.

"Maybe he can do my will," Lucy said softly, sounding as if she now wanted to drop this subject, too.

We stood together for a few more minutes. When the choirs changed, Lucy said, "I should get back to my friends. They'll think I abandoned them again." She stepped back, then she put her mittened hand flat against my stomach as if she were pushing me away. In fact, she was intending just the opposite. "I'm going down to Madison tomorrow to spend Christmas with my sister," she said. "Why don't you come along? It's her and her husband and their new baby, and they've got a big new house with a guest room, so we'll never even hear the baby at night. It'll be fun."

As I ran the calculation in my head—Bow was counting on me to drive him to his meeting with Pete Asmus in the morning—I could see from her face that I'd squandered her spontaneity and already lost her. Another slippery moment. "Oh, never mind," she said quickly. "It probably wouldn't work." She dropped her hand and backed away.

"Maybe I can drive down in the afternoon," I offered.

She looked at me with exasperation. "It's Christmas *Eve.*"

"I promised . . . my job . . ."

"Merry Christmas, Charlie." She wheeled and crashed into a thick man in a huge down coat, then bounced from him into his chunky wife. Lucy kept going, in her hurry to get away ricocheting like a pinball through the crowd, until I lost sight of her.

CHAPTER 31

Marcus Laney's baritone echoed through the amplification system. "While we've got a short break," he was saying as the next choir filed onto the Opera House steps, "let's take a moment here to remember our boys in Vietnam. Right now, where they are, it's damp, filthy, and bug infested. They're probably lonely right now, and miserable and scared. Yet they're putting their lives on the line for us. Please join me in a moment of silence for our boys in Vietnam." Heads bowed all across Main Street; the sea of people crowding the plaza sank by six inches. Over the sudden stillness, the bonfire crackled and spit, the oil-soaked ties firing artillery bursts of sparks into the sky. It occurred to me: Maybe Vietnam is an answer for me. Get myself out of here. Just sign up. Who cares if I'm for or against the war? Make a change, as Bow said. Start over.

Without waiting for Laney's little ceremony to end, I slipped over and planted myself at the back of the line snaking up to the glogg table. Fifteen or so people stood waiting to buy a drink, all of them now with their chins buried in their chests. The two men behind the table selling the stuff were also frozen in respect. Getting a drink was going to take forever. In my father's day, they knew how to keep things moving.

"Thank you all, and thank you, boys," Laney rumbled at last, and the plaza returned to life. Ox wandered by, his tent of a coat unbuttoned down the front, a full cup of glogg in each bare hand. "Charlie!" he cried. "I didn't think you liked glogg."

"I usually don't."

He saw me eyeing his double-fisted providence. "I'd give you one, but I'm bringing it to Eddie Belcher," he explained apologetically. "We got a bench in the back of the park. Why don't you come on back when you get yours?"

I told him I'd see how things went. Ox's round, flat face had turned almost scarlet with the cold and the alcohol. Without thinking, I asked him, "Do you have any idea—how old is too old to join the army?"

A ridge of deep lines creased his forehead, and his lower lip popped out. It was a neutral enough question, but Ox's battered brain still made connections. Maybe it made them better because it was battered. "You're not thinking of joining the army, are you?"

"Not really. I was just wondering."

"'Cause that would be pretty crazy. Ha, ha." The lines on his forehead melted. "I don't know," he went on. "I was too old for Korea."

"That was the draft. I meant, what about enlisting?"

Ox's eyes became two little blue dots. "You're too fucking old, Charlie. Besides, why would you want to get shot at?"

"Forget it." I realized I should never have brought it up. "It was just a thought." A stupid thought, but now Ox would never let go.

"A lot of guys are getting killed over there."

"I said forget it."

The glogg line crept forward. Ox walked backward, staying face-to-face with me. "A lot of guys are trying to get *out* of going to Vietnam. Why would you volunteer?"

"I wouldn't. I was just thinking out loud."

"You know what the worst thing is?" Ox was getting agitated. He wanted to gesticulate, but the drinks in his hands held him back. Still, the glogg sloshed over the tops of the cups. "The worst thing is they all look alike. How the hell do you tell who's the enemy and who's friendly? That's what I don't understand."

"Hadn't you better get that drink to Eddie?"

"We should just leave 'em alone. Let 'em settle it among themselves."

"Eddie."

"Yeah, right." Ox surveyed the mess he'd made. The red, sticky glogg was dripping from his hands like blood. "But don't you get any more dumb ideas."

"Don't worry."

Ox lumbered away. "And come on back when you get your drink," he called over his shoulder.

I was within ten people of the front of the line. Big, stainless-steel vats of glogg simmered over a long grill, churning up fragrant clouds of steam. The air reeked of cinnamon, too sweet, too thick. On the Opera House steps, another big choir ran through a medley of modern Christmas songs as syrupy as the glogg. My father would have insisted on the nineteenth century or earlier. None of this pop crap, tainting everything with its inane, jingly optimism. *Here comes Santa Claus, here comes Santa Claus, right down Santa Claus Lane.* I was starting to think like Bow.

"Hey, Charlie, what's up?" Ginger's soft voice came from behind me. He was standing in the blocked space between the glogg table and the line of customers, and for a moment I tried to figure out how he'd got there.

"Not much," I said, still slightly startled. "What are you up to?"

"Trying to keep busy." He seemed oddly isolated, a lone figure in the crowd. "I'm pretty jumpy, in fact. I can't stop thinking about Bow's meeting tomorrow with Mr. Asmus."

"I don't blame you. I'm surprised you're even in the mood to be out."

He glanced around. "Bow's not here, is he?"

"No."

"I don't see why I can't go along," Ginger said.

"That's not the way Asmus operates. Things are easier this way."

"But it's *my* life. You'd think I'd get the chance to participate."

"You'll get your chance."

Ginger had removed his cap, and he kneaded it now, worrying the coarse wool. "Listen," he said, stepping closer, "come with me. I want to show you something."

"Now?"

"You'll like this. It'll surprise you." His face, catching the glow of the bonfire, seemed lit from inside. "Come on, Charlie," he pleaded, "who else am I going to talk to?"

I caught a glimpse for a moment of the helplessness that had swept through his body, loosening all the joints, that day he'd fainted in the fetid prison. He leaned toward me, rising slightly on his toes, as if expecting me to catch him if he fell, and the thought struck that he'd come looking for me.

He took my hesitation for assent. "Great!" he said. "Let's go." Without glancing back, he scooted around the glogg table, then headed east, away from the crowd. I glanced down the stagnant line of people waiting for glogg. What the hell, I figured, Bow would probably want me to keep an eye on him.

I caught up with Ginger as he turned onto a side street toward the river. Halfway down the block, he cut into the dark alley behind the Opera House. The huge, brick bulk of the building stood between us and the concert. Ginger stopped in front of a battered metal door, braced open by a wedge of wood. Behind the door, concrete steps led to a long basement hall that skirted the boiler and service elevator and eventually opened into the cavernous storage room for sets and props. I knew the space well from my days of wandering the building while my father organized his shows. Years ago, the basement had been a shadowy, filthy maze.

"This way," Ginger said. He gave the door a yank and plunged in. The steps and the hallway were dark, though someone had propped lit flashlights against the wall at intervals, creating a trail of light. The path led past bolted doors and stacks of lumber and assorted junk. The air smelled just as I remembered from years ago, heavy with the odor of damp wood and paint. In the storage room, illuminated by a single, dying flashlight, dropcloths covering the piles of old props created dinosaur shapes against the walls. Once there'd been opera sets down here, even a Wagnerian mountain that I'd dreamed of climbing.

A skeletal spiraling staircase led two flights up, past the first-floor landing to the back of the stage, and a shaft of soft light flowed down over the rickety structure's thin metal steps. The air stirred with the throb of rock music coming from above: "The House of the Rising Sun," by The Animals. "Away we go," Ginger sang and bolted up the rattling stairway.

The climb was dizzying, round and round the spiraling steps. We emerged in the middle of a party, thirty or so people standing around, lounging in the flimsy folding chairs used by the basketball teams, dancing in stocking feet on the hardwood stage floor. Most of them were high school kids, Ginger's friends and teammates, but I recognized a few older faces, a couple of college students, a junior salesman out at the auto lot, even the mayor's nephew, who'd recently filled the latest opening for a mailman. Nobody there was anywhere near my age. A record player churned out the music, and an array of liquor bottles and snacks covered the scorer's table. Ginger disappeared into the crowd. A lone camp lantern cast a shadowy light.

"What do you think?" he asked, coming up behind me again. He'd shed his coat and grabbed a can of beer.

"Aren't you worried about being caught?"

"We do this every year. It's a tradition, the Alternative Revels." He studied my face. "I thought you'd be amused. I know how much this place means to you."

With my head still spinning from the climb up the stairway, and now the shadows and the rock music pounding, I couldn't get my thoughts straight.

"You want some scotch?" Ginger offered.

I stared at him.

"I found you in line to buy glogg," he said, as if to wave off any protestations.

"I better get out of here," I told him.

"Don't worry, the cops don't care. Besides, if they raid us, we can scatter in a second." He studied my discomfort and offered an inducement. "Do you want to say hello to Anna? I know she'd like to see you."

"Anna?"

"You know, Anna Sterritt. Macy's granddaughter. Come on." I let him lead me across the stage. As he swung by the scorer's table, he grabbed a bottle of scotch.

Anna was sitting with two other girls on the far side of the stage, almost in the dark. The three of them were drinking out of plastic cups. "Charlie!" she cried as if we were old friends. "Charlie, what fun." She motioned toward the two other girls. "Charlie Stuart, these are my friends Lauren and Kim." Next to Anna, with her dark elegance and poise, the two girls, both blondes, looked unmistakably like high school kids—not so much young as unshaped. "Charlie works for Mr. Epps, the lawyer," Anna explained.

"Oh, he scares me," bubbled one of the girls. "He looks so *weird*."

Anna came to her rescue. "I know what you mean. The first time I saw him I was seven or eight. He was just walking down the street, and you know how slowly he goes. And his face was all two-tone with that scar." She laughed. "And then everyone said he was the smartest man in Laroque."

"What's scary about that?" the other blonde asked.

"I think smart people *are* scary, don't you?" she said. "I mean, you never know what they're thinking."

"But you're smart, too," the girl offered.

"Oh, I'm smart, but not *really* smart, you know?" Anna's gaze drifted from me to Ginger. "Oh, well, we are what we are, right?" she said brightly.

Someone loved "The House of the Rising Sun." The song was playing for the fourth straight time. "Change that record!" Ginger called out uselessly. He noticed me ogling the bottle of scotch in his hand, and he pushed it toward me. Cutty Sark. Not my favorite, but I unscrewed the top and took a long drink. The two blondes made faces.

"Charlie's father used to be the director at the Opera House," Ginger said. "Charlie practically grew up in this building."

"We were just talking about how neat it is," Anna said. "Can you give us a tour?"

In the dim light, her face glowed with the prospect of adventure. In her own way, she was as captivating as Ginger. "There's not really that much to see," I said, fumbling. The slug of scotch had thickened my tongue.

"I brought a flashlight," she offered, digging around in her purse and pulling out a small, black cylinder.

Lauren and Kim announced they didn't want to go. "It's too dusty," said one. The other was going to dance. Ginger said he'd get another beer and catch up with us.

"So, it's you and me, Charlie," Anna said.

All right, I thought, I'll give her the tour and then clear out. Ginger was right about one thing—I did enjoy being in here. Wandering the Opera House backstage was like going home after many years. The viscera of the place hadn't changed much, even with the drop-off in theater productions. I showed Anna the mechanics of the stage— the thin, metal catwalk, cluttered with lights, high over our heads; the thicket of ropes that had once been used to raise and lower sets. In the back corner, my father had kept a flimsy metal typing table, his director's station during productions. I remembered him sitting there, notes spread out, frantically waving and pointing, repressing the urge to shout, as actors flitted on and off stage. He'd seemed so old to me then, but I did the calculations and realized that he was only in his late thirties—my age now as I pointed out his old haunts to Anna.

An opening on the side wall led down several steps to a plain corridor. "You'll enjoy this," I told Anna as I pushed open another door. The narrow beam of the flashlight picked up some chairs, a mirror, and a shiny table surface, but the effect I wanted was missing. I closed the door behind us and searched the wall until I found the light switch. Suddenly, the small space exploded in brightness. Light bounced around the white walls and jumped off the long mirror, which itself was surrounded by bare white bulbs, most of them still working. "God!" said Anna. She pitched slightly. The onslaught of light came like a wave.

"The women's dressing room," I told her.

Everything was padded and frilly—the simple chairs with their cushioned seats and backs, the dressing table with its pink skirt reaching almost to the floor. Even the mirror wore a band of fluffy cloth.

"It's like a little girl's bedroom," said Anna. She moved around absently, touching the frill, examining bottles of makeup, now dried and caked, still sitting on the table. "Can you imagine how much fun it must have been?"

"It wasn't always this lush," I told her. "My father had it decorated to impress an actress he was interested in." Martha Fanning, with startling red hair, who'd come to star in his production of *New Faces of Broadway* in the summer of 1940. She was a proper Catholic girl, taught in a Sacred Heart school, and the functional dressing room that had sufficed for years pinched her sensibilities. My father, smitten, would do anything for her.

Anna sank into a soft chaise longue and swatted at the cloud of dust that drifted up around her. "Did it have the desired effect?" she asked.

"He ran off to New York with her when the show ended. But it didn't last." That was during the endgame for his Opera House ventures.

Anna was thrilled. "What an exotic story," she gushed.

"Not so exotic when you are ten years old," I corrected, and immediately regretted the tone of self-pity. "You want a refill?" I asked, waving the bottle of Cutty Sark at her plastic cup.

She shook her head. "It's only Coke."

I settled into one of the dressing-table chairs and set the Cutty Sark bottle on the floor. Anna watched me with an amused aspect, as if she expected me to say something witty. She had Ginger's way of disregarding the formalities that normally stiffen conversation between people of different ages. Clumsily, I asked her what she was going to do with her inheritance from Macy.

She leaned back on the chaise longue and sighed. "There isn't *that* much money, you know. I mean, there's plenty, but not enough to set you up for life. Besides, I'll give some to my parents."

"What about college?"

"I don't know if I have the patience for college yet. I can go to the U of W, but maybe I'll travel instead."

"Where?"

"Ohhh, anywhere. New York. Paris. London. I feel like moving around. I've never been outside the state of Wisconsin."

"You're getting enough money to travel for a long, long time, if that's what you want." I felt like another drink of scotch, but I was self-conscious about swigging in front of her.

She sat up quickly. "Can I ask you something personal?" she said.

"Go ahead."

"How come you never got married?" She was flirting with me, but the question was serious.

"I'm not *that* old. Maybe I still will."

"You won't."

"How can you be so sure?"

Anna hugged her knees, rocking slightly. "You seem like someone who's looking for something besides a wife." She saw the dismay on my face and quickly added, "Mr. Epps, too," as if having his company would ease my plight.

"You certainly know a lot about us."

"I'm very intuitive," she said cheerfully. "It's my Chippewa side."

"Don't believe everything you intuit."

She smiled. "Also, Macy talked about you."

"You're kidding."

"Oh, she was very discreet," Anna reassured me. "She only told me things because I asked her. And because she had no one else to tell her secrets to." She paused. "Besides that idiot Bill Addy." Another pause. "Macy knew *everything*."

"What secrets?" I churned through my memory to anticipate how bad this could get.

"Don't worry," Anna said, laughing. "Macy adored Bow and you."

"I don't think she even noticed me."

"She told me about your father, too. She said he was a genius but impossible."

With the door closed, the dressing room felt cut off and adrift, a separate planet. I said, "We seem to have lost Ginger."

"He'll find us. He's very resourceful." I couldn't be sure if that was a compliment or an expression of mild irritation. She looked at me closely. "You know, he did it," she said evenly.

"Did it?"

"He smuggled in the knife. In his pant leg. You can't tell him I told you."

For a long moment, I stared at Anna. Her eyes were shining, and I felt almost addled by their glare. Finally, I reached for the Cutty Sark and took a deep swig. Outside the walls of the dressing room, voices bounced around the corridor.

"The night after the trooper was shot, he came to my house," Anna said. "He'd never dreamed it would end like that. He was desperate."

"Why'd he do it?"

"He thought Gary Fontenot had got a bad deal, and he saw it as a kind of protest. I don't know. I'm not even sure he could explain it. Later on, he knew he'd made a terrible mistake."

"He had."

"It was killing him that he'd let Bow down. He thought he'd dishonored Bow."

She was sitting with her legs crossed and her arms out at her sides, palms pressed down on the chaise longue, so cool in her manner that I wondered if I'd understood her correctly. Footsteps scuffled past the door. I asked, "Why are you telling me this?"

"You already knew, didn't you?"

With a bang, the door flew open. Ginger raced in, his face flushed. He hesitated, glancing from Anna to me. I guessed what he was about to say before he gasped it out: The cops had come. He grabbed Anna's hand and yanked her out of the room. A right turn would only take us back to the stage and the shouts of the cops and stragglers. To the left, the corridor disappeared into darkness. I pulled Anna's little flashlight out of my pocket and pushed my way past the two of them, headed left. Once I'd known this puzzle of halls and rooms like my own house. Now I led them past the door to my father's old office, through the small, open space that he'd used as a rehearsal room. When the Opera House was converted to a basketball arena, contractors had torn out the other side of the building and turned it into locker rooms and athletic offices. But this corridor was like an unexplored chamber of King Tut's tomb, dusty and untouched, a museum of the past. Beyond the rehearsal space, the corridor stretched along a big wardrobe closet and then, behind a door, concrete steps led to the ground floor. We were back in the basement maze, but another door with an inside lock opened onto the alley west of the building. I cracked the door; the alley was dark and empty. We slipped outside.

"That was great, Charlie!" crowed Ginger. "We never would have got out of there. You were fantastic."

I gave Anna her flashlight and pointed the two of them toward River Road. She put her hand on my arm. "Take care, Charlie," she said. Ginger gave her a tug, and the two of them ran off.

I waited a few seconds and then turned up the alley toward the front of the building. Marcus Laney's garbled voice bounced around the walls. The Revels was breaking up. Just before I stepped onto Main Street, Ernie Ostberg, a Laroque cop, swung around the corner and almost ran into me.

"Jesus!" he said, startled. "Sorry, Charlie."

"That's okay."

"What were you doing back there, taking a pee?" Ernie was an old guy, within a few years of retirement. He was happy to make up excuses for people.

"Yeah."

"Some kids broke into the Opera House," Ernie said. "You didn't see anyone run out this way, did you?"

"Nope."

"Well, you take care now. Merry Christmas." He pointed his big flashlight down the alley and headed off behind the beam.

In the plaza, the crowd was dispersing, though circles of the hearty had gathered around the bonfire. There'd be a vigil for another hour or so, celebrants waiting for the burning tower to collapse in a glorious eruption of sparks and applause. The ground was littered with crushed plastic cups, the sort of casual mess that would have horrified Laroque in the old days. At Summer Street I turned up to the Bluff, and in ten minutes I was at Bow's door. Aside from the burning porch light, the house was dark. It was after ten and Bow was probably in bed, probably asleep. Still, I pushed on the doorbell, setting off chimes. The hike up the hill had left me panting and impatient. When Bow didn't respond, I kept pushing, eventually overstimulating the chimes, until they got confused and lost their melody, clanking out an irritating cacophony. After two or three minutes, lights in the house popped on and soon Bow flung open the door. "What the hell?" he growled. The chimes took several seconds to calm themselves. "Jesus Christ, Charlie," he barked over the noise.

Countless times I'd slept in a tent with Bow, glimpsed him in his underwear and even naked, but seeing him now, in a tattered, brown velour bathrobe over a pair of thin, flesh-colored pajamas, his white, veiny feet pushed into a pair of expensive leather slippers, I felt acutely invasive, as if I'd caught him in some intimate, private act. A frigid drop of sweat wriggled down the middle of my chest.

"What the fuck is going on?" he demanded.

"I need to talk to you about Ginger," I said. "I found something out."

I expected him to invite me in, but he stood planted in the open doorway, the warm air spilling out of his house. "Well?"

I told him about the party at the Opera House and what Anna had said. He listened, his face concentrated into something between irritation and concern. The expression didn't change when I got to the end of my account. He seemed to expect more. Finally, he said, "Well, what the hell am I supposed to do with that?"

"I thought you'd want to know before you went out on a limb for him with Asmus." As an investigator, I was used to dumping facts in Bow's lap. It was up to him to figure out how to use them.

"So some high school girl at a fucked-up party claims he told her he did it. Has she told anybody else?"

"I'm sure not."

"Why'd she tell you?"

"Maybe she wanted to get a message to you."

Bow had been mad at me before, but now it was as if a curtain had dropped behind his eyes.

"I think Ginger knew she was going to tell me," I added weakly.

Bow took a step over the threshold. "Listen," he said, pressing up close. The frosted air squirted out of his mouth in tight little clouds. "Ginger is my client. He says he didn't do it. He's been saying that all along, and I've been choosing to believe him. That's what lawyers do: They work for their clients. And they don't get all bent out of shape because some chippie at a party starts spouting nonsense."

My instinct was to defend Anna, but I barely started stammering something out when he interrupted me. "You never liked that boy, but I do, and I'm going to tell you something: I'm going to do everything I can to save him." Bow stopped and pulled back. He considered my face. "You've been drinking," he said.

"I had a couple drinks." I felt like one of his clients, trying to explain away a felony.

"You never have just 'a couple of drinks.'" His voice was mocking.

"I didn't have time for more," I said honestly.

He wrapped his robe tighter across his chest. For the first time he seemed to notice that he was standing outside in pajamas and slippers, and he stepped back into the relative warmth of the doorway. "Just make sure you're here tomorrow to drive me to Waterville," he said. "Now, I'm going back to bed."

He shut the door firmly. I stood staring at the bright white paint on the door's front—a new job; Karl Nygaard, Ginger's teammate, had painted the door and the trim just two summers before. Inside the house, the lights went out one after another, following the trail to Bow's bedroom. Finally, only the porch light still burned. The night was quiet, save for an occasional shout drifting up from the plaza, the crowd cheering the imminent collapse of the bonfire. By now, bottles were being passed, and bets were being laid down to see when it would go.

I stood on the porch for five, maybe ten minutes, though I knew Bow wasn't coming back. The cool air braced, and by not moving, by staying absolutely still and meditating like a yogi on the whiteness of the door, I found I could hold my thoughts at bay. Eventually, though, the shouts from the plaza pulled me away, and I headed back down the hill.

Through the years as I've puzzled over what happened that night, I've come to find generous explanations for Bow: He was startled and half asleep when I showed up, a good enough excuse in itself for his foul mood and unpleasantness. More important, he was probably still deciding how to think about Ginger, particularly given the looming confrontation with Asmus. I'd interrupted Bow while he was in the process of building a kind of psychological redoubt around the boy.

Until he had those defenses entirely in place, he stayed on the offensive, and I had happened to step in the way. As for that look of stony contempt on Bow's face—it was probably something I would have seen often in court if only I'd been sitting on the other side of the bench, on the receiving end of his appeals arguments. Around the state, the judges respected Bow, but they resented him, too, and they were even a little frightened by him, and now it was easy for me to see why. Of course, over the years I've also come to understand that Bow loved Ginger—loved him in the same lonely, crabbed, unexpressed way he loved me. I was all he had, and then Ginger came along and there were three of us, an odd little triangle cobbled from need and hope, but glued together by Bow's unwavering loyalty.

Eventually, all those thoughts passed through my head. But that night, as I trudged back down from the Bluff, I only thought that Bow had finally seen into my fears and weaknesses and cut me loose.

Back on Main Street, Officer Ostberg lurked in the shadows near the park, trying to avoid coming across anything illegal. "Have you seen Ox?" I asked him. He pointed me toward Duffy's.

CHAPTER 32

The mortar shells hit in the distance. They came in behind me, moving closer, each explosion a flash of brilliant rainbows across my eyes. I had to concentrate on staying down, but this rice paddy, this stinking patch of earth, was dry and hard when it should have been wet and forgiving. I was a plump, clumsy mole groping on concrete, everything exposed. The bursts of fire got closer. They shook the ground, setting off winds. I was going to be hit. I saw it the way you see an accident coming, your mind making that instant, sure calculation through the hysterical scream of scraping rubber that these brakes and tires won't stop this car in time. This was my father's fault. Even from the grave, he'd driven me to offer myself to this deadly nonwar; he'd made me die for Vietnam.

The explosions were coming faster now. My hand snaked down protectively between my legs. *Please, not there.* I turned my head, there was another flash, and then it came—a sort of tug and a searing in the cheek. I waited, but at first it wasn't so bad. My feet and hands were icy, but I was floating free, released, swimming away in the rice paddy. Then I felt a fierce, thick needle of pain shooting through my head, and I was blinded by the agony. Let me faint, or die, I pleaded, screaming, anything to get that needle out. Suddenly, two sweet, soft hands were cradling my head, babying my ragged flesh. Ginger. Ginger's sure, surgeon's hands were promising help, going after the needle.

I opened my eyes, and there was Duffy's kid Jimmy, his puffy, round, ten-year-old face taut with wonder and concern. "Mister, are you all right?" he asked, letting go of my head. "I thought you were having some kind of fit."

I blinked. I tried to sit up, but the edge of my cheek, near the ear, was still attached by a paste of beer and saliva to the green Naugahyde of Duffy's banquette. With an effort, I ripped it away, and the needle pain shot through my head again.

"I guess you must have had too much to drink, huh?" said the boy. He grabbed an Old Style bottle from the table and dropped it into a trash can full of empties. Another shell exploded.

"Can you hold off on the empties for a second?" I begged. My voice was metal scraping metal. I swung my feet to the floor, trying to clear my head. Someone—Ox, maybe—had tossed the throw rug from Duffy's back office over my legs for a spot of warmth, and a layer of dust had settled on my pants. The air got scratchy.

Duffy's kid grew suspicious. "Are you supposed to be here?" he asked, his eyes narrowing.

Something in his expression broke through, and I realized where I should have been. "Jesus Christ, what time is it?" I cawed.

Jimmy jumped back. I'd scared him. Duffy didn't keep a clock in the bar, but Jimmy ran to the office.

I stared at my watch, squinting the hands into momentary focus: seven-thirty. At seven, I had been due at Bow's to drive him to the meeting with Asmus.

A guardian angel had folded my coat and draped it over the back of a nearby chair. Ox again, probably—in love with domestic order. Grabbing the coat, I rattled to the door, then out into the pounding morning sun. Thirty yards down River Road, Jimmy's wavery alto called after me: "Seven-thirty-two and forty-six seconds!"

Left on Ellis, right on Main, scudding down the middle of the street. Eyes not working, I needed space, the sidewalk dangerously narrow. *No one here can love and understand me.* A terrorist car bore down, honking like an angry goose. A cruel shout. Sorry, sorry, but whasamatta, ain't you ever seen a drunk in panic before? *Oh, what hard-luck stories they all hand me.* Left on Summer. The grade mounts. Chest exploding, legs failing, face awash with liquid. Sweat, tears, drool, snot. All engines in reverse. Hideous, shrieking siren sounding. Fire alarm. No, just me sucking air. *Make my bed and light the light, I'll arrive late tonight.*

Shut down, finally, beside the thick, gray oak in front of the Wickers' house. The cold, scaly bark soothing against my face. *Blackbird Bye Bye.*

This was the resting spot for Bow's old man—the place he paused to catch his breath in his daily walk home from the bank. Five-thirteen. You could set your watch by it. He'd turn, gasping, waiting for his lungs to settle, and look down over the town, the Agnes visible in ribbony patches between the buildings, the curving roof of the Opera House a relief against the flat surfaces. Then one time his breath didn't come back, and he collapsed and died, his arms open to the sky, his hat blowing into the street, his mounding belly still locked in behind his brown suit coat, here at the foot of the Wickers' oak.

A fit of vomiting seized me, great, wrenching spasms of vomit emptying into Summer Street, flowing down the gutter toward the town. I leaned against the tree for support. A young mother came toward me, leading her son by the hand down the sidewalk. Poor child, he was dressed like an elf, probably on the way to a holiday pageant. They detoured around, looping way across the Wickers' lawn to avoid me, and still I heard their low, disapproving whispers. More spasms and vomit. I watched it run off, my tearing eyes painting the world in Impressionist canvases. Where did all this liquid come from? I tried to tick back the night. Duffy had made us drink beer.

A car came rolling down Summer Street, its engine clicking in the cold air. Passing me, it slowed but kept moving. I raised my eyes. A yellow smudge. Murphy's cab. Blinking, I made out a silhouette through the back window, a wide head.

Emptied, soaking with cold sweat, I walked the last fifty yards to the Bluff and down the street to Bow's house. Mrs. Gehrke, the housekeeper, answered the door. "Oh, Mr. Stuart, he's waiting for you before," she said, her pale German eyes studying my condition. "He's calling a taxi."

"Oh." Her mangled syntax left me a sliver of hope. "Has the taxi come yet?"

"Just left," she said, pulling her thin lips tight across her teeth, feigning regret. Did I only imagine her accent had miraculously disappeared?

"Thank you, Mrs. Gehrke." I turned away before she could shut the door on me.

The sun was rising over Laroque, reflecting off the gold and silver Christmas decorations knitted around the Main Street light posts and scattered over other shopping blocks. The townscape was gilded. Heading down the hill, I walked toward the painful light.

Back in Bow's office, I prepared the bath. The faucet coughed water in rusty spurts. I let it run clear, then dropped in the stopper. I took off my clothes and stood naked on the cold tile floor of the bathroom, waiting for the tub to fill. My filthy, damp pile of clothes offended, though. Down the hall, the bank had been renovating several empty offices and left behind a big cardboard trash bin. I bundled the clothes in my arms and walked naked down the corridor, leaving footprints in the construction dust, then buried the pungent evidence in a mound of broken-up plasterboard. Finally, I climbed in the tub and soaked until the water turned cool.

There were spare clothes in a file cabinet. I got dressed and packed my other things in a shopping bag we used for hauling stacks of transcripts into court. By now it was after ten, and I was feeling pressed. I sat at Bow's desk and left him a note on a legal pad, though I found I didn't have much to say. I apologized, and I quit the job as his assistant, but my brain wasn't working right, and I couldn't form the sentences to express the failure and disappointment I felt. At the end, I thanked him for his many kindnesses and scratched in my name.

Outside, Main Street was hopping. Maybe business would catch up after all. Toting my shopping bag of clothes, I headed east out of town. At the Route 53 intersection, I stopped and put out my thumb, pointing north. After about ten minutes, Bud Chaltain, a milk hauler, stopped his truck and opened the cab door, beckoning me in. "How far you going?" he asked when I was settled beside him on the seat.

"Spirit Light."

CHAPTER 33

In the summer of 1939, as Hitler was menacing Europe and the world outside Laroque lurched toward disaster, my father put on a production of *The Merchant of Venice*. I was nine, just old enough to be tuned to the anxieties that drifted out of adult conversations and seemed to hover in the air wherever people gathered that summer. Or is it just the layers of subsequent history that have turned the memory so acute? *Merchant* was the last show produced by my father that busy season. The huge cast drew on the entire summer-stock troupe, as well as various people from Laroque, but to play Shylock, Dad imported an old pal from his theater days in New York, an actor named Rodney Fiske. After enjoying some minor successes on Broadway, Fiske had gone to Hollywood and for a time found a calling in B movies. He was a big, black-haired, handsome man, with puffy cheeks and features perhaps a bit soft to carry him into Hollywood's elite. Instead, he got typecast as the rich, impeccably mannered, but slightly befuddled friend. In movies, he was always dressed for polo or about to embark on a sea voyage. In real life, he was a prodigious drunk and a cad, qualities that had made him a dear companion to my father back when they were roaring around Greenwich Village together. By 1939, Fiske's bad behavior had banished him from most studios, so he was available again to Dad. The tale they told *Variety* and then repeated for the Milwaukee and Chicago papers was that Fiske wanted a recess from film to reexplore his theatrical roots. What better place than a community theater in the heartland? Casting him against type as the tormented Jew emphasized the sincerity of his quest.

The night he arrived, my father took my mother and me to the station to meet his train. Word was out and a small crowd of curious fans waited in a light summer rain. The train pulled in, and Fiske didn't get out. There was a commotion, and conductors scurried up and down the platform. Finally, a knot of people emerged from a train door—a retinue Fiske had picked up during three days in the bar car. For several minutes, the knot careered around the station, to my nine-year-old eyes a huge, dazed centipede scampering in one direction, pausing, then legging off somewhere else. At last the knot pulled itself apart near a wood bench in the waiting room. At the center was the star himself, borne by his arms and legs, a suitcase plopped on his stomach. His new friends laid him on the bench before scrambling back to the train. My father pushed his way through and shook his buddy by the shoulders. Fiske didn't recognize him.

Things deteriorated from there. At night, the star mowed his way through the bars on River Road. He insisted on borrowing my family's car, and by one or two in the morning, wanderlust would overtake him and he'd go roaring off to another town, weaving along the country roads in search of more bars and new acolytes. Day after day, before rehearsals could start, my father would have to retrieve him from a jail or a ditch.

Whether drunk or recovering, Fiske couldn't resist a woman, the younger the better, and many of the college girls swarming around the Opera House were happy to have an adventure with a handsome celebrity. Here was the first Shylock to seduce Nerissa, Portia, and even his own confused daughter, Jessica. When he moved beyond the imported cast and started chasing Laroque high school girls, however, my father got visited by Mr. Epps, Bow's father, the first of countless warnings issued that summer.

Meanwhile, the show was a disaster. The girls in the troupe who'd been charmed and then discarded by Fiske all blamed one another for breaking up a love that should have lasted a lifetime. On stage, they bounced apart like opposite ends of magnets. The local cast was alternately awed by the star and confused by the chaos. And Fiske himself was having trouble with his delivery. Perhaps the endless nights of drinking had finally affected his senses or maybe he was recalling some ancient, fixed notion of technique—whatever, he was incapable of modulating his voice. Every statement, on or off stage, was declaimed in a thundering baritone as if, my father once ruefully remarked, he were permanently performing before an audience of the hard of hearing. During weeks of rehearsals, Dad tried to work his way through these problems, but, in the end, the emotional climate rarely fell below hysteria whenever Fiske appeared.

I saw all this happening, and, in my childish way, I became a seismograph of the summer's intrigues and traumas. One day when I was innocently exploring the Opera House, I burst into a small, out-of-the-way room used for storing old costumes and props. Before me, on a miserable, cold, Formica table was a great mound of squirming flesh. I had only a moment to notice the remarkable bulges and the mysterious dark places before the forms focused into Patsy, the chunky assistant director, and Fiske. While she hopelessly tried to cover up, he aimed a cruel stare at me, and for several seconds his dark rummy eyes held my small ones. I slammed the door and dashed away, certain I would get in trouble, but quite the opposite happened. Fiske seemed to think the encounter had created a kind of fraternal bond between us—we'd shared a manly moment, and ever after we were equals and intimates. In the following days, he'd take me aside and in his booming voice confide his great unhappiness— his dismay with the level of talent in the production, his certainty that my father was favoring the other actors, his agony at the noisy tribulations of his intestinal tract. I always nodded and tried to appear sympathetic, and he'd put his big hand on my shoulder and look enormously relieved. Soon, I started to feel an awful responsibility for the terrible tensions around the production.

In a pitiful effort to get a grip on the show, my father stopped coming home at night and began sleeping at the Opera House on a cot made up in the men's dressing room. Fiske disappeared entirely for a few days (he later told me he'd been helping a young lady in Kawnipi to move), throwing the production into even greater chaos. Mr. Epps, who knew how the play was taxing the town's budget, started coming over in midafternoon, with rehearsals in full swing. He would take a seat in the audience, place his hat on the chair beside him, and watch silently.

Finally, one day, my father snapped. He was directing from the front row when something went awry. He leaped onto the stage, raging at the top of his lungs. Everybody watched in horror. He marched up and down, roaring nonsensically. My mother tried to calm him, but he pushed her away. He ended up on his back in the middle of the stage, flailing the air like an overturned beetle. Eventually, my mother got him home and into bed. By the next morning, he seemed to have recovered, but in the middle of the next rehearsal he exploded again.

I saw it all and was deathly afraid. The second time it happened, Fiske came up beside me. I felt that huge paw on my shoulder. "Son," he confided, "your father has lost his mind." It was the first time I'd ever heard him whisper.

The production was due to open the next night. I recall huddled discussions among Mr. Epps, my mother, and the other adults connected to the troupe. Too much was at stake to cancel. The question became how to keep my father away. Everyone was certain that at some point he would jump in front of the audience and throw another fit. Mr. Epps wanted to put him in the hospital. My mother wouldn't allow it. Someone else suggested buying him a weekend in Milwaukee and simply pushing him onto the train. By morning, though, he was rational again, and he insisted on being present.

So the show opened in a state close to panic, the whole troupe waiting for my father to rush out from the wings into the middle of the stage. He never budged, of course, and his *Merchant* turned out to be a smash. As soon as the curtain went up, the chaos assembled itself into a tight, electric show, the actors sparking one another to keep the emotions high and the scenes moving quickly. Fiske's Shylock took over the dark center of the drama, and I saw the wretched, rheumy, self-pitying, 11 A.M. hangover—Fiske's signature state of being—perfectly filling out the tortured personality of Shakespeare's sad villain. *Life* magazine came out and did a little story on him. The studios called again. And the show was extended for two weeks, paying for itself several times over. My father's fits of madness had produced a triumph.

One day years later, after other bouts had left him ragged and homebound, I asked Dad if he remembered his stunning *Merchant*. Of course, he said, I think of it every day. And what had driven him over the edge like that and then brought him back? It's all just acting, said the little man in the bathrobe. Everything hangs on how you play it. You mean, you were faking it? I demanded. He smiled at my surprise. Few things brought him joy anymore, but he could still find amusement in the credulity of his son. Sometimes, he told me, acting is all you've got.

CHAPTER 34

few days after Christmas, a storm blew through northern Wisconsin, dumping fourteen inches of damp, heavy snow. The county was slow getting around to clearing the secondary roads, the only access in and out of the Spirit Light camp, so I was marooned there with Bob and Margaret Morgan. They'd just come back from their annual December vacation in Sarasota, Florida, and Bob's leathery face had taken on a pinkish glow from the semitropical sun. They seemed pleased to have me around, eager for the diversion. In fact, I detected a slight stiffness between them, as if there had been a tectonic shift in the marriage, even a betrayal, and each was still groping through the adjustment.

Since the unheated bunkhouse was closed for winter, they put me in a guest room of the big house, and Bob and I spent several mornings shoveling the paths between the buildings and pushing snow off the roofs. A few parties of ice fishermen were coming up just after New Year's, and Bob was glad to have help staying ahead of the chores. Margaret couldn't get to the grocery store, so she dug into her freezer for ducks, pheasants, and venison left behind by hunters, and for several days running she prepared huge game meals that kept us at the table for much of the afternoon. By evening, we'd be exhausted from the shoveling and sated by the meal. Bob would get a fire going in the family room, a clubby space with old, soft furniture and high-beamed ceilings, and we'd sit around and play Clue on an ancient, tattered game board.

In the pleasant isolation of the camp, I came to regard the snowstorm as a sign, falling into the habit my father acquired of reading the world for validation. In that way, the storm was a blessed curtain on my past, an argument for closing out the long, first act of my life. I thought I had it all figured out. Working for Bow had been a privilege, but it had also anchored me in a losing pattern: He dominated me with his intelligence and money, and my only way to break free and assert myself had been to go on a binge. Now that was over, I told myself; I was on my own.

I took comfort in my analysis, and for several days I didn't much exist beyond the circle of undulating heat from the fireplace and the Victorian rooms of the Clue mansion. Then one night, to catch up with the outside world, Bob turned on Marcus Laney's radio show. In among the pop songs, the talk of who was visiting where for the holidays, and the gloomy news of the war, Laney mentioned that Ginger Piper had quit the Laroque Lumberjacks basketball team. "Don't know why yet," Laney said in his clipped and haughty radio voice. "We'll try to find out. But that's sure the end of an era for the Lumberjacks."

I considered trying to call Bow but reminded myself that I was beyond that now. The next evening, Laney had more news: Ginger had quit school.

Overnight, a narrow warm front blew through the area, followed by another blustery wave of cold. The top layer of snow melted, then froze. The landscape turned to ice. In the morning, Bob and I went out to look around and ended up sliding in our boots down the long, sloping lawn from the big house to the lake, a gentle ride of fifty yards or so. Then we couldn't climb back to the house on the slick surface. Finally, we used sticks to chop toeholds in the glassy snow and took half an hour clawing our way home. Meanwhile, the wind came up and the ice-coated telephone and electric lines snapped all over the county. By noon, the camp had lost electric power and the phone was dead.

We were completely cut off. For the first time I could remember, Bob turned sour. He walked around the house, checking the pipes and shaking his head. "Too much weather," he kept muttering.

For two days, the three of us lived in front of a constant fire in the family room, the only place we could heat. We put candles around for light. Margaret cooked in the fireplace, and at night we bedded down in sleeping bags on the hearth. Bob and I managed to drain the pipes before they froze; afterward, we had to make frigid excursions to the privy behind the bunkhouse.

On New Year's Eve, Margaret cooked up a rich venison stew in a big iron pot. She clipped evergreen boughs to make a fragrant wreath for the center of the table, and with the candles burning, the scene was rustic but festive. Bob's mood lightened for the first time since the power went out. Halfway through dinner, he exchanged a glance with Margaret, then turned to me. "We've been meaning to tell you something, Charlie," he announced. "We're thinking of selling the camp and moving to Sarasota."

"It's still just talk, so we weren't sure whether to bring it up," Margaret interrupted nervously. This was the issue that had been gnawing at them. "We didn't want you to worry," she added.

"The custodian at our church down there is about to retire, and they're looking for someone to take his place," Bob went on. "We could get a nice little house near the water." He paused to taste another spoonful of stew. Margaret and I watched as his jaw deliberately crushed a cube of meat. I felt a stab of envy at his patience. "I'm fifty-two years old," he continued. "I love it here, but I feel like I've been chasing fish all my life. It's not that I can't do it anymore. It's just that I think I deserve something else. You know what I mean, Charlie?"

I nodded. Margaret's eyes were brimming with tears, shining in the candlelight.

"Margaret here doesn't disagree, but she wonders what will happen to the boys that work here. She's particularly worried about you."

"I've always thought we were more than just a fishing camp," said Margaret.

"I'll be fine," I told them. "I don't blame you for wanting to get away."

"I just want to sit on my porch at night and listen to the frogs without having to worry about what's going to happen tomorrow. And without having to swat mosquitoes." Bob's voice rose in indignation at the memory of the years of needy fishermen and the relentless hordes of insects. He soothed himself with more venison stew.

"Can you always work for Mr. Epps?" Margaret asked.

"I'm sure I can," I lied.

"He's been good to you," Bob said, starting to ask a question but deciding, in the space of his natural drawl, to make a statement instead.

"He sure has." I could feel the chill of the room pressing my shoulders and got up to put several logs on the fire.

"Such intelligence," sighed Margaret. "Maybe he's a genius. You must learn so much from him."

I could have told her I was an expert on geniuses. I was the son of one, I'd worked for another, and perhaps I'd seen yet another begin to blossom. But in the end their greatness had done nothing but diminish me, and I'd disappointed the one true good man among them.

"Who do you think would buy the place?" I asked.

They glanced at each other. "We've been talking to an outfit," Bob said. "They want to turn it into a boys' camp."

"You're kidding."

"I guess there's good money in that these days. It's steadier than fishing. And there may be some tax deals they can work."

"When do they want to take over?"

Another troubled glance. "They'd like to get started this summer," Bob said. "Apparently they've got the campers lined up and need some place to put them."

"We haven't signed anything yet," offered Margaret quickly.

"Jeez," I sighed, thinking about the long summer evenings when a handful of fishermen would troll the lake after dinner, the only sound the occasional clunk of a paddle against the side of a canoe or the slap of a leaping fish falling back against the surface. "Imagine this place overrun with kids."

"I'll take Florida," said Bob.

The electricity came back the next day. The phones were still out, and we hadn't seen any sign of the county's snowplows yet, but I fibbed and told Bob and Margaret that I had to get back to Laroque, that I was on a deadline for Bow. My plan was to hike down to the first cleared road, then hitch a ride. "But you'll freeze to death," Margaret said. Actually, the weather had turned pleasant: Patches of sun were breaking through and the temperature was headed for the high twenties. Bob lent me a good pair of boots and Margaret sent me off with a thermos of coffee.

The going was treacherous at first. My feet kept punching through the frozen surface of the snow. The shards of ice were sharp, and when I sank in over the tops of the boots, I scraped my shins. Before long, I had bright red circles around each pant leg, and I was leaving a bloody trail in the snow.

After an hour or so, I came out of the trees onto Wilmington Road, the county road leading up to the Spirit Light. On a hill looking across a snowy pasture, I could see traffic moving on Route 53 a mile or so away. Once I got there, I would stick out my thumb. Route 53 led south, toward Laroque, but I wasn't going to stop. I'd keep heading south, through Illinois and all the other forgettable states until I got to Florida. South, away from the weather and the bugs and small-town geniuses. Someday, maybe, I'd find out what had happened to Ginger. Maybe I'd catch up with Bow. But Bob had it right. I'd beat him and Margaret to Florida. I had a few hundred bucks in my account. Enough to start over. Leave all this behind. Florida.

The sun softened the icy snow. My feet were cold, but the hike got easier. Coming down off the hill, I could hear a heavy truck grinding in the distance. It cleared a rise, and I could see the truck on Wilmington Road, pushing a plow, clearing a neat one-lane furrow. I went a bit farther and then stood by the side of the road to wait. A familiar white Pontiac crept along just behind the truck. As the procession got closer, I could see two heads in the car. I stepped back to let the snowplow pass. The Pontiac stopped in front of me. Ox Mueller was driving. Bow rolled down the window. "Get in," he said. "It's a new year. Time to get back to work."

CHAPTER 35

Ginger had joined the army. A few days after Bow told Asmus the deal was off, Ginger walked into the recruiter's office on Hutchins Street—the same place he'd picketed a month before—and signed up. "It was his idea," Bow said, as if I could have imagined anything else. "I tried to talk him out of it."

"Ruined the basketball team," said Ox over his shoulder as he laboriously turned the Pontiac in the single plowed lane. "'Course, they never won anyway."

With an effort, Bow twisted to face me in the backseat. "He came up to my office the next day," Bow said. "He told me he'd been thinking a lot about the war, and he'd finally decided I was right: It *was* a just cause. It stood for something—honoring commitments, standing by your allies, protecting the hope of democracy. I heard all my old arguments coming back to me. It was extraordinary. I nearly fell on the floor."

"But why now?"

"That's what I said. At least finish high school. Get the diploma, then do what you want. But he said he had it in his bones. He wanted to get over there, be part of it. He wanted to test himself." Bow shrugged and forced out a smile that never made it to his eyes. In his gauntness and with the tension of the last few months, I'd seen that familiar face toss up entirely fresh expressions, as if someone else were occupying his ravaged body. "He just turned eighteen," Bow said.

"I can understand how he feels," Ox offered. "Sometimes I wanted to climb into the ring and get the hell beat out of me just to say I'd done it."

"He's punishing himself," I said.

"That might be part of it," Bow allowed uneasily. Even now he couldn't bring himself to acknowledge that Ginger's scheming had set in motion a series of deadly events. "Of course, Asmus was thrilled," Bow continued. "He was happy to drop the whole thing as long as Ginger cleared out."

"So it's over?"

"It's over. Fontenot's dead, and that's the end of it."

Bow and I stared at each other. "So maybe enlisting's not such a bad idea after all," I said.

"There's no proportion in it," Bow responded softly. "He was free and clear with the deal I'd worked out."

"Then why?"

"The war. He'd really changed his mind. We talked about it a long time. For all the abstract arguments, he had a very personal response. Why should *he* escape when others were being asked to fight? Why should *he* get a deferment just because he got better grades and could go to college? Losing two buddies over there had a lot to do with it."

A second plow nosed over a small hill in front, clearing the shoulder of the road. The crusted snow flew off the blade in chunks the size of pizzas. The scraped earth looked raw where the machine had passed.

Bow said, sounding resigned, "Well, Holmes fought—in the Civil War, saw terrible action. Got wounded. It stayed with him his whole life and in the end probably made him a better lawyer."

"Ginger's making a terrible mistake," I said.

Ox searched for me in the rearview mirror. "I thought you was *for* the war," he said.

"The funny thing is," Bow mused, his voice lifting slightly, "I was starting to come around to *his* way of thinking. The war really *is* a quagmire. We aren't making progress, and the best thing would be just to settle and pull out. I told Ginger that, and for a few minutes we argued on the exact opposite sides of where we'd been before. I wish you'd been there, Charlie. It was quite amusing. He was the hawk, I was the dove. Then we shook hands and he left. He's taking the train to Milwaukee tomorrow morning."

"Vietnam, here I come," crooned Ox.

Bow turned back to face the highway, a silver slash in the white landscape. "Quite amusing," he repeated gloomily. "It's about the funniest thing I ever heard."

At five the next morning, I walked in the dark down to the train station and found Ginger sitting alone in the small waiting room, an old canvas suitcase at his feet. He was surprised to see me. He'd already said his assorted good-byes—to Anna the night before, to his father minutes earlier. He wanted to avoid sentiment, he told me— as much as suggesting I leave him alone, too, allow him to make this escape without having to look into any familiar faces. But I sat down on the wood bench opposite him, and we chatted for a few minutes, trading gossip. The waiting room smelled of old cigarette smoke, and with sections of yesterday's newspapers scattered around, the place had the distant, brittle aura of history about it, a site captured in sepia where many lives had passed by. Finally, I told him, "You can probably still get out of this."

"Now, why would I want to do that?" he asked.

"Because there's no proportion to it," I said, echoing Bow.

He smiled. "Proportion never meant that much to me." After a moment, he added with a laugh, "I guess I wouldn't have made much of a lawyer after all."

"Bow still thinks you would."

"He's always been too generous," Ginger said, and managed another laugh.

"I know why you're doing this," I told him.

He stiffened. "No, you don't, Charlie. At least give me that much. No one knows why I'm doing this. That's mine, and not you or Bow or anyone else can own it." Just as quickly as he'd slipped to the edge of anger, he pulled back. "You and Bow were born different from me," he said. "I see the world in opposition, I've been that way as long as I can remember. Maybe war is where I should be." He shrugged. " 'The life of the law has not been logic: it has been experience,' " he offered brightly. "I'm getting my experience. I want to go."

I stood up. It was silly to argue with him. He knew himself better than we did—he recognized the perils and limits in his inflamed sense of right and wrong. "Well, good luck," I told him.

Down the track, the train whistle sounded. I followed Ginger out to the platform and stood beside him as we watched the headlight on the engine grow larger in the darkness. Bundled against the cold in his ski parka, he seemed slight and boyish, far too innocent to be fodder for a war. For a moment, I was flooded with an urge to wrap my arms around him and squeeze, as if I, in all my weaknesses, could offer protection to his vulnerable flesh. The moment passed. The train pulled up in an eruption of screeching metal. The door slid open. Ginger pulled off his glove to shake my hand. " 'Bye, 'bye, Blackbird," he said before bounding up the steps. I watched as the train pulled away. The lights inside glowed garishly bright against the early morning blackness. Ginger was alone in the car.

My plan to decamp for Florida got delayed or abandoned—I wasn't quite sure which yet—and I went back to work for Bow, though there was much less to do. His criminal practice continued to dwindle, and he actually turned down a few cases that judges tried to assign him. Popping in and out of probate court to settle Macy's estate, he picked up some trusts work, and the bank started referring people who wanted to have a will drawn up. I did a fair amount of typing for him—deadly dull documents I could hardly bear to proofread—but there was rarely a call for the kind of investigating I used to do.

In fact, our workdays were entirely different. Instead of traveling to prisons to interview men who indignantly protested their innocence, we were visited by a string of old people worried about dying and anxious about getting their affairs in order. Or sometimes the client was an earnest young couple whose squirming infant had propelled them to draw up a plan for the future. More than once, I was assigned to walk the kid up and down the empty corridor outside, trying to keep the lid on while Mom and Dad conferred with Bow.

I think Bow got some satisfaction out of the work. He was a craftsman, so simply doing the job well kept him occupied. And though he never would have admitted it, he enjoyed the interview process—rooting around in people's circumstances teased his lifelong voyeuristic impulses. He saw what his clients owned, what they earned, how their family loyalties broke down. Bow's curiosity was about the only thing that energized him anymore; it was as if amassing enough facts about others would somehow help him explain what he'd been doing all those years.

As for me, I still longed for criminal law. Every case was a tale of some sort, animated by a narrative, a plot, developing characters, a beginning, middle, and end. The best had much more—drama, mystery, a moral sense. There was action in crime, something woefully lacking in the tedious lists of assets, the numbing collection of insurance forms and beneficiary statements that were the heart of the wills business. Once when I grumbled to Bow that I missed the old work, he snapped back that what I really missed was the "criminal element." He was right, of course—I'd never really got over a puerile fascination with bad guys and bad behavior. But neither had he. Being a defense lawyer had bolstered Bow's idea of himself. It gave him a bit of swagger. He was a disfigured, overweight intellectual who'd nonetheless come to feel slightly dashing.

Now he seemed determined to put that behind him. Looking back years later, you could argue that Ginger represented a clear break in Bow's life, a last flirtation with all the childish ambitions bottled up in his clumsy body. When things fell apart Bow, in his logical, lawyerly way, shut out the past and embraced his middle age and decline. That's certainly Lucy's analysis of what happened. But Lucy had always regarded Bow as more immature than complex. She never came to know him and she never gave him credit. And her analysis doesn't begin to appreciate how special Ginger was.

From my vantage, I could see that Bow couldn't put the past behind him. He'd invested too much in the idea of Ginger, in the intoxicating allure of the boy's promise—a notion of heroism that probably equaled Bow's unspoken and unfulfilled dreams for himself. Of course, Ginger thrived on that idea, too, once he'd sensed what was going on. He was similarly intoxicated, which may account for his terrible misjudgment. Afterward, he used his wonderful gift for giving and inducing empathy to push Bow to the edge of his principles, perhaps beyond. Even then, Ginger couldn't abandon Bow's vision. He made himself pay for his failings, changing his position on the war, giving up part of himself. In the end, he avoided the debilitating self-justification that spoiled so many of his generation. But Bow had paid, too, though he didn't owe anyone. Both of them had made an offering of themselves. In their toughest moment, each honored the other.

Around February that year, after hearing everyone tell him how gray and listless he looked, Bow decided he needed a vacation. I drove him to the Far Flung Travel Agency in Waterville, and he collected a file of brochures on cruises. He spent a week plotting courses and calculating rates and finally settled on one of the fanciest trips, a three-week journey that touched port at a dozen Caribbean islands. He bought himself a new set of luggage and a tropical wardrobe, packed a bundle of books, and in early March, I drove him down to Milwaukee for a flight to Miami, the port of embarkation. The weather was miserable—slashing rain that periodically turned to sleet as the temperature dodged around freezing. We got soaked just loading up the car.

In Milwaukee, the storm delayed the flight. We sat around the airport reading magazines and waiting for word on the departure. Instead of benches, the airport had recently installed row after row of fiberglass bucket seats, formfitted to a far sleeker physique than Bow's. He took his discomfort as an omen. "Now I know why I never went on vacation," he groused. "What am I going to do for three weeks?"

"Maybe you'll find romance." Since Macy had got sick and her place shut down, Bow hadn't slept with a woman, at least as far as I knew.

"Ha." He snorted.

"A beautiful young widow eager for an adventure."

He snorted again. But he enjoyed the idea. He folded his arms across his chest and smiled to himself. From certain angles now, with his narrowed, craggy face, he'd begun to look almost handsome.

After a few seconds I said, "Hell, maybe you'll meet your future wife. You'd make a pretty good catch, you know—settled, responsible, rich."

He gave me a sideways glance. "You mean, the older I get the more normal I seem—just another fat, arthritic, middle-aged man."

"I'm serious."

"By the time I'm eighty, everyone will be as decrepit as me. That's something to look forward to."

"You were married at twenty-five. There's no reason you can't be married at forty-eight."

"I'm wiser now," Bow said. He watched a young soldier make a bed for himself, stretching out between his duffel and the wall. Soldiers were wandering all over the terminal, many of them looking blank and unshaven, as if they'd been there for days.

I said, "It was just about exactly a year ago that you were telling me you were ready for a change in your life, a new direction."

"I don't remember that," Bow lied.

"You thought you were in a rut."

"I did say that, didn't I." He pretended to be bored by the memory. He stretched, trying to get comfortable, and the fiberglass seat groaned under his weight. Bow said, "It's amazing, isn't it—how arrogant you can be about life?"

The plane took off after a three-hour delay. He called me from the hotel in Miami, worried about a couple of last-second details on a will I was typing up. Then I didn't hear a thing for two weeks. Finally, a postcard arrived, mailed from the island of Dominica. The picture showed a lush, jungled cliff bisected by a delicate waterfall. On the back, he wrote, "I'm tan, trim, and rippling, a vision in Bermuda shorts. The tropical air does wonders. Plus, the ship is overrun with widows. All systems go!!!" Under his signature, he added a postscript: "You're a dear and loyal companion, Charlie, everything a friend could be. And I've been a jerk. Please forgive my stupidities."

I thought I knew where the sentiment came from—he was probably stretched out on a lounge chair on the deck, too much time on his hands, chewing on the past. I hoped the cruise wouldn't kill him.

While he was gone I kept an eye on the office and checked the mail every day, but once I'd typed up and sent off a few leftover documents, there was absolutely nothing to do. So I started dropping in on Lucy downstairs at the bank. She was working as a teller, and I'd cash a small check, then stand around her window, leaning on the cold stone counter, chattering with her fitfully as people came and went. I didn't care that I was making a pest of myself, and she didn't seem to mind, but after a week or so, her boss complained. After that, she'd come up to Bow's office occasionally on her break. We'd have pleasant, innocuous conversations—about people we knew, things we'd done together, even the latest news from Vietnam. We seemed to be in a kind of contest to see who could keep going the longest, wringing all emotional inflection out of our interactions while staying lively and amusing. Once the rules of the game had been silently established, I found it hard if not impossible to break them. She was good, and I wanted to prove I could be her equal. Besides, it was rather fun working to keep up; I felt, in my clunky way, like a character in a Noël Coward play, though it worried me that I didn't know how you'd pick a winner or even how the game would end.

Once I nearly faltered. Lucy walked in, full of complaints about the bank's management, and flopped down on the sofa, stretching out as if she were spilling it all to her psychiatrist. As I watched her there, her lovely legs balanced atop one sofa arm, her skirt settled at midthigh, I couldn't help recalling the many times we'd made love on that sofa. While I coolly talked her through her job crisis, my chest was pounding with desire and anxiety: Should I go sit on the edge of the sofa? Stroke her stockinged legs? Lean down, kiss her? I wrestled with my ambivalence for several minutes. Clearly, a brazen show of affection would break the rules of this odd charade, but perhaps that's what Lucy secretly wanted, and she was waiting for me to take the lead. On the other hand, maybe she preferred to stay at an emotional distance—she certainly had seemed contented over the last few days—and I dreaded to see dismay on her face again directed at me. We continued to gab. She wasn't even looking at me. She was staring up at the grimy ceiling of Bow's office, waving her hands in exaggerated expressions of frustration at her idiot bosses, seemingly oblivious to the lush history of the office, the sofa, the two of us alone together. Finally I decided, Fuck it, I'll go for it. But just as I tensed to push myself out of my chair, she swung her legs to the floor and bounced to her feet, pronouncing herself refreshed and ready to go back to work. I had no clue whether she'd sensed what was coming.

Around that time Lucy heard they needed a hand over at the library while one of the librarians was off on vacation, and she thought an extra job would do me good. Jeanie Blanchard, the head librarian, had roused me enough times from a table in back that she wasn't keen on my application. But the morning I presented myself, the library's lone public toilet was stopped up, and I knew something about plumbing. She took me on, and once I got the toilet running again, she assigned me to shelve books.

The work was easy and agreeable. Following Melvil Dewey's great tracking system, there's nothing uncertain in a library; every book has its place. I'd put in a few hours every day. Sometimes I'd pause to flip through a volume, even sit down and read a couple of pages. Jeanie didn't appear to mind. One of the odd things about shelving books—you could work frantically or take your time; no matter the effort, it seemed there was always a new cart of returns filling up at about the pace you cleaned one off.

One day I wheeled my cart out of the canyon of the biography section into the open area around periodicals and found Errol Piper sitting at a long reading desk studying *Newsweek*. He grunted hello but was typically unfriendly, so I didn't try to talk. A few days later, I found him there again, this time looking over the *Christian Science Monitor*. If you didn't know him, he would have made a nice Norman Rockwell image, something suggesting the hearty American drive for self-improvement—a leathery fellow in worn and stained work clothes beavering away in a small-town temple of knowledge.

I was curious, so when Piper got up to leave, I followed him out-side. The late-March day was mild and breezy, but he had an old felt hunting cap pulled down to the tops of his ears. I caught up with him on the sidewalk just in front. "Hello, Errol," I said.

He knew I'd been following him, and he turned to me warily, as if I were about to accuse him of something—stealing a book, perhaps.

"What do you hear from Ginger?" I asked.

"He's at Fort Campbell, Kentucky."

"How does he like it?"

"It's the army. It don't make any difference if you like it or not."

"Is he going to Vietnam?"

"I suppose." Piper stared off down the street and let the silence settle between us.

I felt like slugging him just then. It wasn't only that his reticence was infuriating—I wanted to discover how deep it went, to see if at his core I'd find method. Instead, I wheeled and started heading back to the library.

"I miss him," Piper called out. He wanted to talk after all. Standing alone, his hands dangling at his sides, he looked as plain and denuded as one of the maple saplings planted the year before along the library's sidewalk. "It was just him and me around the house. The place is pretty empty now." Piper spoke in that slow, country way he had, every word a morose little ballad. But I sensed an accusation there: He probably blamed Bow for driving Ginger into the army.

"That must be quite a change for you," I said.

"He misses home."

"Did he say that?"

"He wishes he was here for the spring."

I stared at him. Wisconsin doesn't have a spring. It goes from winter to summer. In between are a few days of mud.

"The soft weather," Piper continued. "It's already hot down there."

"Oh."

"He writes two or three times a week," Piper said.

Before leaving for his cruise, Bow had watched for the mail every day, looking for a letter from Ginger. Not a word.

"What's he talk about?"

"The weather, the other boys. He finds things to say." We were standing a few feet apart, and Piper leaned toward me, lowering his voice. Talking about his departed son scratched up a sudden cordiality. "He used to be like that when he was little. He'd talk to his mother about everything. His feelings. He was a regular chatterbox. He didn't hide nothing." Piper searched my face, looking for confirmation. "I think a boy needs a mother for that, maybe more than a girl does, you know? Someone to relax with. With a father, with me, there was always more to prove, showing me he could act like a man. After his mother died, I missed hearing him chatter."

Piper leaned back. A faint crown of perspiration had appeared at his hairline, and he took off his cap and used it to swipe at the moisture. I don't think I'd ever heard him string together more than a terse sentence or two before, and I wondered if he'd been drinking. But his small, dark eyes were clear. "He didn't chatter around us, either," I offered, thinking the father would appreciate knowing his son wasn't different around others. "He and Bow discussed the war a lot."

"That interested him," Piper said coolly. I could sense him closing up again. He didn't like to hear about Bow.

"He read things. He was smart about it," I said quickly.

"I've been reading about it myself." With his chin, Piper indicated the library.

"You a hawk or a dove?" I was trying to josh him.

"I want to know what to expect," Piper said, ignoring my question.

"Do the magazines help?"

"I wrote him and told him, 'Work in a kitchen. Learn to type. Count rolls of toilet paper. Whatever you do, don't be a hero.' "

"He's a smart kid. He'll figure his way around."

Piper thought about that for a moment and seemed to conclude that he'd had enough of this conversation. He pulled his cap down to his ears again, and his face fell back into its usual mask of blankness. "He should never have gone," Piper said. It occurred to me then that Ginger hadn't confided in his father. The two of them probably had gone up to Bow's property, but stashing Fontenot there was something else. Piper gave me a little nod and headed down the sidewalk to his truck.

Bow came back from the Caribbean looking better than I'd seen him in years. The color he'd picked up helped hide the scar on his face, and he remained trim enough that he had to buy a new wardrobe—his old suits bagged too much. As it happened, he did meet a widow on the cruise—a woman from Connecticut, a few years older than he was, rich in her own right. In a picture taken on board the ship, she was wrapped in a white bathrobe, looking soft and chesty and quite attractive. For several months, a flurry of letters and calls sailed back and forth. She had three children, the youngest just starting college, and there always seemed to be a crisis, an unwanted pregnancy, an arrest at an antiwar rally. Bow was often on the phone, giving his best lawyerly assurances, talking in the same firm, quick voice that I'd heard him use on dozens of prisoners over the years, a voice designed to throttle emotion. Sometimes when he talked, he'd cradle the receiver on his shoulder, take notes on a legal pad, and roll his eyes at me. The conversations often lasted an hour. Eventually, they arranged for her to come visit. Bow sent her plane tickets, and he and I made plans to drive to Milwaukee to pick her up. The day before, just as I was on my way out to clean the Pontiac, she called to cancel. Her dog was sick. A golden retriever. She couldn't leave it. "At least it's a good breed," Bow told me. Afterward, her letters piled up unopened, and soon they stopped coming.

The vacation bronzed Bow over, but it didn't do much for his spirit. For all his logic and honesty, he had no antidote to profound disappointment. Losing Ginger and all he stood for was sapping him. Bow kept busy, but he seemed lethargic, certainly compared with the old days. His silences dragged on longer than ever, and when he did talk, the edge was disappearing, as if he didn't have the energy to be cynical or even enthusiastic. He'd light a cigar and then forget to smoke it; at the end of the day, two or three beauties would be lying forlornly intact in Bow's big ashtray; their fire had simply burned out.

By early summer, I was worried enough that I started to urge Bow to see the doctor or maybe go to the Mayo Clinic. My nagging irritated him, which I took at least to be a good sign. Still, he didn't get around to making an appointment. To cheer him up, on the Fourth of July I drove him over to Kawnipi, which was known for having the best fireworks display in our area of Wisconsin. It had rained that day, however, and the show was late getting started. The Kawnipi city park was infested with mosquitoes. After twenty minutes or so, Bow said he wanted to leave. On the way home, I again urged him to see a doctor. "I'm all right," he said, this time without sounding irritated. He knew I'd tried hard to entertain him. "I'm just kind of . . ." He hesitated, searching. "Uninterested."

"Well, it's probably got some physical basis. That's why you should see someone."

"I feel empty." He smiled weakly, amused at least that he'd been able to express his symptoms.

"Tell the doc."

"I'll give it a little more time," he said. "I think it will pass."

A day or so later, a letter came from Ginger, neatly typed on onionskin paper, two pages single-spaced. He'd befriended one of the clerks at the base and cadged use of a typewriter. It was a good letter, but a bit arch in the youthful way of someone articulate who hasn't yet learned to relax on paper.

Ginger explained that he was about to ship out for Vietnam. He'd be going with a number of buddies from basic training. Everyone was nervous, but no one would admit it; they were treating the prospect of combat as a great adventure. He told Bow that he didn't know how he felt about the war anymore—he'd swung back a bit from the hawkish views he'd held when he enlisted. "I'm eager to take a look for myself," he wrote. "Either way I come out, I'll be able to make a better argument."

Bow was reading out loud to me, and he paused in pleasure at that remark; Ginger was thinking like a lawyer.

Most of the letter stuck to talk of basic training and the war. In the last few sentences, Ginger came around to his real point. "I'm sorry I rushed off so quickly without properly being able to thank you for all you've done for me," he wrote. "But now I've also had a little time to think, even in this lousy place. You probably won't be surprised when I tell you that most of the thinking has been about me. I've realized that my mother and to a larger extent my father have made me who I am, and I'll always love and cherish them. But I also know that the principles that matter most to me—straight talk, clear thinking, fairness all around—are things I learned from you, Bow. They are simple things, and very 'Wisconsin,' but they are easy to lose sight of. Forevermore, Bow, when I'm uncertain, I'll think about you to guide me through."

Bow read that last section twice to me, then he put the letter down. He was sitting at his desk and behind him, a high July sun washed through the window, bleaching the solemn gray of the office. "What do you make of it?" he asked.

"I think he's sincere, if that's what you're wondering," I told him.

"He was always good at sentiment. Remember his eulogies."

"He was smart enough to be candid."

" 'Straight talk,' " Bow read from the letter. "He said he got that from me. Of course, that's one quality he applied selectively."

The letter had opened something in Bow, allowing him to admit what he knew. "You're being too hard on him," I argued. "He was working his way around to coming clean with you. Enlisting was part of that."

"Look who's defending him," Bow teased. "You were the skeptic."

"I was careful. But I decided he was all right. A few more years with you and he'd be able to do anything."

Bow folded the letter and slipped it into his inside jacket pocket.

"Are you going to write him back?" I asked.

"Eventually, I suppose. I'll let it stew a bit. But what would I say? That I've hardened in my new view of the war—that I'm convinced now it's a terrible mistake? Sort of an inopportune moment to say that, just when he's being shipped out."

"You could tell him what you think of him."

"I liked his instincts," said Bow, smiling. "He had the instincts of a hero." After a moment, he pushed himself up from his desk. In his trimmer, subdued incarnation, he didn't so much stand as unfold, various parts stiffly separating from others. He stood beside the window, staring down at the street. The bank had finally bought a shredder and started destroying its old documents, dumping the scraps in the alley below, huge piles of tiny paper flakes. The garbage cans couldn't contain them. On windy days, even now in the dead of summer, the pavement seemed to be covered with snow. "What the hell do I know, Charlie?" Bow said finally. "I've lived alone too long. You, too. Without a family around, you forget how people act."

He looked up and answered his own question. "I'll write him. I'll tell him he's a great kid, he's got a great future. And I'll tell him to watch out for his ass over there. We need him here at home."

CHAPTER 36

On a warm, damp day in August, I spent the morning shelving books and then stopped by the Wanigan to pick up sandwiches for Bow and me. He'd called the library to say he didn't want to go out because of the rain. By noon, the worst of it was over, but Main Street was slick and puddled and almost empty. A ceiling of dark clouds hung low over the town. I entered the Bank Building through the alley, and walking down the corridor to Bow's office I had what my father would have insisted was a premonition—though I didn't so much sense the presence of death as of lifelessness. Something was missing.

Bow wasn't at his desk. With the gloom outside, the office seemed pitched into night, and for a moment I imagined Bow had gone home for the day. It was a second or so before my eyes drifted to the floor. He was lying facedown in the middle of the room, his arms stretched at his sides with his palms up, like a swimmer preparing for a racing dive. Death looked uncomfortable.

Bow may have lost weight, but still he was big, and in the cluttered office I had to step high over his mountainous bulk to get to the desk and set down the bag of sandwiches and drinks. When I kneeled to touch the veins on his neck, I saw a trickle of blood trailing from his face, and for a moment I thought he'd shot himself. I've always

regretted that reaction and felt it was a kind of betrayal, since everything about Bow, even over his last, glum summer, affirmed the logic
of carrying on. The blood was from his fall. His heart had burst and
he was probably dead before his face pounded into the floor.

Working with someone that long, you get to know his habits like
your own, and I could easily reconstruct Bow's final moments. As it
happened, he'd been fussing with one of his leftover criminal cases—
an appeal of an appeal for a car thief named Steve Hollenshead. Bow
didn't like him. Hollenshead was a gassy little guy, but he was just
smart enough to be a nuisance. Rooting around in the prison library,
he'd found a 1923 case that he imagined would be helpful, and there
on Bow's desk was a scrawled letter from Hollenshead with a cita-
tion. Bow had circled the cite in pencil, then stood to find the use-
less case in the appropriate volume of *Wisconsin Reports* in the
bookshelf across the room. He fell beside the chair in front of his
desk. He'd been smoking a cigar, and this time he'd kept it lit: I found
it under the chair, where it had burned a small hole in the rug before
the fire went out.

Small towns can be like families in the sense that basic, quotidian
proximity forces a kind of cooperation that can't quite be distin-
guished from affection and respect. Thus, in the absence of any near
relatives, Marcus Laney, as the next ranking intellectual in town,
assumed the chore of helping Reverend Olson organize Bow's
funeral. Laney lined up as speakers two appellate judges who'd
worked with Bow over the years and Harry Eliot, a law school classmate who taught criminal procedure at Madison. At first they
planned to hold the service at St. John's, but within a day it became
clear that seating would be a problem—in addition to the many people of Laroque, lawyers from around the state were planning to
attend. So, once again the Opera House was unlocked and dusted
out, the first it had been used since the final basketball game the
March before.

The old place holds 923 ancient wood seats, and almost all of
them were filled the day of the funeral. I waited out front for Ox,
who was late, and by the time we got upstairs to the auditorium, we
had to squeeze into a back row. For the second time in a year and a

half, I found myself sitting next to old Mrs. Pangborn at a funeral. Her health had wilted since I'd seen her last, and she mumbled something indistinct to me. "I beg your pardon?" I said.

"You must be very sad," she boomed, summoning all her strength to her voice. For rows around, people turned.

"He's holding up good," Ox thundered back.

Mrs. Pangborn put her fragile, liver-spotted hand on my thigh and kept it there, where it twitched occasionally like a small, nervous bird for the entire service.

Reverend Olson served as the master of ceremonies, as it were, but Laney put himself on a chair on the stage, and I watched him puffing out, the proud producer, as he periodically surveyed the crowd. The three featured speakers told overlapping stories documenting Bow's brilliance and his pioneering role in developing criminal procedure in Wisconsin. Each of the men offered a handful of anecdotes. Several I knew to be apocryphal. Nobody wept. In fact, it was the least sad funeral I've ever attended. Not that people were unmoved—they knew that someone special had died too young. But it was as if, for once, on a sunny, late-August day, when the last drops of summer were being squeezed out of the weekends and families were preparing for the start of school, the people of Bow's world accepted an unsentimental logic worthy of Bow himself: He'd led a limited but useful life. Now it was over. Time to move on.

Afterward, in the milling second-floor lobby outside the auditorium, Anna Sterritt pushed through the crowd to find me. "I didn't see you," I told her.

"I got here early and was way down front," she said. She'd turned brown over the summer. She was wearing a sleeveless black dress, and when she moved, I glimpsed the glowing whiteness left on her shoulder by her bathing suit strap. She reached out and made a sandwich of my hand between her palms. "Why didn't *you* speak?" she wondered. "You knew Bow better than anyone."

I shrugged. "Nobody asked me."

"Charlie, what a waste."

"I'll save it for my book," I said.

"I got a letter from Ginger. He's in the infirmary. He landed in

Vietnam and got sick the next day. I hope he stays there all year. It's probably the safest place."

"I was going to write him about Bow. This afternoon," I told her. She squeezed my hand. "I was hoping you would."

Ox had gone ahead. The crowd was pushing toward the stairway. Anna and I were being jostled apart. "I'm moving to California," she said, dropping my hand. "Los Angeles. Next week."

"What about college?"

"Maybe out there. Maybe UCLA." She was holding her ground while I was being swept toward the stairs. "I'll send you a postcard," she called out. "At the library."

Outside, the crowd spilling from the Opera House had overrun Main Street. A Coke truck that had come upon the scene was trapped in the plaza, surrounded by heedless pedestrians. The driver had stepped out and was leaning against the cab, smoking a cigarette, waiting for the route to clear.

I came across Lucy sitting on a bench in Veterans' Park. The bank had shut for the funeral, but she'd told me she wasn't going to attend, she'd rather spend the gift of a few free hours on herself. Now here she was. "I couldn't stay away," she told me, and she slipped her arm through mine. It occurred to me that I went days without physical contact with anyone, and now she was the third woman in an hour to touch me. We sat together in the park, watching eddies of people form and break up on the Opera House steps. "They don't look very sad, do they," she said.

"I was noticing the same thing."

She studied my face. "Are you all right?"

"I don't know yet," I told her. "I'll have to wait and see."

"Do you want to go down to Duffy's?"

"No, not that."

"There was nothing you could have done, Charlie."

"I know. It's only things I wished I'd said."

"You didn't have to," she told me.

After about ten minutes, the street was clear enough for the Coke truck to move on. I walked Lucy back to the bank. It wasn't supposed to reopen for another half hour, but when we got there, Sher-

iff Kurtz was just coming out of the glass door in front. "I was looking for you, Charlie," he said. "I thought you might be in Bow's
office." His face was flushed. He leaned close to my ear, as if to shield
Lucy from what he was going to say, though she could hear perfectly
well. "I wanted you to know," Kurtz said. "Ginger Piper's dead. The
army sent two casualty officers. They stopped by the station looking
for directions to Errol Piper's house."

Perhaps because I'd just come from a funeral, I was prepared for
death. Lucy grabbed my hand, but I was calm. "How did he die?" I
asked.

"Shot in the neck crossing a rice paddy. Bled to death before they
could get a helicopter in, but he wasn't going to make it anyway.
Spinal cord was nicked." Kurtz relished his command of the details.
I was impressed with the efficiency of the army, furnishing the
hometown with an immediate account of the casualty.

"He hadn't been there two weeks," the police chief mused. "That's
the third boy Laroque's lost. And to think—six months ago he was
protesting the war. Vietnam is bad luck for this town."

"It's a stupid, boys' war," said Lucy furiously.

Kurtz stared at her, uncomprehending. After a few seconds, he
said, "I thought you'd want to know, Charlie. The three of you—you
and Bow and him—you seemed to be so tight."

"Thanks." I took a deep breath. "We should tell Anna Sterritt. She
was his girlfriend."

"Right, right," said Kurtz. "I'll drive you there." He seemed eager
to get away from Lucy.

"Well, I've got to go back to work," Lucy pronounced, still sounding angry. She took a step toward the bank and saw herself reflected
in the glass door. Suddenly, tears were washing down her face. Standing behind her, I put my hands on her shoulders. When she sobbed,
her arms shook limply at her sides. "You should marry me, Charlie,"
she said through her sobs. "You really should."

"I'll get the car," said Kurtz.

I closed my eyes and rested my cheek on her head. She was using
a new shampoo and her hair smelled like lilacs. My mother used to
keep a row of lilac bushes in the yard behind our house, and for a

week each spring the air back there radiated with a heavenly fragrance. Holding Lucy on the sidewalk in front of the bank, I remembered sitting on the damp grass as a little boy, looking back at our boxy house, already the scene of so much turbulence, and feeling safe in the luxurious aura of the lilacs.

Bow died without a will, of course. He'd never got around to that detail. His closest relatives were a handful of second cousins, all quite elderly, most of them living in Florida. While the bank worked at tracking them down, it asked me to straighten out his papers—right away, the law school at Madison put in a request for his files. So one day a few weeks after the funeral, I was back in the office when Archie Nye suddenly appeared at the door. He'd apparently been looking forward to a warm reception, and his dark, hatchety face sank as he surveyed the cardboard packing boxes piled high around the room. "Is Mr. Epps here?" he asked, not sounding hopeful.

I shook my head. "Died last month."

"You're shitting me."

"Heart attack. Right here in this office."

"Jesus." Archie shook his head, though not particularly out of sorrow. "I had something I wanted him to take care of."

"A legal matter?"

"Yeah. I traded this guy my pickup for the fishing rights to his lake over in Clearwater, and the lake don't have nothing but a bunch of little-bitty crappies in it. Now he won't give the truck back." Archie scowled at his bad luck. "Dead, huh?"

"Big funeral. I don't know how you missed hearing about it."

"I been away," he said cryptically. He eyed me thoughtfully. "Say, Charlie, you aren't a lawyer are you? I want to sue that guy."

"Nope."

"What about that kid, that hotshot? Is he a lawyer?"

"He's dead, too."

"Jesus!" Archie stepped back as if the room held something contagious.

"Killed in Vietnam."

"Mother of Christ." Archie clomped in a kind of Frankenstein's-monster walk over to the sofa and sat down heavily between two boxes of papers. "Mr. Epps I could see, maybe. He was so overweight, you know. But the boy, he was like me, he was the picture of health."

"A bullet doesn't care how healthy you are."

Archie thought I was rebuking him. "I hate guns," he said.

"I know."

"Jesus Christ." Archie sat back on the sofa. For a moment he forgot the predicament of his truck. "Those two were all right, you know?" he said. "At first I wondered what the hell they were doing together, but they were all right."

Bow would have been pleased. A compliment from Archie Nye didn't come much higher.

"Say, what's that?" Archie asked, pointing to a wastebasket where I'd tossed Bow's bottle of Chivas Regal, still half full.

"You can have it," I told him.

He fished the bottle out and held it up to the light. "Really?"

"Take it."

"You don't want it?"

"It's not strong enough."

He looked at the label. "Jesus, it's probably ninety-proof."

I laughed. "That's not what I meant."

"Hey, thanks," he said.

Archie stayed for an hour or so and helped me move boxes. At about six, I locked the office and we walked down the back stairs. He'd parked his truck in the alley, and now a ticket sat on the windshield.

"I thought you traded the pickup," I said.

"It was another one." He tossed the ticket onto the floor in front and set the bottle of Chivas Regal on the passenger seat. "Tell you the truth, that one I traded's a heap," he said, smiling sheepishly. "I'd like to get it back before it dies on the guy."

He let that confession settle, and then hesitated. Something was on his mind. Standing uncomfortably beside the truck, his eyes searched the dark length of the alley. "I meant to tell you, Charlie," he said after a moment. "Remember that time we ran into you guys on the lake up at Mr. Epps's place?"

"Sure."

"You know, we never would have done you any harm. That was just sort of our way of getting a conversation started."

"I think we figured it out."

Poor Archie, his eyes scanned the alley again as if absolution were hiding out there somewhere, in the dust and paper scraps, behind the battered garbage cans, under the rusty, jagged stack of discarded sheeting that the trash department refused to pick up. "I hate to think they both went to the grave not understanding," he said.

I touched his forearm, wiry and hard under his sleeve. "Believe me, Archie, they didn't have a problem with it."

"Okay." A flash of that huge, muskie smile. I thought of the effort and muscle it must take to expose that endless lineup of teeth. He hopped into the truck, and with a wave he was off down the alley and around the corner.

I walked down to River Road and then west toward Turner Bridge. It was a gorgeous, early-fall evening, and the sunset was turning the Agnes into a strip of gold. I stopped on the bridge to watch a man with a spinning rod on the far bank cast over and over into the water. He was a skilled fisherman, and his easy, rhythmic motion caught and held me—the gentle arc of line, the distant, silent splat of lure on water, the lazy metronome beat of the rod. For the first time since Bow had died I felt my heart slow down. Archie's guilt had been like a huge blanket, and he'd lifted up a corner for me to crawl under. I stayed on the bridge until the fisherman reeled his line in for the last time and the Agnes had turned from gold to black.

As it turned out, I did marry Lucy. Bow was fond of quoting Mencken to the effect that of all escape mechanisms, death is the most efficient. In my case, though, that honor belongs to marriage, in the best possible sense—escape from stagnation, from the empty notions of my past. Lucy and I will celebrate our thirty-fourth wedding anniversary next year. We tried to have children, but it didn't take. There was a miscarriage, then Lucy fought off an illness. Finally, we adopted, though in those days we were one of the oldest couples in Wisconsin ever to get the green light. Eric was eight weeks old when he came to us—a robust, happy, curly-haired blond. He filled up the little house we'd bought just north of town. There were moments over those years, when the three of us would be sitting around at home, usually plunked in front of the TV—I recall one evening watching the moronic gyrations of *Dallas,* which for a year or so we never missed—and I'd suddenly have to fight off a surge of anxiety when I thought back to how untethered I'd once been.

We used to remark on how much Eric looked like Lucy's branch of the family—the blond hair, the lanky, athletic build—but as he got older, his chief interest hooked back to my side: He fell in love with the theater. I don't know how it happened. He certainly didn't get any encouragement from me. Now he's in drama school in New York City. Not long ago, I pointed out to him that by going east he was reversing the route taken three-quarters of a century before by his stage-struck grandfather. The connection didn't interest him. "New York's where the *work* is, Dad," he said impatiently, as if the past, even its ironies, didn't count for anything.

Lucy left the bank to care for Eric when he was little, but when she returned to work, six or so years later, her bosses—having realized what an asset she'd been—made her a loan officer. Today she's a vice president, responsible for all the bank's residential mortgages. I often wish Bow were around to see her success. There were no women officers in his day. I think he'd be amused and a bit chagrined that he hadn't spotted her talent himself.

His bank, of course, has been sold several times over, and now it's part of a huge operation based in one of those booming cities of the Southeast. The last I saw, Bow's old office had been converted into the computer back room. For curiosity's sake, I peeked in a few years ago and found three kids barely out of high school hacking away at a wall of machines. Downstairs, however, one piece of the old decor has made a comeback. Trying to connect to the local market, the new owners had the smart idea to anchor the public space with portraits of the early owners. So they pulled the picture of Bow's father out of storage someplace, and now he and some turn-of-the-century predecessors, their faces riots of jowls and hair, hang again from a lobby wall, reassuring depositors.

As for me, I've stayed at the library, moving up through the years to deputy head librarian, second in command. I could retire at any time, but I think I'll hang on a bit longer. It's been a good place to work. The hours are easy and the pace is gentle. I like the feel of a library, pressed in by the walls of books, calmed by the quiet intensity of the place. Frankly, it reminds me of those long days up in Bow's office when he'd be buried in a transcript and wouldn't look up for hours.

Also, through the library, I've officially become what Bow always said I was—an archivist of Laroque. Early on, I saved some of Bow's family papers, and over the years I've gathered other documents and memoirs about the town and the development of this part of Wisconsin. I've even donated that chaotic trunk of my father's things. Now our little library has an entire alcove devoted to local history, one of the finest collections of original materials in the state.

I suppose you could say this book is a part of those archives, or, more, an extension of them. It came about because a few years ago we were converting the big, bound volumes of the Laroque *Daily Sentinel* into microfilm, and I found myself wandering through the back issues. Turning the broadsheet pages, I'd trip over the headlines, then drift through the stories, struck in hindsight by their odd approximation of truth, all ambiguity and motive falling into the yellowing white space between the lines of type. My father arrived in Laroque just about the time the paper started making aggressive use of local photographs, and in the summers, just about every week, there was a picture of Dad promoting a show, often enough with one of his imported stars. Rodney Fiske was there, even Broderick Crawford, looking impossibly young and handsome, a startling ancestor to the weathered, paunchy man on *Highway Patrol*. Still, my father outshone them all. He had great newsprint features, jet-black hair and very light skin, and the crude, black-and-white reproduction relished the contrast in his face. Beyond that, the photos seem to register his unsettling vitality. The people around him usually look slightly upset or off balance, as if they've unwittingly stepped into his energy field and the laws of gravity have changed slightly.

Going forward a decade or so in the paper, I started coming across pictures of Bow—nowhere near as many, and they were mostly tedious shots; Bow at the ribbon cutting for the bank's new drive-in teller window, Bow introducing a state supreme court justice at a county Chamber of Commerce dinner, that sort of thing. Unlike my father, Bow was tortured by the camera. He was naturally uncomfortable in the spotlight, and, in any case, his lumpy body and misshapen face come out gray and unfocused in print, as if *his* energy field muddied the negative. Nothing in those pictures suggests his singularity; for all they tell the casual observer, he was just another burgher—someone *fungible,* to use one of Bow's favorite words. In fact, apart from the G. Bowman Epps Papers at the U of W law school and a handful of files here at the library, there's little to memorialize him. Everything I read and hear tells me that even many of the procedural reforms he built into case law—the protections for the accused—have been dialed back by the courts and the legislature in response to the fear of crime. It's what Bow secretly dreaded, I suspect—that too soon his mark would turn invisible.

For what it's worth, Ginger has a memorial. His name, along with the names of his two pals killed in Vietnam, was finally added to the war monument in the park downtown. Those three early casualties turned out to be the only victims from Laroque, though the town didn't get around to recognizing them until 1981, well after the passions over the war had cooled. The day after the ceremony, the paper ran the high school yearbook pictures of the three boys. Ginger looks so much younger than I remember him. In my memory, he's virtually a contemporary, but in the picture, he's a child with a clumsily knotted fat tie and a soft, innocent face. I stared hard at that picture, but I couldn't find any evidence of the spareness and grace that expressed his style.

One other photograph gets closer to my memory. It's a remarkable shot, though I'd forgotten it existed until I leafed through an ancient edition of the *Sentinel,* March 14, 1966. The photographer snapped it just seconds after Ginger sank the basket to beat Kawnipi. The Opera House stage is a mob of celebrating players and students, and even crooked old Coach Gourdon looks as if he's about to take a joyous swan dive off the front edge into the arms of more fans.

Ginger stands at the center of the commotion, but he alone looks motionless. His shoulders droop and his face is drawn. He seems misplaced, as if someone with a modern-age computer had cleverly planted an anomaly in the picture—a pious counterpoint to the roaring emotions everywhere evident. I have to remind myself that Ginger was exhausted at that moment. Still, the picture in its objective genius caught his uneasiness, his disconnection, standing at center stage, staring into the wings. I'd seen that look on others—on Bow so often, even on my father. Heroes, all of them, measuring their lives in misses.

ACKNOWLEDGMENTS

For their generous assistance with this book, I would like to thank Pierre Snyker, Daniel Cummings, Kaarina Salovaara, Locke Bowman, Molly Friedrich, Lucy Childs, Sarah McGrath, Joe Babcock, and above all, my wife, Gioia Diliberto.

ABOUT THE AUTHOR

RICHARD BABCOCK is the editor of *Chicago* magazine. He lives in Chicago with his wife, the writer Gioia Diliberto, and son, Joe. This is his second novel.

19093072R00196

Made in the USA
Lexington, KY
05 December 2012